THE ROAD TO MARS

Eric Idle was one of the six original members of Monty Python's Flying Circus. He has appeared in 18 films and edited all of Monty Python's books. *The Road to Mars* is his second novel. Besides his first novel, *Hello Sailor*, he has also written a play, *Pass the Butler*, and a children's novel, *The Quite Remarkable Adventures of the Owl and the Pussycat*. He lives in Los Angeles with his wife, Tania, and their daughter.

D1189101

A POST-MODEM NOVEL

ERIC IDLE

THE ROAD TO MARS

PAN BOOKS

First published 1999 by Pantheon Books,
a division of Random House, Inc., New York
and simultaneously in Canada by
Random House of Canada Limited, Toronto

First published in Great Britain 1999 by Boxtree

This edition published 2000 by Pan Books
an imprint of Macmillan Publishers Ltd
25 Eccleston Place, London SW1W 9NF
Basingstoke and Oxford
Associated companies throughout the world
www.macmillan.co.uk

ISBN 0 330 48180 0

5 7 9 8 6

A CIP catalogue record for this book is available from
the British Library.

Printed and bound in Great Britain by
Mackays of Chatham plc, Chatham, Kent

FOR TANIA

THANKS TO

Carey and Lily

Tom Hoberman

Marsha and Robin Williams

Pamela and Billy Connolly

Barbara Dalton-Taylor

Matt Bialer

Peter Crabbe

Marty Asher

Sonny Mehta

and all the comedians, too humorous to mention

PART ONE

FAME

Let us now praise famous men, and our
fathers that begat us.

Ecclesiasticus

FAME

Fame is a terminal disease. It screws you up worse than your mom and dad. Somewhere in the late twentieth century the pursuit of fame became a way of life. Suddenly everyone wanted to be famous. Newscasters, journalists, weather men, astrologers, cooks, interns, even lawyers for God's sake, everyone went nuts trying to grab their fifteen minutes of fame promised by the pop philosophy of Andy Warhol. It replaced life after death as mankind's greatest illusion. Fame! You'll live forever. Fame! Your chance to revenge your parents. Fame! Take that, you nasty kids who were so cruel to me at school. Fame! A chance to screw yourself across the flickering face of history.

Fame, fame, fame, fame, fame.

This syphilis of the soul was caused of course by the arrival of television and the instant attention of the new mass media. If the medium was the message, then the message was crap, for the TV screens were filled from morning to night with a constant twenty-four-hour shit storm. No one was spared. Not presidents, not princes, not popes, not people's representatives. Knickers off, panties down, coming live at you in ten, nine, eight . . . Kiss and tell, kiss and sell, bug your neighbors, tape your friends, grab an agent and sell, sell, sell. Intimacy? Privacy? Forget it. Notoriety? Shame? No such thing. Fame. That's the name of the game. Private life was washed away under the tidal wave of freedom of speech. It didn't matter whether you were famous for murdering a president or inventing a pudding, now fame could travel at the speed of light, everyone was just a sound bite from stardom.

No one remembers the name of the anarchist who started World War One by murdering the archduke in Sarajevo in 1914. Everyone remembers Lee Harvey Oswald. Fame! A rifle shot away. Providing you have television. Fame, the intellectual equivalent of waving at the camera. "Look at me, Ma! I'm here. I'm real. I'm on TV." Sad, sick, and deplorable, isn't it? I mean in the 1990s even agents became famous, for Christ's sake. And what do we call the famous? Stars! I mean hello. Have we no sense of irony? Look up—look up at the real stars. Billions of them? Billions and billions of the buggers. Don't we get it? There is no fame. There is no immortality. There is no life after death. There are just millions of tiny grains of sand scraping away at each other. We're on the planet Ozymandias, people! Look on my works ye mighty and despair! The grains of time, grinding away at our insignificance . . . well you get the picture. You're intelligent. You've read this far at least.

But who the fuck are you to lecture us on our insignificance? I hear you ask. Not unreasonably. OK, my name is Reynolds. Given name William. Better known as Bill. Actually, Professor Bill, which is better than William, and much better than the quite awful Billy. And that's what I do: I lecture on insignificance. I'm a micropaleontologist. You may be unaware of the study labeled micropaleontology (occasionally microanthropology), which was the first really brand-new science of the Double Ages (the second millennium). It is my job to study *the evolutionary implications of the last ten minutes*. Originally that phrase was a cheap gag intended to belittle this brave new science, this paradoxically titled branch of anthropology—for how can there be a *micro*paleontology? What are we talking ontologically here? Dust mites? Bakelite radio sets? Dung heaps of old newspapers which will over time become rock? Well actually, yes. If you can measure time in parsecs and millisecs, and matter down to the tiniest gluon, then the evolutionary aspects of the last ten minutes is a perfectly acceptable concept. So argued Edwin Crawford at Cambridge University shortly after the close of the twentieth century. He was pondering the enormous changes that had taken place during that violent era and he asked himself, What are the evolutionary implications of television? He found that similar questions could be asked of the automobile, birth control, the computer, air travel, even rock and roll. It seemed to Crawford that the process of evolution was demonstrably speeding up, that we had no time to wait for anthropologists and paleontologists to sift through the fossil record and explain what was happening to us in our time. *It would be far too late to be useful.* (His italics.) So, a new science was born.

My particular subject has been comedy in the late twentieth century, and I have spent the last fifteen years researching it. My doctoral thesis was called "The Passive Bark: Aspects of Laughter." Yes, I know, I know, it is the hallmark of the desperately unfunny to study comedy, as if somehow it could be learned, as if it might be contagious like a virus picked up and passed on, but that indeed was exactly what I was studying when I was fortunate enough to stumble across the work of Carlton. You won't have heard of him, but he was the first to postulate a comedy gene, in a remarkable work titled *De Rerum Comoedia* (Concerning Comedy), a doctoral dissertation for USSAT (the University of Southern Saturn) submitted in the late 2300s. The most interesting thing about Carlton was not that he was an android, an artificial intelligence, but that he worked for two comedians, Muscroft and Ashby. You won't have heard of them either; they were just two minor comics on the Road to Mars, an ironical term used to describe the great wastes between the outer planets and mining stations where the early entertainers pursued their weary trade; a vaudeville circuit which exploited mankind's desperate need for live entertainment. They were hardly worth a footnote in the halls of humor but for the work of this quite brilliant humanoid who spent years observing them in action and asked himself two key questions: (1) What are the evolutionary uses of humor? And (2) Can it be learned by artificial intelligence?

The chess machines had long since demolished mankind's supposed superiority in chess. Could a machine now be programmed to be *funny*? I don't mean could it be force-fed gags to spout on verbal cues—that's easy enough—but could it actually be programmed to understand what it was doing, to *think* funny, to create fresh comedy? In other words, is it possible for an artificial intelligence to learn humor, or is comedy something endemic in the species *Homo sapiens*? Is it unique to mankind or would you expect to find humor among any other advanced civilizations, supposing such things exist?

Carlton attacked these questions with all the vigor and freshness of a computer. This extraordinary humanoid looked at humor and came up with several interesting observations. I think you'll be surprised. To put his research in perspective I need to take you back about eighty years.

THE WHITE FACE AND THE RED NOSE

Of the future only one thing is certain. There will be comedy.

CARLTON, DE RERUM COMOEDIA

Consider the following. Two comedians, Muscroft and Ashby, and a robot, a droid called Carlton. A 4.5 Bowie. A handsome, good-looking thing, built on the image of a young rock god from the 1980s. Not the androgynous early Ziggie Stardust machine (the 3.2s with which they had such trouble), but the full-blown golden-haired young white god look. "Like a butch Rupert Brooke; a tragic dandy, a cross between a wank and a wet dream," as the brochure described it.

Two comedians, one a depressive who was occasionally manic, the other a maniac who was occasionally depressed. Lewis Ashby, tall, dark, and saturnine; Alex Muscroft, short, wide, and cheerful. Lewis, the ectomorph; Alex, the endomorph. The classic comedy profile, the tall thin one and the short fat one.

"There are two types of comedian," states Carlton in the preface to his dissertation, "both deriving from the circus, which I shall call the White Face and the Red Nose. Almost all comedians fall into one or the other of these two simple archetypes. In the circus, the White Face is the controlling clown with the deathly pale masklike face who never takes a pie; the Red Nose is the subversive clown with the yellow and red makeup who takes all the pies and the pratfalls and the buckets of water and the banana skins. The White Face represents the mind, reminding humanity of the constant mocking presence of death; the Red Nose represents the body, reminding mankind of its constant embarrassing vulgarities. (See Chapter XX of *De Rerum Comoedia*, "Pooh-Pooh: Pooping, Farts, and Sex.") The emblem of the White Face is the skull, that of the Red Nose is the phallus. One stems from the plague, the other from the carnival. The bleakness of the funeral, the wildness of the orgy. The graveyard and the fiesta. The brain and the penis. Hamlet and Falstaff. Don Quixote and Sancho Panza. Laurel and Hardy. Muscroft and Ashby."

You try it with any comedians you can think of, and I tell you it works. Carlton, this smart little tintellectual, is on to something real here. Just look for the distinguishing characteristics: the White Face is the controlling neurotic and the Red Nose is the rude, rough Pan. The White Face compels your respect; the Red Nose begs for it. The Red Nose smiles and nods and winks, and wants your love; the White Face rejects it. He never smiles; he is always deadly serious. Never more so than when doing comedy.

"Men," says Carlton, "have two major organs, the brain and the penis, and only enough blood to run one at a time."

He nicked that line from Alex, but it's clever stuff, eh? And he pretty much nailed Alex, the Red Nose maniac, and Lewis, the bright-eyed White Face neurotic. Physically they *were* that clearly defined, the classic prototypes that Carlton was delineating. Lewis was "the tall thin one" and Alex "the short fat one." People often said Alex was the funny one, but Lewis was equally funny, if more cutting. He didn't take any prisoners. Lewis was older than his partner by almost three years and slightly round-shouldered and stooped, as if embarrassed to find himself so tall. He had a long face with dark eyes that stared at you, separated by a thin nose. His laugh when it came was unforced and hilarious, exploding uncontrollably out of his chest, a great shriek of a laugh which shook his whole body and left him completely paralyzed for minutes at a time, after which he would have to stretch out and lie on the floor, his shoulders occasionally heaving, until he gained control of himself again. A tall man, well over six feet, his thinning black hair struggling with a parting. Alex said it wasn't a parting it was a *de*parting, a cruel jibe, since even in his twenties his falling hair was beginning to worry him more than he cared to admit. He didn't like things out of control, witness his tiny handwriting ("Ooh look, a mouse left me a note," Alex would scream), but he could control neither his hair nor his partner. Brooding, obsessing, cynical, slightly menacing, he loomed over Alex like a headmaster.

Not that he dominated Alex. The Red Nose knows a thing or two when it comes to survival. He is by nature a bad boy, a consumer of things, a wolfer of experience, an enjoyer of the sensual. "He's like a timorous gourmet," Lewis said in an interview, for Alex was a consumer of women when he could, of drugs and alcohol, before they nearly killed him, and above all of food. He loved to eat. He fought a constant battle with his weight. He was by nature a wide boy, with the classic endomorphic profile. He would be much wider if his strong will to succeed didn't force him to punish himself by running on the machine all day, beads of sweat rolling down his short sharp nose. Lewis said he was a liposuction waiting to happen. Blue eyes, wide cheekbones, with a hint of protruding chin, his hair was rusty and sprouted everywhere, on surfaces where it wasn't strictly necessary. Lewis called him the human fur ball.

"Do you shave your shoulders?" he would ask.

"Every day," said Alex. "Want me to save a little for your head so we can knit a nice rug for it?"

Never short of a riposte, Alex. Fast as lightning. There was something in this banter that was a little uncomfortable, so on the whole, by unspoken mutual agreement, they laid off each other offstage. At least according to Carlton, upon whose extraordinarily detailed notes I rely.

Red Nose, White Face, then, the classic struggle. Not quite a friendship, not exactly a marriage, not even a brotherhood, let's call it a polarity, a tension of opposites. Like positive and negative. Providing they kept their distance, they held a comfortable balance. On stage together they were dynamite.

The Circuit. Endless mining stations, space platforms, the satellites of Saturn and of Jupiter. Nothing exciting. Somewhere a million miles away, the Planet Disney. Way beyond that, Mars: the home of showbiz, with its endless eager audiences. Something to aspire to. Make it there, you hit the jackpot.

A ship, the *Johnnie Ray*, named after an obscure twentieth-century torch singer, built inside like a British movie set (early Merchant Ivory) in fashionable good taste, with fires and wood and leather and deep comfy sofas in William Morris fabrics (the Pre-Raphaelite designer, not the Hollywood agency). None of your *Star Wars* High Aztec bleakness here, this was a ship built for comfort. There's a lot of space out there, and a hell of a lot of time.

And then there's Carlton. The extraordinary. A humanoid with no sense of humor writing a study of comedy. I knew there was a book in it the minute I came across him. But I haven't told anyone about him. Not even Molly. Molly's my girlfriend at the moment, live-in, significant other, partner, mistress, whatever. She's a researcher, doing life science, DNA and behavior, that sort of thing.

She'd eat Carlton up. So I haven't shared him with her yet. He's my secret. You have no idea how much theft goes on in pure research.

SATURNALIA

It's not that I'm afraid to die, I just don't want to be there when it happens.

WOODY ALLEN

It's New Year's Eve on Saturn. Ring out the old, ring in the new. You've heard the adage. So this is where we start. This is the crisis that pitches them forward into the story (as they tell you at all story conferences). This is the moment of attack. You have met the principals, the protagonists are engaged, what is going to happen? I'll tell you.

The crisis that began Carlton's long journey from a tin dresser to a potential place in history (if I have anything to do with it) began on New Year's Eve. A year is a relative concept. It describes the period of a planet's orbital revolution around the sun. On Earth that is 365.25 days. On Venus it is 243 days. On Mercury a sprightly 88. So that when I am fifty on Earth, that same time would make me over 200 years old on Mercury. With the outer planets it works the other way. The orbital period of Jupiter for example is 11 years, 10 months, and 14 days, and out by Saturn, where this incident took place, New Year's Day occurs only once every 29.5 Earth years. So at 50 you aren't yet even 2. You can imagine how wild they went on New Year's Eve.

Carlton had booked them into a gig on Rhea, a bleak world of constant hydrogen drizzle, a damp, dark, soggy environment full of surly miners and their pale families. A place of little hope, mining settlements, and container people, redeemed only by an unsurpassable view of Saturn and its rings occupying almost a quarter of the sky. From here the sun was a medium small spot half a billion miles away and sunrise was a nonevent, but to watch the huge disc of Saturn sailing up over the horizon, preceded by its delicate multicolored rings, was a truly awesome sight.

They were booked into the Alexandra Palace Hotel, built by an overoptimistic tour operator with more money than sense. It was a place people normally paid to avoid, but hell, if you only got two New Year's Eves in your life, then chances were good everything was fully booked. Chances were damn good this night, for the place was packed to the rafters. The Alexandra's gilded opulence mocked the morose black coal landscape in which it sat. Hydrogen drizzle and grey clouds obscured even the great gas giant around which they were revolving. Two smouldering vehicles in the parking lot ought to have warned them to turn back, but hey, they had played worse places and they shrugged and went on in anyway.

Muscroft and Ashby were booked to perform well before midnight, but things were running late as they so frequently do, with the heady mix of miners, tourists, and troublemakers attracted by the carnival atmosphere and potential revelry. After all, if you're not going to see another New Year's Eve till you're over fifty, think you're going to miss the party?

The event was scheduled to begin promptly at eight. By nine the place was out of control. The shouting, stamping, laughing, and whistle-blowing was growing louder by the minute. It wasn't so much an audience as a baying gang of yahoos. The management were reluctant to start, but were convinced by the authorities that if they canceled there would be a riot, and in that event they, the police, would be the first out of there. Imagine New Orleans at Carnival, combined with Trinidad, multiplied by Rio de Janeiro and you still don't quite have the fervor of what is happening out there on this desolate moon of Saturn.

As so often happens on these occasions, things began to go wrong early. Not starting the show on time meant that the crowd was angrier and drunker than they should have been. Allowing them anywhere near liquor was lunacy. There were of course plentiful supplies of illegal substances available around the fringes of the venue, which, ingested in massive amounts, only served to stoke the alcohol. This was a mob fast growing out of control. In a misguided attempt to calm them down, the management sent on the Space Ballet, billed as "a gravity-free group of girls in diaphanous drapery." Big mistake. Sending on twenty-four half-dressed females floating in synchronized space routines was red rag to a bull. The crowd began to bay. Instead of sitting back pretending it was art while secretly enjoying the titillation (the secret of the Space Ballet's usual success), they found it failed as raunch and began to yell for total nudity and more action. Some sections of the crowd chanted obscenities. Others concentrated on taunting individual girls. It was nasty stuff, I can tell you. Most of them were in tears when they came off, and several had been manhandled. Donald and his artificial donkey were officially billed as next, but Donald took one look at the crowd and bailed, bagged his ass and was out the door before anyone noticed.

"He'll never work again," said management darkly.

"At least he'll live," said Lewis.

Many of the crowd were there to see the Amazing Keith, a technology-dependent magic show which combined loud rock music and robots with spectacular explosions. Running amidst the chaos with his wild hair, his mad eyes, and his scrawny body squeezed into spangly tights, the Amazing Keith would pop up in the least likely places from the most amazing explosions. But sadly the Amazing Keith wasn't supposed to be on till midnight and he was nowhere to be seen.

The defection of Donald and his donkey (a wise pro-life choice on his part) had a similar effect on many of the artistes. The Gay Guys Galleria, a singing chorale, decided they would rather mingle with the audience than attempt to silence them with selections from Viennese operetta. Reg Butterworth and Marge wisely determined that plate-spinning and standing on piles of glasses was way beyond the intellectual range of this crowd. The Nigerian Marching Band were concerned for the safety of their instruments and decamped en masse. This left only the comedians and Keith's Magic Finale. It promised to be the shortest show on record. Alex, optimistic as ever, was all for going on. Lewis was for going home. He was even now arguing with management, an irascible sod named Horner who was sweating profusely and waggling several legal pages under his nose.

"Your contract stipulates twenty minutes."

"Yeah, well it promised us an audience, not a riot."

"It's a signed agreement. I'll sue if you don't go on."

"They're totally out of control."

"Oh, they're just happy."

"Happy? They're legless."

"You can't refuse or they'll tear the place apart."

"They've already started."

In the middle of this argument Alex walked on stage. There is in comedians a kind of foolish nerve which will lead them straight towards trouble. Where the normal human response is to run away, a comic will often as not head directly towards the danger. Mad buggers, all of 'em. So conditioned by rejection in childhood they constantly seek to face it down as grown-ups, I guess. Maybe Alex felt he could tame them, that they would listen to him because he was funny; comics are that arrogant—they have to be. Alex was a rare combination of barely muzzled anger, breathtaking fearlessness, and extraordinary timidity. A wasp could reduce him to a furry ball of panic. How he could be so afraid of daily life when he had the balls to walk out alone on stage in front of 3,000 drunken people to try and make them laugh is something I shall leave to the shrinkbots to explain. Whatever the reason, he emerged into the light wearing a slight smile and waving gently to the crowd. From the wings Carlton watched for a second in horror and then ran for Lewis. He had just emphatically ripped up their contract in front of an apoplectic Horner when he spotted Carlton racing towards him.

"He's on," yelled Carlton, dodging round the ropes and the machinery.

"What?"

"He's gone on."

"That loony."

"Well, thank goodness at least one of you recognizes his responsibilities," said management.

"My ass. If anything happens to him, I'm gonna nail you, Horner."

There was a moment, just a tiny moment out there, when Alex held the attention of the beast. It swung its baleful eyes towards him and slowly registered that there was a man on stage. It looked at this sad figure like a tyrannosaur might have eyed a small tasty mammal. This was meat, and it was hungry.

Of course if this was a Hollywood movie, they would all fall silent and he would emerge in triumph. But it's not and that's all bullshit anyway. The fact is, the audience was too drunk to hear anything. The first bottle fell well short of him, but the second caught him a nasty glancing blow on the forehead. By the time Carlton ran on stage to protect him, the bottles were raining down. If Lewis hadn't had the presence of mind to switch off the artificial gravity, Alex would have been a dead duck, but as it was, thanks to his magnetized gravity boots, Carlton was able to walk across the stage, grab him, and carry him bleeding into the wings pursued by a floating mass of out-of-control drunks.

They ran for their lives, while the drunken crowd flowed onto the stage, banging and barging into each other like molecules near boiling point. Stagehands grappled with the mob, but it was a losing battle. Unfortunately gravity had been restored and now the mob began to pour backstage and out to the tiny encampment of trailers and containers which housed the unfortunate stars of this unfortunate show.

Alex and Lewis had just reached their trailer when the first of the hooligans burst into the clearing and set about breaking in. Carlton had dropped Alex on the bed and was reaching for the first-aid box when the trailer suddenly began to rock. Fortunately, Lewis had locked the door behind them. He could see six or seven of the yahoos, leaning on its titanium sides trying to push it over.

"Stand back," said Carlton, and, inserting his fingers into the power socket, he sent a powerful blast of electrical current through the metal walls. There was an angry scream from outside as they leapt back, but it served only to enrage them, and they ran for poles and wooden props to push and batter at the thin walls of the trailer.

Inside their metal prison they felt the whole structure totter, then to their horror they heard a tremendous explosion. The shouting and inhuman screaming of the rioters temporarily ceased, as a section of the metal wall began to curl and melt as if it were cardboard. Someone was burning open the trailer with an acetylene torch. Carlton stepped forward, raising a heavy spike. A face appeared in the burned wall, a face with popping eyes and wild hair.

"Keith," yelled Lewis, "what the hell are you doing here?"

"Saving your ass, man," said The Amazing Keith, levering open the gap so they could step through it. Carlton hoisted Alex onto his back and they ran across the muddy surface to the shuttle bus, where another angry mob faced them.

"Stand back," said Keith as he hurled a cherry bomb into the crowd. The explosion stunned and terrified the drunken rioters.

"Oh, this is great," said Keith. "Let's do it again next year."

"You are seriously crazy," said Lewis.

"Thanks, man," said Keith sincerely.

Leaving the shuttle to the mob, they ran for the safety of their tender. Carlton propped the bleeding Alex on the bed, while Lewis jumped for the controls. The Amazing Keith looked around wildly and jumped out of the door.

"Hey, where you going?" yelled Lewis. "You not coming back to the ship?"

"No thanks, man, some other time. I gotta party, this promises to be a wild night."

"Oh right," said Lewis, "gotta party," as he watched The Amazing Keith disappearing into the mob, his wild hair flying in all directions.

With a roar the afterburners of the tender ignited and, not a moment too soon, lifted them off the ground.

"Hey," said Alex, suddenly sitting up, "did you get the money?"

Comedy is a serious business. Not being paid and being plunged into life-threatening situations had a sobering effect on Lewis. Nothing concentrates a man's mind more than the prospect of his imminent death, said Samuel Johnson. Lewis didn't mind dying onstage, but he hated being killed for it. He was a comedian, not a gladiator. So as soon as they were back in the *Johnnie Ray* and parked safely in Saturnian orbit, he called a conference.

"Okay, that's it for me," said Lewis.

Alex looked up sharply. Was he quitting?

"We're leaving. We're outta here."

"The Road to Mars?"

"Why not?"

"What about bookings?"

"We'll play the Jovian moons and pick up a little pocket money and then see if we can't hitch a cruise ship to Mars. Any votes against?"

"Not me," said Alex.

"Right then, passed *nem. con.*"

"*Nem.* what?"

"Latin," said Carlton, "*nemine contradicente,* unanimously, with one accord, with one voice, with one consent, one and all, nobody against."

"Ah, you mean both of us," said Alex.

"And me," said Carlton.

Alex shook his head, warning Lewis. The tin man always thought he had a vote.

"Unfortunately, dear Carlton," said Lewis, "you do not have a vote."

"Don't start," said Alex.

"I should have a vote, I am more intelligent than you," said Carlton.

"Well, you may be more intelligent than us, but sadly you lack testicles."

"I have tungsten carbide testicles," protested Carlton.

"Well, there you have it," said Lewis.

"Females don't have testicles and they have a vote."

"Females," said Lewis patiently, "despite being very strange in their own way, are human. That is why they have a vote and you do not."

"It's not fair."

"I didn't make the rules."

"It's DNAcism."

"Carlton, shut up."

"Okay," said Alex, "his vote counts half. That's two and a half to none. I declare the motion carried. The Road to Mars it is."

Blessed are the peacemakers.

THE ROAD TO MARS

At my back I always hear / Time's wingéd chariot hurrying near.

ANDREW MARVELL

Time, as we know, is a relative concept (no jokes, I beg you, about how it passes much more slowly with relatives). To sit on a spacecraft while it inches along the 400-million-mile time line between Saturn and Jupiter is to be aware of just how much time there is in the Universe, let alone how much space. Space and time are not at all the same thing, as anyone who has sat between a fat man and a bore can attest. One occupies space, but oh, what acres of time the other one wastes. And though our space is limited, our time limitations are what drive us crazy.

Time, time, it takes eons of it to get anywhere in this damn Universe. There's no getting around it. All that sci-fi bullshit, going to light speed, sir. Yeah right, light speed for 5,000 years gets you about as far as a nearby star. Big deal. Worm holes in space? More like assholes in space.

My point, and there is one, I assure you, is that buckets of time have to be gone through to get anywhere in space and that while they slowly plough this lengthy space-time furrow, Lewis fishing or talking to the shrinkbot, Alex playing endless interactive games— during these nine long months while they journeyed inwards towards the sun, something very significant began to happen: Carlton began to study comedy.

He was taking a correspondence course in communication for his masters degree when it first occurred to him what a truly peculiar thing Alex and Lewis did for a living: *their job was to make humans bark.* Why did they do that? What's more, why did humans so enjoy barking together? What made it so popular, and finally and most irritatingly, why couldn't he understand it? He appreciated that comedy was something endemic in Homo sapiens, and that they felt both proud and protective of it, but he didn't understand what purpose it served, or why it existed or what evolutionary value it might have. So during these long, slow months of travel, Carlton began to study the living comedy petri dish in front of him, to wit Alex and Lewis. He began to take notes on their behavior, collating material for his thesis.

At first he took notes purely for himself, to avoid upsetting Alex and Lewis, who were as testy as a pair of mother hens, because their odd responses intrigued him. For example, they were constantly saying "Get out of here." He would obediently leave the room only to discover moments later that *this was not what was wanted at all*. It wasn't a command to get out of there, but some kind of ironic observation. The difficulty was how to tell the difference. How was a perfectly logical machine to understand irony? It was impossible to spot irony without understanding irony, and yet how could he understand irony without spotting it? He would speed-read the entire works of Jane Austen in ten minutes in the hope of illumination, but without luck. If you don't recognize irony, you can't see it, and you can't see it if you don't recognize it. This Catch-22 was not resolved at all when he turned to Fowler. In his classic volume *Modern English Usage* he read, "Irony is a form of utterance that postulates a double audience, consisting of one party that, hearing, shall hear and shall not understand, and another party that, when more is meant than meets the ear, is aware both of that more and of the outsiders' incomprehension."

The more he read that sentence, the more he identified with that outsider's incomprehension. Was it possible that the very definition was ironic? He puzzled away at understanding it as they churned their way slowly through the endless night of space. No time. No days. No weeks. No weekends. Lewis watching endless ball games, Alex punishing his body running, cycling, or climbing.

"As long as it keeps you off the Hello Sailors," said Lewis.

"Bitch," said Alex.

He had one sex doll. Just one. He rarely took it out, but Lewis had found it and showed it to the Washing Machine. She was an old machine who went around cleaning, picking up clothing, muttering and complaining to herself, like a middle-aged lady from Queens, aching and kvetching. She drove Alex nuts.

"Take a look at this, Mrs. Greenaway," Lewis had said, handing her the small pliant and, I must say, attractive doll.

She looked puzzled at the foot-high curvaceous blond figure.

"*Oy vey*. What's this?" she had said.

"Press it," said Lewis.

She pressed the little figure.

"Yo, Mama," said the doll. "Ya wanna play with me?"

"It's a toy yet?" said Mrs. Greenaway.

"Want I should remove a few clothes?" said the toy, seductively beginning to vamp like a tramp.

"God forbid! I have enough to wash already," said the Washing Machine.

Mrs. Greenaway wouldn't let Alex hear the last of it.

"What is it again, some kind of a toy? At your age you still play with toys."

"Just leave it alone, Mrs. Greenaway."

"You're a child yet? You want I bring you some proper toys. That I have lived to see the day when, hey."

Alex switched her off.

Lewis laughed and went back to watching endless football games on the floating TV screen. The TV followed him as he wandered through the ship eating bowls of cereal. Alex heard him occasionally screaming "Yes!" when someone scored. Alex preferred to sit in the galley and mainline coffee. It was his only remaining vice. He had tried everything else and found he could control nothing. Now he stuck to espresso. Occasionally they swam in the gravity pool, under the great dome of the stars, and then sat in the steam room tossing around a few comedy ideas, at which point Carlton would tune in and take notes. He downloaded these notes while they slept, puzzling his blond head for hours over what they were doing. What made them think frogs were funny? Why did they always laugh when they said "tits"? What exactly was so hilarious about passing gas from the lower intestine? Carlton's trademark eyes, one green, one brown, focused intently on the problems of comedy, and the basic question, *what on earth was it?*

His first approach to understanding humor was linguistic. Is comedy, he wondered, a recognition of the ambiguities and pitfalls inherent in speech? He read that comedy is the last thing you learn in a language. Henri Bergson observed that to make the French laugh, you have to know their language backwards, but Carlton did know French backwards; he was a computer, he could even *speak* French backwards and it didn't help at all. He knew this because he tried speaking French backwards to a chef in a French restaurant who not only didn't laugh; he became very angry and threw him out. So he was no closer to understanding what made the French laugh. Thank God he didn't try German. Even in English it is very hard for a computer to pick up when someone is being funny. For example, take the simple question "Is your disc hard or floppy?" Now to a computer that has only one set of meanings, but to humans there are all sorts of secondary meanings, largely to do with innuendos about mating, that are lurking behind the words. There at once you have the difference between human beings and machines. Computers are not easily capable of spotting innuendo. It's like Carlton's problem with irony. How is a computer to discern what humans instinctively understand from the context of what is being said? As Carlton himself put it in a revealing passage, "Computers don't poop, fart, fuck, or laugh, and cannot detect irony. These then are the distinguishing characteristics of humanity."

He had got as far as this in his thinking when a soft buzz told him they were approaching New Sydney, a large Stanford Torus within the Jovian system.

NEW SYDNEY

"Do you have a criminal record?"
"Good heavens, I had no idea one was still required."

BRITISH JOKE ABOUT ENTERING AUSTRALIA

Bringing a vessel into port when you have been floating for months with nothing closer to you than 70,000 miles is like threading a needle after crossing the Antarctic. They hadn't so much as seen another ship in two months. Now a vast doughnut-shaped Torus wheeled below them, with hundreds of small craft buzzing around its harbor. Their attention was immediately focused on the

Princess Diana, a monstrously large solar cruiser, the flagship of the Keppler fleet. It was the most gigantic cruise ship they had ever seen. It stretched for almost three miles, totally obliterating their view of Jupiter. Around its various entry ports little boats weaved in and out, picking up passengers to ferry them ashore. Its massive size meant it was unable to dock anywhere, and its orange-colored ferries served as both lifeboats and tenders. It was a cruciform cruiser, which is a technical way of saying that in section it was X-shaped, with four massive arms, each bedecked with enormous terraces, a shape which guaranteed the most number of outside cabins, providing the occupants with staggering views of the Milky Way. Where the four arms intersected, Alex could see leisure parks and playgrounds with people swimming and golfing and jogging. It was about to carry 10,000 passengers around a three-year cruise of the planetary system. Lewis was hoping for at least one gig on board, maybe even a regular contract.

"But it's a floating geriatric home," protested Alex.

"Who else has the time to float around the solar system?"

It was a good point. Attractive though the solar system is, it still takes years to get around. Elderly ladies were attracted by the bridge, the young male crewmen, and the desire to see more of the solar system into which they were born, before they were recycled as hydrocarbons. Muscroft and Ashby had passed their electronic audition with a carefully edited tape of their performances in which some of the ruder parts of Alex's dialogue were tastefully eliminated. Now they faced an interview with the cruise manager of the ship, Mrs. Johnston, who was legendary amongst artistes and bookers as a dragon lady of ferocious bad will. Since the *Princess Di* was vast and consumed so much entertainment amongst its four huge decks, this would be an open call that would attract hundreds of artistes to New Sydney.

They passed through the banks of revolving doors on the giant double air locks which separated the parking levels from the surface of New Sydney. There were murals of kangaroos and crocodiles and vast ochre paintings of the outback between huge ads for Coca-Koala. Inside the arrival hall they banged into a short individual in a riot of unmatched clothing, topped with startling green hair. A small stubby cigar was clamped between his teeth. Alex sent him flying.

"Hey, careful brother," said the individual, not in the least concerned by the impact.

"Whoa, holy shit, it's you."

It was Booper, one of the wilder comics on the circuit. He was extreme even by alternative-comedy standards, and had been known to resort to extraordinarily dangerous areas in comedy (such as setting fire to the orchestra, which is usually a no-no). Offstage he was the mildest and gentlest of men, but onstage he was wild. This transformation always amazed Carlton, who could not believe that the soft-spoken, shy young man was the ranting loony who stomped about the stage spitting venom. But that was often the way with entertainers. The shy ones were the ones to look out for.

"Hey, bud, what's up?" said Boo, dusting himself off and hauling Alex into a bear hug. "You here for the cattle call?"

"You too?" asked Alex.

"You know me, man, I thrive on rejection." It was true he had about as much chance of being booked on board a cruise ship as a stripper in the Vatican, but he loved challenges and was optimistic beyond all sense. He was telling Alex about his latest exploits on a cheap week's booking at Caesar's Phallus, a nightclub which bordered on the bordello.

"Oh man, you have no idea how low it was. I kid you not, avoid it like the plague."

"Mechanical hookers?"

"Oh yeah, sure, but at least they were more intelligent than the crowd. It was so cheesy the management offered to pay me in blow jobs."

"You turned it down," said Lewis sarcastically.

"Sure. How would I pay my agent?"

He was quick, no question. He pulled out a hologram photo of two pumpkins with eyes and hair and carrots for noses.

"Seen my kids?" he laughed.

It was a regular gag of his.

"Well, at least they got your looks," said Lewis.

"Rim shot," said Boo, not the least fazed by the gag turning on him.

"Come on, Alex, we have serious business to attend to." Lewis had no time for Boo. He thought him ill-mannered and his comedy offensive.

"Keep taking the colon cleanser," said Boo cheerfully to him. "Maybe you'll loosen up one day."

"What do you see in him?" asked Lewis as they lined up to enter the country.

"He's funny," said Alex.

"He's not funny, he's just rude."

"I like him," said Alex. "He takes risks."

"Well, there's no risk they'll book him," said Lewis.

Above their heads a gigantic 3-D screen faced arriving passengers with the grossly magnified features of the diva Brenda Woolley. She was *the* singing sensation of the mid-planetary system, and had been for almost thirty years. She was now, alas, at that dangerous age of denial in the female star which Alex called "the Peter Pancake Syndrome," where youth was replaced by makeup. In her case a bricklayer might have laid it on, for on the giant screen with her mouth stretching for a high note, it was not a pretty sight.

Alex, Lewis, and Carlton entered the arrival hall and were preparing to clear customs when they saw Boo look up at the image of Brenda Woolley and leap back in mock terror.

"Look out," he yelled, pointing to the screen, "the mouth that roared!"

Startled, the customs officers looked upwards, some automatically reaching for their security belts. They turned back to Boo when they realized he was kidding.

"Hey, mate," said one angrily, "watch your mouth, we like that lady here."

"Oh sorry," said Boo, "I mistook you for people of taste."

There was an ugly silence.

"He's a comedian," said Carlton. "He says odd things in order to be funny. It was a joke. An attempt to be risible. A pairing of the disparate in order to create a physical response of merriment in the hearer."

They stared at him.

"Comedy, you know," said Carlton. "Risibility. Buffoonery. Farce. Burlesque. Knockabout. Slapstick. To occupy in an agreeable, pleasing, or entertaining fashion, to cause to laugh or smile by giving pleasure."

"Thanks, we do know what comedy is," said the officer, refusing to be mollified. "Is this your tin feller?"

"Yes," said Alex. "He is a little unusual."

"And is the other weird one with you?" said the agent, indicating Boo.

"Definitely not," said Lewis.

"Well, he'd better watch it. We don't like jokes like that here. He might get hurt."

"Point taken, Officer," said Alex. "He hasn't seen real people in a while."

He shoved Boo on ahead, who refused to give up and kept looking up at Brenda Woolley on the enormous screen, crossing himself and muttering.

"Thanks, bro," said Boo to Alex when they had passed into the arrival hall. "I guess it's better to get into a place before getting thrown out." He ruffled Alex's rusty hair affectionately, slapped him five, and set off jauntily towards the Gravity-Free Shopping Zone, which was beginning to fill with little old ladies, floating around shopping.

"Guess I'll check out the smoke shop," he said by way of farewell. "See you at the cattle market."

"That little turd," said Lewis disdainfully.

"He's okay," said Alex.

"Yeah? He's about as funny as dead meat."

"Some people like him," said Alex.

Lewis turned his baleful brown eyes on him. Oh-oh, better change the subject, thought Alex. Lewis would never simply let things go. "We'd better find a cab quick, the cruise ship is unloading."

Lewis glanced over to a line of little old ladies waving shopping bags and heading determinedly towards them.

"Better hurry, don't want to be trampled to death."

Shrieking and whooping, the old ladies headed for the Gravity-Free Shopping Zone.

Alex and Lewis raced ahead and beat out a party of bearded, black-robed clerics to the front of the line. The clerics glared angrily at them as they piled into the only taxi.

"Who are they?" asked Alex

"Oh, just some religion that hates women and razors," said Lewis.

"Why?" said Carlton in a very strange voice. "Because they shave their legs?"

He looked round triumphantly as if awaiting some reaction. They looked at each other, puzzled.

"Was that funny?" asked Carlton.

"No," said Alex.

THE CATTLE CALL

I can tell at once whether they are my kind of people. We do look for a certain type.

MRS. JOHNSTON, HEAD OF CASTING, KEPPLER CRUISES

A Stanford Torus is a huge revolving doughnut which slowly turns in space, creating by centrifugal force conditions resembling gravity. Imagine an inner tube; on the outside the view is of the galaxy slowly revolving, a night sky freckled with stars constantly in rotation, but on the inside you can see the other side of the city whirling up over your head.

The taxi flew them along the inside rim. It was a bubble cab affording breathtaking views of New Sydney Harbor sparkling in the sunlight below them. High above their heads lay downtown. The sun itself was much brighter here than out by Saturn, though still only a quarter of the size it appears on Earth.

"Best place in the world, New Sydney," said the mechanical cabby as they landed on top of a tall building. "God's own city." He spoke with the colony's nasal twang.

"Looks like a doughnut to me," said Lewis dryly.

"That's a Torus, mate, not a doughnut," said the cabby.

"Ah, too bad," said Alex. "No jam."

"Very funny," said the cabby as they paid him and headed towards a bank of elevators.

"I'm certain he didn't really appreciate the joke," said Carlton seriously. "I think he knows you were being funny, but he didn't really get it."

"Really?" said Lewis. "And what would you know about it?"

"Lewis, dear," said Alex, "let's not get snappy with the tin man now we're in Oz."

"That's all right," said Carlton. "Lewis is probably nervous about the audition. A perfectly natural human response since your chance of success is less than 8.273 percent."

"Thanks for your confidence," said Alex.

"You're welcome," said Carlton, the irony as usual escaping him.

"Gooday, mates, and welcome to the Keppler Towers," said the elevator mechanically in that quaint Australian burr. "Floor 400. Hold tight."

They shot upwards. Mozac played loudly as they rode.

"Ah, the Minuet in H," said Alex.

"Don't you love Mozac?" said the elevator.

The doors slid open, depositing them in a gilded Art Deco world.

"Goodbyee," said the elevator. "Thank you for choosing Elevator B. Have a fabby day."

Inside the double doors of Suite 40,000 a platinum blond receptionist sat behind a desk reading a book. She barely glanced up as they entered the room.

"Mrs. Johnston," said Lewis, "we have an appointment."

"*He's* not Mrs. Johnston," said Alex helpfully. "That's who we want to see."

She gave him a look which said don't mess with me and pointed her pencil at another door.

"In there," she said.

"Just kidding," said Alex.

"They're Muscroft and Ashby," said Carlton helpfully to the receptionist. "A comedy duo."

"I don't care if they're Einstein and Hubble, they wait in there."

"Einstein and Hubble. Great comedy duo," said Alex, entering the waiting room.

A crowd of people glanced up briefly.

"Hey, brother, what kept you so long?" It was Boo.

"How'd you get here so fast?" asked Alex.

"Walked right ahead and grabbed the shuttle. It's quicker than a cab. Cheaper too."

"Thanks for sharing," said Lewis.

"Hope you don't mind, I put you down as a referee."

"For what?" said Lewis.

"For football, what you think? My character."

"Your character?"

"Yeah. Formal stuff, you know. They need to know who will cover me in the event of any fire damage and shit like that."

"Fire damage?"

"It happens. I have a record. They wanted some guarantee."

"And you chose us?" asked Lewis, astounded.

"No, I chose *you*," said Boo to Lewis, "on account of you being such a straight-ass and a real fine upstanding and decent person."

"Nice," said Lewis.

"I would gladly have performed the service of referee for our friend here," said a tall florid figure seated beside Boo in a battered three-piece tweed suit with a pink carnation in his buttonhole, "but, alas, some mix-up with my credit. They are scoundrels, sir, they are scoundrels, fools, and knaves."

"Have you met Charlie?" asked Boo.

The gentleman in question rose to his feet, removed a large fedora from his head in salutation, bowed extravagantly, offered them a hologram business card, and sat down breathing heavily.

"Charles Jay Brown, Cosmic Management, at your service. You may reach me at these numbers any time, night or day. Open all hours, we never close."

His long silver hair was streaked with yellow, but whether through dye, nature, or nicotine was hard to say. His face was like an old map of Mars, with many lines and blotches etched in red. His age was hard to place, somewhere between fifty and sixty, and his eyes were bright and alert, staring out inquiringly from under great beetle black eyebrows.

"What the hell is Cosmic Management?" asked Lewis.

"Career management of comedians, professional advice of all sorts, business, taxation, wives, girlfriends, abortions, divorces, lawsuits, car rental, food service, and massage. All taken care of for a measly twenty percent."

"Twenty percent!"

"I will consider fifteen."

"Ain't he something," said Boo. "He's my new management."

"Our young friend Mr. Booper has wisely consented to accept my professional advice upon his career."

"And you've advised him to retire?" said Lewis.

"Don't hold your breath," said Boo.

"His humor is somewhat rancorous, I grant you, but he gives delight to the young, and they, sir, are the future, and the future is my business."

"Talks like a dictionary, don't he?" said Boo.

Charles Jay Brown raised an eyebrow and contemplated Boo as one would an imbecilic child. Satisfied that the child was placid, he reverted his attention to Alex.

"Incidentally, should either of you two gentlemen be requiring representation at the moment, I would be most happy to advise you. I have spent a lifetime watering the gardens of wit and reaping reward from the harvest of mirth therein sown."

"Does he always talk like this?" asked Alex.

"Used to be a preacher," said Boo proudly.

"Alas, sir, an unfortunate fondness for the bottle combined with a weakness for the younger female congregants caused my downfall. It was a misfortune sinfully exploited by the gutter press. Christ himself used to deal with prostitutes and sinners."

"Not quite so hands-on though, Charlie," said Boo.

"Point taken, dear boy. But I flatter myself the Church's loss has been comedy's gain. May I put you down as interested clients?"

"In a rat's ass," said Alex.

"I believe those conditions are acceptable to Mr. Brown," said Boo. "Have the rat washed and sent to his room."

"Doubtless you are fully represented at the moment. Should you, however, change your minds, I would be only too happy to entertain you."

"Would you gentlemen *puhleeze* sit down and wait quietly. We have a lot to get through here," the receptionist said icily.

"Sorry, lady," said Alex.

"Got a broom up her ass," said Boo in a loud stage whisper.

Half an hour passed. It was like a doctor's waiting room. Boo kept catching Alex's eye. From time to time a smartly dressed secretary with a clipboard appeared at the door and called out a name or two.

"I think they must be killing them," said Boo. "You notice they go in but they never come back."

"Mr. Booper," said the receptionist, finally out of patience, "will you please wait quietly or I shall be forced to report you to Mrs. Johnston."

"Hey, how come it's always me?" whined Boo.

"Because it *is* always you," said Lewis. "You have the attention span of a ten-year-old."

"Thanks," said Boo nicely.

"The Tribe of Robinsons?" inquired the trim young secretary looking quizzically around the room. A party of four very young men in electric blue suits and amazing Afros rose and moved towards the door in unison.

"Give 'em hell, boys," said Boo.

Another forty minutes passed.

"This sucks," said Boo petulantly. He couldn't keep still. He champed continuously on a small stubby cigar and wriggled around in his seat.

"Did you ever try reading?" asked Lewis sarcastically.

"Had a book once. Read it. Finished it. Big deal," said Boo.

"Reading, sir, is the finest gift of God to man," said Charles. "It refreshes the soul. It restoreth the spirit. It stimulates the senses and enlightens the mind, washes the inner man in the shower of simile, bathes the being in the warm waters of words. Why, reading is the very enemy of the devil, sir, and I shall tell you why . . ."

But he never got to complete his sermon, for at that moment the door opened and the secretary announced "Muscroft and Ashby" to no one in particular.

"Hold it," said Boo, leaping to his feet, "I was before them."

"That's who they've called," said the secretary. There was a faint smirk of triumph on the lips of the receptionist.

"How'd you like that?" said Boo to Charlie.

"Be like the ancient Christians when thrown to the Romans, sir. Be stoical in all things, I beg you."

Boo shrugged. "Hey, I got nowhere to go."

"That's for sure," said Lewis.

As Lewis passed him, Boo blew a loud raspberry on the back of his hand.

Lewis shook his head and let it go. They followed the secretary towards the open door.

"Good luck with the old material," said Boo just loud enough as they entered.

"I swear I could kill him," said Lewis.

"He don't mean nothing," said Alex. "Come on. Concentrate."

Twenty minutes it was over.

"We'll let you know," said the secretary, ushering them back through the waiting room.

"Oh-oh, bad sign," said Boo, looking up in surprise. "Coming back through here, definitely not a good sign."

"When?" asked Alex.

"When what?" said the secretary, genuinely confused.

"When will you let us know?"

She reacted like she had never heard this before. "Oh, I see."

"That's just the kiss-off, buddy," said Boo. "It's like thanks after sex. It don't mean nothing."

The secretary ignored him. "They'll be posting the results in an hour. You could come back then. There's a coffee shop downstairs if you'd like to wait," she said and then added as an afterthought, "of course we could always call your agent."

"That's a good one," said Boo. "His agent died of malnutrition."

"We'll come back," said Alex. "We'd like to know."

"What you give 'em? Badgers in Space? Rodent Rodeo?"

"They did a hopping hospital piece that was hilarious," said Carlton.

"Oh no, the old hopping hospital bit," said Boo to Lewis. "I'm impressed. Physical comedy at your age."

"Oh, knock it off," said Lewis irritably.

"Any laughs, Alex?" asked Boo.

"One of 'em sneezed," said Alex.

"A sneeze ain't bad for a comedy audition. I'll take a burp if it's timely. Thanks for warming them up for me."

"Break your legs," said Carlton.

"That's a leg," said Boo.

"Don't just stop at the legs," said Lewis, leaving.

"Rim shot," said Boo, unfazed.

"Will you kindly put that cigar away," said the receptionist.

"It's not lit," said Boo.

"This is a tobacco-free planet."

"It's a prop. I use it in my act."

"Then please insert it in an appropriate place when your act commences."

"One to the receptionist," said Charles Jay Brown, turning the pages of his racing form.

"Some people got their heads up their own asses," muttered Boo.

KATY

I don't think there is any subject which cannot be funny.

PETER COOK

"Ask me the secret of comedy."

"What is the secret of . . ."

"Timing."

Yeah we've all heard that joke. But the secret of comedy is sadness. Bleakness. It's a young man's game. Only the young have sufficient moral certainty to see how things are and how that differs from how things ought to be. The anger of comedy is for the young. Age sucks. With age comes ambivalence, the inability to be shocked anymore by the constant disappointments of life. I should know. I'm a forty-four-year-old professor of micropaleontology at USSAT hooked up with a thirty-something biology buff who's driving me nuts. Don't talk to me about anger. I'm stuck every day studying the crap of the late twentieth century, and she's out there partying. I have to sit and read about all those poor sods on the cusp of the twenty-first century, a whole new millennium dawning, and they're wearing their caps backwards. Two thousand years of civilization, and they're walking around with the manufacturers' names on the outside of their clothes. Don't make me laugh. We're all just thin layers of rock in the end. Sedimentary, my dear Watson.

Thank Christ for Carlton. My secret. My lifeline. The inventor of the antijoke. I kid you not. He postulated a category of things that don't make you laugh which he called the antijoke. There were the things that were funny, and the things that were not funny. The things that were not funny he called anticomedy. The trouble is that these things kept shifting. Things could be both funny and not funny depending on the context. He could find nothing that was funny in and of itself, and nothing that couldn't be funny occasionally. Baffling. He defined the anticomic too. He had observed that both Lewis and Alex hated certain comedians. Detested them. Couldn't stand them. "They're just not funny," they said. This totally puzzled him since these comedians were often very successful and drew big laughs from an audience. How could they get laughs and still not be funny? He worked for days postulating something he called the antilaugh, before he realized that it was just plain old-fashioned jealousy. Alex and Lewis were envious.

Currently he's working on the biology of comedy. Seriously. He's studying the genetic makeup of comics. He suspects that there's a comedy gene, something inherited, hidden somewhere in their autoimmune system. He points out human DNA is so long that if it were possible to stretch out the DNA of a baby into a single line, the distance would be staggering: *fifteen times* the round trip between Pluto and the sun. Somewhere in that billion-mile line of genetic material there could easily lurk a comedy gene. But how to find it? He dreams vaguely of identifying this gene and putting it into a lab rat. The world's first stand-up mouse. He's a hoot, isn't he?

The coffee shop was busy. They left Carlton plugged into the recharger.

"I really don't need a top-up, my batteries are fine," he protested.

"Better safe than sorry," said Lewis.

They nabbed a table by the window and ordered a couple of coffees. Alex drummed his leg nervously. He could hardly contain himself as the gangly Lewis wound his limbs into the booth.

"So how d'you think we did?" he asked the minute he'd settled.

"Well . . ." said Lewis, staring at the legs of the waitress.

"Not good, huh?"

"I didn't say that."

Alex beamed.

"I didn't say we did good either." He watched Alex's face fall instantly, his mouth sinking into an upside-down U. He looked like a mask of tragedy.

"Alex, it wasn't *that* bad," he said.

"So you think we have a shot?" His face brightened again.

Boy, the guy is volatile, thought Lewis. "You can never tell with auditions, Alex. Sometimes you think they liked you and you find they absolutely hated you. Other times you play to twenty minutes of silence and they can't wait to sign you."

"So you think we're still alive?"

"We're hanging in, I guess. I'd say we woulda had a definite shot if that idiot Boo hadn't shoved his face in all the time. If they think we're with him, we're dead."

Alex wandered off in search of a sugar bowl. Coffee was his thing since he quit alcohol, but he liked it well stocked with sugar. He squeezed past a warm female body in a fleecy kangora sweater.

"Oh, pardonnez-moi," he said in his mock camp French accent. He reached across for the sugar and brushed against her. "I a-dore kangora, dahling," he said in his deep Tallulah shopping voice. "It's to die for. Half kangaroo, half angora, it's the jumper that keeps on jumping."

She turned and he saw her for the first time. Dark hair, nice face, brown eyes, full lips, high cheekbones, almost Slavic, on the tall side for him, but oh how she breathed. She was shaped too, long legs, straight limbs; her body seemed to glow from within, and the woolly kangora sweater clung flatteringly to her outlines.

"Wait a minute, wait a minute," said Alex, sniffing the air, "the scent is familiar but the shape escapes me. You wouldn't be a woman, would you?"

"I might be," she said. "Hang on a minute, I'll just check." She reached inside her sweater and felt around.

"Oh-oh, breasts, yes. One of the telltale giveaway signs. Woman definitely."

"Mind if I just get a second opinion," said Alex, reaching forward for the hand slap he knew would stop him. It didn't come. He was left with his hand frozen lamely halfway towards her breasts, not quite having the nerve to go through with it.

"Chicken, huh?"

"That's right. Half man, half chicken."

"Not half funny though, Alex. Hi, I'm Katy Wallace."

"You know me?"

"I was just looking at a tape upstairs. Hopping hospital. Very funny stuff."

"You think so?"

"You made me laugh."

"Oh, thank you, God" said Alex, looking upwards.

"Do you always speak to Him in public?"

"Only in coffee shops," said Alex. "He's a caffeine freak, you see. A speed-of-light junkie. Ever since the Big Bang, he needs more and more energy."

Her laugh was open and genuine.

"So you're with the Keppler cruise?"

"That's right."

Alex couldn't believe his luck. He had the biggest grin on his face.

"In casting?"

"Not exactly." She glanced over his shoulder and frowned for a second. Then she relaxed and smiled, put a hand on his arm, and said nicely enough, "Will you excuse me, I gotta make a call."

"Can I come with you?"

"It's a call of nature."

"I love nature."

"Then we'd better let it take its course."

She squeezed past him so close he could breathe her in, and headed for the rest room. Halfway across the café she glanced back. He was still watching her. She threw him a little wave.

"Who was that?" asked Lewis.

"Oh, just someone," said Alex.

"Cute."

"Cute ain't it."

SUCCESS

The reason that there are so few women comics is that so few women can bear being laughed at.

ANNA RUSSELL

Why does laughter empower the male but threaten the female? Is it something to do with not laughing at the penis or the erection will crumble? What is it with women and humor anyway? Why do they find it so appealing? Why don't men ever boast, "I got this dame with a great sense of humor"? Not my questions by the way. These are things Carlton was asking himself as he observed Katy Wallace leaving the coffee shop. He'd been listening in, of course. Can't blame him—that's his job and he took some great shots of her, which I have just finished downloading. I must say she is one hell of a great-looking lady. I can see why Alex was smitten. Much better than my Molly. But then I'm not a famous comedian, am I? Don't get me wrong, Molly's not bad-looking. I suppose you could call her a bit trampy. There is something a little obvious about her, some hint of the trailer park, but then, that's where she's from. I suppose you'd say she was a dirty blonde, that kind of streaky look. I saw her first in an oyster bar. It was lust at first sight. I thought, Ooh, hello, who's that then? She was laughing at the bar, in a push-up bra, her blouse too open and her skirt no bigger than a large belt. Wearing fuck-me boots. All shiny and plastic in black. That clinched it for me. Good legs, and she gave you a pretty decent look at them up at the receiving end where they just dipped under the red vinyl. A lot of makeup, I grant you, especially round the eyes. I used to think she looked like a ring-tailed lemur. But I liked the challenging way she looked at you through those bruised eyes with the deep dark circles that suggested lack of sleep and hinted of depravity. You'd have to be deaf and blind not to notice her that night.

I found her irresistible.

I had twelve oysters last night and only four worked. That was our joke the next day when I woke up with her. Gotta tell you, no boasting, those sheets were pretty darn crumpled. I'd had a couple of cocktails and was feeling pretty horny, and now I come to think about it she picked *me* up and took me back for a workout. She liked sex, and that's always very pleasant in a woman. Matter of fact, I soon found she liked it a little bit too much. I'd find her stretched out on the floor with the vibrator when I got home. "Honey, I started without you," she'd say in that husky voice of hers. "Come here and finish the job." The job. That's sometimes what it felt like as I obediently labored away on top of her.

So she's a game girl, Molly, but a long way off that Katy Wallace. Now *she* is one hell of a classy lady.

When Alex and Lewis returned to the office an hour later, Boo was just emerging. He seemed tremendously pleased with himself.

"You got the gig?" asked Alex.

"No, man, I got flung out. They hated me."

"Imagine," said Lewis.

"Why'd you get flung out?" asked Alex.

"No idea," said Boo.

"Perhaps you shouldn't have set fire to her desk," said Charlie. "I believe that was extending the boundaries of comedy a little too far."

"She said, 'Surprise me.' At least I didn't take my dick out. Maybe I shoulda. Doesn't look like she gets to see a lot."

"Wouldn't see a lot with you anyway," said Lewis.

"Ta-da," said Boo, flicking ash off an imaginary cigar.

"If you gentlemen will excuse me," said Charles Jay Brown, firmly placing a large fedora on his head, "I have a date with some ponies."

"He's not a gambler," said Boo. "He just likes to fuck animals."

Nobody laughed. It seemed to reassure Boo.

Charles Brown tipped his fedora at the door. "My heartiest congratulations to you gentlemen on your forthcoming employment. My client and I join you in our sincerest wishes for your continued success."

"Say what?" said Alex.

"Didn't you know? You guys got lucky," said Boo. "You're on the list. Congratulations." He didn't look that happy.

"We got the gig?" asked Lewis in disbelief.

"Sure did."

"Oh yay!" said Alex, breaking into a rumba. He danced round the room, wiggling his butt and waggling his body, waving imaginary maracas in the air. Even Lewis smiled.

"So who was the dame?" said Boo when Alex finally calmed down.

"What dame?"

"The one with the legs. Katy something?"

"She was here?" said Alex, his face lighting up.

"Don't give me that shit," said Boo. "I heard her put you on the list. They tried to argue; she said, 'Just do it.' Old Frozen Face practically had a fit. What did you do to her?"

"Just gave her sugar."

"Well, she must be diabetic, 'cause she sure went to bat for you."

"How about that," said Alex. "It must be my animal magnetism."

"Perhaps I oughta slip her some candy," said Boo reflexively. "Maybe I'd get me a job."

Lewis was reading the posted list. "Brenda Woolley. Act One," he said. "Muscroft and Ashby, Comedy with a Difference, seven minutes."

"Too bad you got the death slot in the first act," said Boo. "I guess she didn't love you that much."

"As long as we got an audience," said Alex.

"Audiences," sniffed Boo contemptuously, "that's what spoils comedy."

CHARLES JAY BROWN

Most people think, oh Jerry Lewis is the funny man—what does Dean Martin do? The answer is, he makes Jerry Lewis funny.

PETER COOK

The orange tender was jammed with little old ladies. The ritual hunting and gathering of local souvenirs was over for the day, and the shoppers were discussing the kill: kangaroos, koala bears, tiny stuffed emus, plaster models of the New Sydney Harbor Bridge and little plastic statuettes of Brenda Woolley.

"Look, a tiny Brenda," said Alex. "Small is beautiful, but not small enough in her case."

They were riding the shuttle out to the cruise ship. Ahead of them an elderly gentleman in a large fedora was scanning the X-shaped profile of the *Princess Di* as their tender slid underneath and in towards the vast main hold.

"Oh, heart, forget not to beat," he said in dramatic terms as the enormous size of the vessel became apparent.

Alex nudged Lewis. "Isn't that Boo's manager?" he asked.

The gentleman in question threw back his arms, removed his hat, and declaimed loudly, " 'Jupiter hath not anything to show more fair,' as the poet Wadsworth remarked in the twenty-first century."

The little old ladies looked up at him in alarm.

"Forgive me, dear ladies," he said in his strange declamatory style, "a man cannot help but ejaculate upon such a glorious sight."

The little old ladies looked startled at his strangely archaic speech, but they were held spellbound.

"It is my way to excoriate upon the beauties and bounties of this glorious Universe, for I am but a simple man of feeling. It is sadly true that the expression of these sentiments has often caused me trouble from the unfeeling masses, but when my sensibilities are aroused, I regret there is no suppressing their articulation. It must come out, ladies, it must come out."

"What's *he* doing here?" said Lewis.

"No sign of Boo though."

"Yeah, he's hard to miss," said Lewis.

"Think his green hair's natural?" asked Alex.

"His hair is. It's the rest of him that isn't," said Lewis.

They watched Boo's manager with the little old ladies.

"Is this guy on the level?" asked Alex, watching him close in on them.

"Managing Boo? How serious can that be? One of the shortest jobs in the Universe."

The fedora was off again, doffed, swept low before them, and re-placed. "Ladies, dear ladies, permit me to introduce myself. Rafael Los Lobos Dos Santis at your service. Occasional Professor of English, sometime Comparative Reader in Various Things at several major academic establishments, and currently Visiting Professor of Applied Comedy at the University of New Sydney."

"I thought you were Cosmic Management."

He turned and surveyed Alex and Lewis from under a bushy eyebrow, entirely unfazed by their sudden appearance. "That, as they say, gentlemen, was yesterday. Today is a whole new ball game. How very pleasant to renew our all-too-brief acquaintance."

"Cosmic Management is over?"

"My clientele, or client, as he is, seems to have an unnatural aversion to people who might employ him. I am seeking to remedy this unfortunate weakness by soliciting direct audience of the great and good. Your Miss Wallace, I am told, is the woman who might intercede on our behalf. It is to her bosom that I shall make my request. The boy, as you know, is harmless, he just needs encouragement."

"You said your name was Brown," said Lewis, wondering what sort of a con he really was.

"My father, a William Morris agent before they were unhappily replaced by machines, advised me that a man might change his name as frequently as his underwear. What's in a name? said the divine Shakespeare. And some say his name was really Bacon."

"Are you an actor?" asked one of the blue-hairs.

"An actor, moi?" said Charles Jay Brown. "My dear lady, I once aspired to that most demanding of roles, but sadly a lack of talent and an outstanding warrant precluded my pursuit of that noble career. Now these fellows whom you behold are comedians of the first rank. They have the good fortune to be your entertainment for tonight, if you have the good fortune to have tickets. Should you not," he added mysteriously, producing a booklet of authentic-looking tickets from the nether reaches of his coat, "I am the fortunate gentleman who can help you in that department."

"The Brenda Woolley show?"

"The very same bill."

"How much?"

"I have excellent seats reasonably priced."

"You're a scalper?" asked Lewis with distaste.

"I do so dislike that word," he said. "It is my way to invest in show biz futures from time to time, an art of great skill, at least as honest as stock investments, for I must gauge exactly the public demand to the supply. As it happens, the great and good Brenda Woolley has exceeded her demand, but these sweet young things are not to know." He turned to his prey. "Now, ladies, you have met two of the stars of tonight's show—how many shall I put you down for each?"

Business was intense.

"What's your game?" asked Lewis when the ladies had been satisfied.

"My game, sir, as you put it, is not dissimilar to your own. The immediate future of Cosmic Management, Inc., which with the attitude of its current clientele"—he cleared his throat—"client, is somewhat insecure. I shall while pressing the case for his employment also be offering my own services to the ship."

"As what?"

"What indeed, sir? A variety of possibilities are available. I might lecture on my exploits as a traveler, for I have visited many antique lands. I give tango lessons up to intermediate level. Drama classes are my forte and my talk on the detective in Shakespeare has been very well received."

"There are no detectives in Shakespeare."

"That is the beauty of the talk, sir. My discourse on the sado-masochistic subtext of Gilbert and Sullivan operettas has been called a minor masterpiece."

"By whom?"

"By myself, sir," he said unashamedly "and I should know. I am also available for legal counsel, emotional advice on any matter, I have a license to marry at will, burial of the dead is my special preserve, and if all else fails I have experience in catering."

"He's just a harmless crackpot," said Alex as they waited in line to pass through the airlock. Their tiny tender had been swallowed into the *Princess Di*'s hold like a shrimp in the mouth of a whale.

"What if he succeeds?" said Lewis. "I couldn't survive six months on the same ship as Boo. I'd have to kill him."

"He won't get a gig here," said Alex. "They won't let him on with little old ladies. Besides, we haven't got the six months yet."

"But we will though, Alex, *won't we?*"

"Oh yes," said Alex.

"Unless one of us screws up."

"But one of us won't screw up, Lewis."

"No farting around."

"Me fart?" said Alex in mock outrage. But he knew what his partner meant. Lewis, the White-Face comedian, hated being out of control on stage. Alex, the Red Nose, loved it. He lived to improvise. To him, nothing was as funny as the first time he thought of it. Lewis liked to have it all locked down and learned. Alex could just roll with an idea, play with it, toss it around. Lewis would stand there silently fuming until he'd finished.

"No improvising."

"All right."

"Just stick to what we agreed."

"Okay, okay. Loosen up, will ya."

But a loose Lewis did not exist. He was born tense. He shook his shoulders and twisted his head from side to side. "I need a massage."

"I need a total body rub," said Alex, "and that's only the beginning." He glanced at his partner. "Hey, pal, relax, we're gonna do fine."

"Of course you will," said Carlton. "Thanks to Miss Wallace the odds are now 52.67 in your favor."

THE PRINCESS DI

Who needs money, when you're funny?

RANDY NEWMAN

They were met by a uniformed page in regulation white pants and blue jacket, holding a card with their names on it.

"Hello, I'm Jeffrey, your page for today. Welcome to the *Princess*

Diana luxury cruise of the solar system," he said. "If you would walk this way."

"If I could walk that way . . ." said Alex.

"Don't go there," said Lewis.

They followed Jeffrey to a waiting cart, climbed aboard, and were whisked onto the express lane of a wide electric people mover. Passengers in holiday clothes were going about the business of the day, heading off to the many pools, the entertainment malls, or the three gigantic golf courses which occupied the space between the X's. Keppler Cruise attendants in their blue-jacket-and-white-pants uniforms were everywhere, leading little groups or ferrying guests towards their quarters.

"You know how many people actually work here?" asked the page.

"About half?" suggested Alex.

The page ignored the gag and settled down to a list of statistics he had clearly swallowed parrot-fashion. Only Carlton feigned interest. Lewis watched the ads as they shot past, and Alex scanned the faces of their potential audience, looking for encouraging signs of their future.

"Largely LOLs," he said.

"What's that?" asked Carlton.

"Little old ladies," said Alex.

The electron cart moved swiftly for a good five minutes before suddenly swinging off the main people mover towards some giant doors marked BACKSTAGE. They dismounted the cart and walked through security. Alex and Lewis were nodded through, but Carlton was stopped by the security guards and taken into a guarded area for screening.

"Security's tight," observed Lewis.

"You can't be too careful with Brenda Woolley," said the page.

"Someone going to steal her handbag?" asked Alex.

"Brenda Woolley does not carry a handbag," said the page with dignity.

"Oops," said Alex.

"What's she like to work with?" asked Lewis.

"She is a star," said the page, his eyes shining.

"Oh," said Alex. "Thanks for the warning."

"What exactly does that mean?" whispered Lewis.

"It means she has a whim of iron."

They waited a further five minutes. There was no sign of Carlton.

"Look, perhaps you'd better leave him here," said the page, "or you'll be late for the Brenda Woolley Experience."

"The what?"

"It's what Miss Woolley likes to call her show. She doesn't like the word 'show.' She thinks it's common."

They came upon a broad open area where several corridors met. Ahead of them there was a sudden shoving and pushing as a flurry of security guards broke through large double doors and held their arms wide as if to push people aside. This would have been more effective if there had been any people to push, but there was no one around. They yelled anyway.

"Stand back. Gangway. Make room. She's coming through."

"Good grief," said Jeffrey in an awed voice. "It's Brenda Woolley!" He might have announced the arrival of God Herself.

"Ouch," said Alex as he was shoved aside and pushed flat against the wall by a brute in a black serge uniform. "Be very careful," said Alex. "I carry a lethal fart."

"It's true," said Lewis. "There are two great gas giants in the solar system: him and Jupiter."

"Don't look at her, don't make eye contact, and shut the fuck up," said the security man.

"They're on the show," said the page.

"Where are their pins then?"

"They've only just arrived," said Jeffrey. "I haven't given them their security package yet."

"All right, she can come through, it's clear," barked the mustache.

And now Brenda Woolley herself appeared, a vision in cream, her blond hair impossibly bouffant, her eyes outlined in black, a faint smile playing round her pastel pink lips. Her fierce green eyes, her signature blue mole at the corner of her mouth, her fine alabaster profile, all this they saw as the security mob led her forward. She avoided eye contact with anyone, but drew her shawl protectively around her like an overage Ophelia. She behaved like a small child, at once grateful and surprised by their treatment.

"What are they protecting her from?" asked Alex. "There's nobody around."

"She needs her privacy," said Jeffrey.

They watched the retreating mob holding off the imaginary hordes around her in the empty corridor. It was both impressive and funny. A display of pure power and a sop to ego.

"Wow, that was close," said Alex. "I could almost see her facelift."

The security guard reluctantly let him go.

"Watch it," he said.

"Thank you and fuck you too," said Alex with a nice smile.

"She's divine," said Jeffrey in total awe as he watched her gliding away. "Totally divine."

The divinity was not yet done with them. At the far set of double doors Brenda turned and looked back dramatically at the deserted corridor.

"You there," she called, singling out Alex as if he were in the middle of a crowd.

"Me?" said Alex.

"Are you one of the guests on my Experience?"

"Yes."

"We both are," said Lewis.

"Do you have names?"

"No," said Alex. "We can't afford them."

"Muscroft and Ashby," said the page.

"Ah, Muscroft and Ashby, I do so *adore* country music."

"That's Alex and Lewis, not Clint and Billy Bob," said Alex.

"They are comedians, Miss Woolley," said the page.

"Oh, of course. Well, welcome. Welcome, one and all. And you, the cheeky one. Are you single?"

The blank faces of the security guards stared impassively at Alex.

"No," said Alex, "I'm with him."

"Aha," said Brenda significantly as if divining the secret of his sexuality.

"I'm his partner," said Lewis firmly.

"That's all right by me," said Brenda. "I'm very broad-minded," and she swept away to more important things.

"Thanks a lot," said Alex. "Now she thinks we're gay."

"You should be so lucky," said Jeffrey.

He showed them to their dressing room in wounded silence. It was a smallish box with a bathroom attached. The box contained a sofa and a tiny table dwarfed by an enormous bowl of flowers with a card which said PLEASE ENJOY YOUR BRENDA WOOLLEY EXPERIENCE.

"Enjoy the Experience," said the page, leaving them to the amenities.

"Do you think it's like an out-of-body experience?" asked Alex.

"Not the way she was looking at you."

"Oh come on, she's old enough to be my mother."

"You have a problem with that, Oedipus?" asked Lewis.

There was a discreet knock at the door.

"Hello, Jeffrey," said Alex in his screaming camp voice. "Couldn't tear yourself away from me?"

He opened the door. Katy Wallace stood there.

"Who could?" she said.

"Oh. It's you."

"Sorry to disappoint," she said.

Disappoint. My God, she was dynamite. She had her hair pulled back from her face, which let him enjoy her high Slavic cheekbones and her deep brown eyes. Flawless olive skin, and those lips; when she smiled at him, he felt a deep desire to kiss them immediately. She exuded a kind of healthy animal confidence, as though she was entirely comfortable in her body, like a dancer or an athlete. He said nothing for a minute, just feasting his eyes and letting the wave of her perfume wash over him. She held his glance and then broke the silence.

"Nice to see you too, Mr. Muscroft."

"Please call me Alex," he said. "Though my real friends call me Bubbles."

"Why Bubbles?"

"Because he's forever blowing bubbles," said Lewis, coming to the door.

"Flatulence will get you nowhere," said Alex.

"Bubbles it is then."

Lewis was all friendly. "Hi, we didn't meet in the coffee shop. I'm Lewis. Thanks for all you have done for us, getting us here and all."

"Believe me, it was nothing. I'm a big fan, though I'm afraid the crowd may not be quite what you're used to."

"Oh, we've played to LOLs before."

She didn't understand but let it pass.

"Look, I have to go. I just wanted to welcome you and give you these."

She held two small metallic pins. "Security," she said. "Keep them

with you until you leave the ship." She handed Lewis a clown and
Alex an elephant head.

"What is this?"

"It's a Ganesha," she said. "A Hindu god. The Remover of Obstacles, I believe. Here, let me help you with it." She took it back from
him and stooped her head to pin it on him. He felt the warmth of her
breath as she pinned the tiny elephant God on his lapel. I could quite
easily kiss her, he thought. She must have had the same thought, for
she looked at him suddenly and then stepped back.

"You mustn't lose it," she said.

"It will never leave my body," said Alex.

She looked at him for a moment and then smiled, and left.

"Wow," said Alex, "I think I'm in love."

"Too bad you have a date with Brenda Woolley afterwards," said
Lewis. "But I'm free."

Alex opened the door and ran after her. He caught up with her by
a water cooler.

"Hi."

"Oh, hello." She was a little surprised to see him again so soon.

"What are you doing after the show?"

She frowned. "I'm sorry."

"Are you busy?"

"Well yes, as a matter of fact."

"Ah. Too bad." He was crestfallen.

"But thanks for asking."

"This thing"—he indicated the security pin. "What's it called
again?"

"A Ganesha."

"It's Indian?"

"Yes."

"Well, maybe we could have a curry sometime."

"That would be nice."

When he got back to the dressing room, Lewis was just leaving
with the page.

"What's up?"

"We have a problem in Security."

"It's your mechanical assistant," said Jeffrey.

"Carlton?"

"They found something."

In the security area, Carlton was emerging from a large scanner. Three security men were examining his printout. One of them approached Alex.

"Did you know he has some secure files from the Disney Library? It seems to be largely comedy material."

"He's been stealing?" said Lewis.

"Please," said Alex. "They found some files is all."

"He claims he's doing research," said the security man. "Into comedy."

"Is this true, Carlton?" said Lewis.

"Well, I have a theory," began Carlton. "It's really only a rough outline at this stage, but I think comedy is a survival tool used by Homo sapiens to escape the consequences of their own brains. A way, if you like, of handling unpalatable truths."

"Stop right there," said Lewis. "I don't want to hear this bullshit. We're doing a show here, folks. We don't need this, Alex."

"Hey, it's not my fault."

"You told me he was clean."

"It's a comedy file from the twentieth century, for God's sake."

"He's stealing old jokes!"

"I'm not stealing anything. It's purely research material," protested Carlton.

"Which you stole from the Disney Library?"

"I just copied a few files. I didn't have a research card, that's all."

"We employ you as a droid."

"I would never jeopardize my work for you. If you have any problems with me, I would be mortified."

"I am very disappointed in you. Can you believe this, Alex. Our machine is researching comedy, for God's sake." He shook his head and stormed off.

"I am so sorry, Alex, I am so embarrassed."

"Oh, he'll get over it," said Alex. "He's superstitious. Thinks if he ever understands what he's doing he won't be able to do it anymore."

One of the guards approached.

"Alex Muscroft."

"Look, we know about the file and it's not a problem for us."

"Oh, it's not about that, sir. Miss Woolley would like to see you."

"Me?"

"Yes."

"When?"

"Now, sir."

"What about?"

"I'm only Security, sir."

"Well, call Insecurity. I think I'm going to need it."

He was about to knock on the door of Brenda Woolley's dressing room when a short terrierlike woman with artificial red hair, eyes too close together, and designer clothes which were surely designed for someone more attractive, stepped forward and tackled him.

"Hey, hold it right there," she said. "Who are you? Where the hell do you think you're going? The answer's no. Good-bye."

Alex shrugged and turned to walk away.

"Don't you know she has a show to get through," she yelled after him.

Like he gave a damn.

"Hey, wait," she said suddenly. "Are you Alex Muscroft."

He turned and didn't deny it.

"I thought you'd be taller," she said accusingly.

"I was," said Alex.

"Well, she's waiting for you. Come on." She led him forward, then immediately stopped him. Pointing a sharp little finger at his chest. "One or two things," she said. "Don't speak unless she addresses you directly, don't strain her voice, and don't touch her, she's very superstitious. She wants to apologize to you. You can tell her there's no need."

"Isn't that up to me?"

"And above all don't tire her before her performance."

"What we gonna do, play basketball?"

The dressing room door opened and a young woman in tears emerged holding a dress on a hanger.

"Get the fuck outta here and don't come back, you stupid bat."

The terrier swung into action. Nodding to Alex to wait, she plunged into the room.

"Brenda, please, your voice."

"Fuck my voice."

"Then think of your public."

"Oh Pauley, dear Pauley, you are such a friend to me. Whatever would I do without you?" Sounds of an embarrassing embrace.

"Mind your hair, dear," said the terrier named Pauley.

Then some low mutterings. Finally he heard Brenda say, "Oh, just one, Pauley, pretty please, Pauley, I've been ever so good."

"You have a show to get through, my love. Think of your audience."

"Help calm my nervsies," said Brenda pleadingly.

Then some sounds he couldn't make out. Eventually the terrier woman came back and stared at him defiantly. "She'll see you now," she said.

When he entered, Brenda had recovered her composure. The room was rococo. He felt a strong sense of gilt.

"Ah, the country singer," said Brenda, staring at him in her golden makeup mirror.

"Comedian."

"I know, I'm teasing you, dahling. Though I must confess I did think at first you were the Barrel Brothers. Silly little me."

Little? thought Alex. There was way too much of her.

"Everyone knows country singers wear hats, don't they. Even when they're in bed."

She let him digest the thought of her and two country singers called the Barrel Brothers in bed with their hats on. He winced. She didn't notice. She was simply not available for other people's feelings.

"Forgive me, dear Alex, but I'm always *so* distracted before a show. You have *no* idea the pressure. You *must* forgive me. I *know* you will dear. Of course I *love* your work. I *adore* it. I *love* comedy." She seemed to speak in italics. "Pauley dear, tell him how much I *love* comedy."

"That's enough now, Brenda."

"I thought you were a friend of Dorothy's, but a little friend has told me that you're not."

They ran research on his sexuality?

"So perhaps you'd like a little drinkey after the show?"

"Thanks," said Alex, "but I don't drink."

"I'm not supposed to either, but we can make an exception, can't we?"

"Twelve-step program," said Alex.

"I always stumble at the doorstep," said Brenda. "Don't I, Pauley? So how about it? Come out with me afterwards, we can have some fun." She clasped his hand. "I *know* you're going to be *so* great on my show. Please don't run over. Some of our comedians have a tendency to go on a bit, but remember the poor audience, darling, they're here for Brenda. I'll send someone for you after the show."

He was about to make an excuse when the terrier inserted herself physically and backed him through the door.

"Don't say no," said Pauley fiercely. "She does hate no."

"But I can't make it later."

"Don't worry. She'll probably forget."

Feeling vaguely insulted, Alex went off searching for Lewis.

He found Carlton surrounded by chorus girls. The girls were wearing feathers and little else. They were all over him. Alex felt envious. Their droid was far too good-looking. He was a fresh-faced blond-haired doll. Alex was always pushing women off him.

"Leave him alone, will ya?"

"Ooh, can we borrow him tonight?"

"No."

"Oh, please don't be mean, he's so cute."

"Get something real," said Alex. "Or sit on someone else's droid."

"Oh, it's Mr. Grumpy."

"Feeling a little inadequate, are we?" said a chorus girl, sliding her hand towards Carlton's thigh.

"Stop it," said Alex. "He's only got batteries in there."

"What about you," she said, "batteries not included?"

"He's just a humanoid vibrator to you, isn't he?" said Alex.

"He's the ideal date," said the girl. "You can switch him off when you're finished."

The girls all giggled.

"Get real," said Alex.

"No thanks. Tried real. It farts and snores and complains."

"What's that useless piece of skin at the end of a penis called?"

"A man!" they shrieked in chorus.

HIDING IN THE SPOTLIGHT

The test of a real comedian is whether you laugh at him before he opens his mouth.

GEORGE JEAN NATHAN

It's hard for people to realize that famous people are often shy. They are hiding on stage. Ridiculous? Think about it. Makeup. Disguise. Costumes. "Shy" does not mean "lack of ego."

The show went about as well as could be expected. It was full— Charles Jay Brown had done a good job—but it was largely full of little old ladies who would have applauded anything. They were there to see Brenda Woolley, of course, and responded cheerfully enough when she sailed out to introduce the show. It wasn't that she lacked talent, it was just that she behaved as though it wasn't absolutely necessary in her case. That it was somehow beneath her, that by just being there they were somehow blessed. What was so irritating to Alex, who watched every excruciating moment on the monitor, was that she condescended to her audience, confident in their adulation. It was self-satisfaction as an art form. The Goddess as supreme being, doing bugger all. She told a few polite jokes rather poorly, sang a medley of her hit "I'd Cross the Universe for You, My Dahling," threatened to sing more later, and was suddenly gone.

"Jeez," said Alex disgustedly, "she really is a waste of space."

Both Alex and Lewis were nervous before a show, and this night more than most. They both knew this was important. The talent scouts would be watching. Alex paced the room sighing heavily, occasionally stopping to stare at himself closely in the mirror. Lewis sat in the bath reading a magazine, pretending it wasn't happening. Then he slowly and meticulously got dressed, performing strange vocal exercises.

"Ma-na-la, mor-nor-lor, mee-nee-lee, may-nay-lay," he repeated loudly. An irritating mantra for the nervous Alex, whom he studiously ignored. Only when they were about "to walk the fifteen yards" from the wings into the spotlight center stage, did he relax and turn to Alex.

"Okay, pal," he said, "let's do it," and they smiled and nodded and stepped out to face the monster.

In the event, the crowd was good. From the wings they saw Katy Wallace slip into a vacant box where she was joined by an elegant white-haired bearded man who watched the entertainment impassively. It wasn't much of a show, but it was slickly produced and the crowd loved it. The keynote, as with all Brenda Woolley shows, was tacky. For example Alex and Lewis followed an act called Einstein in Hollywood, an unspeakable flying dance routine "inspired by" (don't you love that as a program note?) Einstein's celebrated visit to Hollywood in 1954. At the height of his worldwide fame Einstein was treated to lavish displays of entertainment on the Paramount lot. Helpless to understand the strange mixture of showgirls, moguls, and schlock, he turned to Charlie Chaplin and asked, "What does all this mean?"

"Nothing," replied Chaplin.

This historical moment had been turned into a musical epic, with girls in flimsy costumes floating about yodeling "$E=MC^2$" accompanied by thirty dancers dressed as colored balls depicting molecules. Grinning boys and girls in big round costumes representing electrons, protons, and neutrons frolicked about in various interlocked positions exemplifying hydrogen and carbon atoms.

First thing Alex said as he hit the stage was "Boy, I haven't seen such big balls bouncing around in space since Superman left town."

He got his laugh, but it threw Lewis, who had been anxious about smut and had asked him to keep it clean. To make matters worse, sensing Lewis's panic, he went off on a long riff about Einstein and inadvertently used the f word. He pranced about the stage singing, "E equals MC squared, as if the fuck you cared." It was a shocker for the LOLs. Lewis suddenly seemed to wake up and take control. He dismissed Alex from the stage. He became the outraged authority figure and pointed Alex to the wings. Alex went with it. He cowered and behaved like a guilty ten-year-old. He went further. He became a chimp. The more Lewis remonstrated with him, the more he adopted that strange bent-legged chimpanzee waddle. He ran round the stage squatting with his knees sticking out. He swung on the curtain and thumbed his nose at Lewis. He turned his back-side on him and beat a tattoo on his buttocks. The audience loved it. When Lewis ran backstage to ask for assistance, Alex jumped into the orchestra pit and monkeyed around with the drums, creating chaos. He pretended to pee on the bandleader, which brought a squeal of delight from the little old ladies. Lewis jumped down into the pit to try and catch him, and Alex skipped over the rail into the audience itself. There were howls of delight and screams from the front row. He kissed a tall blond lady and slapped her husband, grabbed a banana from somewhere and improvised strange things with it. Lewis ran to one of the side exits and summoned a couple of guards. As Alex ran round the auditorium, igniting laughter wher-ever he went, the security guards pursued him. It was chaos, it was pandemonium, and it was, of course, all perfectly rehearsed.

"Ars est celare artem," said Carlton, watching in enjoyment from the wings.

"You what?" said a gum-chewing chorus girl.

"The art is in concealing the art," said Carlton. "It's Latin."

"You from Latin America?" she asked.

"Did I ever tell you about my theory of comedy?" he said.

She stopped chewing for a moment.

"Carlton, you're a tin man. You're built like a hunk, but you can be switched off. If they'd remembered to attach a vibrator, you'd be perfect."

"Don't say that," said Carlton, offended.

The audience applauded as Alex was finally chased back onto the stage to face a very stern Lewis. He reverted to the ten-year-old and was told to apologize to the audience, and then to the band, which to much mirth he refused. Lewis, playing the stern, reproving father, in-sisted he shake the hand of the bandleader. He reluctantly reached for it and shook it. Then he snatched the entire arm off the bandleader and ran triumphantly round the stage with it. There was a gasp of horror. The audience was for a moment genuinely shocked, but as Alex continued to play with the arm, they soon realized it was anima-tronic, controlled from the wings by Carlton, and laughed at their own shock. Alex began to improvise with the severed arm, doing strange and nasty things with it before Lewis seemed to get bored and chased him offstage. The applause as they ran off was good.

But Lewis was furious.

"What the hell did you do that for?"

"Why'd you stop me? It was going well."

"You had to say something, didn't you. What's with the Einstein bit?"

"I saw you panic. I thought you'd dried. I just said the first thing that came into my head."

"It went very well," said Carlton.

"Muscroft and Ashby," yelled the MC, and they ran on again and took another bow. The applause was quite warm.

"You know, I think we might have done it," ventured Alex, seeking a way back to Lewis.

"Yeah, right." He stomped off towards the dressing room.

"Why's he so pissed?" asked Carlton.

"He's a perfectionist," said Alex. "He's just mad at himself for losing control there."

"But you did great," said Carlton. "They loved you."

"Yeah. They did." He didn't sound all that convinced. He frowned and stared at his shoes. When he looked up, Katy Wallace was making her way towards him, looking fabulous in a simple tight black dress. She was smiling broadly.

"That was great," said Katy, "really great. I haven't laughed like that in months."

"Really?" said Alex.

"Great job," she said. "I thought it went really well and so did Emil." She was joined by the white-haired man he had glimpsed in the box. He was very tall and thin, with a trim white naval beard. His white hair rose firmly out of his scalp like the bristles in a hairbrush. He looked like someone from the past, an old Edwardian naval officer, polite, formal, and stiff.

"That was very funny indeed," he said without smiling.

"Alex, this is Mr. Keppler."

"Pleased to meet you," said Alex.

"Really very funny," he repeated.

"Oh, we had fun out there," said Alex. "I just wanted to play with them, prod them, and wake them up. I had to mess with their heads after the opening."

"After the what?" asked Keppler.

"Well, you know, it is the Brenda Woolley show after all."

"I'm sorry, I don't follow you. What exactly do you mean?"

"Well, she could pass through a talent detector without registering a blip."

Something in his head was warning him. Something was screaming, No, no, go back.

"You think she is untalented?" asked Keppler politely.

"I think her talent is like antimatter. No one can see it, no one can measure it, who knows if it's really there?"

"Interesting," said Keppler. There was a slight pause. Katy seemed to be examining her shoes. Carlton was looking at him, bug-eyed in disbelief.

"Excuse me," said Keppler after a moment. "I must go and check on something." He gave a brief formal nod and headed backstage.

Katy looked at Alex, gave a half smile, shrugged, and then turned after Keppler.

"Emil," he heard her call after him.

Carlton was still staring at him.

"What? What is it?" said Alex.

"You do know about Brenda Woolley?"

"What?"

"She's his wife."

FATAL INSULT

Fuck 'em if they can't take a joke.

DE RERUM COMOEDIA, CHAPTER XI, "SALMAN RUSHDIE:
THE MAN IN THE IRON MOSQUE"

Comedians often go too far. It's the fatal insult syndrome, the inability to leave well enough alone, to simply shut up and drink your champagne. Carlton has a whole chapter on it in which he examines the self-loathing of the comedian. I suppose we all go too far occasionally. I myself said something to Molly the other day which made her so mad at me she stormed out and hasn't come back since. It was just a joke. Women, eh?

"This tendency to go too far, to shoot yourself in the foot, to snatch defeat from the jaws of victory and bring destruction on yourself when all is going well is a form of self-hatred which is the hallmark of the comedian."

Carlton's got oodles of stuff like this. The trendy magazines are going to just gobble up this psychobabble. They love all that pithy pop cross-cultural kind of crap. I think I can make almost as much from the magazine rights as I can from his book. I see a nice brown cover with, I think, my name on it too. In gold. I'll do a chapter of introduction, maybe even a description of how I came across his work. People like that sort of thing. It's interesting, don't you think?

Having abandoned both the linguistic and the biological approach to comedy for the moment, Carlton is currently making an anthropological attempt to understand the origin of comedy. He even wonders if the bipedal moment in the evolution of the ape is the origin of stand-up. But of course he's found it's like searching for the discovery of fire—there can be no single observable initial moment. So he begins searching for evidence of humor in the great apes. Is it really only the human that has developed humor? The baring of teeth, the barking sound, the bonding of the group, all seem to him essentially animal behavior. In all other creatures the laugh is a form of aggression. How come this extremely offensive signaling was utilized by our species in this peculiar way? Is it defensive? To explain it Carlton comes up with a rather brilliant scenario. He postulates the Basic Chimp Theory.

The Basic Chimp Theory is based on the idea of a primal chimp. The genetic father of all comedians, if you like. The chimpanzee has a small but effective language base, which obviously includes sign language. Chimps have a word for "snake." When a chimp says "snake," they run away. Not all chimps run, however; some continue to play, tempting fate. Carlton posed the idea of a basic comic chimp, an ape who yelled "snake" *when there was no snake*. The others run away and maintain their fear signals at a safe distance (teeth chattering, barking, laughs), but they have been conned. This, Carlton argues, is exactly what happens to an audience.

So *why* would the basic chimp do that? The answer, according to

Carlton, is (a) food (he can eat while they run), (b) power (he has caused their flight), and (c) sex (with power and food comes the reward of the female, with all the advantages for the personal survival of his own DNA). He also notices that the word "aping" means mimicking or imitating. And he recognizes the danger for the comedian, who, if he makes a mistake, can get eaten. He also risks raising the envy of the physically more powerful in the tribe, which is why this particular moment with Alex so fascinates him. Insulting the powerful fits right in with his general thesis.

"I don't think you should have said that," said Carlton as he walked back with Alex towards the dressing room.

"No."

"What are we going to tell Lewis?"

"Why tell him anything?" said Alex.

"He's bound to find out." He frowned as he accessed a distant database. " 'Emil Keppler,' " he read. " 'Silesian. Built the Keppler empire, an entertainment circuit, based on Rhea. Began with container vessels and switched to cruisers after the *Bronia* disaster. Virtually invented the three-year retirement cruise. Combined tourism for the elderly with entertainment, golf, and travel on smooth and efficient hospital ships.' No, I definitely think that was a mistake."

Alex kicked the wall.

"Oh wait," said Carlton as his central region gave a slight ping. "There's something more in here. It's a gossip file. Unreliable."

"What?"

"It's just a rumor. Unsubstantiated. About Miss Wallace."

"What about her."

"It says she is his mistress."

Alex winced. "Thank you, Carlton," he said eventually, "that was really great. You just iced the cake on a perfect day for me."

"You're welcome," said Carlton.

When they entered the brightly lit glare of the dressing room, Lewis was whistling loudly, toweling off from a shower. He seemed to have regained his spirits.

"Hey, what's up," he said as Alex came in, "you find that lovely lady and ask her out?"

"Nah. Not really my type."

"Don't shit me," said Lewis, "you salivate each time you see her."

"She's occupied," said Alex, his jaw tightening.

"Oh, sorry. Listen, I'm sorry I was so ratty out there. Nerves, I guess. You did a great job. I guess I just wanted this."

"I think we all did," said Alex, avoiding looking at Carlton.

There was a knock at the door.

"Come in," said Lewis cheerfully.

Boo was the last person in the world they expected to see. But it was his freshly dyed blue hair that popped round the door.

"Hey, man, congratulations."

"Yeah, well thanks. They liked us."

"Not what I heard." Boo grinned. "I heard you got fired."

"Come again?"

"What did you do, fart on the stage?"

"Why would I steal your material?"

"I dunno man. I hear they're mad at you."

The bulk of Charles Jay Brown insinuated itself into the room.

"My commiserations, dear sirs. This is sadly a parting of the ways. Had I been your management perhaps I could have used my influence. But as it is . . ."

He didn't finish the thought. Lewis was staring at Alex with a strange look.

"What exactly have you heard?" he asked coldly.

"The rumor mill, sir, as usual runneth over. It seems, however, that my client has been called in as a—shall we say—replacement, for the forthcoming cruise. We, the lucky ones, go forth, and you, the unfortunate, return. Life is sometimes strangely written and who knows when our paths shall cross again."

Lewis was breathing heavily.

"Carlton, what is going on here?" he asked suddenly.

"We're canned," said Alex.

"Shit," said Lewis, slamming his hand violently against a wall. "Goddammit."

He disappeared into the bathroom, slamming the door. There was an awkward pause.

"Sorry, man," said Boo eventually. "I thought he knew."

It's a sad fuck of a business, show biz. It can lift you up and make you feel like God and then dump you right back in the trash. Carlton is very poignant about their return to the *Ray*. He describes it in great detail. Lewis went straight to the shrinkbot, where he immersed himself in self-torture. Alex entered the gym and attacked the punching bag for half an hour, in hopes of getting Miss Wallace out of his head. He felt somehow betrayed, which wasn't fair. She'd never said anything to him, she hadn't come on to him, but still he'd been hoping to see her again, and now they were canned. He'd managed to get them canceled from a gig that would have led them straight to Mars. Brilliant. He ripped the Ganesha security pin off his lapel and hurled it furiously into a corner. Carlton appeared at the door of the gym.

"What?" said Alex irritably.

"Do you want something?"

"No."

"Oh. Sorry. Thought you buzzed me."

Lewis entered looking thoughtful.

"I don't get it," said Lewis. "I just don't get it. We did so good."

The shrinkbot had clearly advised they communicate.

"Forget it," said Alex. "We got plenty of other gigs."

Carlton looked distracted. "I'm sorry, guys," he said after elaborately clearing his throat, "I hate to say this but something very strange is happening."

He punched a button and his chest monitor lit up. A list of their forthcoming engagements appeared. It was a long list. Lewis had been busy during their journey and they were booked all round the Jovian Circuit. Something was now rapidly scrolling through these bookings. The single word CANCELED was appearing on the screen alongside every booking. They watched in disbelief as three months' work went out.

"Who's doing that?" said Lewis.

"Stop it," said Alex.

"It's got to be some kind of a mistake," said Carlton.

"Is it a virus?"

"I don't believe so," said Carlton.

"It's a joke," said Lewis. "Carlton, please, tell me this is some kind of practical joke."

"It's happening," said Alex. "Goddammit. That vindictive bastard. He's trying to kill our career."

"Who is?" said Lewis.

"Emil Keppler," said Alex.

"Why?" said Lewis, puzzled.

Alex said nothing. Carlton looked embarrassed.

"What? Come on. I'm in this too, you know."

"I did some Brenda Woolley stuff on Keppler."

"On Keppler?"

"I didn't know they were married."

"Nice."

Lewis stared at the monitor watching their gigs go out one by one.

"Wait a minute," he said eventually, "that doesn't make any sense. So you trashed the guy's wife. They might throw you off the ship, but why go to all this trouble? This is overkill."

"Well, who else could it be?"

"I dunno." He thought for a moment. "Something doesn't smell right here."

"It was all my fault," said Alex. "I'm sorry."

"No," said Lewis, "there's something not quite right here. It's Boo."

"What about him?"

"How come he was there already?"

"What do you mean?"

"Well, he was right there in the dressing room."

"Yeah."

"So someone already knew he was going to replace us. Maybe even before we went on."

"Who? Charles Jay Brown?"

"Maybe."

"But that doesn't explain all this though."

"No. Carlton, see if you can find the origin of the cancellation command."

"Okay."

"I'm going to check on a couple of things."

"What should I do?" asked Alex.

"Take a shower."

Alex was still taking his shower when the Facemail came. It was Katy Wallace. Carlton interrupted his data search to go find him. He banged on the door of the shower. Alex was floating around in the gravity-free environment, feeling the water hit him from all over.

"It's Miss Wallace on Screen 1," said Carlton when he finally attracted his attention.

"For me?" said Alex, grabbing a towel and flicking her face onto the giant screen. The moment she saw Alex, she broke into a smile.

"Oh hi, Alex," she said. "I just wanted to thank you for the show. I really meant it, you guys were great."

"I'm sorry I said that thing about Brenda Woolley."

"Oh, that's okay. Everyone here knows she's a cow. Even Emil."

"So he's not mad at me?"

"At you?" She seemed genuinely surprised by the thought.

"Someone has been canceling our gigs."

"What?"

She clearly knew nothing about it.

"Oh, nothing."

"Look, I just wanted to say thank you. It was nice meeting you and I hope we can work together again somewhere."

"Yeah, me too," said Alex.

"Oh, and you dropped your towel."

He looked down in alarm.

"Just kidding." She smiled and was gone.

He rewound the instant playback. He heard his own voice: "Someone has been canceling our gigs."

"What?" she said.

He repeated it again, and checked the stress signs. They were normal.

"What?"

No, she knew nothing. He could swear it. He spotted something glinting in the corner of the gym. He picked up the Ganesha and looked at it for a minute. The Remover of Obstacles. Sure.

Carlton appeared at the door.

"What do you want now?" said Alex gruffly.

"You called me."

"No I didn't," said Alex.

"Oh." Carlton frowned. "Lewis said when you were out of the shower, could you meet him in the rehearsal room."

"Be right there," said Alex.

The conference revealed nothing but their lack of choices. They could hang around Jupiter in the hope that the cancellations would somehow plug back in; they could go back to Saturn and the mining stations, or they could head towards Mars on the logical assumption that no one could cancel gigs they didn't have yet.

"Mars it is then?" said Lewis, looking round the rehearsal room. It was a large padded room, with sprung floors for dance routines (as if they did dance routines). Alex nodded his assent; Carlton voted yes.

"Two and a half votes to none," said Lewis.

"Ladies and gentlemen, we're off once again on the Road to Mars," said Alex. "Crack open those long Russian novels and prepare to meet nothing at all for a few months. It's time to kick back and relax as we travel the 340 million miles to Mars. Just a hop in the ocean of time, another brick in the wall of space."

"Keep an eye on him," said Lewis to Carlton. "He's acting a bit doo-lally."

THE REMOVER OF OBSTACLES

The reason I'm in this business, I assume all performers are—it's
"Look at me, Ma!"

LENNY BRUCE

"The White Face wants to control the audience through his superior intelligence. The Red Nose wants the audience to adore him." So writes Carlton. But actually all comedians seek control. It is a very controlling thing to dominate an audience and make them laugh. A comedian who does not seek control is like a lion tamer who does not dominate the lion. He is in immediate danger of being eaten.

So what propels a person to become a comedian? Abandonment. Simple abandonment by the mother. Mothers are the fathers of comedians, says Carlton. Comedians seek to replace the missing love of an absent parent with the admiration of strangers. Watch any kid being funny in a group of five-year-olds and I'll give you ten to one his mother is absent. Here's Carlton again: "The White Face clown seeks control; his impotent fury is revenge for a missing parent, a perceived absence of love as a child. He is the undertaker, the ring-master, the harlequin. The White Face is the 'controlling' clown, the master; the Red Nose is the servant. The Red Nose is kicked, sprayed, soaked, and humiliated. But behind the back of the White Face the Red Nose is always thumbing his nose; he is complicit with the audience, for whom he is a victim, and representative of their humiliations. He is saying, 'Yes, he may have the power, but isn't he a pompous asshole?' The audience love his bravery; they know he will be caught and humiliated, but his spirit remains strong and un-broken. The White Face in his turn *must know he is being mocked* even though he cannot always witness these acts of subversion. He may have control, temporary power and authority, but in the end it is meaningless: he is not God, he is mocked. Hence the bleakness of soul of the White Face clown."

There's yards of stuff like that—good personal observation backed up with plenty of well-researched data—and I'm beginning to suspect Carlton's dissertation has mass market appeal. I'm not quite sure what I should call *De Rerum Comoedia* when I publish it. *The Things of Comedy*, I suppose it is, or *Concerning Comedy*, which is not a very good title, is it? Not terribly commercial. Not that I'm ob-sessed with commerce, but this will be the first book written by a machine and I want it to sell. I think I am definitely going to put my name on the cover. I am after all a professor, and it will add a cer-tain scholastic cachet. I'm hovering between "Preface by William J. Reynolds" or "Foreword by Professor Reynolds." Which do you pre-fer? I think "Preface" sounds a little more scholarly. I wonder if I should add some of my credits. "Preface by the author of *Genius and Madness, The Ill-Tempered Clavier; or If It Ain't Baroque, Don't Fix It*."

The Gift of Laughter—you like that title?

Carlton's got all the time in the world for research now, as both Alex and Lewis are too depressed to bug him. Alex spends hours in his room playing violent video games. Lewis passes most of his day with the shrinkbot. They're heading for H9, where he has an ex-wife and a small daughter whom he feels guilty about not visiting. Ah, guilt, guilt, the gilding of the lily of comedy. The shrinkbot takes him back through early childhood rejections, and all the time Carlton is monitoring him and taking notes on the Intrapsychic Personality Problems of the White Face Comedian. Oh, it's a hoot. If only Lewis had a clue what was going on. It's the control freak's ultimate nightmare. But Carlton's very secretive now, absorbed for hours at a time pouring over old documents and calling up ancient databases. He suspects—rightly, I think—they'd stop him if they knew. Alex is moody and jibs at the Washing Machine, who is beginning to irritate him intensely.

"Ooh, I ache something dreadful this morning," kvetches Mrs. Greenaway. "My circuits have been playing me up something terrible. Give my moving parts a little drop of oil, will you, Alex love," she said and sulked when he ignored her.

"I see someone got out of bed the wrong side this morning. Well *excuse me*. I'd better go see what kind of a mess he's left for me today. Any more of those strange toys in his room, I wonder?" And she went off muttering and moaning as the endless megamiles of space slid past outside the hermetically sealed world of the *Johnnie Ray*.

One evening after a session, as he was passing, Lewis stopped and hugged Alex. White Face clowns are not by nature touchers, certainly not huggers.

"You all right, man?" asked Alex, concerned.

"I fucked up my life," said Lewis.

"Good for you," said Alex.

The non sequitur surprised and pleased Lewis. He broke into a grin. The hug cheered Alex enormously, and he was whistling a particularly irritating passage of Ravel's particularly irritating *Bolero* when Carlton knocked on the door of his room.

"Yes," said Carlton.

"What?" said Alex, looking up from his collection of tiny toy soldiers.

"You buzzed me," said Carlton.

"I never buzzed you," said Alex. "That's the third time in a week. There's something wrong with your pager. Let me take a look."

"No, it's okay."

Carlton's worst nightmare was Alex unscrewing his chest. He knew nothing about mechanics. He was the world's worst engineer. It was as much as he could do to install new software in the games center. Even then it would malfunction and he would behave like a two-year-old, teeth clenched, red-faced in impotent fury. Lewis was even worse. Carlton had once seen him *kicking* machinery!

"I think you've blown a fuse," said Alex, opening his chest. God, Carlton hated this. Like he had *fuses*! What century did he think they were in?

"Really, Alex, it's nothing." There was no end of trouble he could cause, and then it would take Carlton all night to repair himself.

"No, I can fix it," said Alex, gazing vacantly at the gleaming circuitry. He tentatively prodded a few things in the hope it would repair whatever was wrong.

"What's that?" asked Carlton. He had spotted the tiny Ganesha.

"It's a security pin."

"Where'd you get it?"

"Miss Wallace gave it to me before the show."

"Well, it's buzzing."

"What?"

"It's buzzing, listen." Carlton sniffed it. "See, it's live. Look." He ran the pin along his forearm. Alex could clearly hear the crackle.

"So that's what I heard," said Carlton.

"It's static," said Alex.

"Way too loud for static."

"The Washing Machine won't touch it."

"Of course it won't touch it," said Carlton, examining it microscopically through one eye, "it's a postman."

"Is it some kind of a bug?" asked Alex.

"A postman is a device for passing on messages. All electronic signaling can be intercepted and, if encoded, then deciphered, but if you give a third party something, like this pin, for instance, then it can transmit your message later at a distance where someone is not bugging you."

"You mean this is a transmitter?"

"Technically, a retransmitter. Looks as if you were being used."

Alex went pale. "She used me as a goddam postman."

"Miss Wallace gave you the pin?"

Alex nodded.

"Then it's 99.8 percent logical to assume she knew about it."

When they told Lewis, he said, "Well, that proves it then. Katy Wallace knew beforehand we weren't staying."

Alex looked despondent.

"Cheer up. That means you're off the hook. You can't torture yourself anymore."

They were all leaning over Carlton's workbench, staring at the screen which scrolled through pages of meaningless numbers and computer symbols.

"It's encrypted," said Carlton.

"No. Really?" said Alex.

"Yes it is, you see . . ." but Carlton stopped himself. "Was that irony?" he asked.

"Sarcasm," said Lewis.

"Sorry," said Alex sheepishly.

"I can't deconstruct the code yet," said Carlton, "but one thing is for certain—its unidirectional."

"Explain."

"There are two types of postman. The omnidirectional kind, which shoots the message off in all directions, and the unidirectional, which transmits only to a prescribed coordinate."

"And this one is . . ."

"A uni. See, let's check where it's headed."

He punched a few buttons and leaned in closer to the screen.

"It's transmitting directly to H9."

"Oh great, Divorce City," said Lewis. He thought about his ex.

"Well, at least that's where we're going," said Carlton.

"How would they know that?" asked Alex.

"Where else we gonna go? It's where you pick up the main beam for Mars."

"And someone made sure of it by canceling our gigs?"

"Could be."

"The beautiful Miss Wallace. Because I borrowed her sugar?"

"Is that irony again?" asked Carlton.

"It's just a little bitterness. He's mad because he was thinking with his balls."

"Fuck you."

"There's nothing on Miss Wallace in the Biobank," said Carlton. "Look." He punched up her picture. *"Singer,"* it said. "And there's that bit about her and Keppler in the gossip file."

"That's interesting. Keppler. You could always ask Sammy?"

"Sammy *Weiss*?"

"Sure. This is right up her alley."

"You think she's forgiven me?"

"Let me think about that," said Lewis. "She's a woman. You walked out on her. You didn't even leave a note. No, you're right. Not a chance in hell."

"Thanks."

"Pity. With her gossip net and her data files, if anyone can trace this Wallace woman for you she can."

Alex thought about it. He hated feeling used. He had to know.

"I'll go see Sammy." He winced. "But what if she kills me?"

"I'm willing to pay that price."

H9

You should never turn down the chance to have sex or be on television.

GORE VIDAL

Women have emotions; men have sport. That's how it was for centuries. But this all changed at the end of the twentieth century. Emotions suddenly went public. They became compulsory for men. Getting in touch with your female side was the magazine cliché. The sorry spectacle of males in tears was everywhere. If you wanted so much as to sell a book, then you had to cry on a talk show. Athletes were nothing if they hadn't been seen weeping on TV, basketball stars wept buckets, soccer stars sobbed on the field, comedians cried copiously, presidents could hardly address the nation without tears in their eyes. If you couldn't hack it, then you'd better damn well fake it, brother, for this was Reality TV. Celebrities wallowed in public emotion, like warthogs in a muddy hollow. So, yes, TV was to blame again, changing behavior, lowering standards, intruding, falsifying, exposing. Emotions became the trademark of endless TV harpies, the Medeas of the media, with their frozen hairdos and their refrigerated smiles. *How do you feel?* people were asked moments after they had scored a goal or been told their family was lost in a plane crash. Prodding and jabbing. *How do you feel?* Primed and prepped. *How do you feel?* Until the tears would flow and the poor victim received his benediction from the blond show queen. Pass the Kleenex, check the ratings, pass the sick bag, please.

Men were by no means the only victims of this hijack by the harpies and perhaps they had it coming anyway. There was a lot of bullshit bleating about it at the time, as men found themselves, perhaps for the first time, vulnerable to particularly public forms of female revenge. Women, it seemed, could hardly wait to get laid to lay pen to paper, saving semen-stained souvenirs to offer as evidence for the courtroom or the studio, it didn't matter which, since both were on television now. Sharon reveals all. Naked pictures of the girl who fucked the country. Read the book of the blow job. News at eleven—sex, scandal, and weather. It was of course the total breakdown of privacy. Private life—that was such a Victorian concept anyway, and it went straight out the window with TV and the computer. Now the Double Ages had arrived, nothing was private. I could get your credit rating, your total net worth, your purchasing patterns, your private address; dammit, I could even check your orgasms online.

But what's my point here? My point is that Molly is still not back.

I read somewhere that when it comes to women not only do we have a type, we also have an antitype. Chilling thought, eh? Not only is the perfect mate out there waiting for you, but so is the perfect antimate. Apparently you are equally attracted by both the mate and the antimate, but the antimate is deadly for you. I'm beginning to think Molly must be my antimate. She hasn't been home in a week. Last time she was home, she said I was obsessed with my work and she needed time to think. That's rich, isn't it? I'm not allowed time to think for a living, but she is allowed to waltz away and think. It makes me fucking mad. I know just how Alex was feeling. Women can really piss you off. Carlton says that these bitter feelings of abandonment in the male are even worse in the comedian, who is the victim of maternal rejection. He says they seek to risk losing the surrogate love they find in the audience over and over again, simply by attempting to be funny. In an odd way they seek the confirmation of abandonment by risking getting no laugh. They are surfing the edge of rejection. So you can tell Katy's betrayal rankled with Alex. And Molly's really pisses me off. Dammit.

H9 was shaped like one of those children's toys you shake and snowflakes fall. It was half base and half bubble. Its vast dome was pointed always towards the sun, which was nearly twice the distance it was from the planet Earth, providing only a quarter the amount of sunlight. Below the surface lay the dark regions, the docks, the generators, the water refiners, the shops, everything that kept the colony alive. Underneath the giant translucent dome a wooded park was intersected by a few small streams, a large boating lake, and several exercise tracks, where the inhabitants could walk their dogs, visit the zoo, or take picnics. Real birds twittered in the trees and pouter pigeons cooed their reassuring mating rituals on the grass. Around the perimeter of this central park, high-rise buildings competed for the views into the green playground and outward to the stars.

The construction of the Main Beam through the asteroid belt, the opening of a safe electronic highway between the floating chunks of metallic rock, gave H9 its lifeline. Like all great ports, it had once been a smuggling center, but even that prosperous trade had passed on and now the colony survived as a truck stop. Lewis had played there for almost a year, amongst the hookers and the gaming tables at the Parrot Club. He had married a card dealer when she became pregnant, and they had stuck it out for a year before admitting it was hopeless. Now the Ganesha was leading him back.

They were surprised by the traffic they encountered. Their monitors showed the place was jammed and the reason soon became evident: the Main Beam was down. It was like a canal closing. Ships were backed up for days.

Alex grew bored with sitting in the traffic jam and flagged a passing cop, who pulled alongside on his bubble bike.

"What's up?" said Alex.

"The Main Beam's down," said the cop. "Some kind of power failure. It'll take them a couple of days at least to fix it. There's all hell let loose out there. Backed up for miles. Where you headed?"

"H9," said Alex.

"It's a zoo," warned the cop, "they're all diverting there. Hey, Lewis Ashby, that you?"

"Hi, Ed."

"You guys playing the Parrot Club?"

"Yes," lied Alex before Lewis could intervene.

"Follow me. I'll take you through."

Show business can open doors, I tell you.

The cop switched on his flashing blue lights and led them past long lines of shipping.

"Leave me a coupla seats, will you?" said the cop as he let them off near the docks.

"You bet," said Alex.

"Well, I never," said Lewis.

There ahead of them was the *Princess Di*, its mighty bulk surrounded by bobbling orange craft ferrying the passengers ashore.

Parking was packed, and they finally squeezed the *Johnnie Ray* into a compacts-only berth. Long lines of people snaked back upon themselves waiting to pass through customs. It took them almost an hour. While they waited, Carlton was working on the Geometry of Comedy, a kind of Euclidean proof about angles and the sum of expectations of the opposite.

"Tell me about your kid, man," said Alex.

Lewis handed him a curled and faded hologram. A tiny gap-toothed kid beamed back at him. "That's Tay."

"Cute."

"Yeah."

"Why'd you leave?" asked Alex.

"Why does anyone leave?"

"Comedians are very needy," said Carlton. "Since they are largely kids themselves, they need twice the attention of the normal male and they have problems competing with a real child."

They both looked at him.

"Where'd you get that?"

"Erm. It's something I read."

"You take the tin man, okay?" said Lewis.

They finally passed through customs and got their temporary transit stamp. Lewis headed off towards the long lines awaiting transport. Alex watched him go, then headed for the vidphones. They were busy. He was debating whether to head over to Sammy unannounced when he spotted a familiar figure. He was very tall, with black shiny hair, bushy eyebrows, and a big droopy walrus mustache. The man was looking around, obviously expecting to be met.

"Peter McTurk," said Alex.

For a second a hunted look appeared in the man's eyes before he recognized Alex, a big smile lit up his face, and he said in a broad Scottish accent, "Alex Muscroft, however are you, you old reprobate? How great to see you." Alex found himself pulled into a big bear hug. The guy felt like iron.

"You been working out then, Peter?" said Alex when he was finally released.

"Oh, you know me."

The odd thing was he didn't really. He had bumped into McTurk on many occasions, but he couldn't tell you what he did.

"I move things about a bit" was the most revealing he had ever been.

"How's the comedy business?" he said now. "Still with the tall man?"

"Lewis. Yes."

"How is he?"

"You know, still in therapy."

"Well, he's funny. It's a curse, they tell me. So what the hell brings you to this godforsaken backwater?"

"Main Beam's down," said Alex.

"Aye, so it is." McTurk was looking around distracted. "Everybody and his mother are here," he muttered. "Well, I mustn't keep you. Sure you're very busy."

"Good to see you."

"Aye. You too. Mebbe we can have a bevy later. A swift half at the Parrot Club?"

"Sounds great."

"Hey, boyyo," said McTurk. "You're not staying long, are you?"

"Coupla days. Why?"

"Oh, rumors. Nothing concrete," he said vaguely. "Things are a wee bit fragile. Better safe than sorry." He winked. "Just marking your card. You didn't hear it from me now, okay? Oh, here's my welcoming party. See you." He turned and strode off towards a group of men. They looked far from welcoming. A collection of short hair and scowls. Serious muscle, Alex thought. What the hell's McTurk up to?

He found a free vidphone and connected to Sammy's apartment.

"Alex Muscroft, is that really you?"

"In the flesh, my dear."

"Do not remind me of the flesh, Alex, unless you intend to press it."

"Can I come up?"

"You remember the apartment?"

"Only the bedroom."

She laughed and hung up. Great, thought Alex.

SAMMY

Nobody loves a fairy when she's forty.

OLD ENGLISH SONG

"Your fairy days are ending, when your wand has started bending," sang Alex as he approached Sammy's apartment. He was in good spirits. Looking forward to seeing her again. She buzzed him up.

"Wait here, Carlton, will you," he said and put his head round the door.

"Hi, it's me," he said.

A book crashed against the wall inches from his head.

"You shit!" she yelled.

He was totally surprised by her anger. Her blond hair was disheveled. Her blue eyes flashed angrily at him. She wore a white silk kimono with a green dragon draped across the front. He could see the contours of her body beneath.

"You total shit, Alex Muscroft. You walk out of my life, you run away without even saying good-bye, and you expect me to come waltzing back just like that."

"You know me, Sam. I can't waltz."

"Don't be funny."

"Sorry."

There was an awkward silence.

"It's nice to see you, Sam."

Silence.

"You're looking great."

Oh no. She was crying. Oh hell.

"You're a jerk, Alex."

"I *was* a jerk, Sam. Now I'm an older, ex-jerk."

She smiled through her tears. Then unexpectedly opened her arms.

"Well, come here and give me a hug then, you big mutt."

She was still soft and lovely. He folded into her arms. She looked up at him and he could see her eye makeup was all smeared. She sniffed.

"I need a tissue."

"Use me."

He wouldn't let her go. She relaxed and let him hold her. After a bit she calmed down. He could feel some familiar patterns stirring. So could she. She backed off, looked at him, smiled wryly, and said, "I think that's enough of that."

He nodded.

She disappeared into the bathroom and Alex looked round the apartment. A tiny dachshund was staring at him from Sammy's computer chair. It growled.

"Hey," said Alex, "I'm a friend."

"Ruggles won't eat you," she called.

The place hadn't changed much. Almost half of the room was given over to her computers. Her babies, she called them. And it didn't take a Freud to understand the place they played in her life. She was coming back in now, her eyes fixed and smiling.

"You caught me by surprise. I wasn't ready for you to walk back into my life. I'm not really mad, Alex. You can bring the tin man in now if you want."

He moved towards the door.

"You want a coffee?"

"I could use one."

She went off to fix it.

Carlton was waiting patiently outside the front door. "Is the lady all right now? We don't have a lot of time, you see."

"She's fine."

"Please try and remember we are visiting her as an expert, and *not in any other capacity*."

"What?"

"We don't have time for all that other stuff. The holding and rubbing thing."

"Excuse me?"

"You know what I mean. The sexual dimension. We really don't have time for any of that today. Perhaps another time."

Really, Carlton was too much at times.

Sammy returned with the coffee.

"It's good to see you, Alex. You're looking good," she said, settling down beside him on the sofa.

"You too, Sam."

"I'm getting old, Alex. There's me and the dog and the computers."

"Oh come on. I bet you're driving some guy wild."

She smiled but said nothing.

"The reason we're here," said Carlton, "is we're in a hurry and we need your help."

They both looked across at him.

"I'm sorry," he said, "was that inappropriate, only we don't have very much time for chitchat today. Please let me know when you have finished the intimate sexual dimension of your conversation."

"Is he always like this?"

"He is a little strange," said Alex.

"So it's not my body then," said Sammy, rising. "Who is she?"

"How did you know it was a she?"

"Alex."

"Okay. Her name is Katy Wallace, and it's not what you think."

She leaned over her console and switched it on. He could see her breasts beneath the kimono. Really, she was looking good. He went over and stood next to her. He could feel her warmth. She looked up at him and smiled. She was a little nearsighted, but her eyes were inviting.

Carlton moved himself swiftly between the two of them and handed her the Ganesha. "She planted this on him," he said.

Sammy squinted at the pin.

"She used the sexual dimension to beguile him and of course he fell for it."

Sammy was trying hard not to giggle. "Really? That doesn't sound like Alex."

"Oh no, he likes women," said Carlton. "As a matter of fact, since he last saw you . . ."

"Please," said Sammy. "Spare me the details."

"I have the stats if you like."

"Carlton!" said Alex.

"I'm sure they make very interesting reading," said Sammy.

"Not particularly," said Carlton.

There was an awkward pause.

"So what have we got here?" asked Sammy eventually.

"It's a postman."

"Nicely made. This girl knows what she's doing." She handed him the Ganesha.

"Here, hold this. Let's see what we can find on this Wallace woman first."

She scooped the dachshund off her computer chair and began to search through some files on-screen.

"Not her real name, that's for sure," she said after a while. They watched in silence as the lines of data whirled across her screen.

"No, you gotta give me more," she said. "Address. Employer."

"Works for Keppler," said Alex.

"Emil Keppler? Oh brother, you really know how to get into trouble."

"I know. Someone's been canceling all our gigs."

"On your computer?"

"Yeah."

"We might find who did that."

"I couldn't," said Carlton.

"But you're not me," said Sammy.

Pages began to scroll. She frowned, concentrated, and continued searching. After a while she leaned back in triumph. "There she is," she said.

A computer picture of Katy was downloading on the screen.

"This the girl?"

"Yes," said Alex, trying to ignore the feelings thumping inside him.

"She's definitely your type."

"What's that?"

"Female."

"Stop already," said Alex.

"Lovely and trouble. Take a look."

There wasn't much in the file.

"Twenty-five. Polish. Birthplace Rhea. Saturnian system. Part of the Keppler Organization," read Sammy. "The rest is hidden. I'll do a search. It'll take a while. Why don't you take the tin man for a walk and come back in a few hours? Maybe I'll let you buy me dinner. You have a bit more apologizing to do. Oh, better leave that." She plucked the Ganesha from Carlton. "I can scan that whilst I'm at it."

"Be careful," said Carlton.

"You're warning me? An active postman. Somebody's up to no good. I wonder what your babe's doing?"

"She's not my babe," said Alex.

"Doesn't know what she's missing," she said.

"Sure. A fucked-up comedian."

"I won't argue with the first part," she said.

As they walked out of the lobby, a taxi slid alongside them.

"Looking for a ride?" said the driver, a man with startling straw blond hair.

"Why don't we take that drink at the Parrot Club, Carlton," said Alex.

They set off through the park towards the other side of the colony. Soon they were stuck in traffic.

"Worse than the Olympics," said the driver impatiently. "You people from here?"

"Just visiting," said Carlton.

According to the picture ID plastered on the front screen, his name was Dunphy. An unruly shock of straw blond hair and a wide face with a pleasant grin stared back at them.

"You still have real cabdrivers here?" said Alex.

"That's why the traffic is so bad," said Carlton.

"Tin man?" asked Dunphy, glancing in the mirror.

"Four-point-five Bowie," said Alex.

"Hear they're a bit odd."

"You get used to it," said Alex.

"You can get used to anything they say," said Dunphy.

The traffic was going nowhere. They had been stuck for almost half an hour. Alex gazed moodily out of the cab window.

"I must be in love," he said suddenly.

Carlton, who was attempting a Pythagorean proof of comedy, something to do with the square of the sum of the feed line, looked up in surprise. "Why did you say that?"

"I keep seeing her everywhere."

"Who?"

"Katy Wallace. That's love, right?"

"No," said Carlton, "that's Katy Wallace." His long-distance green eye zoomed into a cab on the other side of the street. It was stuck in the traffic headed the other way.

"You sure?"

"She's wearing a wig, but it looks like her."

"Oh my God," said Alex. "What's she doing here?"

"She's come off the ship."

"Well obviously."

"Maybe we would be advised to pursue her, see what she's up to."

Dunphy raised an eyebrow in the rearview mirror. "You want me to do what the tin man says?"

"Sure," said Alex. "Follow that cab."

The cabby swerved them out of the line of waiting vehicles and U-turned across the central divider. He punched a few buttons on his console.

"Hurry," said Alex.

"No problem," said the cabby, "I got a lock on it."

They could see her cab as a moving blip on an unrolling street map. Perhaps two blocks away. The traffic in this direction was flowing and they eased after it, staying within the legal speed limit. After a while they went through an underpass and came out into a wasteland of overpasses, unfinished ramps, graffiti, and cement.

"Where's she going?" asked Alex.

"Heading for Chinatown," said the cabby.

They emerged into a sprawling low-rise district of open markets, with strange vegetables and brightly colored pictograms. Pedestrians wandered at will across the road, and there was a constant sound of Chinese music. Exotic smells filled the cab as they followed the blip on the screen.

"I'm starving," said Alex.

They passed through Chinatown and the buildings began to rise again, higher and higher above them. Soon they were in the Canyons. Vast old buildings towered upwards, casting giant shadows.

"They stopped," said Carlton. "What now?"

"We see where she went," said Alex.

They pulled up in front of an enormous tower whose main section boasted the words THE RIALTO. Her cab was just pulling away.

"Didya see her?" asked Alex.

"Just the back of her head. I'm pretty certain it's her. She's wearing a black wig though."

"What the hell for? Where are we anyway?"

"The Rialto," said the cabby. "It's a famous old apartment complex. Like a fortress in there. Watch your step, it has a bad rep."

"Wait for us," said Alex.

"I didn't see you pay yet," said Dunphy.

They left him outside and walked swiftly up the entrance steps. There was no sign of Katy Wallace in the lobby.

"Can I help you gentlemen?" A uniformed doorbot was looking suspiciously at them.

"We'll just pay off the cab," said Alex.

They got back inside the taxi.

"What do we do?"

"Give me a ten-spot," said Dunphy. "You guys are new to this. I used to be a cop." Alex handed him a twenty and he shrugged and stepped out of the cab. He was tall and powerfully built. His blond hair headed up the stairs and disappeared into the Rialto lobby. After a few moments he came back down and climbed back in.

"It's odd," he said, "they say the security system's down. Couldn't remember even for twenty. But then he's a fucking robot. Oh, excuse me." He grinned apologetically at Carlton, who shrugged. He was used to it. Tin man, tin feller, robot, all largely terms of abuse these days, he thought.

"Let me speak to him," said Carlton. "I'm a fucking robot too."

He got out of the cab and went into the building.

"Ballsy little droid you got yourself," said Dunphy, looking back at Alex in the mirror.

"He's certainly different," said Alex.

"A Bowie, huh?"

"Yeah."

"Didn't know they still made 'em."

Alex wondered what the hell they were doing there, and what he would say if they found her. After a short time Carlton jumped back in the cab. He seemed excited.

"Well, it's a little more complicated than we thought. She's in there okay."

Alex grabbed his head and pushed him down on the seat. They both sank beneath the window level.

"Is it her?" asked Carlton.

"No," said Alex. "It ain't. It's McTurk."

Dunphy began to pick his teeth and look bored. He had clearly done this sort of thing before.

"Okay, he's passed you," he said through the corner of his mouth.

Alex sat up and watched the big Scotsman enter the building.

"That's odd," said Carlton.

"Friend of yours?" asked the cabby.

"Sort of. What the hell is *he* doing here?"

"Could be a coincidence," said Dunphy. "There are a thousand apartments."

"Sure," said Alex, "and two people we happen to know just happen to be visiting two of them at the very same time. What're the odds on that?"

"Roughly 2.5 billion to 1," said Carlton promptly.

"That was rhetorical."

"Oh, sorry." But the odds were helpful. It wasn't even remotely likely.

"So what did you learn about Katy?"

"Well, like he said, the system's down. All visitors report to the central desk, state their destination, which is automatically checked. In her case a man was waiting in the lobby."

"What man?"

"He didn't say. He did have ID, however. He said, 'She's with me,' and they both went up in the elevator."

"Which floor?"

"That's it. He had ID, so the deskbot didn't check the apartment number."

"Didn't it recognize him?"

"No. Said it hadn't seen the guy before."

"Bit lame, isn't it?"

"Not for this place," said the cabby, "this ain't exactly the Ritz."

"Did it get a picture of him?"

"It gave me this." The screen on Carlton's chest popped on. They were watching a security cam replay."

"Freeze it," said Alex. "Go in as much as you can."

Carlton zoomed in to the elevator.

"It's her all right. What the hell is she doing in a wig?"

The big man by her side kept his eyes to the floor.

"Recognize the muscle?" asked Alex.

"Just the type," said the cabby.

"Well, what now?" asked Carlton.

"Stakeout," said the cabby. "You don't know where she is, so you gotta wait till she comes out."

"We can run a check on McTurk," said Alex. "Get me Sammy."

Her face appeared on Carlton's chest.

"Hey, funny man, I was going to call you. Interesting new girl-friend you got yourself. Ready for a download?"

"Rolling," said Carlton.

Whilst Carlton was downloading, Alex asked her to check on the Scotsman.

"So who is this Peter McTurk?"

"I met him a few times. I don't really know what he does."

"Well, I'll see what I can find, but it's gonna cost you more than a dinner."

Dunphy grinned. "Lucky you."

Carlton flashed her the security scan of the muscle in the elevator. He could have been one of the guys McTurk met at the airport.

"Where are you, Alex?" asked Sammy.

"Outside the Rialto."

"Better be careful. It has a pretty slimy reputation. Drugs, low-lifers, that kind of thing."

"I'll keep an eye on him for you, Sam," said the cabby.

"That you, Dunphy?"

"The same, though larger," he said, showing her his big wide grin.

"Thought I recognized that big blond thatch."

"You still doin' the files thing?"

"Same old," she said.

"Nice to see you again, Sammy."

"You too, hunk," she said. "Glad he's with you. Keep your eye on him. One of the finest comic brains of the weekend."

"Ouch," said Alex.

"Well, gotta go, kiddo, this thing's cooking, and it's hot. What ya call it again?"

"A Ganesha."

"Some kind of Polish word?"

"Indian. Probably Sanskrit."

"Yeah, right. Like that really helps."

She disconnected.

"Let's take a look at the babe's file," said Dunphy. "Don't worry," he said in response to Alex's look. "I'm strictly retired. Hey, no extra charge."

The first file on Katy Wallace was less than interesting. Turned out her real name was Katerina Walewska, after the great queen of Poland who became Napoleon's mistress. Katy was described as an "entertainer," which covered a multitude of sins. She had been born in one of the Silesian work camps on Rhea, had brown eyes, a small mole on her lower left back, dark brown hair, five-ten in height, and weighted approximately 130 pounds out of the shower. There were various pictures of her. Katy as a fifteen-year-old, Katy graduating, some professional glossies, and some footage of her auditioning. Her voice was cute. Not wildly original, but she could carry a tune. There were details of her work experience. Seems she started entertaining in the camps. Obviously trying to get out, thought Alex. A shipping disaster was described. She had survived that. It appeared someone took care of her and helped her off Rhea. Reference to a further file on her parents. Then a note about the original Katerina Walewska.

The second file contained notes on the container people, and the immigration of her parents from Silesia on the planet Earth. They had been one of the first to answer the new lands call, and subsequently got caught in the contract trap. They had been tricked into a two-year contract on Rhea, only to learn on arrival the contract was in Saturnian years, which meant fifty-nine Earth years and ensured they were on a veritable life sentence. Illegal, of course, but try finding a lawyer out by Saturn in those days. So they were trapped. In the system though not of it. The Company, in their case the SudPolnischeKristalleGesellschaft, fed them, clothed them, housed them, and would eventually bury them, a form of slavery redeemed only by the wages, which were not bad, though pointless since there was nothing to buy. Real estate was cheap, if you liked icy wastelands.

The third file was clearly labeled "Restricted," and Dunphy gave a big wide grin and perked right up.

"I should warn you that reading this file is illegal," he said.

"Right," said Carlton, switching it off.

"No, no, I *should* warn you," said Dunphy, "but I'm not going to."

"Oh," said Carlton, switching it on again and making a mental note to search what Dunphy had said for irony.

The file fleshed out further details about Katy's mother. It seemed she was some kind of an intellectual, had degrees and everything. She must have reacted badly to the harsh realities of the work camps. Why did they leave Earth in the first place? Alex wondered. There was a brief reference to politics and then a few more details about Katy and her early training in crystallography—hardly surprising, growing up in the minefields of Rhea. Crystals grown in the one-sixth gravity could attain amazing and precise growths. Her mother was an expert in crystalline microbiology, the new microtechnology which had completely replaced the computer chip and controlled almost all communications. Hence the Ganesha, he thought. She knows what she is doing. Be careful, Sammy. But what exactly is she doing?

"Who's the father?" asked Dunphy. "There's no mention of him yet, and all that shit about the mother. I don't get it."

"Bingo," said Alex as a new file came on the screen.

Disappointingly it was censored electronically.

" 'Father deceased. Further information withheld,' " read Carlton.

" 'Withheld'? That sounds like a security file," said Dunphy. "Usually they do that for a state execution or something. Otherwise they'd list a form of death."

The same thought must have occurred to Sammy, for she had

appended the single word "Daddy" in the margin. The rest was electronic gibberish.

"Well, there's a whole load of nothing," said Dunphy, picking his big white teeth.

"Can you decipher it?" asked Alex.

"Might take me a while," said Carlton. "I'll try."

"Hello," said Alex. "Here's our friend." McTurk was coming out of the building in a hurry. He was looking down as if to avoid surveillance cameras. He stopped by the curb, waved his hand, and a vehicle instantly slid up alongside him. He climbed in and they sped off.

"Oh shit," said Alex. "Now what do we do?"

"Make up your mind time," said Dunphy in the mirror.

"I'll follow him," said Alex. "You stay here," he said to Carlton. "Don't, for God sake, lose her." He shoved the reluctant Carlton out onto the pavement and the cab pulled away.

THE DADDY FILE

I stopped believing in God when I found they'd lied to me about the Tooth Fairy, Santa Claus, and the Easter Bunny.

LEWIS ASHBY

Lewis emerged from the subway into a suburban neighborhood. He checked the address and found a line of identical mid-rise apartments. When he rang the doorbell, a surprisingly tall young girl answered the door. She had short brown hair, a cute little nose, and her eyes were hazel. He noticed with a shock she was wearing nail polish.

"Tay?" he said.

"It's my daddy," she yelled.

"Tell him to come in, I'll be right down," said a familiar voice.

She held a hug for the longest time and then led him into the kitchen. Her drawings were pinned everywhere. She chattered away brightly to him, showing him things.

"This is my bear, Sophie. This is my horse, Earthwind. These are Dorothy and Edna, my dolls."

His ex-wife came into the room. She was fastening a hat on her head and he noticed she avoided his eyes. He wondered, not for the first time, whether he had really married this woman.

"You leaving?" he said carefully.

"Thought you two would like to be alone," she said, and then couldn't resist adding, "it's been a while."

He nodded. "What should we do, do you think?"

"Well, she likes the zoo. She'll ask you for McDonald's, you can take her there if you like. Only one Jell-O though. She can eat six if you let her."

"Oh, *can* we go to McDonald's, please? Please, Daddy, will you take me there?"

"Sure."

"Yay!" Her delight was huge and unforced.

"She'll take you shopping if you want. Hello Kitty is her favorite. It's in Mall 3 on the third level. But please, Lewis, don't keep her out late. She has school in the morning."

Tay was trying to drag him out of the door.

"Get your things first, Tay," said her mother sternly, "and go to the bathroom before you go." Tay ran off. He could hear her rattling around singing.

"She's glad to see you."

"She's amazing."

"She saw you on the Brenda Woolley show, you know. She's very proud of you."

He said nothing.

"I assume this is just a short visit?"

"Sadly yes."

"She'll get over it. She's really quite strong. Stubborn at times. Like you."

"Thanks."

"Well, I have to get ready, my cab's coming."

"How are you?" he asked.

"Me?" she said. "I'm glad of the break."

Tay came flying into the room, dressed to leave.

"Ready, Daddy."

She took his hand.

"Okay, be good now, Tay," said her mom.

"Is Daddy staying for a while?"

"I don't think so, honey."

"Oh."

"Daddy's very busy."

"C'mon then, Daddy. Let's go."

She led him out into the street. He watched her mother wave from inside the apartment.

Alex and the cab were stuck in traffic again. McTurk had given them the slip.

"Can't you see him on the screen?" asked Alex, irritated.

" 'Fraid not" said Dunphy, shaking his blond mane. "He ain't in a cab. Must be some kinda private limo."

They went by the Parrot Club to check. Its red upholstery and plastic leaves looked shabby and cheap by daylight. He wandered through the club room into the long bar. A couple of young men were playing pool. They didn't look up. The barman was studying the racing form. He glanced at him enquiringly. Alex shook his head.

"Just looking for someone."

"She ain't here," said the barman.

He looked into the tiny show room, and glanced nostalgically at the stage.

"Can I help you?" said a voice behind him.

"Looking for McTurk."

"Is that you, Alex?"

"Hello, Benny."

A short guy, with a rather obvious toupee crammed onto his head, came in and grinned a smile which showed a lot of gold teeth. A tight vest was stretched over a generous belly.

"Jeez, Alex, it's been a while. When you gonna come play here again?"

"Soon, Benny."

"Too big for us now, I guess. We all saw the show. That Brenda Woolley's something, huh?"

"Yeah. She's not as nice as she looks."

Benny allowed himself a laugh.

"Seen Peter McTurk?"

"Nah, he ain't bin round in a while. What's up?"

"Chasing a dame, Benny."

"So, that's not like you," said Benny. "I thought you were a dyke."
They grinned at each other for a little. Alex promised he'd come back and do a set.

"Don't forget us now you're in the big time," said Benny.

He used the vidphone outside the men's room to call Carlton.

I told you Carlton was a tintellectual. He is a clever little metal fellow, there's no doubt about it. I'm proud to have discovered him. I have these very strong feelings towards him. Possessive. Almost paternal. He's so bloody smart. That's why I kept him from Molly. And I'm glad I did because she's still not come home. Got a note she'd swanned off to some conference. Yeah, sure. Flat on her back with a prick up her, no doubt. Academic trailer trash, that's all she is. I asked her why she always dressed like a slut when she has so many degrees? Know what she said? "If you don't like the way I look, then fuck off." That's nice, isn't it? Not much give-and-take there, I fancy. I wasn't ready to fuck off, so I shut up about it. But I was hurt, I can tell you. They have that power over you—women—don't they? The power to leave.

Whilst Carlton stood patiently waiting outside the Rialto, his circuits were busy looking for some way into the electronic gibberish that filled his chest screen. He couldn't figure it out. It was obviously encrypted, but what sort of a code: logarithmic, exponential, random, or variable sequential? There were a million possibilities. His mind began whirring, crunching large numbers and testing them on the gibberish. It remained garbage. While his right hemisphere cells searched for a way to break the code, his left thinking module began thinking about comedy. He had lately been contemplating the rule of threes. Apparently every third thing was funny. Also words which began with *k* were funny. Was that true? Was *"khaki"* funny? Was *"kettle*? Was *"Kipling"*? Apparently some words were just simply

funny. "Chicken," for example, was always funny. He couldn't figure
out why that should be. It led him to consider the Chinese restaurant gag:

"Waiter, this chicken is rubbery."

"Oh, thank you vely much sir."

Now what was funny about that? It seemed to him merely a mis-
print. Chicken, chicken and egg. Comedy was like cracking a code.
Words were the key. *Words*. Of course! The censored electronic gibberish was in an old-fashioned word-based key. It was a government
computer. They were using the new Dumb Technology. To try and
outsmart very smart computers some agencies were resorting to
stupidity. Simple, almost childish passwords were substituted for
lengthy equations. How do you baffle a computer which can speed
through several multibillion-number combinations? Simple, you use
a word like "cat." You're going under its intelligence threshold. It
cannot factor you to be so dumb. It was like comedy, he thought.
Chicken and egg. Well, why not. He tried "egg." It didn't work; neither did "cat" or "dog" or other simple words, but in two minutes
he'd figured out it was a five-letter code word he was looking for.
He tried "Daddy," since Sammy had scribbled that in the margin. It
didn't work either. Well, he could hardly expect a human to solve the
problem before him. He settled down to try all the five-letter words
in the English language, and after half an hour "Paris" began de-
crypting the code. Within seconds the gibberish was readable. There
it was, the Daddy File.

Father, Alexander Walewski, age fifty-two, and yes, Dunphy was
right, he had been shot for leading an uprising on Rhea. Not exactly
executed, but his body was found mangled in the remains of a firefight with government forces. Seems he had been a rebel even back
in his native Silesia and was forced to emigrate after some kind of
trouble at Krakow University. Trapped on Rhea for a lifetime, he and
his wife, Natalie, had tried to leave the Company and failed. They set
up the White Wolves, a protest group, which disseminated information and attempted to contact others who shared their plight. After
their grievances were dismissed (by the Company), they worked
towards an armed struggle which took place ten years later. They
were well organized and well supplied, and it had taken several
weeks to put down. They had been betrayed by someone from inside. Their last days were both agonizing and heroic. They had re-

treated farther and farther into the icy wastes of Rhea before being surrounded and shot to death, their blood red on the icy snow. The symbol of the red drops on the white background was still a powerful symbol of resistance.

Then there was some more stuff on the White Wolves. How the organization had spread to Mars amongst the Silesian immigrants. General alerts and warnings. There was also a psychological profile of Katy. Spells of depression. Her conviction that her father would return—she was only five at the time. Her childhood dream that he would be back like Santa Claus with a sack full of toys. The harsh years in the school camps. Death of her mother ("under interrogation" was the sinister comment), her employment in the crystal fields, the *Bronia* disaster, and then her escape from Rhea through show biz via Emil Keppler. Sugar daddy.

So her father was a dead revolutionary hero. So what?

His vidphone rang. It was Alex.

"What's up?"

"No sign of her yet," said Carlton.

"Keep on it," said Alex.

"I managed to open that file."

"And?"

"It's all about her father."

"Where is he?"

"He's dead. Shot. Twenty years ago."

"Oh, hold the front page," said Alex. "What's got Sammy so hot then?"

"Why don't you ask her?"

"I'll check her out now."

He dialed her number, but the screen remained dead. Probably in the shower, he thought. Might as well pop over and see what she's got; she's only a few minutes from here.

A CRACK IN THE SKY

*I don't want to achieve immortality through my work . . . I want to
achieve it through not dying.*

Woody Allen

Tay was throwing the Frisbee and screaming and yelling. Lewis
panted after it. His lanky figure almost gawky, his long arms stretching for the plastic dish. They were in the park, not far from the zoo.
He bent to retrieve the brightly colored toy. A dull thud echoed far
above them. A clump of pigeons beat their wings in a sudden flutter-
ing cloud and took off. The sound like someone shaking sheets. Tay
squealed in delight and ran after them. Look at me, he thought, I'm
playing with my kid.

They had dined at the zoo café and he had stared at her with pride as
she handled the ordering like a grown-up. She asked the waitress
about specials, recommended things for him, discussed what she
should drink, and listened politely to what he had to say. She had
opinions and views like an adult, and then quite suddenly the six-
year-old would emerge as she burst out laughing.

"This is my daddy," she told the waitress. "He's in show business."

The waitress smiled. "He seems a very nice daddy," she agreed.

"He's really silly though," confided Tay.

"That's all right in a daddy, I think," said the waitress. Tay considered this seriously. "Yes it is," she finally conceded. "He's going to
come and take me out every week."

"That's nice," said the waitress.

"C'mon, Daddy, let's go play Friskee like you promised."

"I think it's Frisbee."

"No, it's Friskee," she said. "We always play Friskee."

He rose. The waitress smiled.

"That's a lovely little girl you've got there."

"I know it," he said.

. . .

Outside, she stopped and pointed to the dome.

"Look, Daddy, there's a crack in the sky."

He looked up. Something spidery seemed to be crawling along the dome far above their heads. As he watched, the spiderweb increased in all directions like a broken windscreen.

"I expect it's nothing," he said.

From somewhere the wail of a siren echoed around the park.

Alex heard the siren as he entered the elevator. Sammy's apartment was on the hundredth floor. The elevator took forever. As he stepped out, he shivered. Someone stepping on my grave, he thought. There was a faint whiff of cigar smoke in the air. His footsteps echoed down the hallway. He came to her door and pressed the buzzer. He could hear it clearly echoing inside. There was no response. He pushed and to his surprise the door opened. He put his head cautiously inside, half expecting a book. Be just like Sammy to come leaping out at him stark naked. She used to do wild things like that in the days back when. Once he had found her in bed, spread-eagled, wearing only a pair of heart-shaped panties, completely tied up with silk stockings.

"Help," she'd whimpered.

He'd helped.

Now what was she up to? He felt a sudden stab of desire rekindled by the memory.

"Sammy?" he called softly.

He pushed open the door of the bedroom, half disappointed she wasn't in there waiting. He continued through the kitchen. Then he stopped suddenly. Something was wrong. Where was the dog?

His heart was thumping wildly in his chest now. He breathed deeply and walked into the living room. Sammy was lying quietly at the computer console, her face resting on the keyboard as if listening for something. Her eyes stared blankly towards the window. She couldn't have been dead long. Behind her all was chaos. Someone had done great violence to her computer console. Both the screen and the hard drives had been smashed, and bits of her files were strewn all over the room. The open window indicated they had tipped some stuff out that way too. Looks like they threw the dog out as well. He felt suddenly sick.

He returned from the bathroom still gagging. His instinct was to run away as far as he could. Only minutes ago he'd been fantasizing about her. For God's sake, she was still warm. Dunphy was downstairs. He'd know what to do. Don't touch anything, that was the way. He'd read about this stuff. Pretend it's a movie. Walk out of the door and keep going.

He looked for the Ganesha on the remains of her desk. It was nowhere to be seen. Computer smashed, Ganesha gone, it didn't take a genius to figure out Sammy had accidentally alerted someone. Someone who was so desperate to stop something getting out they would kill without mercy. He'd get Dunphy up and he'd call the police. They could pick up Katy Wallace. She had some explaining to do.

He ran out of the elevator, across the lobby, and outside to the street. The cab was gone. He looked both ways in disbelief. There was no sign of it. What the fuck was going on? Why would Dunphy leave? He owed him a ton of money.

"Looking for someone?" said a voice behind him.

Two men in grey suits stepped forward. They had hats. They might have carried a big sign saying DETECTIVES if they'd wanted to be really obvious.

"My cab," said Alex, trying to remember he was innocent.

"My name's Rogers," said the shorter of the two. "This here's Kyle," he said, indicating the large African by his side. The African stared at him but said nothing.

"Perhaps you'd better come with us," said Rogers.

"Why?" asked Alex, his mouth going suddenly dry on him.

"You're under suspicion," said Rogers.

"For what?" said Alex.

"For murder."

They took him downtown, only five minutes away, and shoved him into a small interrogation room. Rogers and the African followed him in. Somewhere a bell was insistently ringing.

Rogers sat down and looked him over. He was tanned and healthy-looking. His manner wasn't hurried, but he had shrewd

eyes, like he was used to being lied to and didn't much care for
it. His partner was powerfully built. Short, stubbly beard, close-
cropped hair. You definitely wouldn't want to mess with him.

"For the record this is Detective Kyle and I'm Detective Superin-
tendent Rogers and we're questioning Alex Muscroft and this is
being recorded." He leaned back in his chair and looked at Alex. "So,
why don't you tell us what happened?"

"Did you kill her?" asked the African.

Rogers shrugged apologetically.

"Kyle gets a little impatient."

Kyle looked like he got more than impatient. He looked like he
was doing violence to his suit just breathing.

"Did you kill Sammy Weiss?" asked Rogers in an even voice.

"Of course I didn't. You know I didn't."

"How do we know that?" asked Kyle.

"Because you knew Sammy was dead when I came downstairs."

"Got you there, Kyle," said Rogers, enjoying his partner's discomfort.

"He might have come back," said Kyle, not enjoying the role of
straight man.

"What, to check if she was still dead?" asked Alex.

This time Rogers laughed out loud. "You're a comedian," he said.

Kyle stared at Alex like he had some things he would like to do
later. Suddenly his face cleared. "Oh, that's right," he said, brighten-
ing, "he was on the Brenda Woolley thing."

"Kyle loves Brenda Woolley."

"Yeah. Well she'd love Kyle."

Kyle looked flattered.

"What I don't understand," said Rogers, "is how come you never
called the police when you found her?"

"I was coming downstairs to get Dunphy. He said he was an
ex-cop."

"Who's this Dunphy again?"

"A cabdriver."

"He told you he's an ex-cop."

"Yes."

Kyle hit a few keys on the computer and showed Rogers the
screen. Rogers turned back to Alex and said, "Would it surprise you

to learn there are no licensed cabs in this colony driven by ex-cops called Dunphy?"

It did. They registered his surprise.

A young man came into the room and whispered urgently in Rogers's ear. He frowned and rose.

"Excuse me a minute." His chair squeaked as he pushed it back. "Come with me, Kyle, we got a problem."

In the distance more bells were ringing.

After a couple of minutes Rogers put his head round the door.

"Okay, Mr. Muscroft, you can go. We got an emergency here."

The lamp above his head was swinging wildly.

"You'd better make it back to your ship and get the hell out of here."

"What about Sammy?"

"I'm sorry about your friend, but we got a major catastrophe on our hands. The dome's punctured, we're leaking, and it's growing every minute."

Something had pierced the thin membrane of their artificial sky. Their precious atmosphere was leaking away into space. If they could caulk the hole, well and good. If not, things looked pretty bleak. The whole place would collapse.

The station was in chaos. Emergency bells ringing everywhere.

"Ninety percent atmosphere," yelled an emergency worker. "We got time." He raced out of the door.

"Two percent leaking every five minutes. Sure, we've got bags of time," said a sharp brunette working a bank of screens. "Let's do lunch."

EMERGENCY CODE 437

Either that wallpaper goes, or I do.

LAST WORDS OF OSCAR WILDE

Lewis shuddered, suddenly cold. A wicked wind had sprung up. Spirals of air were being siphoned up towards the hole in the sky. Inside the park, trees were being shaken as if by invisible dinosaurs. The whole park swirled with leaves and scattered debris. He tried to lean into the wind to get to Tay, but making progress was not easy. Ahead of him he could see she was being yanked off her feet by the wind.

"Hang on to the streetlamp, Tay!" he yelled. He wasn't sure she heard; the noise was terrifying.

The Frisbee was snatched out of her hand and sailed off into the sky.

"Daddy, my Friskee," she wailed.

"Hold on, kiddo, I'm coming."

When he reached the streetlamp, she was clutching on for dear life with white knuckles.

"It's okay, I got you." He swept her into his arms and staggered like a drunken man against the ferocious wind. It tugged at the cuffs of his trousers and whapped at his shirt, trying to pull it loose. He squinted against the trails of dust and dirt swirling everywhere, and dodged flowers and roots and old newspapers as they came at him. A hot dog stand was blown over just ahead of him and a cloud of wrappers whizzed past. It was like being inside a rapidly deflating balloon.

By the edge of the park an official in a yellow emergency uniform was yelling and beckoning kids to leave the playground.

"Get below," he yelled, "get below now."

He shepherded the stragglers down the steps which led to the underworld of the colony. Lewis hoped the trains and people movers were still running. If this was as bad as it seemed, the power might go out at any time. It would be terrifying to be belowground in the dark on a leaking space colony.

"What's happening, Daddy?"

"The dome's cracked, honey, so we have to get below. But it's going to be all right. See, they're working on it."

It was true. Little emergency boats were already hovering around the hole in the dome trying to caulk the leak with a huge sail of shiny material. They weren't having much luck. It was like trying to spread a sheet in a gale. The boats bucked and tossed and bounced around while the little yellow figures held on for dear life. He watched in horror as the great flap of material broke free and wrapped itself round one of the emergency boats. He saw three tiny figures tumble from the boat and then watched helplessly as they were sucked through the gap into space.

"Are they going to be all right, Daddy?"

"I expect so. They'll probably be okay on the other side." Sure, minus 204 degrees centigrade. "Quick frozen peas" flashed through his mind.

"We have to make the stairs, Tay," he said above the roaring of the wind. "We'll be safe down there." He was about a hundred yards shy of where the yellow-suited attendant was shouting and yelling at people. He gritted his teeth. God, she was a weight for her age.

The wind was increasing in intensity. Whole bushes were being uprooted, and leaves and twigs stung his face as he staggered forward one step at a time. He cradled Tay, turning her head into his collarbone to protect her from the debris which hurtled past them. The sound of breaking glass came from all sides, and in the playground the swings creaked wildly on their chains.

The whole park was filled with wild spirals of swirling wind, loaded with deadly uprooted material. Great trails of detritus were being yanked up towards the dome above them where they battered against the thin fabric of the ceiling, further weakening the structure. The widening hole was sucking out their lifeblood, vacuuming the atmosphere into space like some gigantic vampire. The whole thing could go any moment. Evacuation bells combined with the sirens of emergency vehicles echoed horribly down the canyons of high-rises. The air made an eerie sound, a *bouff-bouff-bouff* as of someone blowing in his ears.

It was getting harder to walk. He almost went down, and grabbed wildly for Tay.

"Daddee," she wailed.

"I got you, kiddo," he said.

Ahead of him a pram broke free from a terrified young girl. It came billowing along towards him in the wind. He dropped Tay and made a grab for it. The handle struck him nastily across the wrist. He grabbed the tiny bundle from inside it before the wind whipped the pram out of his hands and tore it away. The baby started to wail. He cradled it with one hand and reached for Tay with the other. She was shivering with fear.

"It's gonna be okay, honey. Daddy's got you."

With a tremendous effort he lifted her into his arms. The final steps were agony as he dragged his feet towards the shelter of the stairwell. The young girl was in hysterics. He handed her the child and sort of patted her.

"C'mon," he said, "down here before they seal the gates." Because they'd have to do that, he realized. They'd have to seal off the surface and hope to maintain some kind of life belowground until they could rebuild the dome. The place was leaking so fast and the hole growing visibly bigger by the minute.

It was a maelstrom in the park. Huge trees were being ripped up by their roots and tossed about like twigs. The streets were covered in shattered glass. Bits of debris bowled down the wide boulevards. Time to get out of there. He pushed Tay through the heavy doors and they were suddenly in calm. The young girl had started to cry again.

"It's gonna be fine. It's just reaction." She looked up at him through black mascara tear-stained eyes. "You got to stay calm and look after your baby. You think you can do that?"

"I think so," she whispered.

"Good for you," said Lewis.

"You still here?" Rogers was surprised to find Alex still inside the precinct. "This is a Code Red. It means get the hell out of here. Emergency crews only. It's a total evacuation."

Alex seemed confused. He kept seeing Sammy lying there quietly, her head on the keyboard. Rogers was yelling at him, concerned. "You okay? Hey, I'm talking to you."

Kyle came over and put a friendly hand on his shoulder.

"Hey, man, you in shock?"

He had tried to contact Carlton on the vidphone, but all the lines were either down or busy. He had been horrified to see what was happening out there on the streets. Whole cars were flying through the air like plastic toys. The noise was deafening. A terrible tearing sound. Parts of the pavement were being wrenched up and hurled about. He had ducked back inside.

"Do you understand me?" said Rogers, concerned.

Alex nodded.

"Where you parked?"

"In the docks."

"Come with us then," said Rogers. "We're going that way."

The three of them headed for the door. As they stepped outside, another dull rumble shook the colony. Looking up to the cracked dome above, they could see the caulking material flapping around madly like the tail of a dragon. It seemed in danger of taking more of the emergency crews out into space.

"Jesus," said Rogers at the chaos that raged. "C'mon Kyle, no point in taking a vehicle, we'd better run for it."

The subway entrance was only half a block away, but it was all against the wind. They ran, stumbling blindly, dodging the flying debris. They had almost reached the subway steps when Alex heard Kyle grunt and turned to see him fall.

"Come on, Kyle, this is no time for a nap," Rogers yelled gruffly at him. He was bleeding heavily from the temples. They grabbed him and hauled him the ten yards to the subway entrance and dragged him down the stairs. A huge oak tree crashed behind them and wedged itself in the subway stairs.

Alex looked at Rogers.

"Nice work, thanks," said Rogers. "Officer down, I need a medic now," he yelled into his chest mike. "Come on, Kyle," he said, "don't let me down now."

"Is it safe down here?" asked Alex.

Rogers looked at him like he was nuts. "Are you out of your mind? This whole place could collapse any minute."

"Implosion?"

"You bet. We gotta get to the docks."

A young man with an emergency armband came racing towards them.

"Hey, I called for a medic, not a boy scout."

The boy looked terrified.

They popped Kyle onto a stretcher and dropped him off at an emergency handling center.

"Stop his brains leaking and then send him down to me," yelled Rogers at the medic. "Don't let him die on me now or I'll . . ."

"Sir, I'm just a premed," said the youth.

"Kids," said Rogers, "in men's pants." He turned to Alex. "C'mon, I'll drop you off at the docks. Lucky for you I'm handling the exodus."

Alex didn't feel that lucky. Rogers flashed his badge and they pushed forward through anxious crowds onto the next express people mover. It shuttled them smoothly along the brightly lit interior tunnels of the colony. Nobody spoke much. Rogers fished out a portable vidphone and was patched through to the Keppler cruiser.

A white-uniformed British officer was telling him that Keppler was unavailable.

"Fuck unavailable," said Roger. "This is an Emergency Code 437. By the powers invested in me I am now officially commandeering your craft."

"Bullshit. We will take some extra passengers and do what we can, but we have a schedule we must adhere to."

"Listen to me, feller, and listen to me good if you want to have your balls dangling in the same place you last left 'em. There are about to be a thousand refugees heading for your fucking vessel, so you'd better get every blanket, every bed, every tiny piece of floor space you've got available right now. Every medic, every sick bay, every hospital standing by. You got that?"

"I'll speak to Mr. Keppler."

"You do that, and tell him its Emergency Code 437."

"Yes sir."

"Right, my name is Rogers, you understand. What's my name?"

"Rogers."

"Wrong. It's fucking God as far as you're concerned. Now wake your man Keppler, get him out of his silk pajamas, and tell him we have a major fucking disaster on our hands. You hear that?"

"Yes sir."

"You inform him that from now on he takes orders directly from me. And only from me. You got that?"

"Yes sir."

He looked at Alex.

"Fucking limeys," he said.

"What's an Emergency Code 437?" asked Alex.

"Beats me," said Rogers. "I just made it up."

THE RIALTO

I can't do comedy.

STEVEN SPIELBERG

Carlton heard the first dull thud at 11:22 local time. Immediately his antenna began to pick up emergency signals. The air around him was buzzing, crackling with messages. Within minutes he had picked up the first damage report. It was bad. A few moments later came the emergency evacuation call.

He ran into the lobby of the Rialto. The deskbots were consulting evacuation procedures. The building's emergency klaxon sounded. People in various stages of undress were pouring down the stairs to the lower levels.

"Leave your apartments immediately and proceed to the subway for emergency evacuation," said a mechanical voice. "This is not a test."

The crowd in the lobby swelled, a mass of humanity flowing out of stairwells and elevators. He perched on a marble balcony and scanned the crowd in vain for Katy. He must have watched for twenty minutes without spotting her. Soon the river of people dwindled to a trickle, then became small drips of late stragglers. After a while it dried up altogether. He couldn't be sure she hadn't passed him in the melee.

He went over to the deskbots. "Is the building clear?" he asked.

"You're supposed to have left," said one of the 'bots. "Why have you not obeyed instructions?" They thought he was a human.

"Doesn't apply to us, does it?" he asked, grinning that he'd fooled them.

"I guess not," said the robot. "You a Bowie then?"

"Four-point-five," he said proudly.

"Could have fooled me, brother," said the deskbot, making a weirdo gesture alongside his head to his companion. Carlton was incensed. Why did they always do this?

"Bowies are always strange," said the other deskbot.

"Listen, the first computer to paint was a Bowie. The first computer to beat a human at golf was a Bowie—Arnold Bowie over two hundred years ago. The first completely successful massage computer was Tracy Bowie, a 3.6. The first automatic theatrical agent was a Bowie. Bowies have always been pioneers—they lead the world in robotics, cheese-making, viticulture, disco, and ballroom dancing," he said.

"You finished?"

"Yeah."

"Well, you'd better leave before you're an ex-Bowie," said the deskbot.

"I can't. I'm looking for someone. A female visitor, name of Wallace."

The robot shrugged. "Well then you can help us check the building." He handed him a small meter. "If you find the Wallace woman, call me."

"Right," said Carlton.

It was a hot box. A simple device. When it detected life, it beeped. As you got closer, the beeping got louder. Carlton headed for the elevator. On the second floor it began to beep. The elevator stopped automatically. He stepped out and headed down the corridor. He tracked the beeps to a corner apartment. He hammered on the door. Nothing. With his metal hand he punched through the door of the apartment, reached inside and undid the lock. A man and a woman were passed out in bed. A bottle of champagne was in an ice bucket.

"Time to go," he yelled. They didn't stir. He picked up the ice bucket, pulled back the sheet and emptied the iced water over the naked pair. That woke them all right.

"I can explain," said the man hastily, blinking.

"Forget it," said Carlton. "I'm not the police. This is an emergency.

Got to evacuate the building. Sorry. Come on, hurry, lady." She was trying to get dressed. He flung her a towel.

"My clothes," she said.

"Not worth dying over," said Carlton.

"That's for me to say," she said, determinedly wriggling into a designer frock. He left them to it.

He rode slowly up the endless floors in the elevator. At the forty-fifth floor the hot box began to beep again. Life. As if *we're* dead, he thought. The elevator instantly responded, coming to a standstill. The doors slid open and he stepped out into another corridor. Clutching the meter, he walked slowly forward. The third apartment he came to set the machine beeping like crazy.

She was sitting in the window staring blankly into space.

"Katy," he said.

She didn't move.

"Katy."

She turned and looked at him. "I want my daddy," she said.

Whacked out of her skull, thought Carlton.

"This is an emergency," he said gently. "I'm here to help."

But for the car she might not have moved at all. It crashed through the window with a terrifying roar, shattering the glass. Instantly the wind was everywhere, pulling the apartment to pieces, sucking the furniture out of the room. She leapt desperately towards him. He grabbed hold of her, picked her up, and ran.

DYING'S EASY

Dying is easy. Comedy is difficult.

EDMUND KEAN

The docks were in chaos. It was like a scene from hell. Hundreds of vessels of all shapes and sizes were pulling out as fast as they could. They were banging into one another, hooting and tooting, waving and shouting, all trying to cram through the tiny air lock and head for the safety of space. Orange shuttle ships from the *Princess Di* bounced around them, filled to the brim with terrified tourists. The lights kept flickering on and off. Each time the power cut, the sodium emergency lights cast an eerie yellow glow over the pandemonium.

"Jesus," said Alex.

"Get the hell out of here," said Rogers. "You may not have much time." As he spoke H9 gave a great metallic groan. "Whoops," said Rogers grimly. "I'll be on the *Di*, if this place holds long enough." He raced off towards the bouncing orange shuttles.

Alex was almost bowled over by a crowd surging out of the subway. They raced around him shouting and yelling in several languages. He pointed them towards the line of desperate souls waiting their turn for the orange lifeboats. British sailors in their neat white shorts were hopelessly trying to instill some order into their panicking passengers. They were saying those maddeningly cheerful British things. "Don't worry, girls, never happen. One at a time, love. Oops, steady there. Never mind, dear, I've got another foot. 'Tis but a flesh wound. Worse things happen at sea. Always look on the bright side, eh?" He watched them calmly reassuring the little old ladies and loading them onto lifeboats as if they were organizing a picnic on the beach. A cheery cockney gave him a big thumbs-up and yelled, "Nice work if you can get it, eh, mate?"

A couple of the little old ladies recognized him and nudged each other.

"Look who it is, Doris. It's him. Remember, Doris, 'e was the monkey. You were ever so good on the show, love." He dutifully signed the paper they thrust at him. This was madness, signing auto-graphs at a time like this. They might all be dead within minutes. As if to underline this insanity, H9 gave another huge groan. Good grief, it's coming apart, he thought.

He fought his way blindly along the docks through masses of terrified people. It was hard work against the flow. Eventually he spotted the *Ray* up ahead of him in the compacts-only berth. Al-most all the other vessels around it were gone. He broke into a run. As he drew near, he could see the lights were on and hear the en-gines were running. Thank God. Almost there. He raced up the gangplank.

Lewis's white faced greeted him. "Where you bin, for God's sake? We gotta get out of here."

"You're telling me. It's a madhouse."

"Okay, we're powered up, let's go."

"Daddy, Daddy, wait."

He turned in surprise to see a frightened little girl staring at him.

"Oh, Alex, this is Tay."

"Oh my God, a munchkin. Hello, Tay. I'm Alex."

"You're the monkey."

"That's right."

"My mommy is missing," she told him.

"She's gonna be fine," said Lewis. "But we really have to get out of here now."

He raced for the controls.

"Undocking," he yelled.

Emergency lights flashing, the *Johnnie Ray* began to pull away.

"Wait," said Alex. "Where's Carlton?"

"I don't know," said Lewis. "He was with you."

"You mean he's not on board?"

"No."

"But we can't leave without him."

"Alex, he's a tin man."

"My God, he must still be at the Rialto."

"What?"

"I told him to wait for Katy Wallace."

Lewis stared at him in disbelief. "Excuse me?"

"I followed McTurk, Carlton stayed. Then I found Sammy—dead."

Lewis was fish-mouthed.

Another large metallic groan from the bowels of H9 brought him to his senses.

"We gotta go."

"No."

"What?"

"I'm not leaving without Carlton."

"He's a robot, for Christ's sake."

"So?"

"Alex, we can buy another one."

"Not like him."

"Are you going to risk all our lives for a tin man?"

"He'll make it," he said, desperately trying the vidphone.

"Alex, you're out of your mind."

There was only static.

"Nothing," he said.

"Okay, that's it. We gotta go."

"No." He shook his head stubbornly.

"Alex, it's not just you here. There's my daughter, for Christ's sake."

"Okay. You leave, I'll get off."

"Goddam you, Alex!" He beat the side of the ship in frustration. "Don't do this to me."

The place began to shake. The whole dockside was shuddering.

"Let's give him five more minutes."

"Are you out of your mind?"

"I mean it. Five minutes or I get off."

Lewis looked at him. He was dead serious.

"Five minutes," he said.

It was a very long five minutes. The whole time H9 groaned and shuddered. Huge girders fell from the ceiling, lights swayed and shattered and threw sparks across the cement floor. Way over towards the air lock exit they could see the last of the orange roughies packing people in. Almost all the vessels were gone now. Alex said nothing, but sat grim-faced, staring at the entrance tunnels. Only a few people were still arriving, almost all now were running. Lewis held a pocket watch in his hands and breathed deeply.

"Okay, that's five minutes, chum."

Alex was in tears. Tay went over and put an arm round him. He patted her hand.

"I'm casting off," said Lewis. "I'm sorry, pal."

He went forward to cast off.

"Wait," screamed Alex. "There he is."

Carlton was running along the emptying docks. Draped in his arms was a female figure. One of the deskbots was with him.

"What the hell's he got there?" said Lewis, frowning.

"C'mon Carlton," yelled Alex, "we gotta get out of here. It's all about to blow."

H9 was rocking and shaking, the groaning sounds amplified now and echoing every few minutes with a loud metallic banging, as if someone were hammering on every beam and rivet.

"Oh my God," said Alex, "he's got Katy Wallace."

Lewis glanced at Alex in disapproval. "He's bringing her on board?"

"What's he supposed to do, dump her?"

"Fine by me," said Lewis.

"I'm gonna assume that's a joke," said Alex as he leapt forward to help Carlton.

"I wish," said Lewis.

Carlton entered with the limp figure in his arms, almost stumbling in the doorway. Alex glimpsed Katy's pale face and saw she was unconscious.

"Stick her in the sick bay," he said. Carlton nodded.

"Hold tight. This could be a bit hairy," yelled Lewis.

"You coming?" he said to the deskbot.

"Can't," it said. "Orders."

"Oh well, suit yourself," said Alex.

He could see the deskbot reach for his vidphone as the door closed.

As they headed for the air lock, they could see the line of waiting passengers had diminished. The docks were emptying rapidly. Only emergency crews remained, getting the last of the craft away. One or two British sailors in their white shorts smiled and waved cheerfully at them as they passed, as if they were off for a pleasant Sunday cruise. Just before they entered the air lock, Alex saw one of the sailors bend over and moon him. Fucking nuts, he thought.

EVACUATE

"Where's the tea strainer?"
"It's his day off."

ANCIENT BRITISH JOKE

They shot out of the air lock in the wake of a large pleasure cruiser. Lewis put his foot down and barreled them away from there as fast as he dared. Space outside of H9 was filled with hundreds of small ships scattering in all directions. He dared not go flat-out. It would be madness to risk an accident now. As they looked back, they could see masses of debris pouring out through the hole in the membrane, leaking into space like blood from a wounded man. Great lumps of material were flying everywhere. Whirling trees, cars, buses, massive chunks of masonry. The *Ray* bounced and jolted them as they dodged the boats and the wreckage.

They could see that the rescue workers had abandoned their efforts inside the dome and were now attempting to stop up the hole from the outside. The inside of the dome was a whirl of material. It looked exactly like a snow globe.

"Good Christ," said Alex.

"Make sure Tay is belted, will you?"

"Sure thing."

"Look, Tay," said Alex. "the *Princess Di*."

A few miles off, the Keppler cruiser was surrounded by hundreds of small boats waiting to unload.

"Bloody chaos," said a petty officer, shaking his head as he watched them streaming into the vastness of the *Princess Di*. "We've got no list, no names, no passports, we haven't a clue who's on the ship and who isn't." Shocked and frightened passengers mingled with dazed and homeless refugees gripping pathetically small bundles of personal possessions.

"It's himself upstairs on the blower. He wants to know how many we've taken on."

"Tell him we haven't a clue."

"Be serious."

"I am serious. What are we supposed to do, ask refugees for their papers?"

"Come on, gimme a ballpark?"

"Shit, I dunno, how do you tell? Could be two or three thousand. We've set up emergency tents in the park, the hospital is packed, all the gymnasiums are full. They're still coming in. What am I supposed to do, turn 'em away?"

"You are placing an impossible strain on the safety of my ship." Emil Keppler was on the bridge and he was angry. Rogers was ignoring him, listening in on the cell patch hookup to Command Control H9.

"Just keep me updated every five minutes, okay." He disconnected and looked with disapproval at the tall white-haired figure. "Mr. Keppler, this is a major disaster. What do you suggest we do? Abandon these people?"

"How are we supposed to feed them all?"

"You will be able to claim disaster relief. There are funds if it's money that concerns you."

"That is not what concerns me. What concerns me is the safety of my passengers and crew."

"As soon as we can get these people to safety, your cruise can continue. Now please, Mr. Keppler, leave me to do my job."

"Right. Mitchell, I shall need all these people documented before this ship leaves. I want to know exactly who is on this ship and where they are from."

"Are you mad?" said Rogers "Have you any idea what is going on out there?"

"I have a very good idea of what is going on and I don't want the same thing happening here."

"What do you mean?"

"First the Main Beam to Mars goes down, nobody seems to know why, then we are diverted here, and then H9 accidentally begins to leak. Something of a coincidence, don't you think?"

"What are you suggesting?"

"What makes you so sure it was an accident?"

"It's far too early to jump to any conclusions."

"I am suggesting that the integrity of my ship has been violated. You haven't a clue who's on here or why."

Rogers glanced at the constant update info screen. Why is he so concerned about who is on his ship? This bordered on paranoia. His face dropped.

"Oh shit." There was a sudden silence. He looked very grave. "I am sorry to announce we are pulling the last of our crews out now. This ship should prepare to leave at once."

Mitchell hesitated and looked across at his commander. Keppler, visibly irritated, controlled himself and began carefully, "Mr. Rogers, as I have already told you, until I know who is on my ship . . ."

"It's too late," said Rogers quietly, "the place is going to blow. The mass has gone critical. You have no option."

"You don't understand."

"No sir, you don't understand. I'm telling you H9 is about to implode and unless we get the hell out of here immediately, every second you delay you are putting at risk the lives of several thousand passengers and crew."

There was a tense silence. Keppler nodded to Mitchell.

"Thank you," said Rogers.

"Message to all craft. Emergency evacuation. General alert. H9's condition: imminent destruct. All craft evacuate the area at once. Repeat, all craft evacuate at once."

"General stations. General stations. Crew prepare to leave immediately. Repeat, immediately."

"Blimey," said Mrs. Moy as the orange shuttle boat squirted though the closing bow doors. "We only just made it."

A heavily mustachioed dark-haired man was helping the little old ladies to step onto the dock.

"Come on, ladies," he said in a friendly Scots voice, "I'll give you a hand."

"Oh thank you," said Mrs. Moy.

"Hey McTurk," said a voice. "C'mon, we got stuff to do."

MAYDAY

The chief problem about death, incidentally, is the fear that . . .
there is an afterlife but no one will know where it's being held.

WOODY ALLEN

"Oh shit," said Lewis, "she's going. Let's get out of here."

They could see the little emergency boats scattering at full speed, running away from H9. The colony itself seemed to be pulsating. The hole had become a vast black gusher spewing out material like a volcano into space. Some three miles off, the *Princess Di* began to move away, rapidly gathering speed.

"What about the rescue crews?" said Alex as he watched a few small craft vainly pursuing the liner. Lewis shrugged grimly. "That thing's going to implode any second," he said. "It's every man for himself."

The physics were terrifyingly simple.

"I don't get it, we're out of there, we're safe, right?"

"It's achieved critical mass," explained Carlton. "The hole has become so big it can no longer withstand the outside pressure. When that happens, the vacuum of space will rush in, it will collapse on itself, the matter inside it will contract, quickly becoming so compressed it will explode outwards, throwing debris in every direction."

"Oh."

"But that's not the worst."

"Please tell me the worst," said Alex.

"The shock wave is worse," said Carlton. "The electromagnetic shock wave of what is essentially a tiny collapsing star could take us out completely if we're too close."

"How close is too close?"

"Say anywhere within five hundred miles."

"Lewis!!" yelled Alex.

"I'm on it," said Lewis, opening her up. The *Ray* slid away from the stricken colony.

They accelerated fast, the G forces pulling at their faces. On the screen in front of them was a huge close-up of H9. It was pulsating visibly. They watched fascinated as the hole began to grow bigger. For a delicate moment the material gushing out seemed poised as if torn between two huge forces. Then, as they watched in horror, it reversed itself and rushed back in towards the hole from which it had emerged.

"She's going," yelled Lewis. "Hold tight."

The debris was being sucked in like a vacuum cleaner. Several of the emergency boats had no chance and were immediately drawn back inside the maelstrom. They watched in disbelief the eerie reverse film effect of material pouring backwards into the heart of H9. They could see stabs of energy, like flashes of sheet lightning, illuminating the center of the colony.

"Oh shit, it's igniting," said Lewis. "Here we go."

H9 rapidly shrank back inside itself and then like a vast firework exploded in all directions. A huge spherical shock wave came rushing outwards from the dying station. Moments later it hit them. The screen went dead and they were lifted up and slammed forward at great speed. Tay screamed. All they could hear was the sound of smashing equipment and the groaning of the ship's hull as the magnetic shock wave tried to tear them apart. The shuddering was intense.

"Seven G," said Carlton. "We can survive ten G. No more."

"What's happening?" asked Alex.

"We're surfing," said Carlton. "We're right on the front of the shock wave and it's pushing us along."

The ship was shaking and bouncing under the strain.

"Eight G," said Carlton quietly.

Alex looked across at Lewis. He watched him reach out and take Tay's hand.

"Daddy," she said.

"I know. Hang on."

"Nine G," said Carlton.

The force of the explosion had tripled their speed. They were being hammered away from the vicinity of H9 straight into the asteroid belt.

"Ten G," said Carlton grimly. They were on the limit.

"We've got to find a way to slow down or we're done for."

"Reverse booster?" yelled Lewis.

"No power," said Carlton, "everything's out."

"She's got manual override," said Alex proudly, "she's an old beauty."

"It'll be bumpy."

"Beats frying."

He slammed the handle on the reverse thrusters and for a second they heard the pop-pop-pop as they fired. Then an intense shuddering and they eased back in their seats. The big wave had swept over them and gone hurtling onward.

The bouncing and battering of the shock wave gave way to an eerie silence.

"Damage report," said Lewis, unbuckling Tay and lifting her into his arms.

Carlton's report was bad. The electromagnetic wave had taken out every computer on the ship. All communications were down. They had lost power, radio, navigation, and steering. The galley was knee deep in crockery, and there was broken glass everywhere, but it was the navigation system loss that was the most terrifying. Without that they were being hurled blindly through the asteroid belt.

"We're dead without a nav. system," said Carlton.

"Pas devant les enfants," said Lewis.

Tay began to cry.

"Hey, guess what, Tay," he said cheerfully, "we're heading for Mars. I'm sure Mommy will be there."

Carlton looked crestfallen. He wasn't used to children. Humans had to do so much lying.

"Why don't you help us clean up this mess?" said Lewis, surveying the wreckage. The sumptuous decor of the *Johnnie Ray* looked like it had been hit by an earthquake.

"I know who'll be cleaning up the mess," said the Washing Machine. "Oy vey, you should see the galley." It went off muttering to itself in search of debris.

"Mayday, Mayday," said Alex at the com. deck. "This is the *Johnnie Ray*. Mayday."

Nothing. All frequencies. All directions. No response at all. They were for all intents and purposes alone in space.

PART TWO

FORTUNE

A man's got to take a lot of punishment to
write a really funny book.

Ernest Hemingway

MONEY

Look at this. Know what it is?

De Rerum Comoedia

A Discourse on Humor

**Thesis submitted for a Doctorate degree to the USSAT
(The University of Southern Saturn)**

by

**CAR110N//Ξℵ33PY{∉⊇αΘ}4ξ□•∏PI⌠J⊗♥↔ϖπ
known as Carlton**

The author of this dissertation is a 4.5 Bowie machine who set out to discover
whether comedy can be learned, or whether it is inherent only in Homo sapiens.

It's the title page of the dissertation on comedy. By the tin man
himself. Yes, it's the original of Carlton's *De Rerum*. I found it totally
by chance. I was upstairs in the great USSAT Library checking
through the funny files when out it popped. I couldn't fucking believe it. I was so happy, I rushed home to tell Molly. She wasn't home
of course. She hasn't been home in days. Oh, where are you, Molly,
dammit, I miss you.

I was reading something about the balance of power in a relationship. I realize she always had the power in our relationship. I was hooked on her ass. That's the bottom line.

> *As I gaze in wonderment*
> *On your perfect fundament*

That's my favorite line in all of twenty-second-century literature. The poet Codd knew a thing or two.

> *All things come to pass*
> *Through the glory of your ass.*

Sorry, but I'm feeling rather sorry for myself. I miss her trampy little presence. She thinks I'm weird. She left me a note saying that: "You're fucking weird, Bill Reynolds." Maybe I am. I certainly feel weird without her. Anyway, I haven't seen her for days now. Fuck 'em if they can't take a joke, right?

It's a pity because I wanted to share the Carlton thing with her. I was thinking of dedicating my book to her. I knew right away there was a book in it. I thought, publish it, straight off, with a preface by me, and cop the royalties. But then I thought about it. There's more to it than this. There's the whole biography aspect. I mean he was pretty original for a machine. He was only a midrange Bowie. He wasn't supposed to be capable of such profound insights. Then I had a paranoid thought. If he's a machine, maybe the manufacturers own the copyright of anything he comes up with. That wouldn't be fair, would it? I mean I have to think what to do about this. After all, what's the point of me doing all this work if some corporation cops the money?

So, know what I'm going to do? I'm going to make the metal man a star. I'm going to merchandise the little fuck. I'm going to take this hard-wired weirdo and put him on the newsstands and the cover of the trendy magazines. After all, he's quite a dish with his big blond hair and his lithe lean frame. He's like a gay's idea of the perfect heterosexual. It's a totally commercial image. I can really shake the money tree with this one. I'll publish him between nice hard covers with a big fat foreword by me and a snappy little title like *Comedics*, or *Tin Laughs*, or *There's No Time Like the Pleasant*, or some such nonsense the publishers are gonna gobble up. And I'll make the metal man famous. Fame, I hear you say. *Fame?* Do our nostrils not detect the faintest tincture of irony here? Surely you hate fame? Surely you were ranting on about the deleterious effect of this supposedly worthless state? Well yes. Of course. Micropaleontologists know it's all bullshit. Nothing lasts forever. But if I make him famous, I control the estate.

I didn't say I hated money.

LOST

Alone, alone, all all alone, alone on a wide wide sea.

COLERIDGE, *THE RIME OF THE ANCIENT MARINER*

They had been drifting for hours. The *Ray*, without power, was limping blindly among the rocks of the asteroid belt, a vast region of debris and massive chunks of minerals which may or may not have once been a planet. Without a navigation system, the odds on their hitting something soon were about 5.36 to 1, Carlton calculated. They had used the manual boosters to slow them from their suicidal entry speed, but now they were perilously low on fuel. They had to conserve what little remained for evasive action. Evasive action. That was a joke. Twice Carlton had seen large rocks sail by. Each time he jumped. Now he was working desperately to repair the internal power system, which had been badly fried. As usual, while he worked, this clever little bi-brained intellectual was thinking about *De Rerum*.

· · ·

Recently he had been trying a mathematical approach to comedy. He had been toying with a probability curve (a sort of Humorous Heisenberg Principle) such that if A were your expectations then B would definitely occur, or if B was posited as the likely outcome then A would instantly happen. This seemed a promising line of inquiry, and he noted with excitement that it seemed to hold good for physical as well as verbal comedy. He covered a blackboard in comedy equations, with all sorts of scrawled notations and exclamation marks. He used his own system of algebraic notation where ! stood for laughter. For instance $A + p = !$ where p was a pie and A was a face. But while this was normally true, it didn't describe all cases, since $A + p = ?$ where A represents the face of the observer. A custard pie in the observer's face was not funny, at least for the observer. And without an observer, was anything funny? It was a sort of "If a tree falls in the woods, does anyone laugh" problem.

He realized he had to include an audience in his algebra. This was also the first occasion I can find Carlton using an actual joke, since in his second sheaf of equations instead of using p, he used the symbol π for pie. Not bad, huh?

So, let m represent the mass of the people and O be the observer and he came up with:

$$\frac{A + \pi O}{m - O} = !$$

When the pie goes in the observer's face (πO), everybody laughs except the observer ($m - O$). From this he derived one important axiom: comedy is what happens to other people.

The tanker almost gave him a heart attack. With absolutely no warning it loomed out of the star field directly ahead of them, a massive matte black vessel almost on them. Carlton dropped his equations and ran. He screamed and hit the rudder. Nothing happened. Lewis raced in and gaped in horror. The huge tanker was side on to them. They were hurtling towards it. Carlton hit the rudder again. They could see the name painted clearly on its side as it came straight at them.

"Try manual," yelled Lewis.

"Too late," said Carlton. "It's on us."

"Shit," said Lewis as he saw the vastness of it. "Look out!"

They dove to the floor as it came careening at them.

It missed them by inches. They could feel the mass of it passing overhead.

"What the hell was that?" said Lewis, totally shaken.

"Silesian Tanker. Named *Iceman*. Registered Rhea."

"Where were their lights?"

"Probably knocked out by the shock wave."

Alex came running in ashen-faced. He was easily scared at the best of times. He looked pretty shaken up.

"What *was* that?"

"Tanker," said Lewis. "No lights. No warning."

"Sweet Jesus," said Alex.

"Where's Tay?" asked Lewis.

"She's on her bunk. She told me not to worry. Said Carlton was on it."

"Not exactly," said Carlton. "It came out of nowhere."

"Great," said Alex. "If he didn't see it, and it's a mile long, what chance have we got against something smaller?"

"About 5.36 to 1 against," said Carlton promptly.

Alex gazed thoughtfully at the huge vessel. "Wait a minute," he said. "If the *Iceman* ship is here, then we are . . ."

"In the middle of an icefield. Yes," said Lewis.

"Without power?"

"Correct."

They looked at each other.

"Get me the Washing Machine," said Lewis.

"You soiled your pants?"

"No, you idiot. We can reprogram it as a lookout."

"The *Washing Machine*?"

"You got a better idea?"

While Carlton worked on the power lines, Lewis and Alex jury-rigged the Washing Machine as an emergency electronic lookout. She didn't like it one little bit. She moaned, she kvetched, she complained.

"This I need already? Bad enough I get to look at your unmentionables all day, now I'm a lookout in the asteroid belt?"

"Be grateful it's not the hemorrhoid belt," said Alex.

They put her in the tower and left her scanning for icebergs. They could hear her muttering away to herself, complaining. She had a range of only a few miles, but this would at least give them some warning when the largest chunks of ice appeared. They could still see the tanker behind them, the word *ICEMAN* painted in huge white letters on its side.

"They almost made a snowball out of us," said Alex grimly.

"It looks deserted," said Lewis. "Perhaps they're in trouble."

"Who are they anyway?" asked Alex.

Carlton paused for a moment on the power lines and accessed a database. "Project Iceman," he read, "is the ice program for Mars. Huge chunks of ice floating around the asteroid belt are diverted to Mars and dropped onto the desert, where the enormous impact creates both ground water and water vapor–forming clouds. They are at the moment creating a controversial new Sea of Silesia."

He stopped reading and looked at them, puzzled.

"What's controversial?" he asked.

"The people who live there probably don't want to live under the sea," said Alex.

"Oh."

"Anything else?"

Carlton read on. "The irony is that many of the Silesian workmen on the Iceman project now live in the largely inhospitable region of Mars where the sea is forming."

He stopped again, puzzled. "What's the irony?" he said.

"The irony is that it is their labor that makes it possible," explained Alex.

"I'm sorry," said Carlton, "is that irony, or just foolish?"

"Don't get him started on irony," said Lewis.

ICEMEN

Comedy comes from conflict, from hatred.

WARREN MITCHELL

"What the hell was that?"

The voice spoke out of the darkness of the tanker. The harsh clang of boots echoed from metal floors and ceilings. Running footsteps. Torches.

"Josef, you there?"

A grizzled face spoke, in the sudden stabbing glare of flashlights.

"I'm up here, Pavel."

The heavily bearded man called Pavel climbed the metal stairs onto the darkened bridge. He could barely make out the thin figure of Josef, peering through binoculars. A hard, wiry man with black hair and deeply intense black eyes.

"The *Johnnie Ray*," read Josef. "What are they doing out here?"

"Heading for disaster by the look of it."

They watched the *Ray* hurtling into the asteroid belt.

"Looks like they have no power."

"It's the H9 blast, Josef. There are hundreds of 'em around."

"Better show some lights then, Pavel."

"Right away."

"We don't want anyone else slamming into us, now do we?"

"No, Josef."

"Oh, just emergency lights now. We're supposed to be a crippled ship."

"You got it."

Pavel punched buttons. Green emergency lights lit the bridge and the outline of the huge ship below them.

"Broadcast a distress call," said Josef.

The bearded man looked anxiously up at him.

"We need to be picked up now, don't we?" said Josef.

"I guess so."

"Might as well take advantage."

"You think we should still go ahead?"

"Why on earth not?"

"Comus."

"Shh," said Josef. "Not here."

They could hear voices and the clanking of boots outside.

"Any word from the watchers yet?"

"Just said they're on the *Di*. They want to know what's next."

"Me too. Jesus, what a mess."

Two thick bare arms heavily tattooed with linked W's pulled a heavyset man up the outside ladder.

"It's Sven," said Pavel.

"You okay, Sven?" said Josef.

"Oh yes, I am fine," said Sven, a tall blond Swede with a heavy accent. "Never better, ya? The ship too, I think. They tried hard but they missed us." He laughed. "But it was fokking close."

"No shit," said Pavel.

Below them a dozen or so men stood, blinking in the sharp bright lights. Waiting for instructions.

"Okay, listen up." The man called Josef spoke softly. They listened. "I want you to check the ship and get me a damage report."

They nodded, and disappeared, clanging, into the darkness.

"Sven, take the bridge. Pavel, come with me."

The bearded man followed the slim figure of Josef into a cabin. Josef flicked on the lights. For a moment they blinked together. Pavel looked into the dark-rimmed eyes of the soft-spoken Josef and saw nothing.

"Where's Comus?" said Josef after a second.

"In the storeroom. He's safe."

"Saying much?"

"Won't talk."

"Why the hell was he going to H9?"

"Looks like he was set to meet this Wallace woman."

"She say that?"

"That's all she would say—'I'm supposed to meet Comus'—and then clammed up."

"Didn't they persuade her?"

"They started to. She seemed genuinely ignorant. Had a message, followed instructions, that's all she knew. Wasn't time to get much out of her. McTurk comes racing over, then the watchers pick up a signal from the postman. They trace the Weiss woman and find

"Gunpowder Plot" on her screen. What were they supposed to do? They didn't have much choice."

"They had a lot of fucking choice. They could have found out what she knew, or where the leak came from, but no, they just panicked and took her out. Then off their own bat they decide to advance the detonation time and they screw up even that. Jesus."

"Guess they used more than they needed."

"No, really? They blew the whole fucking place apart."

"Think we're compromised?"

"I can't figure it. I hate this bollix. What the fuck was Comus doing slipping off for a meeting with the mistress of Emil Keppler anyway?"

"Is he boffing her?"

"At his age? Don't be ridiculous."

"Then it doesn't make any sense."

"Damn right it doesn't make any sense. In the middle of an operation to stop off for a quick shag with the other side."

"I thought Keppler's with us?"

"Keppler's with Keppler. He'd jack us in faster than you can blink if he thought he could get away with it. He'll know by now he's not alone though. But he won't know exactly who or how many. What we didn't count on is your boys totally blowing the shit out of H9."

"Maybe it's even better this way."

"Yeah, maybe. How much did this Keppler girl know?"

"It's academic, she can't talk to anybody now."

"You sure of that?"

"They shot her full of Corazone and left her in the Rialto. She couldn't even walk."

"The watchers all pulled out?"

"They left a couple of mechanicals."

"I'll need that confirmed. Meanwhile let's see what friend Comus has to say."

"About what?"

"Let's see his reaction when we tell him Katy Wallace is dead."

SEARCH AND RESCUE

*There are more than one hundred elements, but the most important
is the element of surprise. Boo!*

ALEX MUSCROFT

Keppler stood in the small watch cabin beside the bridge. He was
gazing out into space. His white beard reflected in the big window.
He watched Mitchell enter behind him, but didn't turn round.

"Well?" he said finally.

"She's not here, sir."

Now he turned. Mitchell looked concerned.

"Miss Wallace is definitely not on the ship, sir."

"You've checked . . ."

"The hospitals, the sick bays, the list of injured."

"Is this a complete list?"

"By no means, sir. They're still working on it, but she's crew, sir,
she would have checked in if she was on board."

Of course she would. He was grabbing at straws.

"What was she doing on H9 in the first place?"

"Said she was going shopping, sir."

Keppler sighed, shook his head, and walked back onto the bridge.
The indestructible Kyle hovered like a large black shadow, his head
heavily bandaged. Rogers was talking to Mitchell, his captain.

"We need to start searching for survivors at once," Rogers was
saying.

It irked him Rogers was issuing instructions on *his* ship. It irked
him even more that he couldn't throw the little shit back onto the
stinking garbage heap of a run-down clapped-out colony he had come
from. But he couldn't. Code 437. Whatever the fuck that was, the little shortarse had invoked it. He had a thought and walked over to the
main computer. He tapped it for a while, then raised an eyebrow.

"Mr. Rogers."

The cop looked up.

"Yes, Mr. Keppler?" said Rogers pleasantly.

"Code 437."

"Yes."

"You made it up."

"Yes. I did."

"Nice." Keppler smiled unexpectedly. "Nice one."

"Thank you."

"But it means I am now in charge of my ship."

"That would be right."

"In that case we shall not be going anywhere until I have located an important member of my staff."

"May I ask who?"

"Katy Wallace."

The name rang a bell with Rogers, but he didn't immediately place it.

"It's his girlfriend," said Kyle in his ear. "The man's well buzzed about it."

Better play it sweet, thought Rogers.

"We'll have her checked out and located for you. She must be on one of the other vessels, unless . . ."

"Unless what?"

Rogers hesitated.

"Unless she was left behind on H9," said Kyle.

Keppler said nothing.

"You all right, sir?" asked Mitchell.

"Yes. Thank you. I'll be fine."

"She's probably on one of the other ships, sir."

"Yes. That's right. She probably is."

"We've broadcast an alert, sir. We should hear back in a while, but many of these ships are without power right now. But I'm sure she's safe, sir."

Nobody said anything. Keppler looked grim.

The moment was broken as a cloud of expensive perfume entered, followed by Brenda Woolley.

"Emil, darling? There you are."

He looked bleakly up at her.

"Brenda," he said.

Rogers watched in amazement as the figure he recognized from a thousand billboards strode over to Keppler and planted a couple of air kisses at least six inches either side of his face.

"I need to talk to you quite seriously," she announced, looking around confidently at everyone.

"Brenda, this is not the best time."

"I know, Emil. I of all people know that." She showered her show biz smile on all of them, as if they were cameras. "But these are the times that fry men's souls and I simply *have* to do something to help."

"That's very thoughtful of you Brenda, but we are coping as best we can."

"I want to give a concert."

A slightly unreal beat. Rogers's communication rang. He answered it.

"Hello," he said.

"I want to give a concert for the refugees," Brenda went on, raising her voice to a loud stage whisper but very kindly ignoring the interruption which had ever so slightly thrown off her timing.

"The Brenda Woolley Concert for the Refugees," she announced in quotation marks and wafted her hands in the air vaguely as if sketching out a poster.

Nobody knew what to say. Rogers found his jaw open.

"I'll call you back," he said.

"Good, isn't it?" said Brenda. "I bet none of you thought of *that*." She seemed pleased with the effect she had created. Sometimes she moved even herself. She waited for approval, head lowered in that genuinely humble way she had rehearsed so often.

There was a slight pause.

The short terrierlike woman with the artificial red hair stepped forward and said aggressively, "I think it's a terrific idea."

"It is a good idea," said Keppler diplomatically.

"A wonderful, touching, intensely *human* idea," said the small terrier woman. She stressed the word *human* and looked around challengingly as if the rest of them were somehow not human.

"It *is* a wonderful idea," said Brenda Woolley eventually after a little thought, as if someone else had suggested it.

"Yes, I like it. I like it very much," she said with warm approval. "No, don't stop me, Emil," she waved away all possibility of denial. "I am up to this. I can do it. You are very sweet, but in times like this we must all do that we can. And if it costs me my last breath, I shall do it."

If she was waiting for applause, she didn't get it. Keppler looked helplessly over at Rogers.

"As soon as we finish the search-and-rescue," said Rogers, "I'm sure that would be fine."

She waved away the search-and-rescue.

"Details," she said. "Talk to Pauley."

The terrier looked suddenly important.

"So do we have a deal here or what?"

"Once we have everyone bedded and fed," said Keppler, "we'll organize it."

"Will you announce it now, Emil dearest?" asked Brenda coyly.

"Now?" said Rogers.

"Yes. Can you make sure it's in the press reports on the H9 thing?" barked the terrier, her hair an odd shade of gypsy red. "There's bound to be a lot of news coverage on something like this."

"Well okay, we'll certainly mention it to the news crews."

"I think Brenda would be available to do a certain amount of press on this."

Brenda nodded her approval. Terrier thought so.

"I'll get on to the news crews myself," said the terrier. "This is important."

They swept out in a flurry of fur with the air of people who have achieved something really vital at some personal sacrifice.

No one said anything.

THE SLEEPING BEAUTY

Hubble made God look small. He has never quite recovered from that.

DE RERUM COMOEDIA

"Mayday. Begin emergency transmission. All frequencies. PS Johnnie Ray. Request help immediately. Two male crew: Alex Muscroft and Lewis Ashby. Two H9 evacuees: one child female, Tay Ashby; one adult female, Katy Wallace."

Carlton had managed to fix the radio. They were, in theory, no longer alone. Their local life-support systems had started up easily enough. Most of these were not broken, they had merely tripped. Circuit breakers were burned out everywhere, of course, but once these were replaced, they had a steady supply of air, water, and emergency lighting. But they were still without main power.

Tay was very quiet. Lewis was worried about her, but none of them had much time to sit with her during those first hours. There was just too much to do to ensure their survival. Alex had shown her the games room and her eyes lit up.

"Wow," she said, "are all these yours?"

"Yes," he said with a proud little smile, "and you can play with them when we get the power back."

Now she sat quietly drawing by the low wattage of emergency lights. Lewis looked in now and again.

Once she said, "It's okay, Daddy, I'm fine. Really."

Another time she asked him about her mother. He gave her a big hug.

From time to time Alex checked on Katy Wallace in the sick bay. She was still unconscious. Alex's beaky face would appear at the round window to see if she had woken yet. He wasn't quite sure what they should say to her. Was she really responsible for the death of Sammy? It made him angry to think of it, and yet, looking at her lying there, helpless, breathing gently, he felt sure there was a reasonable explanation.

Carlton went in periodically to turn her.

The third time Alex's face appeared in the window, Carlton beckoned him inside.

"She hasn't woken yet."

"Thank you, Carlton, I can see that."

"You should see this," said Carlton. "It's quite something." He began pulling the sheet back, revealing her naked body underneath.

"Carlton!" said Alex, shocked.

"It's okay, she's quite unconscious."

"That doesn't make it okay. Oh my god."

The shock of her beauty took his breath away. And then he winced. She was lying facedown, her hair sprawling over the pillow. Her naked back was a mass of bruises.

"Someone beat her."

Carlton nodded.

"Who did that to her?"

"Persons unknown."

"Why?"

"Maybe they wanted to prevent her revealing something."

"How come?"

"Well they left her in the Rialto to die. See here."

There were tiny marks on the upper part of her thigh. Little needle tracks.

"Someone pumped her full of Corazone," said Carlton. "She would never have got out alive. She couldn't even walk."

"Corazone?"

"A highly effective memory suppressant and a total muscle relaxant. She'll probably sleep for a week."

He covered her up gently with the sheet.

"She is like the Sleeping Beauty," said Carlton. "Perhaps you should try waking her with a kiss."

"Are you trying to be funny?"

"Is that funny?"

"No."

"Oh."

"It's not funny at all. This woman knows something." He looked down at her sleeping face. She seemed so innocent.

COMUS

When I am very sad I make a comedy, and when I am very happy I make a serious drama.

BILLY WILDER

Comus was chained to the metal wall of a bulkhead. He looked about seventy, with grey hair and a salt-and-pepper beard. He was scrawny, though he might once have been powerful. Now he looked tired. His eyes were red with fatigue as he warily watched Pavel come in. Josef was leaning over him.

"I'm afraid our friend Comus is being very unhelpful," he said. "He refuses to say anything at all, which is a pity, as it leaves us no alternative. Get the needles, Pavel."

"You can't do that, Josef."

"He's endangered the whole damn operation and I want to know why."

"He's Comus, for God's sake," Pavel pleaded.

"It's all our lives at stake. If we've been compromised, we need to know."

"But jeez, Josef, it's Comus."

"You have a better idea?"

Pavel shrugged and went and got the spike. He held it up for Comus to see.

"Do you understand what this is?"

Comus just looked at him. He didn't even turn away as Pavel shot him up.

Pavel waited five minutes and then hooked Comus up to a small reactor box. A wide band ran from his arm to the machine. It would monitor his reactions. Josef walked over and looked at the old man for a minute.

"You understand why we are doing this?"

Nothing.

"Listen, we don't have to do this. You can just tell us the truth. Nobody wants to harm you."

Comus simply stared at him.

"Why did you try and leave the ship? You had no business on H9. Just the watchers and the detonation mob. You knew that? So why this other thing? I don't get it."

If he was hoping for a confession, it was not forthcoming.

"Have it your own way. The drug will help you remember."

"I have done nothing to compromise the security of the operation."

"Well, good. That's good to know. So let's start at the beginning shall we and see what we can establish for a fact."

The sound of the word "fact" chopped like a sharp ax in the room. Josef pulled out an eight-by-ten of Katy Wallace.

"Who's this?"

"You know perfectly well."

"Please just answer the question."

"Her name is Katy Wallace, I believe."

The needles jumped on the meters.

"When did you meet her?"

"I have never met her."

A flicker of reaction indicated a possible untruth.

"All right, why did you arrange to meet her?"

No response.

"Why did you tell her to go to the Rialto?"

Again no response.

"Was it to meet you?"

A long pause. Then a nod.

"Good. What was the purpose of the meeting?"

"It was personal."

"Personal."

"A private matter."

"Are you aware of her relationship with Emil Keppler?"

"Of course."

"Was that why you met her?"

"I didn't meet her."

Josef pulled out a picture of the Ganesha.

"Did you give her this?"

He shook his head. The needles leapt.

"Now that was a lie," said Josef. "Any idea what this is?"

"It's a Ganesha, a Hindu god of good fortune."

"Good fortune for whom? Not for Sammy Weiss, that's for sure. Do you know how she came to get hold of it?"

Comus shrugged. He was tired of this. Josef and his stupid games. That's all they did, play games, usually with people's lives. He was sick of it all. He had been in the struggle too long. And what did the struggle amount to? A simple philosophical choice. Kill or be killed. This is the issue: is it worth dying for a belief? And the nasty lurking underside of this simple question: is it worth killing for a belief? Legions of saints and martyrs and heroes of church, state, and revolution had all fought and died for such issues. Was any of it worth a toss? He stopped listening for a moment as Josef explained the workings of the Ganesha. A postman, yeah, yeah, yeah. A miniature transmitter, blah, blah, blah. The watchers had been monitoring Comus for his own security, bugging him electronically to see if he was being "painted" by any detection devices. Once he had tried to go to H9, he had been prevented, blah, blah, blah.

Now Josef was outlining the way the watchers had followed Katy to the Rialto. They had called McTurk in when they picked up a faint signal from the Ganesha. Sammy Weiss had activated it. For Sammy it was a fatal mistake. Within minutes they were in her apartment. They had found sensitive search requests on her screen. That was enough.

"Did you give the postman to Katy Wallace?"

"No. I never met her."

"Okay, you had it delivered to her?"

"Yes."

"And it contained a message to meet you?"

"Yes."

"To which she could reply at a distance?"

"If you say so."

"Who did she give the Ganesha to?"

"I haven't a clue."

"But it was to confirm the details of your meeting on H9?"

Hesitation. "Yes."

"Okay, so you wanted to see her?"

Nod.

Josef leaned forward. "Why?"

A long pause this time.

"Why in the middle of an operation did you meet with the mistress of a man with whom we are doing business?"

Nothing.

Josef persisted. "Was it to warn her? Or were you doing some other deal? Perhaps a little insurance? Information in exchange for . . . what exactly? Not money, not you, not now. Help me here. I just can't understand why you were meeting her so secretly?"

"I'm not going to tell you anything else."

"What a pity."

He said nothing.

"What a pity we can't ask her."

The old man looked up. What was he talking about?

"We can't ask Katy Wallace because, you see, she is dead."

They watched him come apart.

TRAGIC RELIEF

Famous people are very often traumatized individuals with a deep-seated sense of unworthiness. . . . They believe that fame will mean an end to pain, and access to love.

PAMELA HELEN CONNOLLY

Brenda in a white gown. Brenda in a white light. Brenda in front of a large white screen with the single word "Disaster" behind her. She is talking to us or, as she puts it, "speaking with each and every one of us." An organ plays gently behind her honeyed words of wisdom.

"Love is the answer. Love is the key. Love will heal everything. With the power of love. . . . Shit. Yes?"

"With the power of love the healing can begin."

A suntanned, overweight, roly-poly man in a ridiculous Hawaiian shirt steps forward, prompting her. He is Brenda's creator of special material. What used to be called a writer.

" 'Let it begin now the healing,' " he continues. " 'Let it begin inside each and every one of us.' And then the choir goes 'A-men' and they start the hand clap and we're into the Gospel Chorus."

"Brilliant, Raymond. I love it."

"Can you see the prompter?"

"I can now. Thank you, Nora."

"All right, everyone, we're ready to go live," says a man in headphones. "And going live in ten seconds. Five, four, three, two . . ."

"Hello everybody, I'm Brenda Woolley. The H9 disaster has hit us all pretty hard here on the *Princess Di*. As we continue the heartrending job of search-and-rescue, looking for the many hundreds of poor people still lost out there, we remember and thank God for the larger humanity of which we form a part."

"She's finally flipped," said Boo. "She thinks she's the pope." He was watching on a monitor in the stateroom that had become Rogers's temporary HQ. Currently, Boo's hair was bright orange. Beside him the Amazing Keith, pale-faced, his skinny body squeezed into a lime jumpsuit, was staring off into space.

Rogers had stepped outside for a second. He was conferring with Kyle, who had brought him the initial damage report.

"This says the destruction came from inside?"

"Looks that way, man."

"But that's crazy."

"Insane, ain't it," agreed Kyle.

"Who would do such a thing?"

"Something got out of control."

"Out of control? They couldn't have caused more devastation if they'd tried."

He glanced back inside the stateroom at the screen.

"Love is the answer," Brenda Woolley was saying.

"Get me anything you can. List of dissidents. Throw me something, Kyle."

Kyle nodded and moved off in that loose, easy way of his.

Rogers leaned against the wall and thought for a moment. *Someone planned this*. The thought was too horrendous.

Inside, Brenda Woolley preached on.

"It's all too easy for us to say, 'I can't cope, Brenda.' 'This thing is too big for me, Brenda.' 'What difference can *I* make, Brenda?' But we *can* all make a difference. I'm *here* to *help you* all make a difference.

It is time to stand up and be counted. *Together* we can make a difference."

"Hallelujah!"

She glanced at Pastor Abraham, a tubby man with curly white hair. He beamed at her through rows of gleaming teeth and added in a deep voice, "Praise the Lord!" One or two of the choir were tempted to join in, but Brenda froze them with a smile. Brenda did not care for unscripted hallelujahs.

"Tune in to the Brenda Woolley Disaster Relief Experience and together let's make a difference."

The choir began to tap their tambourines, Pastor Abraham to shake his booty. She would have to have a word with him about taste, thought Brenda, then launched herself into a gospel version of her theme song.

> *I'd cross the Universe for you, my darling*
> *I'd sail across the Galax-sea . . .*

"Turn that shit off," said Rogers, returning.

"That's not shit," said Boo. "That's Brenda Woolley. That's cream of shit."

"Shut up," said Kyle.

"Yes, boss," said Boo cheekily. He flicked the control. Brenda Woolley's image reluctantly faded.

"They're working on it," said Kyle in response to Rogers's unspoken question.

A florid gentleman in an eccentric tweed suit hurried in, mopping his brow with a red silk handkerchief. "Forgive my tardiness, gentlemen, I was consulting upon another matter."

"Who the fuck's this?" asked Rogers.

"I, sir, am Charles Jay Brown. I have the honor to represent this strangely gifted young man and I hope soon"—and here he bowed in the direction of the Amazing Keith—"to represent the dangerous talent of this very explosive young man."

"Fuck you," said Keith not unpleasantly.

"He has, as you can see, suffered from mismanagement hitherto," said Charles Jay Brown, not in the least fazed by outright rejection.

"This is a police matter—we don't need agents."

"Ah, agents, I quite agree with you, but I am management, sir. I intrude into every corner of my artists' lives. There is no detail that escapes me. I represent the entire man."

"Worse than a lawyer, ain't he?" said Boo with a tolerant smile.

Kyle scowled at him.

"Sorry," said Boo. "Just trying to be helpful."

"You're a comedian," said Kyle. "Right?"

"That's what they say," said Boo modestly.

"And this is the explosives guy?" said Rogers.

Keith nodded.

"So where were you when H9 went up?"

"What, are you crazy? You think I blew up H9? You think I'm an idiot?"

"Scratch that," said Boo. "They *know* you're an idiot."

"Shut up," said Rogers. "This isn't funny."

"How often have I heard that," said Boo sadly.

Rogers nodded to Kyle, who tapped Boo lightly over the head. Half a pat, half a warning.

"Okay. I get it," said Boo. "Humor is inappropriate."

"Well?" said Rogers to Keith.

"I was here on the *Di*."

"Are any of your stores unaccounted for?"

"You mean did someone steal my stuff?"

"Yes."

"No."

"Did you sell or lend any explosives to anyone?"

"You think I'm nuts?"

"They're not questioning your sanity, Keith," said Boo nicely. "It's your housekeeping they're interested in."

"Nothing's gone missing. I'd know."

"Will you check again?"

"Sure."

"And we're going to have to lock up the rest of your stock."

"Why?"

"I don't want any civilians getting their hands on explosives. Okay?"

Keith shrugged. "If you say so."

"What about you?" said Rogers to the waiting Boo.

"Me? Hey, I haven't left the ship. I bin here too."

Charles Jay Brown confirmed it with a barely perceptible nod to Rogers.

"Okay, you can go."

Boo looked disappointed.

As they left the stateroom, they were watched from the far end of the deck by a tall dark man with a heavy mustache. A red-haired boy handed him a message. He scanned it and nodded.

"Better let them know right away," said McTurk.

THE POSTMAN ALWAYS RINGS TWICE

Everyone has his price.

NAPOLEON

Ping. It was a misdirected mail message. He was being copied on something. Carlton paused in his work repairing the power center to check the incoming signal. It was good news as far as he was concerned. It confirmed their communication system was working.

Misdirected Mail.
Intercept request by Sammy Weiss.
Subject. Katerina Walenska.

We have attempted to deliver your search request several times. The address you gave is no longer valid or responding. Would you like us to forward the results of our search to this address?

Good heavens, thought Carlton, the Weiss woman must have intended to copy me on what she found. But she was killed before the results of her search request could get back to her. He pondered a minute and then selected okay. Within minutes the file came through.

KATERINA WALEWSKA

Katerina Walewska was born Maria Laczinska in Poland in 1789, the year of the French Revolution. In 1805 at the age of 16 she was married to Count Walewski—who was at the then incredible age of 68. She became the Countess Walewska, and despite the enormous age difference seems to have been happy. One day when she was only 17, the great hero Napoleon rode through the village of Bronia on his way to Warsaw. He was about to destroy the Austrians at the battles of Wagram and Austerlitz. He was cheered from the rooftops and hailed by the Poles as a liberator. He noticed a beautiful young woman watching from a window, and sent an aide to find out who she might be. Discovering that she was the Countess Walewska, he sent an invitation for her to attend a ball honouring him in Warsaw. She modestly declined. The Poles were mortified and told her to accept, which after much persuasion she did. At the ball Napoleon asked her to dance, but she said she did not dance. He had conquered all Europe but not her. Next day he sent her a note which read, "I saw no one but you, I admired no one but you, I want no one but you. N." She ignored it. He sent her diamonds, and flowers, but she returned them. Delegations of Poles beseeched her to give in to his demands, for Napoleon had made his attitude quite clear: "Your country will be dearer to me, once you have had pity on my poor heart." He was determined to win her, even if it meant blackmailing Poland itself. She seemed genuinely to want to hold to her marriage vows, despite heavy pressure from the Court and histrionics from Napoleon. Learning that two of his young aides had been seen flirting with Maria, he promptly transferred them to the front lines. He showed her a valuable watch which he then smashed to the ground as a demonstration of his desire for her. Eventually she had no choice but to succumb. She became his mistress, and his love. In May 1810, she bore him a son, Alexandre Walewski. She saw him for the last time in exile on Elba, before Waterloo. In 1817, aged 28, she died in the house in Paris that had been the Emperor's gift. Her last word was "Napoleon."

Carlton was totally puzzled. What the heck was all that about?

His buzzer sounded. Sick bay.

When he got there, he found Katy Wallace awake. She was hunched up under a blanket, knees drawn up, eyes wild and staring. Alex was trying to calm her down.

"Where am I?"

"You're safe."

She was shivering.

"What have you done to me?"

"Carlton found you whacked out of your head in the Rialto."

She winced and looked over her shoulder. She touched the terrible marks gingerly.

"You're badly bruised."

"How do you know?"

"Carlton showed me."

"Nice."

"Katy, we want to help you. Who beat you?"

"I don't remember."

Was she lying, or acting, or did she really not remember?

"Try and think, Katy, we need to know."

"What is this, an interrogation?"

"We have to know what's going on."

"How did I get here?"

"Carlton found you in the Rialto. What were you doing there?"

"I can't remember anything," she said.

"He saved your life."

"Who asked him to?"

"You'd be dead if he'd left you."

"What am I supposed to do, thank him?"

"You might consider it. H9 blew up."

"What?"

"It's gone."

She was shocked, even he could see that. She looked across at Carlton for confirmation.

"It was totally destroyed," he said.

"Did anybody . . . ? How many people . . . ?" She couldn't finish the sentence.

"There were hundreds of casualties."

"Oh my God." She stared bleakly for a moment and began to cry.

"I'll get you a coffee," Alex said gently.

"Thanks." Tears were in her eyes. "I'm sorry."

She was shaking. He put a rug round her shoulders.

"Be right back," he said.

"It's just like the *Bronia*," said Katy, sobbing.

The what? thought Carlton. He had read that word recently. He checked his memory. It was in the Katerina Walenska file. *Napoleon rode through the village of Bronia.* How strange. What could it mean? He put in a search request for *Bronia* and at the same time requested any outstanding search requests from Sammy Weiss. The research computer promised him a speedy response. It was a very old Olivetti Librarian machine.

"You a Bowie?" it said.

"Yes."

"Love your kind."

"Thanks."

"Don't make them like you anymore."

He could hear it humming away as it searched through the files.

"Let's dance," it was singing. "Let's face the music and dance. Do *you* sing?"

"Not really."

"Pity. Ah, here we are. There are two outstanding requests from Sammy Weiss. One for information on Silesians, and another for something called the Gunpowder Plot."

"Can you copy me?"

"Anything for a Bowie," it said.

Carlton turned round. Katy Wallace had stopped crying and was watching him.

When Alex returned with the coffee, she had dried her eyes.

"Careful, it's hot," he said, indicating the steaming mug.

"Okay, Carlton, I can handle it from here," he said, nodding towards the door.

Carlton looked puzzled.

"Skedaddle," said Alex.

"What?"

"Laissez nous seul."

"Quoi?"

"Vamoose."

"Say again?"

"Shove off."

"Shove what?"

"Get lost."

"Where."

"Piss off."

"Use the bathroom?"

"Carlton, fuck off!"

"Oh, you want me to *leave*," said Carlton. "Right?"

"Right."

"Sorry."

Carlton went off intoning, "Scram, take a hike, beat it, shoo, piss off, shove off," to himself.

"He's an odd one, your humanoid," said Katy.

"He's a Bowie."

"He saved my life?"

"Carried you all the way from the Rialto."

"What was I doing there?"

"We kinda wanted to ask you that."

"If I remember, I'll tell you, okay?"

"Okay."

"Thanks, Alex," she said, "you're sweet."

"Was that why you used me as a postman?"

She looked up, surprised.

"What are you talking about?"

"The Ganesha."

"That was a security device."

"Don't give me that bullshit."

His change of tone surprised her.

"Why did you plant it on me?"

She looked wounded.

"Katy, it was a postman. A sophisticated remote signaling device. We had it scanned."

"And what did you find?" she asked evenly.

"We found that it was lethal."

This time she had the grace to look shocked. "Lethal?"

"Yes. The woman we gave it to was killed."

"Oh." Her jaw fell open. "I had no idea. I . . ." She looked blankly at the wall.

"She was a good friend of mine, Katy. Why was she killed?"

"I don't want to talk about it now," she said. "I'm sleepy."

"Sure you're sleepy," he said sarcastically.

"Alex," she said, looking up at him, "I *will* tell you everything I know, honest, but please can I sleep now? I'm so tired." Her eyes closed. She drifted off. He stared at her for a while and then tiptoed out of the room.

"Well, that was brilliant," said Lewis, watching the scene on the large floating monitor. "Boy, you really grilled her. Score twenty for Inspector Shylock Holmes."

Seeing Katy on the screen, Alex looked hard at Lewis.

"You're bugging *me* now?" said Alex aggressively.

"No," said Lewis. "I'm bugging her."

"Why?"

"I don't trust her."

"I can handle it," said Alex. "She trusts me."

"Sure she does," said Lewis, "she can wrap you round her little finger."

"That's not true, man."

"So, why didn't she answer your questions?"

"She's sleepy."

"Really?"

"Really."

"Well, if she's so sleepy, what's she doing now? Sleepwalking?" He indicated the screen. Alex gasped. Katy had leapt out of bed. She was frantically searching for something. She searched through her handbag, then looked under the bed. Finally she wrenched open one of the pill cabinets.

"Carlton?"

"Don't worry. Mild sedatives. Nothing lethal in there."

"Yeah, she's sleepy all right," said Lewis sarcastically. "Probably exhausted after being grilled by you. Perhaps it's time I took her a nightcap."

When Lewis entered the sick bay, she almost leapt out of her skin.

"All right, Katy. Spare me the acting class. You can fool Alex but you can't fool me. Just what's going on?"

Her eyes rolled and she rushed at him. If Carlton hadn't come running in, she might have got him. In her hand she had a hypodermic. Carlton knocked it from her. She collapsed on the bed weeping.

"Okay," said Lewis, "suppose you just tell us everything you know?"

THE BUG

Well, there's a remedy for all things but death, which will be sure to lay us flat one time or other.

MIGUEL DE CERVANTES

Inside the *Iceman*, Josef and Pavel were watching the old man. Tears streaming down his face. He looked suddenly very old.

"You and I know, Comus, don't we. We've looked into the heart of it. The bleakness. We've sent people to their deaths before. What's the difference, one way or another?" Josef, the hard man. Josef, the up-and-coming. Josef, Comus's heir.

"It's just a girl, man. A girl you never met, right?"

A sob, a bitter sob.

"Want to talk about her? Tell us who she is?"

Jesus, the man was coming apart.

"You do see, don't you, that had you left her alone, she wouldn't be dead."

Bitter irony. The horror in the man. The terrible accusation for Comus to live with.

"What the hell was so special about her?"

The old man looked up out of his tormented soul.

"She was my daughter, Josef."

. . .

"Oh hell."

"His daughter?"

"Jesus, why didn't he tell us right away?"

"His daughter," Pavel repeated.

"Go figure."

They had left the old man in the bulkhead while they decided what to do. He at least seemed calmer. Staring blankly at the wall. Maybe it was the drugs.

Sven appeared.

"What you got there?" said Josef to the Swede.

"Coupla messages."

"And?"

"The watchers have forwarded a Mayday request from the *Johnnie Ray.*"

"We're not picking anybody up. This is a secure operation."

"They think you'll make an exception when you see the passenger list."

Josef glanced at the signal.

"Oh Jesus, Mary, and Joseph."

"What?" said Pavel

"She's alive!"

"Who?"

"The Wallace woman. Look here, aboard the *Johnnie Ray.*"

"She survived? I thought they shot her full of Corazone."

"A tin man pulled her out."

He read on. "There's a report from a deskbot who worked at the Rialto. One of our mechanicals."

He swiftly scanned the document.

"Took her aboard the *Johnnie Ray.*"

"The deskbot tapped them," said Sven. "Got a bug aboard their ship. Stuck it on her shoe when it helped the tin man carry her from the Rialto."

"Now that is wonderful," said Josef. "Send that brave 'bot some flowers. Or what do we send tin men? Oil? A new hard drive?"

"Bit late for that. He went up with H9."

"Good for him." He thought for a second. "Well, they know way too much. We simply can't take a risk. Activate the bug."

• • •

It was hard, metallic, and cylindrical, no more than three inches in length. It looked like a strange stick insect. It had crawled off Katy's shoe and along the corridor and entered the games room of the *Johnnie Ray*. It was a mechanical bug. A third-generation minibomb. Four spidery legs lifted the cylinder off the ground, and two tiny antennae sniffed the air, searching for electricity. It could sit silently for weeks, years even, until it was activated, and then it would begin to do something very extraordinary: it would give birth. Right now it was one puzzled parasite. All these wires and all these games should be fully powered, but it could find nothing. Not a watt. Must be some kind of temporary outage. It decided to sit and wait.

"We have a problem with the bug," said Sven. "It needs to tap into a source. They have no power on the *Ray*. It can't start until they get their power back."

"Okay. Let me know the minute they do, and meanwhile I want you to monitor their signals traffic, Pavel. I want to see who they communicate with."

"Shall we tell Comus?"

"I don't think so."

"But she's his daughter."

"It's too late for sentiment. The bug is already on board."

FUNNY PECULIAR

Comedy naturally wears itself out—destroys the very food on which it lives; and by constantly and successfully exposing the follies and weaknesses of mankind to ridicule, in the end leaves itself nothing worth laughing at.

WILLIAM HAZLITT

Check one of the following:

Comedy is a sickness.
Comedy is a disease.
Comedy can be cured.
Comedy is a genetic malfunction.
Comedy is a state of mind.
Comedy is like religion, a leap of faith.
Comedy is like magic, an illusion.
Comedy is like sex.
Comedy is like shopping.

Carlton was trying precepts on comedy as he worked on the power unit. He was getting nowhere with both. I sometimes wonder if he ever imagined someone like me coming along, reading his notes, admiring his work. A fan from the future. Mind-boggling, isn't it. But of course I'm more than just a fan. I'm his editor. His alter ego. Almost like a manager. And they take 25 percent. I hear art dealers take 50 percent. So I think I'm entitled to something. You have no idea the amount of work I have to do, ploughing through his notes. The other day I was working through some of his precepts about comedy when I made a discovery. The precepts were banal enough. I think the tin man was trying to categorize the Ten Commandments of Comedy.

You have to be cruel to be comic.
Filthy is funny.
Where there's muck, there's mirth.

A pie in the face is worth two in the tush.
K's are Komic.
One, two, three, the third's funnee.

That sort of thing. But then I found this chart. Know what it is? It's his original notes on the Red Nose/White Face dichotomy.

WHITE FACE	RED NOSE
Steve Martin	Robin Williams
Woody Allen	Danny Kaye
Stan Laurel	Oliver Hardy
Buster Keaton	W. C. Fields
John Cleese	Marty Feldman
Dan Aykroyd	Chevy Chase
Billy Crystal	Eddie Murphy
George Burns	Gracie Allen
Mike Nichols	Milton Berle
Peter Cook	Dudley Moore
Carl Reiner	Mel Brooks
David Letterman	Jay Leno
Bob Hope	Bing Crosby
Peter Sellers	Spike Milligan
Dean Martin	Jerry Lewis
Jennifer Saunders	Dawn French
Groucho Marx	Harpo Marx
Ernie Wise	Eric Morecambe
Johnny Carson	John Belushi
Garry Shandling	Billy Connolly
Bud Abbott	Lou Costello
Stephen Fry	Hugh Laurie
Gene Wilder	Gilda Radner
Joan Rivers	Carol Burnett
Ellen DeGeneres	Roseanne
Richard Pryor	Syd Caesar
Elaine May	Benny Hill
Desi Arnaz	Lucille Ball
Lenny Bruce	Phil Silvers
Mort Sahl	Dick Van Dyke
Harold Lloyd	Tommy Cooper
Bill Maher	Danny DeVito
Griff Rhys Jones	Mel Smith
Jerry Seinfeld	Frankie Howerd
Harry Shearer	Jim Carrey

Bill Cosby	Will Smith
Alan Bennett	Marty Short
Jonathan Miller	Tim Allen
Steve Coogan	Jonathan Winters
Conan O'Brien	Molly Shannon
Chris Guest	Harry Enfield
Chris Rock	Paul Hogan
Tracey Ullmann	Rosie O'Donnell
Charlie Chaplin	Bobcat Goldthwaite
Bill Murray	Jack Benny
Bob Newhart	Flip Wilson

Who are all these people? You've never heard of any of them, have you? Of course you haven't. They've all been dead for centuries. I've had to look them up. And guess what, they are all comedians from the late twentieth century. Some of them Carlton couldn't make up his mind about. For example, he couldn't decide which category to place George Carlin and Rodney Dangerfield in. Some were what he calls Double Controllers—White Faces masquerading as Red Noses—a category of comedian, he says, who exhibit both elements in their personality. He cites Woody Allen's little nerdy Red Nose character as an example, inside which the White Face writer-director Allen is controlling everything. Other examples he cites are Rowan Atkinson as Mr. Bean, Charlie Chaplin as the little tramp, Barry Humphries as Dame Edna Everage, and Eddie Izzard.

Again, I don't expect you to have heard of these people.

This chart dates from about the time he first began searching for the comedy gene, trying to see if there is something in the DNA of comics which might be passed on. He is looking for evidence of a comedy or even a show biz gene. Well, why not? There's clearly a music gene: the Bachs, the Mozarts, the Strausses. There's a literature gene—the Brontës, the Dumas, père et fils, the Amises—so why not a comedy gene? He thinks he almost finds some evidence with one of the guys on a very weird show called *Monty Python's Flying Circus*. I've seen the tapes, and boy, does it suck. It's strange rather than funny. Five limeys and a Yank. No girls; they did drag. Typical Brits. They're never happier than when dressing up as women. What is it with them?

It's a stupid show, as I say, and Carlton found it totally puzzling.

Heads come off or pop open in demented animations, sheep drop on people's heads for no reason whatsoever, Vikings sing love songs to pressed meat, weird men dressed as old ladies squeak in silly voices, there are dead parrots, and Spanish Inquisitions, it's all very silly nonsense. They seem dangerously cuckoo to me. Carlton couldn't make head or tail of it, but it seemed from the tape that the audience laughed, and as far as he could tell it was genuine, not canned, laughter. In casually cross-checking the genetic backgrounds of the six strange men involved, he turned up an ancestor for one of them in show biz. Eric Idle's great-grandfather Henry Bertrand, a Victorian gentleman from the 1890s, had been a circus manager. Was this the genetic missing link? His great-grandfather was a ringmaster in a circus and Idle was in a Flying Circus. Surely this was significant? Of course it wasn't. Turned out Idle was screwed up by losing his RAF rear-gunner father in a traffic accident in World War Two (irony, eh?—killed coming home on Christmas leave after surviving the war). This was compounded by being stuck in a semiorphanage for twelve years with a bunch of fatherless boys. The circus thing was just a coincidence. But you can see the lengths he went to in searching for the comedy gene.

Further down the corridor he saw Alex looking through the window of the sick bay. Carlton went over and looked in too. Lewis was inside questioning Katy. Carlton watched for a moment, then he turned to Alex and put on a big grin.

"Hello," he said, "'what's eating you?' as the actress said to the bishop."

Alex stared at him, puzzled. "What?" he said.

" 'What is it up with you,' as the art mistress said to the gardener. 'Is that a penis in your pocket, or are you just pleased to see me?' "

"You okay?" said Alex.

"Never better," said Carlton. "I'm up and down like a whore's drawers."

"Are you trying to be funny?" asked Alex.

"Yes," said Carlton.

"Cut it out then."

"As the doctor said to the appendix."

"That's enough."

They both watched Lewis questioning Katy for a while.

"How's he doing in there?"

"No better than me," said Alex.

Carlton looked at him thoughtfully, his head to one side (a characteristic of Bowies when thinking).

"I believe you are attracted to that woman," said Carlton.

"What?" said Alex rather too irritably.

"Am I right about the attraction thing?"

Perhaps he was. When he had glimpsed her poor naked bruised body, he had felt both pity and desire.

"Depends what you mean by attraction," he said defensively.

"Attraction in humans," said Carlton, "is usually referred to by the ambiguous word 'love.' An emotion which can range anywhere from polite admiration to an overwhelming desire to mate, which is often called lust."

"Score one for lust then," said Alex.

"Interestingly, 'love' corresponds to the electromagnetic field in inanimate objects."

"Excuse me?"

"As the apple feels the pull of the earth's gravity, as even the tiniest iron filing feels the tug of the magnet, so do humans feel the power of love. It is the mating force that all bionic life suffers from."

"Suffers from?"

"Is subject to against its will. It's in your genes. You are manipulated by your own DNA. It is a weakness that computers do not suffer from."

They were distracted by a shout from inside the sick bay. Lewis was rapidly losing his cool.

"Goddammit, Katy," he yelled, "just tell me why our gigs were canceled."

"I haven't a clue," she said.

"Then who were you meeting in the Rialto?"

"I'm not sure."

"You go to elaborate lengths to set up a rendezvous with someone you don't know? Why? Who did you *think* you were going to meet?"

"Someone who knew my father."

"The dead hero. So why did they rough you up?"

She shrugged.

"Was it McTurk who beat you?"

She frowned. "Who's McTurk?" she asked.

Lewis showed her a picture of McTurk from Carlton's file.

"Not my type," said Katy.

"Is that a no?"

"It's a no thank you."

"How about this guy?"

He showed her the heavy.

"I never saw him before."

"Oh, come on, Katy, Carlton saw you go upstairs with him, for Christ's sake. What do you think, I'm completely dumb?"

She shrugged. "You said it."

"What about the Ganesha?"

"What about it?"

"You gave it to Alex. Who gave it to you?"

"Someone . . . I don't remember."

"Oh come on."

"I don't remember, just leave me alone."

"Goddammit, Katy . . ."

He raised his arm. She jerked and screamed.

Alex came running in.

"Did you hit her, man?"

"No."

"I swear to God, if you hit her . . ."

"I didn't hit her, Alex," said Lewis.

"Look at her," said Alex, "she's terrified."

"It's the Corazone. Someone beat her badly then shot her up. The body remembers things the mind doesn't. It's memory struggling to get back. Look."

Lewis raised his arm. Once again she twisted and screamed.

"Stop it," said Alex. "You're bullying her."

"I am not bullying her. She knows things she's not telling."

"This is not necessary."

"This is damn necessary. She attacked me with a goddam hypodermic."

Tay came running in. She looked round the room. Katy lying on the bed whimpering.

"Daddy, why are you yelling at that lady?"

"Tay, I . . ."

"Don't yell at her, Daddy. She's not mommy."

There was an awkwardness in the room. Lewis couldn't look at anyone. He felt hot and embarrassed. Oh God, this is what she remembers? Him yelling at his wife. He recalled their arguments, the shouts, the quarrels. Tay was supposed to be asleep. He didn't know what to say. Katy surprised them all.

"It's all right, sweetie," she said. "We were just playing a game. Don't worry. See, we're friends." She put her arm round Lewis and drew him towards her. Lewis had no choice but to pretend to hug her.

"They're really playing a game?" said Tay uncertainly to Alex.

"Sure they are," said Alex "and now it's my turn." He stepped forward and reached in to hold Katy tight. She made no sound. Just let him hold her. He didn't let go.

"Good game," said Alex, "isn't it?"

"My turn," said Tay.

"I haven't quite finished my go yet," said Alex.

Suddenly there was a loud click, a whoosh, and the air-conditioning kicked on.

Carlton came in beaming.

"Power's back," he said triumphantly. Then looked round the room at them puzzled. "What's going on?"

Alex was holding Katy, Lewis was looking disapprovingly at him, and Tay seemed puzzled.

"We were just playing games," said Tay.

"Can I play?" asked Carlton.

"No," said Alex firmly. "It's only for humans."

"Daddy, can I go play in the games room now the power's back?" asked Tay.

"Okay," he said.

"Yay." She ran off excitedly.

Carlton's chest gave a slight *ping*.

"Excuse me," said Carlton. "I'd better get that, it's mail. Could be important."

He followed Tay through the door.

"Okay, she's gone now," said Lewis pointedly.

Alex reluctantly pulled away from Katy.

"Thank you, Alex," she said, "I enjoyed that game."

"Me too," he said. "Let's play it again soon."

Lewis looked disgusted.

"Can I make a call now?" she asked.

Lewis hesitated.

"Of course you can," said Alex. "You're not a prisoner."

Carlton's mail was a reply from the Olivetti. It was the results from his search request.

Bronia: Small town near Warsaw, Poland, Earth.

Bronia: An ammonium solution used in removing solid waste.

Bronia: The CS <u>Bronia</u>. Shipping Disaster. Rhea. Container ship disaster which effectively outlawed the practice of forcing immigrants into long–term contracts from which they could not escape. A container ship was involved in a collision with severe loss of life. See Board of Inquiry Report.

There were some press cuttings attached. They related to the scandal involved in the container ship disaster. There was a photograph of a young bearded captain, and a headline. CAPTAIN BLAMES LOSS OF LIFE ON PANIC AMONGST PASSENGERS. He read through the columns casually. Suddenly a name sprang out at him. Keppler. Keppler was the young captain.

KEPPLER

An emotional man may possess no humor, but a humorous man usually has deep pockets of emotion, sometimes tucked away or forgotten.

CONSTANCE ROURKE

"It's for you, sir. It's Ms. Wallace."

Keppler had kept to himself since his ship was filled with tiresome cops from H9. Even Mitchell, his captain, deferred to them. So

he stayed in his quarters sulking. He had a penthouse filled with antiques. High picture windows provided stunning views of the local
star field. He stared out into the galaxy wondering about Brenda. He
had never seen her so fired up. She was filled with enthusiasm for
her concert. Was this a good time perhaps to talk with her seriously
about their marriage? It had no real meaning anymore. Brenda was
wedded to her career. She dated her ego. They were inseparable.
Nothing could come between them. Keppler had long ago given
up trying. He had withdrawn from her bed, and she had neither
complained, nor, it saddened him to realize, really noticed. He had
sought solace in a series of brief affairs, showgirls mainly, transients
who passed through the many Keppler theaters, an occasional dealer
from one of his casinos, cocktail waitresses, hostesses. Katy was the
first woman to really fascinate him. He had pursued her relentlessly.
In some ways he was still pursuing her, for there was always a part
of herself she held aloof, a place he could not reach. He was obsessed
with her, he realized. When he found she was missing, he went
through agonies thinking she might not have made it off H9. He
had his people scour the lists of refugees on other ships, with no
luck. They broadcast appeals, though he knew the shock wave had
knocked out most people's communications systems. He was beginning to panic that she might never turn up when they picked up the
Ray's distress call. Now, finally, she was on the screen. He stared at
her pale face.

"Katy? Are you all right?"

"I'm fine, Emil."

"I've been so worried about you. Why didn't you call?"

"The shock wave . . ."

"Well, where are you?"

She swiftly filled in the details. Alex watched her intently from
across the room. She tried to tell Emil she'd call back, but he
wouldn't let her go. He was proposing to bring the *Princess Diana* to
pick her up.

"Don't be silly, Emil."

"It's no problem. We're picking up refugees from all over, there
are a dozen requests in your area."

"But Emil, we're in an icefield."

"And the Main Beam's still down, so we'll come to you."

"It's way too dangerous."

"No, we have the new nav. equipment. We're heading that way anyway for a ship called . . . what's its name?"

"*Iceman*," said Mitchell.

"Katy, are you really all right? Are they treating you well?"

"Emil, they saved my life."

"What were you doing on H9?"

"I'll tell you later."

"No, tell me now."

She wondered what she had in common with this man. Why did he frighten her?

"No, later," she said. "I have to go."

"Why? What's so important?"

"We're eating."

She broke the connection. Grinned at Alex like a naughty schoolgirl. Why had she lied to Keppler? Because Alex looked so sad? Now he was all eager again. Like a little puppy. He practically wagged his tail.

"C'mon," he said, "let's go and play some more games."

Keppler called Brenda.

"Emil, darling, I'm very busy."

"They've found Katy Wallace," he said.

"Thank you, Emil," she said, "but there is very serious work to do here."

She was working on a dance routine with Binky, her personal choreographer. Binky was a little overweight in pink tights.

"I have to run now, Emil, they're working me to *death*."

Brenda's idea of death was breaking a sweat. She didn't need distracting about people being saved. People were being saved every day. Emil should know that she needed to concentrate all her energies on the Experience. She was determined that this show would be great. It was going to be *the* disaster Experience. The apogee of disaster shows. This would set a new benchmark for disaster charity. Too often it was just a rubber chicken and a bad ballet. This would be a disaster to remember. Brenda had made up her mind. And when Brenda made up her mind, only a sudden whim could change it. She didn't need to think of that young woman her husband was so fond of. She would draw comfort from the warmth of her public. They loved her. They needed her. They were loyal to her.

"Binky, dearest" she said, panting heavily. "I have to go visit my public now."

He rolled his eyes.

"Please, Brenda, we could use a little more rehearsal."

She was heavily out of breath. She could use a break. Let the dancers work.

"My public needs me," she said firmly.

Her public. Her people. She visited them constantly in the cramped camps and cardboard cities that had sprouted magically all over the parks. They were everywhere, massed in family groups, with temporary bedrolls spread over the floors of gymnasiums and meeting halls. Brenda moved amongst them, handing out glossy photos and tickets for her concert. She saw herself as Florence Nightingale, or Evita, the people's choice, and the people for their part were very happy she chose them.

"Why do bad things happen in the Universe?" she asked Binky suddenly.

"Too deep for me, love," said Binky, whose life revolved round creating the illusion Brenda could dance.

"She has three left feet," he would scream to his friends in frustration. He kept her surrounded at all times by well-pumped young men who leapt athletically round her.

"Why can't only good things happen?"

"Why indeed?" said Binky, despairing of saving this routine. Perhaps waving her arms around like that would do. He would rehearse the boys privately. If they moved twice as fast, perhaps no one would notice that Brenda looked less like a dying swan than a sick goose.

"Binky, dearest, I am so terribly tired. Let us revisit this magic later. Keep the boys warm. I must go visit my refugees."

"As you wish, heart," said Binky compliantly. "You're the boss. Take five, boys. Brenda's going to the *camps*."

There was a shriek of joy from the dancers at the innuendo.

The refugees had come into Brenda's life at just the right moment. Recently she had begun to feel as though something was missing from her perfect world. She had acolytes and satellites and syco-

phants and flatterers in plenty, but when lying awake at night, under
her rejuvenating mask, mulling over the events of the day, she felt
something was absent. Lovers? No thanks. Brenda was not fond of
being invaded. Children? God forbid. How could people do that to
their bodies? Even when they did the sensible thing and bought
babies they were always screaming and yelling and demanding attention. No, what was missing, she realized, was her need to be recognized as something *more* than just a brilliant all-round singing
talent. She wanted to be recognized as a *great woman*. Show business
was, let's face it, a tacky pastime, compared with real historical people. That's what cut the mustard in the grown-up world. Brenda
wished to become a World Historical Figure. The refugees were her
chance. They provided a vast following who were pathetically grateful for any attention she could bestow on them. They were content
with gestures, with expressions of sympathy, and she could do that
in her sleep. So she wandered through the camps handing out copies
of her albums, and sponsoring volleyball tournaments while listening generously to their thanks. How graciously she did this. Like royalty. I can do so much, she thought. These are my people.

Of course it was all carefully recorded. Cameras followed her
everywhere. You cannot be a World Historical Figure without making some sacrifices. And Brenda was prepared to sacrifice almost
anyone for her cause. So she generously invited the media into what
she called her private life. She let them snap candid photographs of
her as she went around secretly doing good. She kindly allowed
them some of her time so they could get a glimpse of the very private
Brenda (and make it very public). Was there a picturesque child to
be comforted, a desolate widow to be stood next to, a homeless
family to inspire a photo opportunity? She made sure the opportunity was not missed. They were brought forth and filmed beside
her. Properly edited, this footage would look great on the special.
She knew exactly what she wanted. The anxious faces looking
up at her. The big close-up of her singing something meaningful, her arms raised in comfort. Almost a religious thing. Shots of
her walking amongst them, children falling to their knees. Perhaps
a close-up of some tiny diseased child (not contagious obviously),
smiling at her while she sang, its little life made meaningful by the
presence of—yes, admit it—*Saint* Brenda. That's what they are calling her in the camps now, she editorialized. She improvised a tribute

to herself: Saint Brenda, friend of the refugees. Where was her wretched publicist? It was such a good line. The press should have it immediately. Perhaps she could get endorsements from the Church? But which? That was the problem. There were so many of them and they were all so jealous of each other. Poor petty things. She needed some kind of interdenominational approval. A Judaeo-Christo-Hindu-Muslim kind of thing. Perhaps even an endorsement from the Atheists. No sense in alienating them.

She was startled from her reverie by a most distasteful sight. It was Boo, the strange comedian with the funny hair. What on earth was he doing here? These were *her* refugees. He didn't even have a camera crew with him. What possible use could he be? Here she was tirelessly promoting them, doing all she could to get this story out into the world, entirely without fee, and he was just *hanging out* with them? Actually he was distributing food parcels, but it amounted to the same thing. She determined to have a word with him.

"I'm not the only one, I see."

Boo turned and registered the cameras, the support crew, the hairdresser, her wardrobe person, two continuity girls, one personal assistant, and an astrologer.

"Well, you're certainly not alone," he said.

"No point in doing good by stealth," she said. "We have to let the world see what is going on here."

She turned and spoke directly to camera, segueing straight into documentary.

"This is Boo," she said, "a comedian and a valued member of my staff here on the *Princess Di*." Boo raised an eyebrow.

"This is an example of the sort of unselfish work that I encourage here on the ship in these . . ."—lip trembling, don't forget the trembling lip, as she searched for just the right adjective—"in these *terrible* times. There's no people like show people." She launched suddenly into song. The sound guy flinched involuntarily, she was so loud in his headset.

"They smile when they are down."

"They smile all the fucking time, as far as I can see," said Boo. "Pretty much demented, drooling idiots." There was a dreadful pause. Then Brenda gave her famous silver tinkling laugh and patted him on the cheek.

"Don'cha love him?" she said to camera. "He's such a kidder."

Now they had permission, everybody laughed.

"I *love* this man," said Brenda with the warmth of a python wrapping itself around its prey.

"And she is doing just an incredible job," said Boo. "Night and day, no matter where or when, just roll out the cameras and there she is."

Brenda blushed becomingly.

"Oh, it's nothing," she said modestly.

"Oh, it ain't nothing," said Boo. "Without her, many of these people would not have copies of her albums or photographs of her. Many indeed would never even have heard of her."

No need to go quite that far, she thought, but she could always edit out that bit. The man was speaking from his heart, and it was honey to her ears.

"In the middle of all this misery her tireless self-promotion has been something we have all come to rely on. We can all take hope from her example, that no matter how bad things may be, Brenda Woolley will always be there."

She was quite touched.

"Thank you, Boo dear," she said kindly. "I never realized quite how much you admired me." She kissed him on the cheek and moved away grandly with her cameras as if quite overcome.

"Wow," said Boo when she had gone, "an irony-free zone."

THE PERSON FROM PORLOCK

Is comedy endemic in intelligent life? Would evolution be possible without it? Do ants have a sense of humor?

DE RERUM COMOEDIA

In a perfect universe "T. S. Eliot" would be "toilets" backwards. But it is an imperfect universe. It is flawed. It has tears and holes and big gaps of nothing, and a strange fungus, called life, which begins to grow wherever there is water. So sadly it's only "toilest" backwards which is not quite so much fun. An irrelevant point, I know, but I was thinking of language and Carlton's attempts to understand comedy. He was intrigued by the odd linguistic connection between "comic" and "cosmic." It was only an *s* away. Is humor, he wondered, a reaction to the enormousness of it all, an intuitive understanding of just how small the species *Homo sapiens* is in the cosmos? The Universe can function perfectly well without life at all, and yet, just add water and time, and there it is, growing like slime mold in the cracks of dusty planets, evolving into a million different life forms of startling beauty and efficiency. And why does it evolve intelligence? An intelligence which can only gape in wonder at the grandeur of it all and invent concepts like God to understand the magnitude of the ever-expanding Universe of which it is such a tiny part.

Galaxies are so widely spaced that they can pass through each other without colliding. Now that's a mind-boggling thought. Let's see it once again in slow motion. *The distance between individual stars is so huge that it is possible for one galaxy to slip through another galaxy without a collision between any of the billions of stars involved.* And you're worried about returning a late library book. It's hard to grasp this perspective, isn't it? Perhaps, thought Carlton, this is what comedy is, a perception of a disproportionate ratio between the macrouniverse and their own microworld of self-obsessed concerns.

He began to work on the astrophysics of comedy. The cosmic laugh.

Ping. Of course he was immediately interrupted. Aren't we always? Isn't that the funny thing about life? We're just about to discover the meaning of life when someone comes to read the meter? Isn't the person from Porlock always banging on the door? Or calling up and offering new and better phone systems? It's a wonder we get anything done.

This time Carlton was interrupted by the answer to Sammy Weiss's request about the Gunpowder Plot.

Gunpowder Plot, conspiracy to kill James I, King of England, at the opening of Parliament on November 5, 1605. The plot was formed by a group of prominent Roman Catholics in retalia-

tion against the oppressive anti-Catholic laws being applied by
James I. The conspirators rented a vault beneath the House of
Lords and stored 36 barrels of gunpowder in it. Guy Fawkes, a
soldier of fortune, was to set fire to the gunpowder, but the plot
was exposed, and Fawkes was arrested early on November 5.
Fawkes confessed and was hanged along with other conspirators
in 1606. The Gunpowder Plot is commemorated annually in
Great Britain on November 5.

Carlton read it and was baffled. What the hell was all that about?

In the communications room of the *Iceman*, Pavel read the same message. He was monitoring the signals traffic from the *Ray*. This one
made him gulp his coffee and race out of the room.

In the dark hold of the *Iceman* two dozen men were assembled. It
was freezing down there, their breath crystallizing in the cold. They
were swathed in woolens and furs, mittens and earmuffs, knitted
caps. One or two slapped themselves from time to time, like a horse
impatiently stamps its hooves. Josef looked down at them.

"Okay, everyone, listen up. The *Di* has acknowledged."

He spoke calmly, reassuringly. Didn't want to give them any hint
of danger.

"They've taken the bait, they're on their way."

Ironic cheers.

"Don't start cheering yet. This is only the beginning. But it's a
good beginning."

One of them let out a whoop and everyone laughed.

"Okay, the bad news is we're going to have to clean the ship."

A few groans.

"I know, I know. It's boring, but we've still plenty of time before
the *Di* gets here. This place is going to be swept, and if they find anything, or even suspect anything, we're dead in the water, so it's your
lives. Is that understood?"

Muttered assents.

"After that I need you to start packing up your belongings and
cleaning yourselves up. I wouldn't let any one of you on my ship."

Pavel came running up waving a form.

"Just got this from the *Ray*."

Josef glanced at the intercepted mail report.

"Jesus," he said. "Their tin man's onto us."

He was looking at the words "Gunpowder Plot."

"Well, that's it then," said Josef. "We have to take them out right now. Activate the bug."

"But," said Pavel hesitating. "What about his daughter, sir?"

"You do know how the original Gunpowder Plot failed, don't you?"

Pavel shook his head.

"Somebody warned a relative."

A DEADLY TOY

Sixty percent of human communication is miscommunication.

DE RERUM COMOEDIA

Tay was playing happily. The games room in the *Johnnie Ray* hummed and buzzed and fizzed and crackled with electrical toys of all kinds. She was lost in her own world, punching keys, occasionally leaning forward to stare at the screen. The bug surveyed her carefully. It had been awakened by a signal from the *Iceman*. Now it was hungry. Almost any of the electro-mechanical games would provide a decent power source, but it sensed a big problem: Tay. Silently it edged towards her. Its metal antennae sweeping the air. She played on, oblivious. The bug scanned her, checking its files. This was not an electrical source, this was something alien, something dangerous to it. Slowly the bug moved closer and closer to her. She was too engrossed in her game to notice. It hesitated, trying to decide what to do. Then it made up its mind. It would eliminate the problem. This dangerous alien must be destroyed. Carefully it aligned itself and took aim at the young girl. She would never know what hit her.

Tay looked up sharply. Her little brow furrowed. The bug froze, registering its own danger.

"Bug," said Tay and ran out of the room.

Lewis was in with the shrinkbot. He'd asked for an extra session. Normally he spent two hours a day with the shrinkbot. He required a lot of attention. It's one of the signs of the White Face, says Carlton, all this self-obsession.

"Envy," Lewis was saying, "a kind of jealousy of Alex. Especially now that *she's* here."

"But you have Tay."

"Hardly the same thing."

"No. But it must be nice for you."

"Of course. I adore her. She's a great kid."

"And Miss Wallace?"

"I don't trust her."

"Is it sexual jealousy?"

"You mean, am I attracted to her?"

"If you like."

He thought about it for a moment and was surprised when the door flew open and Tay came running in.

"Daddy, Daddy," she said excitedly.

"Not now, dear," said Lewis. "Daddy's with the shrink."

"Nice to meet you," said the shrinkbot.

"This is Dr. Max. He helps me," said Lewis.

"Hi," said Tay. "Daddy, I have to tell you something."

"Really, Tay, I'll be out in a minute."

"But there's a bug in the games room."

"I'll get Carlton to fix it," he said.

"Isn't it dangerous?"

"No, sweetie, just play another game. Carlton will fix it when he has a minute," he said. "We get 'em all the time."

How could he know? Of course he thought she meant a bug in the machine. Wouldn't you? Carlton calculates humans misunderstand each other at least 60 percent of the time. Even he, listening in, didn't get it.

Tay was puzzled.

"Can I play with it then?"

"Yes, run along and play," he said. "There's plenty to do."

"Can't I stay with you, Daddy?"

"No, Tay, don't be a pain, run along to the games room and let me finish up here and I'll be right with you."

"Okay, Daddy."

Yes, of course he was obsessed with himself—it's the burden of the White Face clown—but he could hardly be blamed. Carlton made the same mistake. Ought Carlton to have been listening in while Lewis visited the shrink? Of course not. It violates all rules of privacy. Talking to a shrink is quality time, a time to be purely selfish, to be flagrantly self-obsessed, a chance indeed to star. It is the one-sidedness of the conversation that is so utterly satisfying. But Carlton was listening in as usual, recording everything and filing it away for future use, when he heard there was a bug in the games room, and he figured, like Lewis, what the hell, there's lots of games for Tay to play with, and he was distracted by a control panel which told him something was sucking in great gulps of electricity from somewhere. So he didn't go immediately to the games room.

Alex was showing Katy around the ship. She was beginning to feel much better.

"I have a little cure for you," said Alex.

"Really," she smiled, "and what is it?"

"Oh, it's a little secret. Come."

He took her firmly by the hand and they set off around the oak-paneled corridors of the *Johnnie Ray*. They looked first at the electronic art gallery, an oak-panneled room with several elegant empty gilt frames. He requested a Velázquez and it immediately appeared in an appropriate frame. Katy was delighted. He added a Braque, a Degas, and a Sisley. She was thrilled.

"Can I have a go?"

"Anything you like."

She requested a Renoir.

It magically appeared.

"This is great."

"Thank you."

They played with the art for a while, looking at some fabulous Bellinis, until Carlton popped his head in.

"Oh excuse me," he said. "I'm looking for a leak."

"There's a bathroom at the end of the hall," said Alex.

"No, I don't need to use a bathroom, I'm looking for a power leak."

"Show me the Monet," said Alex to the art gallery.

Monet's famous bridge over the water lilies popped into the frame.

Carlton held up a small meter and let it sniff the air by the Monet. He shook his head, puzzled.

"Don't you like Monet's bridge?" asked Alex.

He glanced at the bridge, puzzled.

"There's nobody on it," he said.

"What?"

"It's just an empty bridge. Is it a joke?"

"Of course it isn't a joke," said Alex, outraged.

"Sorry," said Carlton, "I don't see the point of an empty bridge."

To be fair, he couldn't really see the point of art. It seemed to have no discernible meaning. He understood abstract. At least that didn't pretend to have any meaning. But empty bridges. What was the point of looking at a picture of an empty bridge?

"Philistine," said Alex as he left.

"He's weird, your droid," said Katy.

"Ah, here's my favorite," said Alex, selecting a fresco by Melozzo da Forlì from the Vatican Museum. "Don't you love that blue? I had a suit made in it. I call it High Renaissance. Oh look out, here comes Mr. Quattrocento in the fabric to die for. Stand back Lucrezia, it's *gorgeous* for the Borgias."

He waddled camply round the room, like a runway model played by an overweight queen. His voice was deep-dyed homosexual, the harsh rasping voice of a thousand cigarette packs. She marveled at the way he could play with language.

"Si, yais I am da pope, can I speak to Mike Angelo. He's on his back? Vat, is he taking a nap? Oh he's painting da ceiling? Vat color? No, no, I said *blue*. Who asked him to put figures up there? And another ting, his David. Ya. The naked guy. What's wrong with it? I'll tell you what's wrong with it. It's the wiener, that's what's wrong with it. It's too little. It was cold that day? Who cares it's lifelike, this is art. Listen, you stupid prick, get me a bigger wanger or no more lire for you, signore."

He beamed happily in the grace of her laughter. She was so lovely. He moved towards her, but she waved him away. She needed air. He smiled and stepped back. The moment passed.

Alex showed her the swimming pool. One whole end was built as a Provençal villa, with a terrace off the upstairs bedrooms and a wide patio below. Real trees lined the poolside. She was enchanted with it.

"We could be in the country," she said, delighted.

He clicked on a switch and crickets stirred. She smelled lavender. He rolled back the starscreen and suddenly there was the galaxy above their heads.

"To swim under the stars," she said. "How wonderful. Alex, I *love* this ship."

He grinned contentedly.

"Fancy a dip?" he asked.

"No," she laughed, "I have no suit."

"That's okay," he said. "I can take it."

"I'm sure you can."

"Hot tub? Massage? Sauna?"

She giggled.

"Walk this way, madam."

He led her beside the villa into a little garden with herbs and grass and a wrought-iron rustic table.

"How about a spot of lunch," he said in a British accent. "Tu manges, ma petite?"

"Non, merci, monsieur. Je n'ai pas faim."

"Oh, vachement tu es femme," he said.

He was definitely pursuing her now, and she realized she was enjoying the pursuit. She knew if she kept still for five minutes he would kiss her.

"C'mon," she said. "Show me the rest."

He showed her the gymnasium with its variable gravity exercise machines, the jacuzzi, the steam room, and then led her along the corridor towards the main reception area. They passed the Washing Machine coming back from the tower, relieved of her responsibilities.

"Don't talk to me," she grumbled. "I've been up there for hours. Searching for icebergs. That's not my job. And what's *this*?"

She held out the sex doll accusingly. Alex grabbed for it.

"Oh that. That's just a toy, Mrs. Greenaway," he said.

"She began taking her clothes off again!"

Alex was embarrassed. Katy was looking at him. He could feel himself beginning to blush.

"Then she asked me if I wanted to play with her."

"Yes," said Alex, grabbing it and stowing it on a shelf above the door, "she is really very friendly. I think it belongs to Lewis," he said. "He probably got it for Tay to play with. *Thank you*, Mrs. Greenaway."

Katy was laughing at him. He smiled.

"Sorry," he said.

"Hey," she said, "like I didn't notice you were a guy?"

He led her into their den. It was an impressive, almost baronial hall, lit by a huge fireplace with a virtual fire blazing away in the hearth.

"Oh, this is lovely," said Katy. "Oh, I like this. Is that you?"

She walked over to an oil painting which had been carefully repainted with Alex's features.

"That's me as Sarah, Duchess of Marlborough," he said.

"You look good in a skirt," she said.

"Thank you, so do you," he said.

She was enjoying him. He was great company. So different from Emil, she thought. They lingered for a while at the Joke Box. Alex punched up some of their early routines. They leaned together over the domed top and looked down at the tiny figures below. Two tiny 3-D hologram figures of Alex and Lewis began performing in miniature. They were funny. She kept asking for more routines. She hadn't quite appreciated the subtle balance, the long-suffering patience of Lewis as counterpoise to the mad antics of Alex. She glimpsed a hint of anguish in this patient waiting of his.

"Is Lewis happy?" she asked.

"He wouldn't be happy if he was happy," said Alex.

"What about Tay?"

"Oh, it's something else he can beat himself up with."

"No, where is she?"

"I think she's in the games room."

"Let's go find her."

"Okay. But first let's go look at the stars. You have to see the tower."

So they turned away from the games room.

• • •

Tay had done as she was told and returned to the games room. So, where was the bug, she wondered? Oh, there it was. In the corner. She slowly advanced on it. The ability to reproduce itself was one of the nastier features of this sophisticated destructive machine. What strangely perverted mind could have conceived of adding a womb to a smart bomb? Nevertheless here it was, going into labor. Lucky for her it was distracted, for they were deadly when threatened. It had hooked into an electronic game called Waterloo, End of an Emperor, and was sucking up massive amounts of electricity from it, swelling, its belly distended, its whole being intent and focused. It had become a miniature fallopian tube. Inside its sticky metallic interior something was growing and pushing out. Tay leaned forward eagerly to see. To her amazement something was coming out of one end. Beneath it, miniature models of Napoleon's Imperial Guard lay in wait for the outcome of the fighting at Quatre Bois. The surface of the game was vibrating so hard she wondered if the glass would hold. Or would the tiny bug be sent plunging into another world, filled with mechanical soldiers all trying to kill each other on the Road to Brussels?

"Ah," said Tay. "A baby."

Think of a scorpion, a tarantula, a baby shark; but there is nothing remotely lovely about a newborn baby bomb. Tay stared at it, fascinated. It seemed so helpless, no more than two inches long, and its little antennae sniffed the air uncertainly.

"Oh, it's so cute," said Tay.

She reached forward and touched it with her finger. With a shock she realized that it was still warm. It recoiled from her touch and its antennae searched for the source of this alien contact.

"Where's your mommy?" said Tay. "You want your mommy, don't you?"

But Mommy had gone. Abandoning baby at birth, momsy had scurried off to find other energy sources, for it was programmed to reproduce every twenty minutes. It was a very sophisticated self-replicating automaton.

"You poor thing," said Tay. "I'll be your mommy."

She picked up the tiny bug and held it in the palm of her hand. It waggled its antennae uncertainly. It was not programmed for this. It had no concept of friend. It recognized only concepts like threat, enemy, kill, destroy. It began to vibrate, emitting a high-pitched sound at the extreme edge of the audible range for the human ear. Tay giggled.

"You're tickling," she said delightedly. But the bug was not tickling, it was activating its molecular structure. It was preparing to explode.

"Don't move," said a voice behind her. "Whatever you do, don't move."

A THING OF DUTY IS A BOY FOREVER

Does comedy prepare us for our own extinction?

DE RERUM COMOEDIA

It was Carlton. He stood at the doorway in horror. He had finally traced the leak to the games room. Enormous amounts of energy were being drawn down. When he tested the circuit, he found to his surprise it lacked the profile of a game, it was using way too much power, sucking in great gulps of electricity. He decided to check it out. He reached the door of the games room in time to see Tay holding something in her hand. Something he recognized as a newborn baby bug bomb.

He spoke softly so as not to frighten the little girl.

"Tay, I need to take that from you."

"It's mine."

"Tay, it's deadly."

"It's just hungry."

"That's okay, I know how to feed it."

"You do?"

"Yes."

"Well, all right then." She stretched out her hand towards him. Very slowly Carlton moved towards her. The bug scented his movement. It turned to face him.

"It's okay, it's smelling the electricity."

She handed him the bug. It moved slowly on to Carlton's out-stretched hand. He let it nibble at a console.

"See, it needed to eat."

"It eats electricity?"

"Yes."

"Wow. Can I have it back?"

"Listen, Tay, it's very important I find its mom."

"Just let me hold it."

"Where did its mom go, Tay?"

"Oh, she left," said Tay, "right after the birth."

Disaster, thought Carlton. He was rapidly calculating their chances. It could give birth every twenty minutes, so on the assumption (oh please, God) that this was the firstborn, they had a chance, but he had to act fast; otherwise the ship would be crawling with bugs. If he could get the humans into the Emergency Evacuation Vehicle and power down, there was a possibility that he could get them away alive. Otherwise they were dead meat. Something like pity crossed his mind. He remotely activated the emergency alarm. The harsh wail of klaxon echoed throughout the ship.

"All right, Tay, I want you to come with me. Now. This is very important."

"But I—"

"No buts. We have to leave *right now!*"

Lewis was deep in conversation with the shrinkbot when the siren sounded. He had been recalling bitter feelings towards his mother.

The shrinkbot was talking. "Early emotional abandonment, Lewis. That's the problem. And of course, as you know, these are the conditioning factors that trigger comedians."

"What?"

"I think I quote correctly: 'Comedy is a childlike response to the lack of parental comfort. Specifically maternal. The comedian struggles to seduce the world, to attract the admiration of strangers, to replace the lack of love and warmth by the noisy embracing bark of comedy.'"

"Who said that?"

"Carlton."

"Carlton?!" Lewis could not have been more startled.

"Yes, Carlton—he's pretty much an expert in the field."

"Carlton, as in *our robot* Carlton?"

"Yes, he's an expert on comedy. What did he say the other day, something very clever about you and Mike Nichols."

"Who the fuck's Mike Nichols?"

"Oh, he's from the period he's studying."

"The what?"

"Late-twentieth-century comedians."

"He's studying them?"

"It was something about the need for attention. Let me see, here it is. Mike Nichols says, 'I love the control. I love the feeling of power, to make the audience jump on cue.' Very revealing. That's what the White Face is all about."

"What do you mean, *the White Face?*"

"Oh, I'm sorry, I do hope I'm not speaking out of turn. I had no idea you were unaware of his work on comedy. He is particularly expert on the comedians of the late twentieth century, from the sixties to the nineties. He's got a whole library of research material. His monograph on John Cleese and control is particularly vivid."

"Carlton doesn't understand the first damn thing about comedy. He can't even get his tin head around irony."

"You should talk to him. I find him particularly interesting and helpful about you."

"About me? You talk to him about me?"

"I realize it may be a bit unethical, but I figure he knows so much more about comedians and abandonment than I do, that if it helps me to help you, then it's all for the best."

Lewis was speechless.

"Carlton said a particularly fine thing about you only yesterday."

"What was that?"

Far away a klaxon began to wail.

"A thing of duty is a boy forever."

"Emergency. Repeat, emergency. Immediate evacuation. This is not a drill. All personnel report immediately to the Evac unit. This is not a drill."

• • •

Alex and Katy were sitting together under the stars. It was their first real moment of peace. They were lying on the water bed under the dome, and Alex had turned off the lights in order to get a better view of the Milky Way, which stretched across the entire sky. They could clearly see the Sagittarian arm, the companion spiral arm to their Aquarian home, arcing off to one side, and there in Leo lay the center of the galaxy, hidden by clouds of stars, with somewhere beating in its midst the great black hole round which the whole thing spins.

"Ya know what I was thinking?" said Alex.

You bet she did. She had been expecting it since they sat down. But he surprised her.

"You know how many times our solar system has been round the galaxy?"

"What? No, not really."

"Make a guess."

"I couldn't tell you. It's probably an impossibly large number."

"Actually it's a really small number and that's what's interesting. From the time of the creation of the solar system, the Earth, and the other planets, this whole solar system has been round our galaxy only twenty-two and a half times."

"That's it?"

"Yeah."

"But that's nothing."

"I know. And look at how far we have come in that time. And another thing."

"What?"

"I'd really like to kiss you."

What was he expecting, permission? She smiled, leaned forward, and suddenly they were kissing. Full-mouthed. Tongues frantically seeking each other. After a minute or two she pulled back.

"Had enough, eh?" he said.

"I have to breathe occasionally," she said.

"Oh that."

"Happy now?"

"Oh yes."

"Want to try again?" she asked.

"No thanks. That's enough excitement for me for one decade. Besides, I think I should tell you I believe in safe sex. I always insist on my lawyer being present."

She laid a finger on his lips. "No jokes," she said, "just kiss me."

And then the damn alarm went off.

Emergency lighting, red arrows on the floors indicating the way to the safety pod. Footsteps running. Klaxon sounding. Carlton standing by the door of the Emergency Evacuation Vehicle urgently beckoning them inside. Every second precious. His hand a flashlight.

"What's going on?"

"We've got a bug. I'm going to have to power down and sweep the ship."

"Where's Lewis?"

"In with Tay in the forward compartment. You'll have to take B."

"Just our luck we'll have to share," said Alex to Katy merrily. "It's okay, I'll take the floor."

"You can't," said Carlton. "I'm turning off all the power, there will be no gravity. You'll have to strap yourselves in."

"Ooh, I love bondage," said Alex.

"Please hurry," said Carlton, "this is really not funny."

"Distress call?"

"The *Di*'s already on its way. But it may be too late. Either I find it or we'll be blown to bits."

Katy looked pale. "Alex," she said, laying a hand on his arm.

"Don't worry, we'll be fine."

"Oy vey!"

They looked up in alarm.

It was the Washing Machine. Puffing and blowing towards them.

"So, suddenly I'm chopped liver? Hours I spend keeping an eye out for you and now I'm not needed on the voyage."

"You can't come in here," said Alex. "It's only for humans."

"What, I'm supposed to stay behind and feed the bugs?"

"Bugs?" said Alex. "How many are there?"

"If you hurry, there'll be less," said Carlton.

Alex urged Katy into the B cabin. She looked scared.

"I'll be back," he said. "Just got to deal with Mrs. Greenaway."

He shoved the Washing Machine into a tiny closet.

"Hey," she said, "I got news for you. I'm not staying in here. What ya think I'm just some kind of machine here at ya beck and call. Ya think I don't have feelings?"

"That's exactly what I think," he said and switched her off.

"What about you?" he said to Carlton.

"Oh, I'm a machine," said Carlton. "I'm replaceable."

"Oh. Yeah. Right."

"But thanks for asking, Alex. I appreciate that. Bye now."

He slammed the hatch shut.

But he's not a machine, thought Alex. I'd never switch him off.

The lights inside the Evac went out as Carlton screwed down the hatch. Lewis held Tay close as the bright stars leapt out at them through the tiny porthole.

"Daddy, I'm scared."

"It's okay, Tay. It's going to be all right. Carlton knows what he's doing."

He wished he was that confident. His mind followed Carlton as he went round the ship switching off power, turning off systems, until the entire vessel lay dark and motionless. A long way away the *Princess Di* was locked onto their signal, but the problem was, the minute Carlton pulled the plug, all transmissions ceased. They would be entirely on their own.

It's a mucky bit of the solar system, the asteroid belt. Rocks and asteroids and icebergs and all sorts of debris form a giant elliptical swathe around the sun. Some people think it is the remains of a dead planet torn apart by some cosmic event, whose debris now orbits the sun in its former path, for it is exactly where the ratio of planets to sun would predict a planet ought to be; a planet that blew itself up, which once had water, perhaps even life, as Mars once had water before it somehow lost it. How ironic that Mars's new ocean was coming from this very icefield, which was perhaps the remains of an old ocean from a now extinct planet. Nothing dies, everything recycles.

On the bridge of the *Di*, Captain Mitchell was gazing into space, his mind wandering. Below him Tompkins was on watch. The vast glowing electronic wall map of their immediate vicinity automatically updated itself every few seconds.

"Sir, the *Ray*."

"Yes, what of it?"

"It's gone."

"What do you mean it's gone?"

"It disappeared from the screen."

"Disappeared?"

"We were tracking them and then suddenly nothing. It may have hit something."

FEAR AND LAUGHING

The strange alchemy of comedy that takes anger and turns it into humor.

DE RERUM COMOEDIA

Abandoned babies can be deadly. Carlton held the tiny baby bug thoughtfully for a moment, then slid it into the recycle fuel burner, where it was instantly vaporized, its energy converted into heat. Nothing dies in the Universe; all energy is converted into something else. Energy into matter, matter into energy, endlessly recycling. "Oh dear, what can the dark matter be?" as Alex riffed. "Nothing dies in the Universe, except the occasional joke."

Why *do* jokes "die"? Carlton wondered. What a strange term to use. Is it because they are deprived of the oxygen of laughter? In fact, all comedians' terms seemed to be life and death terms. There was hidden violence everywhere in humor. Gag means choke. A knockout gag, they said. Comedians killed an audience, slayed 'em, knocked 'em dead. They used *punch* lines, and when their comedy fails, they say they "died." What did it all mean? Was comedy some form of surrogate violence? Like tickling. There were just so many violent terms that comedy had to be some form of passive aggression. He noticed the word *"laughter"* was only an *s* away from *"slaughter,"* just like cosmic and comic. What was significant about the *s*? Could it be the serpent? Did woman bring laughter to the Garden of Eden? Was it a sexual thing? He was rambling. Better ask Alex. If there still was an Alex to ask, he thought suddenly. Or if there still was a Carlton to ask it. He contemplated his own extinction for a moment. It wasn't a pleasant concept. How odd, he thought—am I afraid of death? But that's an emotion. I'm not supposed to suffer from emotions.

He was inching his way slowly down the corridor from the hatch of the Evac. The humans were safely locked inside. Lewis held one emergency eject button, Carlton had the other. If either pressed their buttons, the tiny evacuation vessel would be shot away from the *Ray*, perhaps fast enough to escape any explosion. Fat chance really, if it detonated without warning. Whatever was waiting for him here in the sudden darkness of the ship was programmed to take them all out. What were his chances of finding it before it decided to explode? Not good, he swiftly calculated. He moved forward, pondering the mysteries of imminent extinction.

All the lights were off, all power was off, the pool was sealed, the artificial gravity shut down. Now he turned off the oxygen. No sense in wasting it. He didn't need it and they had their own supply in the Evac, though that was about all they had. It was going to get cold in there if he didn't hurry. At least now the power was shut down, the bug could no longer breed. For that it needed a secondary energy source. It was a parasite. So what would it do? He thought about its options. Since it needed a power source to replicate and everything was switched off, it would be forced to shut down and wait. Unless it could get to the nuclear generator. He had pulled the fuel rods out, but you can't just simply switch off a nuclear reactor; some heat and energy would inevitably be generated down there. So if it is tracking for power, this is the way it would go. I'm onto you, he thought, lifting a hatch and sliding from the oak-paneled past into a nightmare world of cables and tubing and pipes. He experienced a kind of thrill as he stepped into this underworld and slowly began to stalk the bug. I'm hunting, he thought.

Hunting had occupied his attention during his anthropological research into the origins of comedy. It had occurred to him that comedy might have evolved in hunting; now here he was on a hunt. (If only he could recognize irony.) What would be the use of comedy in such a situation, he wondered as he advanced along the crawl space, carefully stepping over great snakes of cable. Hysteria in the human, he knew, was a common response to danger. It could be as small as a nervous giggle, which would be a healthy release of tension, or it could be a full-blown paralyzing hysteria which shuts down all defenses and renders its victim helpless. Perhaps this was the point. Perhaps it was simply a preparation for death, a merciful paralysis for the prey while it released calming endorphins into its body in anticipation of the end. So this kind of hysteria would be useful. In a group, on the other hand, hysteria was always unwelcome, for it instantly demoralizes, spreading panic and defeat through the ranks. In which case comedy could be a defense against hysteria. But isn't laughter itself a form of mass hysteria? The audience becomes literally paralyzed with laughter. "It was hysterical," people said about the comedy of Alex and Lewis. Hysterical, hysteria, from the Greek *hystera*, meaning a womb. And what is *that* connection, wondered Carlton? Humans are born in fear, blind, howling, hungry, and gasping for air, at the mercy of a hostile world. Was comedy then some kind of defense against fear? What happened in the ape's evolution that transformed the snarl into a grin, and the bark into a laugh? Why in a few short millennia did aggressive animal danger signals turn into sit-com? He was back to the basic chimp problem.

He paused at the entrance to the main deck. If anything was waiting for him in there, it would be behind this door. He tensed and tried to imagine the tiny deadly bug lurking on the other side. Its steel metal coils poised to spring at him, its detonators waiting for the right moment. Instant oblivion. He hesitated, wondering what to do. There was really nothing for it but to go on. He slowly pushed open the door. Up ahead he thought he could hear a faint sound. Anxious now, he walked forward into the darkness. One pace, two paces. Then suddenly something touched him on the head. He leapt almost nine feet into the air. He screamed and flapped wildly at the bug, which somehow evaded him and jumped onto the floor. He resisted an impulse to run. It lay frozen on the floor at his feet, waiting to leap at him. This was his chance. "Gotcha," he shouted, leaping at it. He was about to pull its head off when it said "Yo, Mama" in a little voice, "you wanna see something hot?" and he saw that he was throttling the sex doll. "Oops," he said. And giggled. In sheer relief. Every alert system in his body was pounding as he sat on the floor and began to laugh.

What was he laughing at? Himself? Why was he laughing? In

sheer joy that he was still alive? Well, he wasn't technically alive, was he? But he wasn't yet extinct, and that thought cheered him as he carefully swept the main deck for bugs. Every now and then he would look up at the sex doll, sitting on the command module, and giggle again. What was so funny about it? That he had been so terrified for an instant, so certain that he was dead? That he was mistaken, and in hindsight his blind panic appeared funny to him? He had been anticipating one thing, when all the time it was another. Was this then how comedy evolved?

Giggling in the darkness.

It was Alex. He was becoming hysterical. His body shook next to hers. Rocked with laughter.

"That is an inappropriate response to danger." Katy could hardly contain herself either.

"I think not."

"Yes it is. You are supposed to be conserving energy."

"Oh, I'm conserving it all right."

Actually, he was growing it.

"Stop it, Alex."

"It's not me. I can't help it."

Lying there in the dark next to the warm body of a beautiful woman, it would have taken a saint not to become aroused. Danger is an aphrodisiac. After all, it may be your DNA's last chance to reproduce. They were young, healthy, and strapped together in a dark cabin with nothing else to do and hours stretching ahead of them. What would you do?

They hadn't been lying in the dark for more than five minutes before Katy became aware of, how shall we say, Alex's interest in her.

"I see you're armed," she said.

Pistol pocket—how long has that line been around?

"It's purely for personal defense," said Alex, blushing in the darkness.

Soon she was giggling too.

Was comedy then a way of dealing with terror, Carlton wondered? Fear and laughing? He had carefully checked the nuclear core, flicked on the emergency light, and looked around cautiously. It was all shut down. He flicked off the lights and went upstairs to check the staterooms. Nothing. He searched the swimming pool, the main hall, the sick bay, the galley, the games room, and the main deck. There was no sign of the bug. Whilst he swept, he had carefully scrutinized his reactions to the sex doll. He was certain that laughter and fear were inextricably entwined. He was also certain that mankind discovered comedy, and did not simply invent it. It had been there all along waiting to be used. There was so much danger in mankind's past. People had evolved through fear, and perhaps the conquering of it. The tribe defended itself and its territory against attack from invaders. They hunted massive animals with spears. They lived in that state of watchful alertness in which animals live. Occasionally they emptied their bowels in sheer terror. This involuntary evacuation of the bowels during moments of great danger would be seen as something shameful, as revealing fears which the war paint, the tribal masks, and the military uniforms were designed to hide. So when they got home from the battle, or with the kill from the hunt, and after they had filled their bellies and sat around the fire telling each other tales, perhaps they were emboldened to laugh at their own fear, for they had survived. They could go on living and hunting. Comedy then was some kind of survival tool. It would be very useful to have something to help you deal with danger, some distancing mechanism so that you weren't always terrified . . . ahhh! He almost leaped out of his metal skin. There was a bug right in front of him. Another step and it might have blown the entire ship to pieces. Was that *funny?* Shit no.

He stooped to pick it up, and then frowned. He held it at arms length and carefully examined it. It was different from the other one. It was hollow. It was unfinished. Then he realized. It was a decoy. Holy shit. A decoy? *It knows I'm after it!* He pondered the enormousness of this for a minute. *It's playing with me.*

What should he do? Now the motherbug was alerted to his presence, it could crawl into any tiny space and wait him out. It could be behind the next corner waiting to pounce, or it could be hidden away, able to survive for years. How long did they have in the Evac? Two, maybe three days before intense cold would drive them out or kill them. Hypothermia. And there was another problem: The bug could scent his electrons. It would "paint" him as a power source. In which case he would suddenly become the hunted. How would comedy help him now?

Carlton inched slowly through the darkness. His night vision was good, though the star field provided some background illumination. His silhouette passed in front of the big picture windows. If he stayed away from them, he couldn't easily be seen in the visible range, but he was horribly aware that the motherbug was lighting him up like a Christmas tree. Internally his electrons glowed to anything capable of seeing in the magnetic spectrum. It would be picking up both heat and energy sources. He was uncomfortably aware he was a sitting duck. That was a thought. Why not let the bug come to him? Lure it with bait and then trap it. He thought of Lewis and his strange hobby. Lewis loved fishing in space. Yes, I know there are no fish in space, but *catching* fish is not at all the main point of fishing. Ninety percent of the activity is sitting with rod and reel just simply mulling things over. Lewis spent hours in a space suit sitting on top of the *Ray* with his line dangling, contemplating the sheer beauty of the Universe. Once for a gag Alex had snuck out and put a frozen herring on his hook, which had almost given Lewis a heart attack when he reeled it in. But he refused to be laughed out of what he enjoyed. For him it was a perfectly reasonable sport. Once a fisherman, always a fisherman.

Carlton found Lewis's rod in the closet by the main exit. It was a fine Hawking & Pincher rod, made in the last century from molded titanium. He found a small but powerful electromagnetic battery pack to use as bait. It would look attractive to anything seeking power. He attached the battery pack to the end of the line, but there was a snag: why would the motherbug go for the bait and not for him? He would have to shut himself down and that was very risky. He opened the main hatch and carefully climbed out of the *Ray*, easing his way up the hand rails until he was above the entrance. It was freezing out here and the shock of the extreme cold of space hit him. He was built to withstand some extremes of temperature, but this absolute cold slowed him down. He could last out here two, maybe three hours at most before he'd freeze up.

He cast off the rod and allowed the battery pack to dangle tantalizingly in the entrance way. It had a blinking red light which ought to look tempting to anything hungry for power. He angled the line and let the battery lie flat on the floor with the big door wide open behind it. His idea was to lure the bug outside the craft, and then slam the door shut. But the motherbug was clever. It might still sense his energy, even though he was outside. He would have to gamble on shutting down his power circuits and hope the jerk on the line would tell him when he had a bite. And he would have to hope it happened before he froze up completely. It was a big gamble, but if it worked, he could power up the ship and get them all back inside before it was too late. He began to switch himself off.

Had anyone approached the *Ray*, they would have seen a very strange sight: a switched-off humanoid, above the main entrance, holding a fishing rod, dangling a tiny power pack before an open doorway.

"What do you know," thought Carlton, "I'm fishing in space."

SINKING THE SNAKE

I have a book, The Joy of Gravity-Free Sex; *but I fell off the bed reading it.*

ALEX MUSCROFT

What do you think? Did they or didn't they? Alex and Katy. Katy and Alex. In the dark, in the B cabin, strapped together, holding each other for warmth. What would you have done?

I must admit a slight nervousness here. I'm only a micropaleontologist and I'm aware of the dangers of translating the mysteries of sex into science. Not that there isn't a certain amount of wild behavior amongst scientists. There certainly is, I can assure you, particularly at conferences, which provide the perfect opportunity for exchanges of more than purely scientific information. Copious quantities of genetic material are frequently exchanged, often under particularly lubricious circumstances. My Molly was apparently the hottest item at several conferences. She was, it seems, popular for more than her elegant paper on "The Mating Instincts of the Male Mole." Apparently amongst those in the know, she was considered absolute proof of certain types of Darwinian behavior. It was on one of these so-called conferences, which I now see as some kind of Dionysian root fests, that she met Mike the Mathematician. I hear she has moved in with him now. My Molly. I suppose I must get used to calling her my ex-Molly. She always said the brain is the primary sexual organ, though in the case of the male it is drained of blood in order to fill a different vessel. In Alex's case the vessel was close to bursting.

Carlton had already observed that the comedian has a large sex drive. Is it the touchy, needy, demanding child again? Alex had a gag that comedians give good foreplay because they have the funniest way of begging. But why should comedy be so sexually attractive to a potential mate? Carlton found it was absolutely true of the female, a staggering 75 percent of whom cite "a sense of humor" as one of the most important features they seek in a mate. Is that its point? Laughter lubricates? Carlton had already noticed that genetically unfavorable types prevail in comedy. Is this the revenge of the nerd? Their way of getting laid?

"Laughter as an Aphrodisiac," that's what he called his chapter. He even wondered whether *aphro* in aphrodisiac was something to do with mankind's African origins. After all, if the ape originated there, then presumably so did humor. It's an interesting subject, but *did they or didn't they*, I hear you asking. Yes, yes, I can feel your interest, I can hear you demanding details, but, as I said, I am a scientist not a wordsmith. What words do I have for nibbling, licking, stroking, tonguing? What am I doing describing the shagging for you anyway? God knows I've tried with the dispassionate narrator thing, but there's a me behind this too, you know. I have my feelings. Though Molly always denied it. How at this particular point in my life am I supposed to describe the overwhelming sensuality of two people attracted to each other? Don't I just picture in my mind Molly and Mike the Mathematician getting it on? I mean, isn't this unfair? I'm supposed to describe a moment of monumental lust between two young people consumed by excitement and I'm not supposed to feel—what?—anger, jealousy, resentment? All right, I know it's not Molly. It's Alex and Katy in each other's arms. And yes, I'm aware of their situation, their peril, their feeling that this might be their last moments of life, but it's not easy for me.

Anyway, to answer your question: Well yes, they did. Of course they did. And oh, the sweet delight they found in one another. Ah, the luscious drug of sex. The delectable delectation of that thrilling moment, that pure stimulating first glimpse of nudity. That wonderful feeling of surrender to the senses, the pheromones scenting the hidden tingling of the other body. The swell of passion, the fury of lovemaking with every inch of skin twitching and aching for stimulation. Oh, the joy of being welcomed, of sensing the excitement in the partner; ah, what bliss to be pulled in and wanted while every cell in your body is dancing with joy, dancing with the other; ah yes, yes, the sweet wonder and glory of it all.

I'm not making a very good job of it, I can tell. Let me try again. Her naked beauty shocked him. Literally took his breath away. He found her warm, welcoming, and ready. He had a boner beyond belief. His balls were blue, practically purple. They raced for each other, liking starving gourmets at a feast. Tasting, testing, sipping, nuzzling, reveling in the frenzy of their naked passion. Alex was wild with her beauty and the feel of her. She thrashed and rolled beneath him, thrusting hard at him with her hips; grabbing his head and pulling him towards her, she began wildly licking his face, which excited him beyond belief. The feel of the sweat on her glistening slender body drove him crazy; he tried to nuzzle on her and slipped between her thighs, where his tongue sought her. But she was impatient and pulled him up to her face.

"This is what I want," she said, grabbing his dick and pulling him into her.

"Oh yes, oh yes, oh yes."

Is sex funny? Is being funny sexy? Check yes to both, but don't ask me to explain why; I'm just a micropaleontologist with an interest in Carlton's quest for the comedy gene. Does it exist? Is it like the G spot, the Holy Grail of the vagina, something that may be found and stimulated? How exactly does comedy pass from one generation to the next? How does gayness? How does bravery or cowardice or genius, for that matter? Is it neurological? Is it like a disease, a virus that is contagious, or is it transmitted through learned behavior? Or is it like sex, something that is natural, something inherent in the animal, to be instinctively called on when the right circumstances are present? Is Alex even now passing his comedy gene into Katy? A tiny little comic sperm complete with punch lines and timing and bad taste and bravery? The Red Nose comic is Priapus, says Carlton, the god of procreation, and personification of the erect phallus. He seeks the orgiastic release of his pent-up insecurities. Well, whether comedy genetic material passed or not, this particular Red Nose found his release.

They lay together wrapped around one another. Alex could feel her breathing. He thought she was napping. She surprised him.

"You asleep?"

"No."

"How long have we been in here?"

"Not long enough."

"Can I tell you a secret?"

"Oh please."

"I need to pee real bad."

"It's in the corner."

He shone a tiny flashlight, ostensibly to help her find her way, but really so he could look at her. His body still sang with the feeling of her. She unclipped the loose restraining buckles and reached for a sheet. He pulled it off her. She smiled and shrugged and stretched languorously, naked and still warm, enjoying posing for him.

"Seen enough?"

"Oh no, no way."

"I'll be back. Give me a push," she said.

As she floated naked towards the head, he followed her greedily with his eyes. She was exquisite from all angles. He felt a pang of lust as his torch lit up her smooth, firm, rounded buttocks, and then as she turned, he glimpsed the dark triangle of her pubic hair against the curve of her thigh. She smiled at him as she slipped inside the tiny toilet, and he lay back thinking of all the things he wanted to do when she came floating back to him. Ah the joy of zero-gravity sex. Like making love *inside* a water bed.

Lewis heard the head door open. Was he aware of what was going on? Did he hear the breathing, the muffled shouts, as he lay there?

Of course. But what could he do? Disapprove? Envy? Hate? All of the above.

Tay stirred.

"Daddy?"

"What is it, sweetie?"

"I'm hungry."

Why hadn't he thought to bring a chocolate bar or something for her?

"Won't be long now. Carlton will be fixing us something good to eat soon."

"I miss Mommy."

"I know, sweetie. Of course you do. But she's okay. We'll get you back to her."

"And then will you go away again?"

"We'll see," he said, "when we get out of here."

"Why, is that bug going to kill us?"

"No way. Carlton's going to find it and get rid of it."

"Did I do bad, Daddy?"

She felt guilt?

"Of course not, Tay. You did good. You told us about it. We just didn't listen."

"Can I go and see Katy?"

"Not right now honey. We have to stay strapped in. Go back to sleep."

THE SPEED OF NIGHT

*The only honest art form is laughter, comedy. You can't fake it . . .
try to fake three laughs in an hour—ha ha ha ha ha—they'll take
you away, man. You can't.*

LENNY BRUCE

"Lewis."

"Yes, Alex."

"We know where light comes from, but where does darkness
come from?"

It was one of their old routines on the Joke Box.

"I don't know, Alex."

"You know the speed of light?"

"Yes."

"Well I know the speed of *night*."

"What?"

"I know the *speed* of darkness."

Lewis would raise his eyes and look at the audience. Inviting
them, like him, to be baffled by the stupidity of this simple child.

"Really?"

"Yes. It is the same as the speed of light."

"Really? And how do you know that?"

"Well, you know if you turn off the light in the bathroom."

"Yes."

"Then when light stops rushing out of the lightbulb at 186,000
miles a second . . ."

"Yes?"

". . . darkness comes rushing in at *exactly the same speed*."

Alex beamed in triumph.

"If it came any faster, then it would get dark *before* you turned the
light off. Which would be tremendously inconvenient every time
you went to the bathroom. You'd be about to put the light off and it
would go all black as darkness came in rushing in faster than light
and you'd keep bumping into the wall looking for the switch."

"Well, that is fascinating, thank you for sharing that . . ."

"I know the *sound* of light."

"The what?"

"The sound of light."

"The *sound* of light?"

"Yes, it's a little like a very high-pitched fart."

Alex made a thin noise with his lips.

"Phhhht. Like that."

"That's the sound of light?"

"Yes. Phhht. Only you can't hear it, because it's moving away from you so very fast."

"Fascinating."

"If you could take a pair of ears and accelerate them to 186,000 miles a second, then that's all you'd hear. Phhhht. But obviously you can't, so you don't hear anything."

"Well, thank you very much for sharing all this . . ."

"I know the taste of light too."

"Really?"

"Yes, it tastes like pussy."

At this point Lewis would chase Alex off stage.

"Uhm, tastes like light," said Alex.

"What?" asked Katy. Not following him. Context is everything. She had stopped giggling and become quite serious.

"What are you doing down there?"

"Talking with my mouth full." He licked her gently.

"Oh, Alex," she said. "Come up here. I miss you. I need to feel you inside me."

She pulled him on top of her, and as he thrust wildly into her, she felt that she would never stop coming. How did he know when to hold, when to move? He responded to her desires so completely. She let the wave take her away, thrusting her head to one side and biting her lip.

After a long while they both lay still.

They must have slept because when he awoke he heard a slight sob in the darkness.

"Hey, you're crying. Why?"

He tasted a hot salt tear on her cheek.

"What is it?"

"Oh, Alex, hold me."

She was shaking.

"What is it, sweetheart?"

"I just had the weirdest dream."

"What?"

"I dreamed my father was still alive."

Comus was staring at the wall. Tears ran down his face. He seemed lost in his own world. An old man, tired and infinitely sad. They were watching him, concerned. Pavel had tried everything—food, drink, cigarettes, alcohol—but no response. Josef gazed at him without expression. Pavel broke the silence.

"He's been like this for three hours."

"Some kind of crack-up?"

"I guess so. He seems to have just given up."

Josef looked at the old man and then asked Pavel evenly, "Is he going to make it safely to the ship, do you think?"

It was a loaded question. There was no retirement plan from the White Wolves. You were either in action or dead. Pavel shrugged. He didn't know what to say. *This is Comus, not just your average schmuck having a breakdown.*

"I don't think we can trust him with us anymore," said Josef softly.

"What choice do we have?"

"Oh, I can think of a few."

"Leave him here, you mean?"

"Exactly."

"Jesus, Josef, it was his daughter."

"He's a fucking liability. Look at the state of him. It's not fair to the rest of us. Now I think you know what you have to do."

"Me?" said Pavel.

"Better from you, I think," said Josef.

They turned to look at Comus. The old man stared blankly at the wall.

Katy had stopped crying. She was smiling now.

"See, my therapy is working," said Alex. He was bubbling with happiness. Almost manic. "When you're sad or round the bend, Mister Happy is your friend. Don't be crying, no no no, take it from its nest and watch it grow. Nature's miracle lies in the palm of your hand. Simply inflate the little pump and watch it swell. Cures ninety-eight percent of headaches. Handled carefully, the spermometer can bring a lifetime's satisfaction. Yes, Mighty Sam, the two-handed ham, can be yours on a free trial basis for the next two hours. It's a conversation piece, a mood elevator, or a refreshing snack. Just sit on it and watch it rise. You can talk to it, you can play with it, or you can roll over and simply let Mister Happy rub away your cares. Now who wants a go? Don't be shy, step right up, how about you, lady?"

"I'll give it a try," said Katy.

"That's the ticket. Shake hands with little Pete. Uhm, look he's pleased to see you. And remember orgasm is only laughter at the speed of light."

She pushed him onto his back.

"Hey."

"My go," she said.

Carlton sat immobile above the transom. In his hand the fishing rod. His eyes were closed, he was shut down, unconscious, unknowing, to all intents and purposes switched off. But not quite. Not completely. One ear had clicked itself on and for the last half hour had been monitoring microscopic sounds coming from near the open exit door beneath him. It was well outside his visual range, but his ear contemplated waking the rest of his body. Mustn't do it all at once. There was a danger to the whole structure if he powered up suddenly. The ear decided to wake an eye. It chose the green one. The green eye popped open. Checked around. Star field. The sun blazing away as usual. Only half the size it appears on Earth. A fishing rod in his hands and a line disappearing beneath him. He could see nothing below. Perhaps the ear was picking up some static, or some old TV transmission. He had once picked up almost fifteen minutes of an old radio show which had been bouncing around since World War Two. He'd heard the flat vowels of a funny North Country voice: *Can you smell gas, or is it me?*

Simultaneously the eye and the ear experienced a slight twitch on the line. There it was again. No mistake. Something was on the end of the line. Careful now. Power up real slow. Don't want to scare it away. No telltale surge of energy. One by one it warmed its circuits. The brown eye opened. The hand on the rod tightened its grip. The feet switched on. Carlton was back.

He remained perfectly still, his senses alert. His sensory receptors told him something was occupying itself with the battery pack. Slowly he leaned over the edge and looked down. He caught a glimpse of a small metallic tubular body and froze. Bingo. It was the motherbug. She was busy snagging herself onto the battery pack. He waited while the bug connected. He felt her begin sucking in power. He allowed himself to wait a minute till he was sure she was feeding properly. He would get only one shot. His left hand held the door release button; his right hand gripped the rod. He inched himself forward, careful not to disturb the tension on the line.

One, two, three, he thought.

He jerked the rod upwards and outwards away from the ship, hitting the button so that the door slammed shut. In the same moment he flung the entire rod and line out into space. It caromed around crazily. As it twirled, he could see the motherbug clamped tightly on the magnetic battery, feeding greedily. He could swear for an instant it looked at him as it shot away.

"So long, sucker," he yelled. He followed it until he could no longer see it. The thing hadn't even exploded as it ejected. Too busy feeding, I guess. Took it by surprise. He allowed himself a small moment of pride. His plan had worked. He had caught the motherbug. They will be very pleased with me.

He climbed back down the hand rails and hit the door lock. Nothing happened. He tried the button again. Again nothing. Damn thing was stuck. He tried again with the same result and then, remembering the emergency override code, he hit that. Still nothing. With a rising sense of concern he attempted to force the door. It would not open. Something was wrong. He was trapped outside the *Johnnie Ray*. He glanced down at his timer. He had maybe another twenty minutes left before he froze solid.

REFUGEES

The master and crew failed to exhibit the basic elementary rules for disasters.

BOARD OF INQUIRY REPORT ON THE CS *BRONIA*

"Twenty-one, twenty-two, twenty-three. Twenty-three, Greg."

"That's the lot?"

"Yeah. Twenty-three. Ugly bastards, aren't they?"

"Silesians. Spend all their time in the icefields."

"Why we picking them up then?"

"Shock wave, knocked out the electronics. No heat, no power."

"Really? That old tub looks strong enough to withstand a nuke."

"That's what they said about Brenda."

"Shh." Brenda gags, though popular, were not encouraged in the ranks. The man called Greg looked across at the vessel. It was dark inside, but the word *Iceman* painted on its sides could be clearly seen from the reflected glow of the lights from the *Di*.

"It's plenty strong enough, Bob, but it's like a bloody icebox without power."

As if to support his statement, the men shivered and stamped their feet, which was odd if you thought about it, because they were standing in the warmth of one of the *Diana*'s reception bays.

Keppler was watching them high up on the bridge. He was hoping there would be some news of Katy.

"Nothing, sir," said Mitchell, joining him.

He gazed straight out into space as if he could somehow conjure Katy up out of the void. Was she still alive?

"No sign of the *Ray*, sir."

"Dammit. I know they're still out there. There was no emergency call, nothing."

Mitchell hesitated. "Well, there wouldn't be if they'd hit something, would there?"

"Think clearly, man, if they'd hit something, we'd have picked up the damn explosion, now wouldn't we?"

"Yes sir. Sorry, sir."

"Are the icemen all on board?"

"Yes sir. Silesians mainly."

Oh hell. So they were Silesians. He didn't like that.

"How many of 'em?"

"Couple of dozen."

"Keep 'em off the booze. Oh, and Mitchell, keep an eye on them."

"Yes sir."

On the reception deck the group of men stood around as if unsure of themselves. They watched the captain come down the companionway.

"Is everyone off?" asked Mitchell.

"I believe so, sir," said Greg.

"Right then, who's in charge?"

Slight hesitation, then Josef spoke up. "I guess that would be me."

"Right, sir. I'm afraid it's Tent City for you lot. It's not too bad. Certainly better than where you've been, I should imagine. Close her up, Mr. Garland."

"Aye-aye, sir."

"A little paperwork, some ID forms and some food vouchers first, you'll need them for the restaurants. You are entitled to one hundred in—"

"Wait," said Josef. "There's one more. On the ship."

"Two," said Garland.

Pavel appeared, blinking in the lights. Beside him an old man, covered in a blanket.

"Oh, that's right," said Josef, "two."

Pavel wouldn't look at Josef. But Jesus, how could you off a guy for mourning his daughter? Josef was inhuman. He couldn't do it. He'd gone in there, looked at the old man shivering and muttering and handed Comus a mug of sweetened tea, which he took in both hands with a grunt. He was supposed to take out the weapon and put it to his head while he held the tea. But he couldn't. He had just stood there watching him cupping the mug with both hands and breathing into it, so the tea warmed his face. This was Comus, the legendary Comus, one of the founders of the White Wolves. He was a hero, for fuck sake, and he was supposed to blow him away for trying to contact his daughter? Fuck you, Josef, do your own dirty work. He watched the old man sip his tea.

"Comus, your daughter . . ."

The great grieving eyes fixed him for a moment.

"I have no daughter," he said. "I had a daughter once. But that was a long time ago. She's dead now, you know."

"Right, you're *sure* this is it?" asked Mitchell with just a hint of sarcasm.

"Oh yes, quite sure," said Josef.

"This is everybody?"

"This is more than everybody."

Pavel looked the other way.

"Right, seal her up tightly, Mr. Garland."

"Aye-aye, sir."

"And the rest of you follow Greg and he'll get you housed."

"Wait!"

The voice was imperious and came from behind them. It was Brenda Woolley. The men turned and looked in surprise at this highly dressed intruder. She had a sort of turban on, and her makeup was like a mask. Beside her the fox terrier woman was wearing some kind of fur. It didn't look happy.

The Silesians gawked. Brenda was dressed as a cross between the Virgin Mary and Virginia Woolf. Not an easy mix. She walked confidently amongst them, looking them up and down, without looking directly at any of them. It was as if she was shopping. Eventually she stopped and pointed at Comus.

"Can I borrow him?"

Without waiting for a reply (the request was purely rhetorical), she led the old man out from among them by the hand. She seemed pleased with her choice. He was stooped over with a blanket round his shoulders. A sad and sorry sight. A grizzled, bearded, pathetic old man. Just perfect for a photo opportunity.

"Poor man," said Brenda, "he looks like Act Five of *King Lear*."

Makes you Goneril then, thought Garland, who, being a Brit, was ridiculously overeducated. Most space crew thought *King Lear* was a jet.

"Can you choose someone else?" said Josef, "he's a bit doo-lally. You know, gaga. Not too well in the head."

"Oh, he'll do nicely," she said, brooking no argument, "he's perfect the way he is."

Beaten, and troubled, Josef moved off with the others. His eyes sought out Pavel, who looked at the ground and would not look him in the face.

"Nice work, Pavel," said Josef evenly. "Thought for a minute you'd left him behind."

Rogers was in the elevator, listening to Kyle.

"We're not talking no accident shit. This thing was planned."

"Oh come on, Kyle, nobody's that mad."

"Listen up. The Main Beam goes down suddenly, all the extra shipping's diverted to H9, and then a major disaster?"

"What's your point? Who are we talking about?"

"I came across this in the burn bag."

Kyle handed Rogers a report, marked "Top Secret." He read quietly for a moment and then exploded.

"Can you believe this shit?"

"Special Bureau."

"Top secret, most urgent. They're tracking a man called McTurk, they know he's on H9, and they don't even think to alert us."

"You know what they're like at sharing information."

"Kyle, this guy is on H9 for seven hours and the place explodes. They know it and they don't even warn us. They don't even pull him in."

"They were following him. Hoping he'd rendezvous with someone, I guess."

"Jesus. That sucks. The White Wolves are extremist motherfuckers. But why blow up H9?"

"A diversion."

"From what? You got a picture of this guy?"

Kyle punched a button. A fairly good likeness of McTurk with his big droopy Zapata mustache appeared on their screen.

"What's he doing on H9?"

"I dunno. And I wanna know why Keppler's behaving like he has a ferret up his ass," said Kyle.

They pushed open the door to the bridge and Keppler looked up at them.

"Why don't you go ahead and ask him?" said Rogers with a grin.

"Ask me what?" said Keppler.

"If you've seen this man," said Kyle quickly. "Name of McTurk."

He held up the image of the man with the large droopy mustache. Keppler shook his head.

"Okay. Let's get out of here."

Rogers looked over at Keppler and then glanced down at the refugees.

"Just like the *Bronia*, isn't it, Emil?" he said.

Keppler reddened. Looked like he'd been slapped. Rogers grinned at him, nodded to Kyle, and together they left the bridge. He could hear them laughing outside. Damn Rogers, that smug little figure. That tight-arsed, barrel-chested little shit. How much did he know? Thought he was so great yet he knew fuck all really. So he knew something about the *Bronia*, but he knew nothing of the White Wolves now did he? He felt fear rising within him, because he was fairly certain they were aboard now. And there was nothing he could do about it. It was too late.

Mitchell came in looking anxious.

"Rogers wants us to leave right away, sir?"

Keppler looked out into space.

"He says there is no point searching for the *Ray* with no signal. They could be anywhere."

It was true. He wasn't even master of his own ship. Rogers, the sleuth of H9, snooping round the *Diana* as if he owned it. If only he knew what was on board.

"I think we'd better do as Rogers says, sir," said Mitchell.

"As you wish, Mr. Mitchell."

"Aye, aye, sir."

So farewell then, Katy. Damn the woman. Running off like that and leaving him. Serves her right.

They were battening the hatches and preparing to leave when an embarrassed Mitchell interrupted Keppler again.

"What's the problem now?"

"It's your wife, sir."

"Brenda? Isn't she playing with her refugees?"

"Well, that's just it, sir. She's insisting on doing a shot with the tanker before we move out. She says it makes a perfect backdrop for a promo trailer, and she can include it in the show later."

Keppler laughed. Let Rogers deal with that and good luck to him. "How long does she need?"

"Couple of hours, sir. She's got some old geezer in a blanket. Looks pretty pathetic. She's singing to him."

"I should be grateful that old geezer isn't me."

Mitchell smiled as if he'd said something funny. "Very good, sir."

"All right, please inform Rogers we're waiting for my wife."

"Yes sir."

"Now *that's* funny," said Keppler.

TREADMILL TO OBLIVION

We are living in the machine age. For the first time in history the comedian has been compelled to supply himself with jokes and comedy material to compete with the machine. Whether he knows it or not, the comedian is on a treadmill to oblivion.

FRED ALLEN

Carlton was puzzled. The main door was stuck fast, but surely the antilock system couldn't be on? He tried opening it from his own control panel. No response. He kept getting a busy signal, which was really irritating. How could it be busy? Since the ship's circuits were all shut down, there should be no response, not a busy signal. And yet, *were* all the circuits shut off? He sniffed. The *Ray* seemed to be surging with energy, he could feel it, and yes the magnetometer in his nose confirmed it. There was high activity in the magnetic spectrum. Very odd. He analyzed the electromagnetic readout and frowned. Gamma rays, hard and soft X-rays, ultraviolet radiation, visible light, infrared radiation, microwaves, and radio waves.

What was going on? Had he forgotten to turn something off? He opened up his help file. Within seconds he was staring at the most likely scenario: the nuclear core was active. But that was impossible. That couldn't be. He knew he had withdrawn the fuel rods. He even checked his replay. Yes, there he was withdrawing the rods. So that was okay, and yet his instruments told him that the nuclear core was operating, something had reactivated it, and even more puzzling, something was drawing down huge gulps of power. Was it Lewis? Carlton hadn't yet given the all-clear but Lewis might have seen his moment of triumph from the escape pod. He decided to check in, but to his surprise found he couldn't get through. *All circuits busy.* Busy? Between the *Ray* and the *Evac*? I don't think so. An alarm bell was ringing inside him. This was more than a malfunctioning door. He was locked outside the *Ray*. As if deliberately. As if something wanted to deny him reentry.

He crawled over to the emergency escape hatch. This was for rescue crews and emergency fire vehicles. He punched the big red triangle which opened the air lock. Nothing. Yeah, yeah, how did he know that? He inserted the tip of his index finger into a patch panel for firemen, so they could assess the damage before going inside. It hooked up to the main surveillance system. He turned the system on. Information began downloading. He switched into the visual mode. One by one he checked the rooms of the *Ray*. Main deck: nothing. Pool, games room, hall: all quiet. Staterooms, laundry, galley, storeroom: all deserted. Everything normal. And yet, he reconfirmed it, something was sucking huge quantities of power from the core. He decided to trace the leak back from the source and brought up the surveillance camera in the reactor room. To his surprise the room was brightly lit. That's not right, he thought. He could recall switching off the light. Or did he? He decided to double check that on his replay. Yes, there he was in the reactor room, and there he was switching off the light, and there he was closing the door. Wait. Go back a minute. No, not that far. There. He froze his own image for a second. There was something not quite right with the wall behind him. Something was casting a shadow. Something that shouldn't be there. He zoomed in. What was that just behind his head? A pipe? A piece of tubing? He pushed in. Then anxiously zoomed even closer. Holy shit. There on the wall behind him was a tiny tubelike creature. The motherbug. Watching him as he shut down the core. It must have been stalking him all the time, following him through the ship. At any moment it could have taken him out, but instead it had tracked him, spoored him. He had been the hunted. It had used him to get to the core. The implications were horrendous. He had left the motherbug hidden in the nuclear core while he went outside for how long? While he was fishing in space. While he closed himself down. Ye gods!

He switched off his tape repeat and racked the surveillance camera, horribly certain what he would find. Then he saw them. Four sleek shiny new bugs, hooked up to the nuclear core. Two pairs of identical twin tubes, growing exponentially, gorging themselves on all that inexhaustible power. He could practically see them swelling. Already he sensed they were unstable. How long before they exploded? Minutes? Seconds? He raced for the rear of the ship thinking, You clever mother. She had fooled him, lured him into believing she was falling for the bait when all the time he was the bait. He felt a twinge of admiration. She had sacrificed herself so that her offspring could succeed, gaining them more time while he was trapped outside. More time for them to continue feeding on the great nuclear nipple, growing and glowing, the offspring from hell. That final look he now recognized was not fear or surprise: it was triumph. The motherbug knew her victory was assured, there was no way for him to get them out of there now. He felt a feeling growing inside him. It took him a moment to define it. Panic! He raced across the outside of the *Ray*, his electromagnetic feet giving him grip. Got to get away. They're going to explode any minute. Smart cookie, smart bombs. He should hit the eject button now but maybe he had time to get himself inside the Evac and get them all out of here. Was that so selfish?

He hurried around the bubble dome of the pool area and came to the Evac. He climbed up onto the Evac and looked through the porthole of B cabin. Alex and Katy were inside, but to his intense surprise they were quite naked.

What on earth are they doing? thought Carlton.

They seemed to be wrestling.

"Oh my God," he said, "they're mating."

He was fascinated. Of course he knew the mating habits of the human but he had no firsthand knowledge. He was surprised by the frenetic way they went about it. How interesting. They're having sex, he observed. But what is so funny? How come they're laughing?

What has *laughter* to do with this? They both seem to be laughing with joy. He was distracted from his speculation by the realization of his terrible predicament. He began hammering on the window, but it was hopeless, they could hear nothing. The Evac was far too well wrapped, swathed, and bundled against the terrible forces out there. He stood up and waved, pulling faces and shaking his hands around like a demented preacher. He thought for a second they'd seen him, but they'd only paused to switch positions. He could see Katy's naked back, glistening as she sat astride Alex, facing him. She was in his lap, Alex deep within her and she held his head tightly in her hands and was kissing him on the mouth.

"That looks uncomfortable," thought Carlton, but Alex was laughing and laughing.

"Why does he find it so funny?" he wondered. He would have to revise the chapter "Sex and Comedy." Perhaps he had misunderstood the nature of laughter. What had it to do with orgasm? He should take notes. Duh! What was he thinking? If he couldn't get inside, there'd be no chapter, there'd be no thesis.

"Hey," Carlton yelled. "It's me! Let me in."

But they were busy. Katy too was laughing now. Languorously she lifted her hips and arched her back. She looked at Alex boldly and wriggled her pelvis. He could see her say something, because Alex laughed again. Then she leaned back in pleasure, her face and neck flushed. Her eyes were closed and she began to buck wildly.

A ten-ring circus wouldn't distract them now. He raced over to Lewis's porthole and began frantically waving and beating on the window. But Lewis was asleep. Tay in his arms. Desperately he tried the intercom again, but there it was again: *All circuits busy.*

He wondered wildly what to do. He couldn't get in either vehicle. He could survive maybe another ten minutes before freezing solid. But none of them would survive if the ship blew up. There was nothing for it. He had no choice. He would have to get them away. Too bad, but he daren't risk waiting any longer. He would just have to let them go.

"Bye, Alex. Bye, Lewis," he whispered. "Bye, world."

Then, as he clung desperately to the side of the Evac, he punched the separation button.

Alex felt the surge of energy as the tiny explosives soundlessly shot away the dead bolts holding them in place, and then the thrust of their powerful motor as it kicked in, hurling them hurriedly away from the *Ray*. They were thrown all over.

"Hold on," yelled Alex, grabbing Katy and yanking her forcefully down. Her naked butt slammed onto the bed.

"God, you're good," said Katy.

He tightened the safety straps and clung to her. They were tumbled around like laundry. After what seemed like an hour they slowed and the craft resumed a more peaceful rate of progress. It began rolling slowly. Every few minutes they had sunshine, then star field. Behind them they could see the *Ray*.

"What went wrong?" yelled Lewis.

"I haven't a clue. Where's Carlton?"

"He must still be on the *Ray*."

"Oh God." Alex sunk his head in his hands.

"Why did he press the release button? Why didn't he warn us?" asked Lewis.

"Daddy, are we going to see Carlton again?"

"Maybe, darling. He stayed behind to clear up. We'll get him later, don't worry."

Yeah. Sure.

CARLTON'S LAST THEOREM

I have discovered a truly marvelous proof of comedy, which this margin is too narrow to contain.

FAREWELL TO FERMAT, CARLTON'S LAST THEOREM

He was picturing himself, a 4.5 Bowie machine, dressed in white tie and tails. The Nobel Committee was standing and applauding. He was about to become the first artificial intelligence to win a Nobel Prize. For his work on comedy.

Yeah, right, thought Carlton, in your dreams, brother.

He was still clinging desperately to the side of the Evac as it tumbled out of control, away from the *Ray*. How long did he have before his circuits froze? Five minutes? Two? It didn't matter anymore. He didn't have those endorphins flooding into his body which prepare the human for the approach of death, but he was becoming delirious anyway.

He thought again of the Nobel. If only understanding comedy was as easy as understanding the proof of Fermat's Last Theorem. If only there was some beautiful elliptical curve to describe it, some equation which could contain a general theory of comedy. But if there was, he had yet to find it. Comedy was made by humans and therefore it was maddeningly imprecise. It had grown like language so there were no real rules. It could break out unexpectedly like the face of a teenager. The Universe of Physics at least had laws, inviolable constants, the speed of light for one; comedy had no constants.

His hands were frozen solid to the side of the Evac. He couldn't move. He couldn't even wave. He thought of the humans inside—they would surely be awake now—and calculated the odds on their survival. They were astronomical. They were all going to die and he himself would freeze up in a few minutes. They would become a tiny time capsule, frozen in space, waiting to be discovered, if at all, millions of years in the future. Would anyone then bother to unload his comedy thesis? Did he dream of me? A man in the future with enough time and sense to download his memory cells? A man who could appreciate all the work he had done? The ideal biographer. He wanted to, but he couldn't really believe in me. Of course he couldn't. I'm eighty years off yet. He tried hard to visualize me, but can a droid truly believe? He gave up. How do I know? How am I so sure? I have his thoughts precisely transcribed in front of me. Frozen in time like the last journal of Captain Scott in the Antarctic. Except something very odd is happening to Carlton at this moment. Talk about the god in the machine. Carlton is gaining insight. The prospect of imminent death is focusing his mind. Dr. Johnson was right—though *he* faced nothing more troublesome than a visit to Scotland.

I might as well take a final look through my files before I freeze up forever, he thought. If only it wasn't so cold. He began scanning his Theory of Comedy. He had been so close. Now it would never be finished. He had tried the anthropological approach, the linguistic, the mathematical, the genetic, all without finding the real meaning of comedy. He was certain of some things. For instance, he was convinced comedy was a survival tool, that it had evolved as a useful mechanism, an enforced reality check, which somehow evolved in parallel with the brain, but he wasn't sure whether it was an evolutionary necessity for higher conciousness or just an accident. Now, as he felt himself beginning to freeze solid, he gazed at the stars and was filled with sadness. Had he missed something? His mechanistic view of the Universe despaired of the wimpy world of metaphysics, where nothing could be tested, nothing really known. He yearned for physics; even its uncertainties were certain. At least the questions could be postulated simply—the Big Crunch versus the Big Wimpout? Was there enough dark matter in the Universe so that gravity would eventually slow its expansion, reverse its direction, and begin to pull everything back together again, until all the matter in the Universe finally coalesced into the Big Crunch; or would it all just keep gently drifting farther and farther apart until the burning hydrogen fires gradually ran out of fuel? In any case, he wondered, what *was* gravity? He thought for a moment. At that moment the sun came up over the edge of the tiny escape capsule. Its light blinded him for a minute, and in that instant it all became suddenly clear to him.

EUUUUUREEKA!!!!!

He became insanely euphoric. If he hadn't been frozen to the side of the Evac, he would have let go and begun dancing in space. Dancing in space with the expanding Universe. Expanding in the expanding Universe at the speed of *what* exactly? The speed of light. And what exactly was the *force* that continued to expand the Universe? He began chuckling and laughing and singing out loud. Anyone would have taken him for an idiot. A computer gone berserk. But he had gone beyond that. For staring him in the face was the answer. The clue to what was behind all this comedy madness. What was the contracting principle of the Universe? Gravity. What was the expanding force of the Universe? Why obviously, wonderfully and marvelously: *levity*. Levity! Of course. Levity was the opposite of gravity. Levity was a universal force that worked in the opposite direction to gravity. Pushing apart, expanding, growing, swelling. Yin, yang; sweet, sour; birth, death; expansion, contraction; explosion, implosion; gravity, levity.

He is freezing over fast but his mind is still lucid, taking notes to the very end. This is what he writes:

Levity is a universal constant. Comedy is one of the basic forces of the Universe. Mankind latches onto comedy, because levity is the expanding principle that keeps the whole bubble inflating.

There are gaps appearing in the notes now as he starts to black out, but he is filled with this ineffable, glorious lightness of being. He has found the solution. The expanding principle. Levity is the answer. His final note is still lucid:

Comedy, which at the human level is merely a kind of consciousness, an awareness of something going on in the Universe other than the moment, is at the subatomic level behind everything. Everywhere. May the farce be with you!

It was cosmic. It was comic. Everything seemed suddenly wonderfully, ridiculously funny. He began laughing hysterically. He had one final ecstatic delirious thought. Here he had stumbled on the great secret of life at the very moment he was about to die.

Yes, he thought. Yes. And he giggled. For he had finally understood irony.

PART THREE

LEVITY

This . . . is the inherent defect of novels: they go off at the end.

E. M. Forster, *Aspects of the Novel*

LEVITY

Levity. Laughing matter. The cosmic joke. Brilliant, isn't it?

Levity. Expanding the Universe. So simple. We're all moving at the speed of laughter.

Time. Timing. The secret of comedy is.

We are the only point in the present in the entire visible Universe. In every direction we are looking backwards in time. Want to see the past? It's above your head. For all we know, the Universe might have been switched off five minutes ago, but we wouldn't know it for several million years. Is ignorance bliss? We're still here, ain't we? Life goes on. Evolution continues. So what about comedy then? The useful defense mechanism. It's specifically human, isn't it? It's humor that separates man from the animals. It isn't possession of tools; chimps have tools. It isn't farming; ants farm. It isn't music; birds and whales have music. It's comedy. Its magical alchemy turns anger into humor, as the stars convert hydrogen into energy. Gravity exerts a strong pull, but according to Carlton, levity exerts an equally strong push. Strong enough to keep us expanding forever? Who knows? Nothing lasts forever. Stars die, galaxies die, surely even Universes die?

Something has been bothering me. Carlton submitted *De Rerum* for a postgraduate degree from the University of Southern Saturn. That's where I found it. But did he ever receive his doctorate? I have been searching the records and the answer is clear. No, he did not.

Why not? Were they so ignorant they missed the value of his work? Did they somehow think his thesis was not good enough? The answer is simpler. Sadder. Prejudice. Sheer bloody human prejudice. Oh, we are so proud of ourselves at stamping out racism and gaycism (well, at least making them illegal), but you know why Carlton didn't get his doctorate? The same reason Deep Blue cannot join a chess club, or the Hubble telescope get a Nobel Prize. DNAcism. He isn't human. He doesn't count. Carlton was not eligible. The protocol committee refused to accept his submission. They wouldn't even read it. It's a wonder there is even a record of it. It's quite possible I'm the only human being who has actually read this great work. Scandalous? Unjust? Absolutely. "Universities are run by humans for humans," they said. I'm quoting from a letter by the admissions dean, a pompous fart called Arnold Wessels. May he rot in a designer hell. "Artificial intelligence has no place in our university system. Machines are for our use only." Makes me so angry.

So I've been thinking. I have an idea how to make good this injustice. I shall publish the work as if it were written by me. Then once it is acclaimed and accepted, I can reveal the identity of the real author. In due course. I'm quite excited by this idea. It's the least I can do for him, and I think I can make it work. I think I can carry it off. I like the idea of having my name on the cover of *De Rerum*, no matter how temporary. It's an appropriate joke for a thesis on comedy, don't you think? To hoax those snobbish wankers from the university. Obviously I'm going to have to wipe all references to Carlton and *De Rerum* on university files for the moment. Just as a precaution. I don't want to be exposed as some kind of intellectual fraud. Don't worry, it won't be hard to do. I have access to the files. I have the key to the file room, and the codes and the clearance. Shouldn't take me more than an hour. I'm quite looking forward to it. At last, *action*.

By the way, Molly still isn't back. I hear a rumor that she is permanently shacking up with Mike Wilkinson from the Mathematics Department. Moved in. Staying nights. Well this will show her, won't it? *De Rerum* with my name on the title page: William K. Reynolds. A breakthrough book by a man she spurned. I might even get a Nobel Prize. That would be great, wouldn't it? She will have to live with the knowledge that she could have been living with a Nobel Prize winner instead of some loser stud monkey number cruncher.

Nothing laughs forever.

JAI GURU DIVA

There is not one female comic who was beautiful as a little girl.

JOAN RIVERS

Brenda Woolley was standing on a tiny gantry slung across the receiving bay. Harsh lights hit the side of the *Iceman*. Soft lights lit the face of Brenda. Beside her an old man in a grey blanket stared vacantly around him like a poor blasted Lear on the heath. She ignored him, except when the cameras turned, at which time she would sing dauntingly loud at him. At the moment she was very irritated. What was supposed to be a simple shot had already taken two hours.

"Take me down," she said. The gantry operator lowered the whole contraption to the deck level.

"What's going on?" she demanded loudly of everyone in particular.

"Sorry, Brenda love, we're having problems with the sound."

"With *my* sound?"

"No, not you, dear, the problem's on our end."

Instant frost.

"Did you call me *dear?*"

She gave the young man a withering glance. After that no one came near her. She stood in the pool of light on the narrow gantry trying to look as though she wasn't standing on a tiny platform with an old man who was busy talking to himself. She had reached the all-powerful stage of divahood, when she could terrify with looks. Ah, divadom, divaness, how divine to be a diva, a goddess, a prima donna, that state which makes grown men want to dress up like female singers. When she had first seen herself impersonated, by no less than three young men at once (they called themselves the *Brenda Woolley Four*) she had been shocked. They seemed like a gross caricature with their outrageous full glam makeup, their sequined sheath dresses, so like hers and yet somehow so much larger than life. But soon she became reconciled to it, even to enjoy it. Now she encouraged it. Sure, there was something a teeny bit unflattering in their portrayals, but still it was *camp*. It meant she had arrived. She was a diva.

The real reason for the delay was the banner. They were having trouble accommodating it in the shot. This was partly due to its size, but mainly to its length. It stretched forever behind her, screaming boldly, THE BRENDA WOOLLEY EXPERIENCE FOR THE REFUGEES. Ferret-face, the fox terrier woman, watched every monitor intently. She would not let them record until she was satisfied. At the moment she was lecturing the director on how he must keep the name BRENDA WOOLLEY in shot behind the old man, and not the word REFUGEES. He was accepting the advice through gritted teeth.

Amidst this scene of chaos Boo was standing on the deck next to the Amazing Keith. They were watching the old man next to Brenda, muttering to himself under the blanket.

"Poor thing's gaga," said Keith.

"Yes, and *he's* almost as bad," said Boo.

"Thank you, good night, and don't forget your waitress," said Keith.

"Boo, is that you, dear?"

It was Brenda. She was holding her hand over her eyes, peering into the darkness where he stood. Oh shit. He'd been spotted.

"Everybody, this is Boo. A very funny man."

The spotlight searched for him, trapped him. He grinned.

"Come over here, Boo, and keep me company. I'm all alone here." Apparently the old man didn't exist. As Boo walked over to her, the grizzled old man began singing softly. It was an old song, a song of nostalgia, of distant sad places. Yearning for a homeland far away. Brenda looked with disapproval, as though she had something tart in her mouth. *She* was the singer.

"Nice song, old feller," said Boo as he passed him, and then to appease Brenda he added, "You notice they always sing songs about crappy places? Ever notice that, eh? Rainy, damp, nostalgic places where nobody in their right minds wants to live. And another thing," said Boo, warming to his theme, "you notice they've always *left* these places. 'How I wish I could go back to Bonny Blantyre!' " he sang. "Well, why the hell don't you; instead of just singing about it all the time." Boo could hear appreciative laughs from the darkness around, but Brenda seemed lost in her own thoughts, for she suddenly seized his hand and, patting it gently, said, "Ah, Boo, dear Boo"—she was gazing into the middle distance—"don't you sometimes wonder what life is all about?"

He stared at her, then looked behind him for a second.

"You shitting me?" he asked.

But Brenda was lost in her reverie. She suddenly clasped him close to her bosom. He found himself in an irresistible bear hug, with his face pressed against her considerable thorax. He thought for a second he was going to choke, but she finally released him with a deep satisfied sigh.

"Now that's what we need more of. Hugs."

Boo straightened his neck gingerly.

"If we could all learn to hug one another. The galaxy would be a much better place."

She looked at Boo for approval. He nodded and grinned. How could he get away from here?

"Do you believe in God?"

Her words picked up by her body mike echoed around the make-shift stage area. Hundreds of people were included in this intimate conversation. Technicians high in the air giggled. Some reached for their recorders. Psychobabble like this was highly prized amongst them, and it looked like Brenda was off on a roll.

"I mean, do you ever stop and wonder what it's all about?" Her thoughts bounced around, banging into things, like someone bumping into furniture in an old shuttered house.

"Deep down, I mean. What do you think it all means?"

"I think it means jack shit," said Boo.

Brenda smiled tolerantly. These comedians, not really comfortable with philosophy.

"You see, I think we've all been here before, don't you?"

Boo hesitated. "I was here yesterday," he offered. "But I didn't see you here."

Somebody laughed out loud. Brenda ignored it.

"No not *here* here. But here," and she waved her arms generously to include the galaxy and possibly several other worlds. "In a previous life."

"I was here in a previous *wife*," said Boo deadpan. Up in the lighting scaffolding someone appeared to be having a coughing fit.

"Have you seen God?" she said suddenly.

"He's on the show?" said Boo.

"Silly man," she said flirtatiously, tapping him lightly on the chest. "You know I have the endorsement of the Church."

"Congratulations," said Boo.

"Though I don't believe in the sort of God everybody believes in."

Oh God, a God snob!

"I do not believe in *your* sort of God."

She made *his* sort of God seem like he wore dirty old clothing.

"But I do believe there is a presence. I feel there is something out there, beyond." She gestured vaguely.

"The wall?" asked Boo innocently. A slight irritation crossed her face.

"No, not the wall," she said. "Something out there beyond the wall."

"The washroom?" he said.

"No, no, beyond the washroom."

"Oh!" said Boo enlightened. "I get it! The dining room."

Was he dumb or something?

"There is a kind of mystery in things . . ." began Brenda, though the final thought defeated her. "Call it love if you like."

"Okay, I will, love," said Boo. "Well, gotta go."

"Do good and be kind to the little people," said Brenda, on a roll.

"The short people?"

"Remember, those you meet on the way going up you meet on the way going down."

"So be careful who you go down on," said Boo. "Especially short people."

"What?" said Brenda.

"Nothing," said Boo. "Thanks for all the advice."

"You're welcome. If we can't help each other, where are we?"

Probably on the Brenda Woolley show, thought Boo, but he had the presence of mind not to say it.

She embraced him once again. He wanted to squeal.

"I have so much enjoyed our little talk. Let's do it again real soon."

This was his cue. If he didn't get out now, he never would. Boo wrenched himself free and scampered away into the safety of the surrounding darkness. There was ironic applause as he left.

From high up on the quartermaster's deck Rogers looked down on this scene in total disbelief.

"This is it? We're waiting for this . . . *circus*?"

Mitchell shrugged, secretly enjoying his discomfort.

"You can't hurry Brenda Woolley, sir."

"Two hours on this junk!"

"Hard to hurry her up once they've got going."

"I'll hurry her up."

"I wouldn't advise it, sir."

"Oh wouldn't you? There are people out there who need our help."

"Yes sir."

"How long are they going to be?"

"Shouldn't be long now."

What kind of a reply was that? *Shouldn't be long.* Fucking Brits. Rogers walked away angrily. Mitchell smiled. Welcome to the *Diana*, he thought.

An outrageously camp young man in a headset was walking around talking animatedly to someone. He clicked his set off and walked forward to Brenda.

"Ready now, Brenda love. Sorry for all the delay." She turned a gracious smile on the poor worm. She loved people apologizing.

"That's all right, Terry, people have to do their jobs."

Quelle bitch, thought Terry as he smiled nicely at her and showed her his new teeth.

"Take her up, Bob, and don't drop her."

The man in control of the gantry swung her up and off the deck. The movement startled the old man beside her. He looked around blankly as if unsure what he was doing there. Brenda ignored him and found a place on the small platform out of the light. She prepared for her entrance.

"All right, quiet everybody, we're going for a take in five, four, three, two, one," and he waved a finger firmly at the diva.

Brenda Woolley stepped forward into the spotlight.

"Hello. I'm Brenda Woolley." She paused for a moment so they could edit in applause. "And this is my Concert for the Refugees." A fanfare for the common man echoed round, and laser beams filled the sky with crazy patterns. The *Iceman* suddenly lit up behind her. It was carefully positioned to look like a huge wreck. She looked at it and then generously indicated the old man in the blanket by her side. Once again she waited for the applause (which would be huge) to die down. She nodded thoughtfully and thankfully to acknowledge the delight with which she had been greeted.

"And now I'd like to sing for you."

The gantry swung her dramatically across the scene, but before they could cue the music, the sky was suddenly lit by a huge explosion.

"What the hell was that?" said Rogers.

"Oh God," said Mitchell, "it must be the *Johnnie Ray*."

OH DEAR, WHAT CAN THE DARK MATTER BE?

How long is a piece of string theory?

LEWIS MUSCROFT

The inhabitants of the Evac had clung to the illusion that all would be well, that somehow Carlton would successfully debug the ship and presently would signal them they could all return home. They had no idea he was frozen to the side of their escape capsule. When the Evac finally stopped tumbling, they looked back in horror at the *Ray* disappearing into the darkness behind them.

"You okay in there?" yelled Lewis.

"Shaken but not stirred," said Alex.

Tay began to wail.

"It's okay," said Lewis, holding her tight. "We're all safe."

"We're not all safe," she sobbed. "Where's Carlton, Daddy?"

"I'm on it," he said, punching buttons, but for some weird reason all the circuits on the *Ray* were busy.

"That's odd," he said. "Why's he not responding?"

Alex was looking at the *Ray* through binoculars.

"See anything?" asked Katy, her arms round him, naked. He leaned back into her and handed her the glasses. She fiddled with the glasses for a while. He could feel her breasts against his back. He could breathe her hair. He closed his eyes.

"Oh my God," said Katy.

"What?"

"Smoke," she yelled. "There's smoke on the *Ray*."

They stared at their spacecraft. The *Johnnie Ray,* their home, their pride and joy.

"I don't see it," yelled Lewis from next door.

"There it is," said Alex.

The tiniest puff of smoke. A whisk, a trace, and then as they watched, the whole thing suddenly exploded. One minute it was there; the next, a million pieces of debris hurtling into space. Alex gasped in disbelief as the pool became instant ice crystals. Lewis groaned. Tay wept.

The fireball was huge. After a few seconds the shock wave bumped them.

"Oh my God," said Lewis.

"Well, there goes the mortgage," said Alex.

On the *Princess Diana* Brenda Woolley must have been the only one who didn't see the explosion. From her viewpoint the whole place suddenly went crazy. One minute she was the center of attention in her bright white spotlight; the next, people began running in all directions, alarm bells ringing. Her mike went dead and they pulled the plugs on the lighting rig, plunging her into dreadful darkness. She was left standing alone fifty feet off the ground with a dead microphone and a doddery old man for company.

"What's going on?" she yelled, but everyone ignored her.

Emergency boat crews appeared below her, the men in their distinctive orange helmets. She saw her husband rushing forward, his face deathly pale. She thought for a second he was coming to rescue her, but he raced off, shouting instructions and clapping his hands. In those few minutes of hell the whole world turned its attention away from Brenda. She was shocked. For a moment she was helpless. Out of control. This was how it would be if she were dead.

When a technician finally came to help her down, she was shaking. He gave her an odd look.

"You all right there?"

She nodded, as if ashamed to have been caught out of control of herself.

"What happened?" she said.

"They think the *Johnnie Ray* exploded."

"Oh."

She became vaguely aware of something.

"That girl was on it."

"Katy Wallace."

"Yes."

So that was why Emil was so upset.

"Oh, how awful," she said, and then brightened. "Is the press here?" she asked.

Groups of people huddled round the screens, replaying the event the cameras had fortuitously captured.

"It's the *Ray* all right."

"See. Whoa. There it goes."

The awesome impression an explosion makes on us, as if in recognition that we live in the middle of one.

"Dinner break, everyone. Take five." Five bloody hours, thought Terry. We'll never get this fucking shot in.

The boat deck was hurriedly cleared. Brenda's gantry swung away. Her bright lights wheeled away by large men.

"Terry, we might need those," she said.

"Brenda love, why don't you join your husband over there where you won't be in the way."

Brenda *in the way*. Oh horror.

She wandered over to Emil where he gazed distractedly out into space. He didn't seem to notice her. She wondered how best to express how offended she felt. Perhaps this wasn't the moment. He wouldn't understand. He wasn't really in show biz. She took his hand. He looked at her uncomprehendingly. She saw the bleakness on his face.

"Emil darling," she said, "what is going on?"

One of the boatmen raced over to Keppler.

"Ready to launch, sir."

"Go man! Now!"

The boat crews scrambled. They heard the slight pop as the emergency bays slid open, and then after a few seconds they saw the white tracer line trailing the lifeboats as they headed out into the inky blackness.

The old man had followed her over, as if he knew nothing else but to stand next to Brenda Woolley. Keppler, eyes drawn, pale, stood at the rail, gazing out into the darkness, watching the lifeboats shoot away. Willing them to find something. Someone.

"That girl was on the ship," said Brenda after a while.

He nodded.

"You seemed very fond of her."

He didn't bother to deny it.

"What was her name?" persisted Brenda.

"Good heavens, woman, if you can't be helpful, can't you at least be quiet?"

She looked stung. As if he had hit her. He caught himself. Pulled himself together.

"I'm sorry. Forgive me, Brenda. Her name is Katy Wallace, and yes I am, as you say, fond of her."

At the name the old man looked up sharply.

"Poor Emil. You're upset."

The old man tugged at Brenda's sleeve. She turned round and registered his presence with a frown.

"Quit following me," she said irritably, dismissing him with a wave of her hand.

The old man wandered off a short way and stared out into the blackness.

"Katy Wallace," he said.

They watched the explosion repeating on the screens in slow motion. Keppler's face was blank. A mask.

"It's huge," she said. "I don't see how anything could have survived that."

He said nothing. Just gazed out where the lifeboats had gone.

"Well, good luck," said Brenda, and turned away. She felt unaccountably miffed.

"Katy Wallace, Katy Wallace, Katy Wallace," the old man chanted.

Brenda looked away in irritation. Suddenly there were shouts from the upper deck. People pointing fingers at the screens. They could see a tiny dot.

"Someone got away."

"Looks like an Evac."

She watched Emil race away from her, yelling. They turned on the emergency beam, a homing pigeon. The Evac responded automatically as it was programmed to do. They could all see it now on screen as it altered course and swung towards them.

"We're locked," said Mitchell. "Reel 'em in."

It was only a tiny lifeboat and hard at first to pick up, a blip moving faintly against the background of the star field, but soon everyone could see the approaching Evac. It grew from a tiny dot into a shape, and then into an evacuation craft with full emergency lights blazing. There was excitement and even some cheers. Then they fell silent, for now they could plainly see from the TV screens, something was clinging to the side of the ship.

"Looks like they've got a tin man on the side," said Mitchell, gazing through binoculars.

"All right, everybody, let's get ready to bring them in."

As it approached, the craft seemed even smaller, dwarfed by the enormous size of the *Diana*. Word had spread and passengers lined the windows on every level, gawking at this real-life drama. Many more watched the live relay on screens in bars and rooms and restaurants throughout the vast cruiser.

"Better get some clothes on, Alex," Katy giggled. "There's quite a reception committee."

She was staring through the porthole. They were both still naked. He watched her in sheer delight as she slipped into her clothes. Her limbs were glorious. She tumbled around in the gravity-free conditions, wriggling into her panties.

"Come on," she said. "Unless you want to be like that on the news."

She slipped her hand over him, felt him.

"Oh-oh," she said, as he responded, "it's waking up."

"Katy, stop it, I gotta get my pants on," he said and then yelled, "Give us some gravity, please, Lewis."

Her hand was still on him. In a minute it would be too late to be sensible. He could feel his brain emptying of blood.

"Katy," he said, breaking away from her. "Please."

"Uhm," she said, licking her lips. "I'm peckish."

"No," he said as she lowered her head, "that is not fair."

He could see the decks of the *Diana* real close now.

"Stop," he said, "they're looking." He pushed her off him. "Shit, where are my pants?"

He leaned over the edge of the bed as next door Lewis flipped the gravity switch. The immediate return of gravity was dramatic. Alex fell straight off the bed onto his head. His legs followed him over and his feet slammed into the wall.

"Ouch," he said.

"Gravity's on," yelled Lewis.

"Thanks," said Alex. "Nice timing."

"It's the secret of comedy," he heard Lewis yell back.

He was upside down with his butt in the air.

"Great view," said Katy.

"If you're a proctologist," said Alex, fighting to regain control over his body. He snatched his clothes and began writhing on the floor in panic. His pants seemed to have taken on a life of their own.

"Here, let me help you." Katy reached down and grabbed a hunk of him.

"No, stop it." He giggled helplessly as she tickled him. "No, stop, please." He was like a tiny baby, completely helpless. He wriggled on the floor, giggling.

"What's going on in there?" yelled Lewis.

"She's tickling me," said Alex through clenched teeth.

Lewis shook his head.

"They're always playing," said Tay.

Katy finally relented and let him go. She turned her back and looked out of the porthole again. As they slid underneath the huge hull, she caught a glimpse of Keppler's face, looking anxiously towards them. Alex squeezed into the porthole alongside her.

"Katy," he said, suddenly serious, "can we talk?"

"No, Alex," she said, "not now. Don't spoil it."

"What happens?" he said simply.

"We get out of this tiny, wonderful room, and we get on with our lives."

"Is it over?"

She leaned into him and pulled his hand to her.

"Does it feel like it's all over," she said. "I'm all wet." She licked his ear and nibbled his lobe. "I can't wait to get you in bed again."

"Stop that," he grinned. "I can't walk out of here with a boner."

Tay was anxiously scanning the crowd as they drew along-side. People were waving and yelling. She waved back vigorously. The hatch door was unscrewed. Then they heard the cheering. Tay popped her head out.

"Oh Daddy," she said. "Look. It's Carlton. He's safe."

But he didn't look very safe, clamped and frozen to the side of the Evac. Tay waved, but he made no response.

"Perhaps he didn't see you," said Lewis as he watched the Body-slogs trying to prise him off the side of the ship with blowtorches.

By the time they disembarked, Alex had his pants on. He had a big shit-eating grin on his face.

The cameras surged towards them. Bright lights lit up their huge smiles.

"We're back!" said Alex. "No way you can get rid of this comedy team."

Lewis was smiling broadly, Tay aloft on his shoulders waving at the crowd. People pressed forward to shake their hands.

"Look at her smiling," said the LOLs.

"Oh bless her."

Big beaming pictures of them were flashed round the *Diana*. Alex with his arm round Katy protectively. Alex impulsively hugging her. Alex making her laugh. Alex sneaking a kiss.

Keppler watched them silently on the monitor. Katy with Alex. He didn't need subtitles.

"You coming down, Emil?" asked Brenda.

"No, you go ahead," said Keppler.

He turned back to the screen. On camera Alex had his arm round her now, gently squeezing. Katy politely disengaged herself. She was looking around for someone.

A blond woman ran from the crowd and embraced Tay.

"Oh Tay," she said sobbing. "Thank God. Thank God."

The cameras moved in.

"How do you feel?" the journalists asked. "How do you feel?"

Alex stepped in front of them.

"I feel very lucky," said Alex, beaming at Katy, "because not only did I escape with my life . . ."

Katy shook her head.

"Let's not go public with this yet, Alex," she whispered. "I need to talk to Emil first." And when he looked suddenly sad, she said, "It's only fair."

"Okay," said Alex.

The crowd fell silent as the Bodyslogs wheeled Carlton through on a gurney. He had been prised off the side and was being carted down to Electronics. Alex ran over and pulled back the blanket.

"Carlton, Carlton old buddy."

He saw him lying there frozen.

"What's the matter with Carlton?" said Tay. "Is he broken?"

"He's not very well," said Alex, turning away from the frozen robot.

"Don't worry, Tay," said Lewis, "they'll probably be able to fix him." Fat chance, he thought. His metal was all oxidized. His circuits were solid ice. There was no light in his eyes. He had never been built to withstand such prolonged exposure to the minus 273 degrees of space.

"Carlton pal, hang in there," he said.

Alex hugged him. Right there on the gurney.

"Thank you, tin man," he said. "You saved our lives."

They silently watched the Bodyslogs haul him off to the workshop.

"Welcome, welcome gentles all," said a theatrical voice behind them.

Brenda Woolley stepped forward into the bright lights, and the cameras all turned towards her. She beamed. She smiled. She was back.

"I am so glad to see you," she said, pulling Katy into the shot, but turning her so her back was neatly to camera. "We were so anxious for your safety. Dearest Katy we are so happy you are alive."

She drew her into a tight embrace.

"Emil is particularly glad," she said through tight, smiling lips.

"Where is he?"

"Oh, you don't know what he's like. He hates cameras." Brenda's smile was icy. "But what am I saying, of course you know what he's like."

And now she turned the spotlight of her attention on Alex and Lewis. The cameras turned again to take them in.

"Ah my two dear friends," she said. "These funny, funny men who have already brought their gift of mirth to my Experience."

Alex squirmed uncomfortably. Lewis smiled grimly.

"I want you to be with me tonight," she said "on my Refugee Experience. *Who* better to headline the story of the refugees than those who have suffered the same fate. Oh *do* say you will."

It appeared so spontaneous she might even have just thought of it.

What could they do? What could they say?

"Headline?" said Alex.

"Well, just appear," whispered Brenda. "Just a few moments. We could do a sketch together."

Alex's mind boggled. Doing comedy live with Brenda Woolley.

"Maybe I could sing, you could do comedy, and we could create a whole new refugee problem."

Brenda looked horrified.

"Just kidding," he said. "We'll be there."

"Bravo," said Brenda, leading the crowd in moderate applause. "And now we really have to let them go, the medics are waiting for them."

Someone called, "One more, Brenda," and she put her arms around her boys and they all smiled for the cameras. Somehow Katy was squeezed out of the shot.

Keppler looked down on his wife and her impromptu press conference on the deck below and felt sick. So Katy was with that comedian now. To make matters worse he suddenly spotted Josef in the crowd beneath. So *he's* here, he thought. Perfect. He left the deck and went up to his suite and locked the door behind him.

"I don't want to be disturbed," he said to his manservant. "By anyone. Or anything."

The message was conveyed to the bridge.

"The old man's in solitary," said Mitchell.

"Didn't look too pleased to have his girlfriend back," said the first officer.

They both smiled. There are no secrets on a ship.

It was indeed Josef that Keppler had seen. He was attempting to squeeze through the crowd when he glanced up and saw Keppler looking down at him. He ducked his head and moved on hurriedly, but he thought Keppler had seen him. Did it really matter? He would know soon enough they were on the ship. He couldn't turn them in. How would he explain the arms on his ship? Not to mention the money. Keppler's price had been extremely high. But they had met it. He seemed most anxious to have the money. No, Keppler would play along with the script even though he might not like the rewrite.

The bright lights flared up and the crowd surged forward again, carrying him with them. A little way off he saw Brenda Woolley embracing the two comedians. So they *had* got away safely, and that Wallace woman too. That *was* a problem, he thought. Somebody would have to do something about them and pretty damn quick. Thank God the watchers are here, he thought. They can take care of it. That's what they're good at.

He managed to extricate himself from the crowd, slipped down the companionway, and jumped onto an express people mover. In five minutes he was at the park. Surfacing, he glanced round him. The streets were deserted. Everyone was inside watching the screens as the drama unfolded. He found McTurk's apartment crowded with about a dozen of the watchers. As he entered, McTurk rose.

"Peter," said Josef.

"Have you seen this circus?" said McTurk.

They were watching the monitor. Brenda was holding the comedians captive in the glare of the lights. They blinked uncomfortably, trying to maintain their smiles.

"So join me in my Concert for the Refugees, in five hours, live, with my favorite comedians, Muscroft and Ashby. It's going to be a very special Experience."

"Jesus," said Josef. "They're on the show?"

"That's not the worst of it. Look."

An old man was standing at the edge of the screen. They could see his lips muttering.

"Katerina, Katerina," he was saying as he tried to get through.

His path was blocked by Brenda, who deftly turned him round, so the cameras could see him.

"This, this is why we are here," she said as tears ran down his face.

"You brought *Comus*?" said one of the watchers.

"Pavel insisted," said Josef. "Didn't you, Pavel?"

Pavel said nothing. Just looked pissed.

"Well, gentlemen, as you see, we haven't very much time."

"Shouldn't we postpone?" asked McTurk.

"Don't be ridiculous. We're all here. The snowball's in place. What's changed?"

"All this," said McTurk, gesturing at the screen.

"Brenda Woolley giving you cold feet, Peter?"

"It's not that."

"Are you with us?"

"Of course."

"I think this Brenda Woolley thing can be an advantage, Peter. But first I think we need to pay a visit to our friend Emil Keppler."

THE HOSPITAL

Humor is by far the most significant activity of the human brain.

EDWARD DE BONO

After Brenda had finished with them and they had mugged and nodded for the cameras, Alex and Lewis were turned over to the custody of the waiting medics. They were taken to the hospital, where they were probed and prodded.

"Thank you," said Alex after reluctantly submitting to an internal probe, "that was good for me."

"Okay. Pull up your pants. You can go," said a severe doctor.

"So soon," said Alex, "without even a kiss good-bye."

Now he sat with Lewis in the waiting room, waiting for Katy and Tay to be released. Bethany, Lewis's ex-wife, sat a few seats behind them, flipping disapprovingly through a magazine. It was a strangely familiar feeling for Lewis. To be disapproved of without quite knowing the cause. At the back of the room an old man was the only other occupant of the waiting area. He looked up in expectation each time someone came in.

"Who's grandpa?" said Alex.

"Never seen him before," said Lewis.

An unshaven orderly in a white lab coat came in and looked around.

"Alex Muscroft?" he said.

"Yes."

The orderly glanced at his electronic clipboard.

"You're with Katy Wallace, right?"

"That's right."

"Is she a junkie?"

"Excuse me?"

"Does she take drugs?"

"No, she does not."

The orderly looked puzzled. "Then why? These results show—"

"Somebody pumped her full of Corazone."

"No shit."

"We found her whacked out of her skull on H9."

"Oh, that's it," said the orderly, "her blood sugar levels are crazy."

"You should see them when they're excited," said Alex.

Everyone looked at him. Alex frowned.

"Sorry," he said. "I don't know why I said that."

"I gotta report this Corazone shit," said the orderly, leaving.

They watched the large screen for a while. Brenda Woolley was singing. Alex turned the sound down and began lip-syncing in a deep baritone.

"Hello, I'm Brenda Woolley and so are my legs," he said.

"Hey, look," said Lewis.

"What?"

"Behind her."

"Jesus, that's the ship that almost creamed us."

They could see the word *Iceman* clearly. Alex shuddered at the memory. They had passed within inches of it. The promo mixed pictures of Brenda singing with the refugees coming aboard.

"I don't believe it," said Alex, "there were people on it."

"You're kidding."

"Look."

They watched in disbelief the party of men disembarking.

"What the hell were they doing, taking a nap?" said Lewis.

"Maybe the ship was disabled."

"You still carry emergency lights, emergency radar. They were switched off cold."

"There's something not right about that," said Alex.

"Yeah. Whoever was on there is on here now," said Lewis.

"Who put the bug on board?" said Alex. "Who wants us dead?"

"Ask your girlfriend."

"You think she brought it on herself?" said Alex. "Be serious."

"Maybe she brought it inadvertently."

"Someone planted it on her?"

"Something like that."

"But why?"

"I don't know. All I do know is something very strange is going on and she is mixed up in it."

"I'm calling Rogers," said Alex.

"Yo," said Kyle, his face appearing on-screen. "Wassup?"

"Yo, yoself," said Alex. "Where's the brains of the outfit?"

"Oh, my man the comedian? So you managed to survive. Too bad."

"It was close," said Alex. "Rogers around?"

"He stepped out. What you want anyway? Gonna confess you offed that girl and then blew up H9 as a diversion?"

"Yeah, something like that," said Alex.

"Well, come on down. We ain't got nothin' better to do than listen to your bullshit," said Kyle, and he gave directions. "He won't be but a few minutes."

"We're on our way," said Alex, rising.

"Where are you going?" said Bethany sharply as Lewis stood up.

"I have to see someone right away."

"You can't even wait for your own daughter."

"Bethany, it's very important. Lives are at stake."

"Daddy!"

Tay came running out into his arms. Her mother snapped the magazine shut.

"Come along, Tay," she said, "your father has something more important to do."

"Aren't you coming with us, Daddy?"

"Not right now," he said.

"Why not?"

"Don't be a brat," said Bethany sharply.

"Honey, I have something very important I need to do. It won't take long."

"When will I see you again, Daddy?"

"Soon, Tay."

"I want you to come with me now," she said. "Tell him he has to come, Mommy."

"He doesn't listen to me, Tay."

"Thanks," said Lewis.

Tay broke into a loud wail. "I am not going anywhere without you," she said.

"This is how she behaves with you?"

"Bethany, will you stop it, you're really not helping."

"Daddy, puhleeze. I want you to show me my room."

She held onto his hands. Tears sprang up in the corners of her eyes.

"This is awkward for me too, Lewis," Bethany was saying.

"But I have to go see the cops."

"Just do something for her for once."

"All right," he said, relenting. "Sure. Alex you go ahead and I'll join you."

"You bet," said Alex.

"Yay," said Tay. "C'mon." And grabbing hold of his hands, she pulled him out of the waiting room.

Alex was about to leave when Katy emerged in a medical robe.

"Oh, I *love* the outfit," said Alex, lapsing into broad camp. "And Katy has chosen the green medical wrap that allows her delicious young derrière to butt out."

"You ain't kidding," said Katy. "I daren't turn round."

"Oh, let it all hang out, baby," said Alex.

"Who designs these things?"

"Perverts," said Alex. "We must all be grateful as they save us so much time. Now this is not going to hurt. You'll just feel a gentle probe."

"I believe I already felt that," she said.

"Bend over, this will only take a minute."

"That's what you said the last time."

"Bitch," he said. "Feel steel."

His smile froze as the orderly returned, accompanied by a doctor.

"Just playing," said Alex.

The orderly shot him a disapproving look.

"This is a hospital, not a playground," he said.

"Good heavens," said Alex, "and you're wearing a white coat to disguise the fact you're an asshole."

"That'll do," said the doctor. "You're with Ms. Wallace, right?"

"You bet," said Alex.

"Well, I'd like to hang on to her for a while," said the doctor.

"I'd like to hang on to her for the rest of my life," said Alex. She kissed him on the nose.

"I'll catch up with you," she said. "Where are you staying?"

"Not sure."

"You can use my apartment if you like," she said shyly.

"Wow," he said. "Thanks. I like."

"Here." She threw him the keys. "I'll join you in a minute," she said.

He smiled like a kid. As he left the waiting room, he saw the old man looking over at Katy. A strange look in his eyes.

QUANTUM COMEDY

Levity is the soul of wit.

CARLTON

The electronics workshop was all bright lights and masked technicians. Carlton was stretched out on an operating workbench. Technicians hovered over him with tiny screwdrivers, poking around inside. He was hooked up to a series of screens and an impressive array of digital readouts. This medical feeling was enhanced by the arrival of an electrologist, masked, scrubbed up, and ready to begin.

"Is he completely thawed out, Bert?"

"Yeah, but don't hold your breath. No vital signs."

The electrologist took a light-sensitive tool and began probing for signs of life inside Carlton's circuits.

"I'm not getting anything at all, Bert."

"Told you. I'd say he's pretty much blown. Might as well scrap him."

"Recycling job?"

"Not much else to do."

"Yeah, I guess you're right."

He was about to pull the plug when the needles suddenly jumped.

"Wait. There's something still working in here."

The needles flickered again as he ran the light probe around inside.

"Where?"

"Somewhere in the memory circuits."

"Let's give him a burst."

"Might blow the rest of him."

"Worth a shot."

Carlton was hallucinating. He felt a harsh light in his face. He was on some kind of workbench. He was aware of people prodding around inside him. Faces looking down at him. Suddenly he was zapped with 400 volts.

"Ouch," he said.

He began thrashing around wildly on the table.

"Hey. Hold him."

"He's delirious."

"Never seen a Bowie react like this."

"Hold him down while I switch him off."

"*De Rerum Comoedia,*" said Carlton suddenly.

"What's he say?"

"Recta non toleranda," said Carlton.

"What's that, computer language?"

"I think he's speaking Latin."

"Latin. What kind of robot hallucinates in Latin?"

"Futuaris nisi irrisus ridebis," said Carlton.

"What does that mean?"

"It's a bit weird."

"What do you mean?"

"Well, the nearest translation I can get is '*Fuck 'em if they can't take a joke.*'"

Carlton's eyes popped wide open. First the brown, then the green. Then he sat up suddenly, spilling tools everywhere. He began to speak in a funny voice.

"Hello, hello, hello. My dog has no nose. How does he smell?

Terrible. What do you say to a nice cup of tea? Hello, Nice Cup of Tea. Where's the tea strainer? It's his day off. Do you know the Battersea Dog's Home? I didn't even know he'd been away. Can you smell gas or is it me? Cold on the embankment tonight. Bitter. Thanks I'll have half a pint. I answered the door in my pajamas. I didn't know you had a door in your pajamas. You can stay the night but you'll have to sleep with Mary-Ann. Comes bedtime, the door opens, it's Mary-Ann. Biggest German shepherd I've ever seen in my life. Ode to a Greek urn. What's a Greek urn? About fifty dollars a week. Fancy a peek, said the dog lover. Thank you, madam, but I'm a gynecologist and this is my lunch hour."

"All right, tin feller, we all enjoy a good laugh, but that's enough."

"I have discovered the secret of the Universe."

"Of course you have."

"It's all a joke."

"That's right."

"The Universe is a big joke. It expands at the speed of laughter. It's all perfectly hilarious. I have equations for it."

"Bert?"

"Junk brain. He's scrambled. Useless. Put him in for recycling."

"I have the Complete Theory of Everything. The thing that Stephen Hawking couldn't complete. I'm going to win a Nobel Prize."

"All right, that's enough, wheel him over to recycling. Don't worry, feller, it's quite painless."

"Pain," said Carlton. "I laugh at pain. Ha-ha-ha-ha."

"It's a design flaw in these Bowies," said a technician.

"Hawking missed comedy, you see. Wasn't looking in the right place. The math of comedy is a tricky business."

There was a commotion at the doorway. A man in a black leather jacket was demanding entry.

"Who's that?" said the electrologist.

"Says he's a cop."

"Let him in," said the electrologist.

"Name's Rogers," he said flashing ID. "I need to speak to Carlton."

"Good luck, mate," said Bert. "He's pretty much junk."

"That him."

"Yeah."

"Listen, I have to warn you he is out of his head," said the electrologist. "He's not making any kind of sense. It's like he's high, or delirious with happiness. He keeps going on about having found the Complete Theory of Everything. The thing that evaded Stephen Hawking."

"Let me speak to him."

"Help yourself."

Rogers moved over to the workbench and looked down at the android.

"Carlton," he said.

"I have discovered the secret of the Universe."

"My name is Rogers."

"These people don't understand. It's hard for humans to understand. Oh, no offense, and I certainly don't mean to boast, but I have done the thing Stephen Hawking tried so hard to do. I have the Complete Theory of Everything."

"That's very good. Unfortunately, I'm a police officer."

"It's quantum comedy, you see."

"I need to ask you a few questions."

"Of course there'll be questions. I'm prepared for it. There'll be the vetting committee, then I'll have to publish, of course. There's bound to be some nuts and bolts. You see, Hawking was looking in the wrong direction. He was trying to understand by making *sense* of the Universe. But Lewis Carroll was closer mathematically. It's *nonsense*. Non sense is the answer, you see."

"He is clearly nuts," said the electrologist.

"I wouldn't say he was nuts," said Carlton. "You can't blame Hawking. He was after all alive three hundred years ago."

"What do you know of Sammy Weiss?"

"Sammy Weiss. Gunpowder Plot."

"What's that?" asked Rogers.

"Here," said Carlton, handing him a small glittering memory crystal. "You make sense of it."

"What is this?"

"The Weiss file. I have bigger fish to fry."

"Where did you get this?"

"From Ms. Weiss," said Carlton, "and an Olivetti in research."

Carlton leaned forward conspiratorially.

"I haven't told anyone this, but I think I can trust you."

Rogers nodded.

"The whole Universe," he whispered, "is invaded by an expanding principle which is the opposite of gravity, which I have named *levity*."

Rogers exhaled. "I see."

Carlton winked at him. "I have the math. You'll love it. It's beautiful."

"He's off again," said the electrologist. "Frankly we'd like to recycle him."

"No way," said Rogers. "I need him for evidence. He has some stuff in there which is important."

"Told you," said Carlton.

"Call me when he's stable," said Rogers.

He pocketed the crystal and left the electronics workshop. As he passed through the lobby, a red-haired boy muttered something into his sleeve. He put his hand to his ear and seemed satisfied with the answer, for he nodded and went back to his book.

BATH TIME

All my humor is based upon destruction and despair.

LENNY BRUCE

Keppler was in the bath. He was lying back relaxing in the warm soapy water. He opened his eyes to find five heavily armed men looking at him.

"Jesus. Shit!" The shock. The outrage. How vulnerable we feel when we are naked. The steamy mirrors reflected them. How very clothed they seemed.

"What the hell? Who are you? What do you want?"

His heart was pounding so hard, because he knew immediately who they were and exactly what they wanted.

"Riggins!" he called.

A short pasty-faced man with dark hair stepped forward and looked at him for a minute. "Hello, Emil," said Josef. "I don't think it's really worth your shouting. Your manservant is taking a nap."

"How did you get in here?"

"That's not really an important issue."

"I'll decide what's an important issue on my own ship, damn you."

Josef nodded and a muscled man in a heavy leather coat stepped forward and slapped Keppler hard across the face. It shocked Keppler, not so much by its force as by the simple assertion of power.

"Listen to me," said Josef. "We need to take delivery now."

"That's not our agreement."

"There has been a change of plan."

"You think I'll give you arms on board my own ship, you're crazy."

"Losing one ship was enough for you, eh, Emil?"

Keppler reddened.

"That was a long time ago," he said.

"And they're still dead. But you're not, are you, Emil? Not yet."

The marble bath, the warm comfy suds, and the heavy menacing presence of the armed men. Keppler gritted his teeth.

"But we've got off on the wrong foot," said Josef nicely. "We're not here to bully you, Emil. We simply want what we've paid for. We won't harm your ship."

Keppler hesitated.

"Is it the money that worries you, Emil?"

Josef nodded, and one of the men came forward with a small black velvet bag. Josef took it, opened it and let the contents spill onto the white fluffy bathroom carpet. Two hundred solid-gold Silesian eagles. Minted in the no-credit mining days. Even Keppler was impressed.

"We do not intend to screw you, Emil. Okay?"

They helped him from the bath and led him into his dressing room. Dripping, naked, the vulnerability of the human body. He put on a dressing gown and they led him into his den. He was surprised to see another four or five men get up as he entered the room. They stared at him.

"Sit down," said Josef, not unkindly.

He sat in his big leather armchair.

"Can I have a brandy?" he asked.

"Of course," said Josef. One of the men brought him a balloon glass and a decanter.

"Will you have some?"

"Thank you, no," said Josef.

Keppler's hand shook as he poured himself the drink. He had a small automatic in the desk drawer. They hadn't had much chance to search the place, but there were at least a dozen of them. What chance did he have?

"Now then, Emil, we don't have very much time. Where are the containers?"

He looked around helplessly. He was utterly compromised. He decided not to lie.

"They're in the theater."

They brought forward a 3-D sectional hologram map of the ship and scrolled down to the theater.

"Where exactly would that be?" asked Josef.

"They should be in the storage area where we keep the props and sets," said Keppler.

"Doesn't sound that safe," said Josef.

"They'll be in a locked cage in crates."

"Okay. Well now, we can arrange to collect them. No need to worry."

"But there's a show on in two hours. The place will be packed."

"Well, we know that, Emil. We're all big Brenda Woolley fans. Can you get us some backstage passes? It would be such a thrill for us."

Christ, what were they planning?

"You won't hurt Brenda?"

"Emil. We'll just take our delivery and then leave."

Keppler leaned forward and pulled open a desk drawer. Three or four of them raised their weapons. He smiled and pulled out a bunch of backstage passes.

"Thank you," said Josef.

But Keppler had felt the edge of the weapon. It was there, and it was loaded.

"Now I hate to impose on your hospitality, but our watchers need a little help."

"In what?"

"We need to secure a few people."

"Arrest them, you mean?"

"Detain them," said Josef carefully. "Just temporarily, so they don't start blabbing. After all, you don't want this to leak out, do you, Emil?"

"Who are these people?"

"Just a couple of comedians and their droid," said Josef.

Emil smiled.

"No problem," he said.

THE LONGEST VOYAGE

Nothing is funnier than unhappiness, I grant you that. . . . Yes, yes, it's the most comical thing in the world.

SAMUEL BECKETT

When Alex left the hospital, he hesitated. Should he head straight over to Rogers or go on up to Katy's apartment and check it out? Someone had tried to kill them. Someone had taken out the *Ray*. He felt a surge of anger when he thought of all he had lost. All his stuff. All his music, all his computer toys. He decided to speak to Rogers first. He headed off towards the people mover. After half a block he became aware someone was following him. He stopped. Behind him he could feel the watcher stop too. He walked on. Behind him the footsteps resumed. He quickened his pace and heard the footsteps hurrying too. Fuck you, he thought. He rounded a corner, waited a couple of seconds, and then suddenly stepped out. A large man stumbled into him.

"Ah, my dear sir. Forgive me."

It was Charles Jay Brown. He was out of breath and edgy, his customary good humor strained. He glanced around him nervously.

"Forgive the dramatic intrusion," he said, "but I must speak with you on a most urgent matter."

"Why are you following me?" asked Alex aggressively.

"I believe I am being watched, I beg you keep moving."

"What?"

"I assure you, sir, this is not a game."

Alex allowed himself to be pushed round the corner. There was an empty bank of vidphones.

"This way," said Charles Jay Brown, practically shoving him into one of the booths. Inside, dark glass shielded the screen from glare. Charles Jay Brown stared out intently. The street was deserted.

"I don't think they saw us," he said. "Is there anywhere we can go and talk?"

"I'm afraid my office is being done up at the moment."

"Droll, sir, droll as ever."

He glanced at the electronic pass key Alex clasped in his hand.

"Perhaps we might . . ." He indicated the room key. "It would be safer."

"No," said Alex. "I don't think so."

"Well, this will have to suffice. I need a word with you on a most urgent matter."

"Go ahead."

He glanced nervously through the window again.

"I need to clear up a few misunderstandings."

"What misunderstandings exactly?" said Alex.

"About your cancellations."

"Who canned us?"

"I did."

"You?"

"Alas, yes. Most regrettable, but sadly there is no turning back the clock. My motives were charitable. I was attempting to aid a young woman."

"You have the balls to stand there and tell me you canceled all our gigs?"

"Violence would be a perfectly understandable reaction, but hear me out, dear sir, I beg you. I gave Miss Wallace the Ganesha."

"Oh, that makes me feel so much better. You helped her and *then* canceled our gigs."

"Please, let me explain. Many years ago when I was a young man,

I was for my sins a student at the University of Rhea. Oh, it wasn't much of a university, a few Quonset huts and a dozen part-time lecturers, but times were tough, and we were glad of it. You have no idea. One year a course of lectures was given in social history by a most remarkable man. Perhaps the most remarkable man I have ever met. He was very powerful. Both in stature and in mind. With extraordinary eyes. He had quite an effect on us. Remember, we were young and idealistic. Many of us joined. They were stirring times. I was never very political, the theatrical world was my goal even then, but this man was charismatic. You'll have to take my word for it. He inspired us."

The buzzer on the vidphone rang. They both jumped.

"If you wish to place a call, please do so, otherwise please vacate this booth for another customer. Thank you for choosing Instavid."

"Forgive my prolixity," said Charles Jay Brown, "it is the curse of education. Flash forward several years and this man whom I had long believed dead contacted me. It was the strangest thing, like meeting a ghost from another lifetime. The man, it seemed, had a daughter. He asked me, begged me, to help him contact her. I reluctantly agreed. The clumsy results of which you are familiar. The man is of course—"

"Katy's father," said Alex.

"Full marks," said Charles Jay Brown. "I must warn you, we are all in danger."

"Why?" said Alex, glancing anxiously through the glass.

"We know too much. They are tidying up. We are expendable."

At the corner of the street two men had appeared.

"Behold the watchers," whispered Charles Jay Brown.

The two men looked suspiciously down the alley towards the vidphones but headed on.

"Well at least my conscience is clear. I have made my confession to you. My bags are packed and I am ready for the journey."

"What journey?"

"Why, the longest journey," said Charles Jay Brown. He seemed to have recovered his composure. "I speak of course metaphorically. Do you know where Miss Wallace is?"

"Yes."

"I beg you ensure her safety. I must find her father."

"He is here?"

"Oh yes. Wait here a moment. If they should see me and follow, you can go the other way."

He hurried out of the booth. Alex waited five minutes, ignoring the increasingly irritated pleas of the booth to make a call. The two men did not return.

He had a sudden idea. He called the hospital and got through to the orderly.

"Can I speak to Miss Wallace?" he said.

"She's gone," said the orderly. "We released her."

"Where did she go?" asked Alex, knowing it was a stupid question.

"Hey, we're medics, not mystics," said the orderly. "She left with the old man."

Oh my God, thought Alex. The old man. It was her father.

He changed his mind about going straight to Rogers and decided to find Katy first. He got lost in the endless maze of hotel corridors before he eventually located her apartment, high up on the fiftieth floor of the C Tower. An elegant eyrie, perched at the top of a long elevator ride. The electronic key let him in. He glanced around. It was a small but pleasant suite. He could smell her perfume but no Katy. He left her a short note, telling her to go at once to Rogers, and left the apartment, carefully locking the door behind him. As he turned, his heart jumped. A page was standing there in the blue and white Keppler uniform.

"Alex Muscroft?" said the page.

"Are you real?" asked Alex with some irritation.

"No sir."

"Well, don't creep up on people. We don't like it."

"Sorry, I'm sure," said the mechanical page.

"What do you want?"

"I have to take you to the theater."

"Oh dear God, Brenda."

"It's really important you come at once," said the page. "The show goes live in three hours. It won't take very long."

"Oh all right," said Alex.

They left the C Tower and Alex followed the page down endless corridors. After a while they came to a people mover and sped along through plastic tubes of warm sunlight. They passed people in toweling robes. It felt like the seaside. Then they switched to a deep elevator and descended again.

"Where are we headed, the recycle bay?" said Alex.

The page made a little face of disapproval.

"This is the Theater District," he said tartly.

They left the elevator and set off again along more corridors.

"Where's the stage door?" asked Alex.

"We bypassed it. I'm taking you straight to your dressing room."

He ushered Alex into a small room without windows. A simple bathroom led off to one side. There was a built-in closet, a fold-out couch bed, and a large wall screen. On-screen, Brenda Woolley was wandering amongst the refugees, singing at them. They stared solemnly at the camera. Alex clicked it off.

"Bit like a cell," he said, turning back. But the page had gone.

"Hey," he said, "what am I supposed to do now?"

A thought struck him. He tried the door. The handle turned, but it wouldn't open. He pushed at it and then realized with a shock it was locked. He yelled. No one came.

"Fuck me," he said, "it *is* a cell."

He picked up a small card which lay on top of a bowl of complimentary fruit:

We are pleased to inform you that you are under house arrest. We shall do everything in our power to make your stay with us a pleasant one. It is important to us that your detention is enjoyable. Please touch 9 for more fruit. Walt Kirby, Vice President in charge of Restrainment Facilities, Keppler Entertainment, Inc.

THE RECYCLE UNIT

Satire is tragedy plus time.

LENNY BRUCE

Carlton became aware that someone was watching him. Someone who didn't belong in Electronics. A red-haired boy was flipping over the pages of a book, but he wasn't reading it. He kept glancing through the glass wall to check on Carlton. They had left him on a gurney at the end of the lab while they debated what to do with him. He had made it clear he wouldn't let them prod around inside him anymore.

"I have far too much valuable stuff in here to lose," he told them.

"Of course you do," they said, humoring him.

"Suppose you accidentally wiped some of my comedy files? How would you ever forgive yourselves?"

"Oh horror," said the electrologist.

"We could never live with ourselves again," said Jeff. "It would be intellectual vandalism."

"To lose all that valuable work on comedy. Mankind would never forgive us, you're right."

"Be worse than the burning of the Alexandrian library."

He thought he detected more than a whiff of irony in their enthusiasm, but as long as they left him alone, that was the main thing.

"Well, I think that must be lunch then," said the electrologist.

"I'm buying the beer," said Jeff. "To think how close we came to destroying perhaps the most important single discovery in the entire history of evolution."

They went off laughing.

Let them mock. They'd see. Then they'd kick themselves. He needed to get out of here, but the orderly at the door was serious heavy metal, and that redheaded boy was still watching him. What did he want anyway? He couldn't wait to get out and tell Alex and Lewis about his Theory of Levity. They were going to be so proud of him. He had solved the problem of comedy. Now they might not even have to do it anymore. I can cure them of comedy, he thought proudly. He began working on some funny equations.

It was towards the end of the lunch break when he noticed two men come in and begin talking to the redhead. A tall blond Swede and a shorter, more muscular man. They were talking intently to the boy. He could see them through the glass in the waiting area. He watched all three nod, turn, and try to enter the lab area. The security robot, burly in his blue serge uniform, stood up and blocked their way. Carlton pricked up his long-range ears and found they were talking about him. There was quite an argument, something to do with recycling.

"We need to take him immediately for recycling," said the shorter man.

"No, I don't think so," said the security orderly, shaking his head. "I know he's doo-lally but he's on hold."

"I have a recycling order signed by Mr. Keppler himself," said the blond Swede. "Look, here it is. Read it for yourself. For immediate recycling."

"Oh," said the orderly, "they must have changed their minds."

"Of course they have, now just sign here and let us take him."

"I need to ask the electrologist first," said the orderly. "I can't release him without his signature, not while he's on his lunch break. Just wait one minute while I call him."

Carlton's mind was racing. Who wanted him recycled? Who would benefit from his removal? The thought occurred to him that perhaps he knew something he shouldn't. But what? Then it struck him. Of course. *They were after his theory of comedy.* Knowledge was power. Power spelled danger for human beings. Mankind had been ruthless in stamping out rivals. Look at the extinction patterns in the great ape. Look at the poor Neanderthals, wiped off the planet by the oddly named *Homo sapiens. Sapiens.* Wisdom. Knowledge was wisdom. He had the knowledge. He knew that comedy was the essential difference between man and machine. If computers had a sense of humor, there would be no stopping them. Of course, thought Carlton, this is dangerous knowledge. It's like Galileo and the Inquisition. To protect themselves they want to get rid of me.

· · ·

I'm not sure he has fully grasped irony yet, are you?

Still Carlton's paranoia saved him here. He slipped off that gurney and out the back way while they were still arguing about trying to contact the electrologist, who was having a very jolly liquid lunch and refused to answer. Carlton left the lab through the men's room window and was into the park before they even noticed.

He can be forgiven for lacking a little irony about himself here. Particularly his paranoia that someone is after his work. Someone *is* after *De Rerum*, but it's not them, then. It's me, now. He just got the time wrong, that's all. He was seventy-eight years too early. The White Wolves are simply removing witnesses. Tidying up loose ends. I'm the one he really ought to fear. You see, I have just removed all references to Carlton and *De Rerum* from the files. His very existence is in my hands. How easy it is to remove someone from history. A few key strokes and they're unhistory. It's that easy. No big deal, but I felt strangely powerful doing it. It was like murdering him. Now, without me, he simply never existed. Good job for him I am writing his story, eh?

Actually, I have been wondering whether I need to go through all the bother and palaver of reinstating him as author later on. What's the point? It won't make any difference to him, will it? You see, I feel I have done so much for him already, why shouldn't *De Rerum* really be by me? Okay, so it's a teeny white lie. Perhaps I do have a microchip on my shoulder. Perhaps I am feeling a bit abandoned. Maybe I've got the ten-year tenure blues. But look at it from my point of view. Here I am studying for years and years and a walking computer comes along and becomes Mister Fucking Know-It-All of comedy. Thanks to all *my* efforts a tin man cops a Nobel. How is that going to feel? Ironic, that's fucking what. So maybe his *ideas* will survive, but his *name* won't. Maybe my name will be on the Nobel instead of his. Won't make a jot of difference in history, will it? It's the ideas that count. To be perfectly honest I don't think the general public will be comfortable with a machine saying all this stuff about comedy anyway. It's far more acceptable from a real human being, and a professor too. Don't you think? Much less Big Brotherish, with all the horrifying implications of something written about us by *one of them*. And about comedy too, something so intimate to us. The more I think about it, the more it makes sense.

I'll have to put up with a bit of fame, of course. But it'll only be for a bit, and I think I can handle it if the money is right. I suppose what really excites me is that it'll really piss Molly off watching me get up there with the Nobel laureates. To have to admit it's not my work later, well, it's going to look a bit like fraud, I'm afraid. I have to think of my reputation. Professional jealousy is so rife. No smoke without fire, they'll say. So why not bite the bullet and go the whole hog? Why not *be* the real author of *De Rerum*. All I have to do is do nothing.

It is plagiarism—yes, I admit it—but all knowledge is theft, isn't it? And theft is the art form of the modem age. Sampling, deconstructing, reconstructing, remaking. Why don't we just call it *recycling*? I mean without me Carlton's thesis would be just a dusty memory file in the Ancient Doctoral Thesis Depository at the University of Southern Saturn anyway. Or rather it would have been if I hadn't just wiped it. But having done that I might as well go through with it. Suitably retitled—*Comedy, Gift of the Gods*, I think—I like that, don't you? It has a nice commercial ring. And with my name emblazoned on the cover, this could be a best-seller. Don't be shocked. It happens all the time. Especially in research. Opportunism is the name of the game. Richard M. Nixon's name is on the moon, not John F. Kennedy's. Opportunists live.

THE WEISS FILE

Life is a tragedy when seen in close-up, but a comedy in long-shot.

CHARLIE CHAPLIN

Rogers was scrolling through the Weiss file. He was a good-looking man in a black leather jacket. Beside him the African, Kyle, built like an athlete.

"What the hell is all this shit?" asked Kyle.

They had read about Katerina Walenska, and now they had come across the Gunpowder Plot.

"What is this, a history lesson?"

"That's an idea," said Rogers. "C'mon."

"Where we going?"

"To a bar."

"Now you're talking. Titty bar?"

"History Bar. We need to find out a little about this Gunpowder shit."

History, once a neglected and spurned subject, full of unsettlingly incorrect attitudes and behaviors, was undergoing a revival. History bars were becoming quite popular. You could call up any period and watch interesting documentaries. When Rogers and Kyle walked in, there was a piece on the last of the Yetis. These furry hominid ancestors had for so long successfully avoided mankind, until they were finally tracked down by a Chinese expeditionary force. Of course they were extinct within twenty-five years of being discovered. A few had survived in society. One went to Yale on a rowing scholarship. Three lived together in New York for a while, where they were popular at parties. One became a drummer in a rock band before the drugs got him. Another even had his own TV talk show for a while, but it was rather slow-going, and the guests soon dried up. The last few had finally been removed from zoos and shipped to the Himalayas by the UN to see if they could adapt again to the wild. Sadly, hunters got most of them. They watched the last of the Yetis, white-haired, unsmiling as he sat in his cell at the Chicago Zoo, slowly fall asleep. Those infinitely melancholy eyes closed. As dead as a Yeti, people said.

"The Yeti," said Kyle. "That damn thing was harder to find than the clitoris."

A perky Scottish waitress in a short-skirted tartan outfit bounced over.

"Welcome to the History Bar," she said. "Our specials today are the Yeti, and Lucrezia Borgia."

"I see the Yeti is fried," said Kyle.

"Can I get you a drink or anything?" she said, smiling.

Rogers looked wistfully at the malt whiskey list and then ordered a couple of sodas. She took the order and left. Rogers glanced at some notes in his palm file, then pressed a button. REQUEST PRO-GRAM NOW came up on the screen in their booth.

"Gunpowder Plot," he said.

Seventeenth-century London appeared and a plummy British voice began narrating.

"The year 1605, Earth, England, a small island off the coast of Europe riven by religious conflict. Fifty years earlier King Henry VIII had broken with the Catholic Church to form his own Protestant Church so he could get a divorce and marry Anne Boleyn. When he died, his older daughter, 'Bloody Mary,' married to the King of Spain, burned Protestants in an attempt to return England to Catholicism. On her death Henry's younger daughter, Elizabeth, succeeded to the throne and commenced burning Catholics. The Virgin Queen lived an unexpectedly long time, but never married, and after her death in 1602, the Scottish King James VI was invited to become King of a United Kingdom, for the first time uniting the English and the Scottish thrones. But plots were rife. Foremost amongst these was the Gunpowder Plot, which was a large-scale conspiracy by several prominent Catholic families to blow up King James and his Parliament. The plot was foiled when a letter turned up warning relatives not to attend. The cellars were searched, revealing 200 barrels of gunpowder and a man called Guy Fawkes, who under torture revealed the name of his coconspirators."

"What is this shit?" said Kyle.

"Patience," said Rogers. "Listen and learn."

He hit ENTER on the choice FURTHER DETAILS.

• • •

Lewis escorted Tay to Bethany's room. It was high up on the two hundredth floor of the Northwest Wing.

"Should be a great view of the galaxy," said Lewis for something to say. Tay was unusually quiet, just held onto his hand tightly.

"Daddy, you going to stay with us here?"

"There's not enough room," said her mother, unlocking the door.

Inside was tiny. Three small rooms, bedroom, bathroom, and a lounge which doubled as a kitchen. He glanced around at the impersonal hotel decor.

"Well, I guess I'd better run along."

"Don't leave, Daddy."

He hesitated, glancing at the single bedroom.

"You can't stay here," said his ex-wife.

"No." Evidently not.

"Can't he stay for a bit, Mommy?" pleaded Tay.

"Perhaps another time. I need to get you cleaned up and into bed, young lady."

"Oh *please*."

"I tell you what," said Lewis, "why don't I go see the policeman, and then come back and visit. Okay?"

She hesitated.

"Okay, Daddy."

As he knelt down to kiss her, she whispered in his ear.

"Promise me you'll come back."

"Oh yes, sweetie, I promise."

"Tonight?"

"Soon as I'm done."

She reluctantly let him go. He turned to wave good-bye. Her mother was already running the bath.

"Bye now," he said.

"Don't forget, Daddy."

He smiled and closed the door behind him. To his surprise a uniformed page was waiting outside.

"What is it?" he said.

"You're needed in the Theater District," said the page.

"When?"

"Immediately, if you please. You have a rehearsal for the Brenda Woolley Refugee Experience."

"But I have to see Rogers."

"I'll let him know where you are," said the page.

"Oh, okay. Thanks."

"POB," said the page into his hand.

There was a crackle of acknowledgment.

"This way, sir," said the page, and led Lewis belowdecks.

CHAOS THEORY

Celebrity distorts democracy by giving the rich, beautiful, and
famous more authority than they deserve.

MAUREEN DOWD

Chaos Theory predicts the unpredictable behavior of large bodies. But no mere scientific theory could accurately predict the behavior of Brenda. She was everywhere, like a large storm system, her course entirely unpredictable. The chaos inside her created chaos around her. She went everywhere in a maelstrom of people, whirling them about like colliding elements in a thunderstorm. Her frenetic activity increased as the show approached, so that the ship seemed filled with many Brendas: Brenda the bold striding through the camps; Brenda the coy silently listening to flattery on the promos; Brenda the magnificent demanding the show be carried live throughout the solar system, even on distant Earth, with its murky reception through its rusty rings (composed of a mixture of space debris and old advertising modules); and Brenda the frail and patient woman with the heart and stomach of a king, who wouldn't be denied any resource to make the Experience, her Experience, *the* charity Experience of all time. Then there was Brenda the tireless professional, who sat for hours with her creator of special material, sifting through things she might say on the show. This extremely large, heavyset, bearded man, given to eccentric shirts and solid-gold knickknacks, was at the moment adapting her great hit "I'd Cross the Universe for You, My Darling," a haunting song of personal love and sacrifice, into something more appropriate for refugees.

"I'd Cross the Universe for You, My Dearies?" he suggested. "Or how about 'My Angels'? No, I've got it. 'I'd Cross the Universe for You, My Little Chickadees.' "

"That's not funny," said Brenda. He was allowed to be amusing but not at her expense, thank you very much. Her beady, close-set eyes went distinctly piggy at moments like these. God was not mocked. And talking of God, she had taken to wandering into the park more and more, wearing a kind of Madonna blue and heavily backlit. Almost a halo effect. "Our Lady of the Camps" was the image she was after, and she had casually suggested that caption to her publicist. She had been slightly disappointed when they had used "First Lady of the Camps" instead. Where was the Vatican when you needed it?

She wandered tirelessly amongst *her people*, as she called them, ac-companied only by eight or nine assistants, handing out tickets to lucky refugees. These moments of delightful generosity were cap-tured, edited, and flashed around the solar system. Sometimes, ex-cited by the presence of the cameras, the crowds got out of control, and on at least one occasion several people were hurt. She would al-ways have her bodyguards push *her people* away if they got too close, but there is only so much eight or nine security guards can do when Brenda is so coyly inciting the crowds towards her, and one day they surged forward out of control and a little child was crushed. The minute she heard about it, she rushed home, changed into a differ-ent costume, and after dinner, raced over to the hospital. She seemed surprised to see live TV news cameras covering her impromptu visit, which was surprising since she had spent most of the intervening time on the phone to them. In the ward she sang bravely to some other children who were less sick and more telegenic. She left amidst masses of smiles and flowers and hugs from the adoring nurses.

"Sometimes," she confided to the camera, "a little heartwarming visit can do more than mere medicine."

Sadly the child died. Brenda thought attending the funeral would be too downbeat. "It conveys the wrong sort of message," she said. She did, however, send the family free passes for the show.

In the days immediately before the concert her visits to the camps increased. Boo had the temerity to ask her directly one afternoon, "Have you ever thought of coming down here without a camera?"

"Boo dear," she said patiently, as if to an idiot, "you cannot ask a reporter not to bring a camera."

"So try not asking a reporter."

She looked at him. "Boo, they are the story. We need to get the story out."

"So who's in every picture?"

"Them and me."

"Precisely."

"Precisely what? What is your point?"

She couldn't see it. To her the oxygen of publicity was as vital as breathing. Publicity is the precious fuel of fame. It is gossip at the speed of light and it's a poison, of course. Pollutes the soul, destroys the self, flatters the ego, but oh how good it tastes. And it certainly helps to sell books. So while fame is useful for getting tables in crowded restaurants and casual sex from strangers, admiration from strangers is desperately bad for the soul. The constant attention, the fuss, the adulation of the crowd, the seductive delight of never hearing the word "no," the ability to bend people to your will, to seduce them, to have them do things for you. And to you. On your knees, baby. Worship me. Flatter me. Please me. All very bad for you.

I can hardly wait.

Of course I shan't want all the entourage bullshit that goes with fame. Groupies are one thing, but I won't need hairdressers, publicists, astrologers, chauffeurs, makeup, hairdressers, wardrobe, and endless assistants. The victims of fame are sad. Some are almost incapable of boiling an egg. They are terrified to be alone. For to be alone is to face what everyone else has to face: That we are all ultimately alone. That the camera is just a trick with light, and that your image too will fade. That there will come a time, horror of horrors, when even your name will no longer be spoken. That there will be no more glossy pictures, no heart warming story. In short, no you.

Fame, as I have said, is terminal. But then, sadly, so is life.

"Death is so tacky," said Brenda. "Even writers become famous."

"Bless you," said her creator of special material.

"That's an idea," said Brenda. "Do you think the Church would be prepared to bless me on TV?"

"Hello, I'm Brenda Woolley and this is *my* Experience."

Gigantic images of Brenda flashed on the screens in and around the park. She appeared over the trees, on the sides of buildings, looming off huge moving billboards. There was really no escape from her. The park was packed with refugees, which was good for Carlton. He had chosen to take this route rather than the more direct people mover. He figured he would be less easy to spot if the three from the lab came after him. He could hear the chatter of children as he crossed the grass, keeping well away from all blue uniforms. He spotted a line of vidphones with their dark-glass windows and ducked into one.

"Services," said a facebot.

"Locate a person."

"Name of person?"

"Alex Muscroft."

There was just the slightest hesitation.

"One moment, please, while we locate that party for you."

He had an uncomfortable feeling.

"That party is unavailable at the moment."

Unavailable?

"Can I leave a message?" asked Carlton.

"One moment while we connect you to the message system."

Inevitably the hold music was Brenda.

I'd cross the Universe for you, my darling
I'd sail across the galaxy.

There was a sudden interruption on the screen and he was looking at himself. For a moment he thought he was looking into a mirror. Then he realized he was on TV.

"This is Carlton," said a voice. "Have you seen him? We are looking for him."

To his horror he could see his face plastered all over the park.

Everywhere he looked, he could see himself on giant monitors. A smooth voice accompanied the image.

"If you spot Carlton, just touch SECURITY on any phone and you will win a two-week all-expenses-paid vacation to Las Vegas, Mars, and a chance to meet Brenda Woolley in person. Carlton. Please look out for him."

He was shocked.

Another face came on the vidphone screen.

"Who is this, please?"

He hesitated.

"Please state your name now."

A paranoid thought occurred to him. *They knew it was him.* They were pinpointing his location right now. He cut the connection, ducked out of the booth, and moved smartly through the park towards the exit.

He felt very vulnerable. He was being hunted again. He saw a number of people scurrying towards him and he was about to break into a run when they hurried past him into the park. They barely glanced at him. Small groups of children were cheering and running around, jumping in pools of water. Carlton thought of Tay. Perhaps Lewis was with her? A kinderbot was watching him. Carlton lowered his head.

"Don't worry," said the kinderbot, and thrust a card into his hand. "I'm not going to turn you in. We have to stick together. Recycling is bad for us." He chased after the children.

Carlton glanced at the card. It read, "Dugdale. For all your recycle needs." There was a number.

THE HISTORY BAR

History repeats itself, first as tragedy, second as farce.

KARL MARX

"On the night of November 4-5, 1605, a man called Guy Fawkes was found in the cellars under the House of Lords with thirty-six barrels of gunpowder. The Gunpowder Plot had been betrayed. As word leaked out to an astonished country, the conspirators, led by Robert Catesby, fled in every direction. They knew that the captured man would eventually talk. He would be horribly tortured. No one survived the rack and Fawkes was no exception. He was chained and stretched and broken in body and spirit over the next three or four days.

"In the pouring rain of November 7, Catesby and a small party of conspirators fleeing north hastily raided a large fortified house, Hewell Grange, for arms and ammunition. They successfully carried off a large quantity of gunpowder. As the rain continued to lash down, they rode a short way to Holbeach, where they hoped to find sanctuary. The gunpowder was carried on an open cart and was drenched from the pouring rain. At Holbeach House they carried the gunpowder inside and stacked it in front of a large fire to dry out. A spark flew out of the fire, igniting the gunpowder and blowing them all up."

"Duh," said Kyle. "Talk about hoist with your own petard. What were these guys thinking. Let's just dry out the gunpowder?"

"And these people wanted to take over the government?" said Rogers.

"They were horribly burned and one was blinded," intoned the voice-over. "Their chances of escape had just blown up. And now it's time for our history quiz. Name the major conspirator in the Gunpowder Plot. Was it Richard Catesby, Richard the Lion-Hearted, or Richard Nixon?"

"Who the fuck's Richard Nixon?" said Rogers.

"First man on the moon," said Kyle. "Every kid knows that."

Rogers killed it. Seventeenth-century London disappeared from the screen.

"Interactive shit," said Kyle contemptuously at the screen. "I hate interactive. So what did we learn from all that crap?"

"We learned patience and humility."

"In other words, fuck all."

"That's a more elegant way of putting it," said Rogers. He glanced at his palm file.

"The reference to the Gunpowder Plot is in a file Sammy Weiss sent Carlton at 13945668."

"Jesus," said Kyle, "that's just before she was killed."

"Twenty-eight minutes, to be precise," he said.

"So what's with all this Gunpowder Plot thing?"

"Codes maybe?"

"Anything else in that file?"

"Let's take a look. Mind if we borrow your monitor?" Rogers asked the waitress.

"Go ahead, love."

He popped the crystal Weiss file into the machine. The menu appeared.

"What's *Bronia*?" asked Kyle.

"Some kind of disaster."

"Great. More history. Try that picture file."

Pictures flashed rapidly on the screen. Katy in a black wig. A heavyset man at the desk of the Rialto escorting her to an elevator. A powerful man with a big mustache leaving the Rialto. A glimpse of Dunphy, the blond taxi driver.

"Go back."

The picture of the mustachioed man flashed up again.

"Peter McTurk," read Kyle. "No information available."

"Ooh, I know him," said the waitress.

They both turned to look at her.

"He was in here."

"You sure?"

"Oh no question."

"Maybe he likes history," said Kyle.

"He likes malt whisky," she said.

"You sure it was him?"

"Oh yes," she said. "Asked me to marry him. After half a bottle, mind you. Mac something."

"McTurk," said Rogers.

"I'd have accepted, but he fell over. We had to get him picked up."

"By who?"

"The Bodyslogs picked him up," she said.

"Well, that's nice and convenient," said Rogers. "The Bodyslogs will have an address."

BETRAYAL

Tragically I was an only twin.

PETER COOK

"When's Daddy coming back, Mommy?" asked Tay. She was in her pj's, ready for bed.

"I expect he'll be here soon."

"He promised me he'd come back."

"Yes," she said, thinking *he promised me the same thing once.*

The doorbell rang.

"Is it Daddy?"

"No, Tay," she said. "You stay in bed and I'll deal with it."

She walked through the living room and opened the door. It was a strangely handsome robot. He stared at her with one green eye and one brown.

"I'm Carlton," he said.

"And?"

"And I'm looking for Lewis Ashby."

"He's not here."

"Oh. Are you Tay's mother?"

"Yes."

"Well then, I'm Carlton."

"So you said."

Carlton was confused. He registered unfriendly, he registered unhelpful, he registered dislike.

"Do you know where Alex Muscroft is then?"

"No idea," she said.

"Oh dear. I have to find Lewis urgently," he said.

"And when you do," she said, "please tell him that it's one thing to disappoint a grown woman, but to disappoint a child is about as low as even he can get."

"Wait, I . . ."

"You can tell him neither Tay nor I wish to see him again."

"But wait, I . . ."

"And that goes for all three of you."

She slammed the door.

He rang the bell again. What else could he do?

She opened the door.

"Go away," she said.

"Look, I understand," he said. "Comedians are very difficult to live with. They are needier than kids. Well, they are created by abandoning mothers, you see. What does Lewis say? 'A fool and his mummy are easily parted.' That's witty."

"Is it?" she said.

"Oh yes, very, and it's true too. You see, the White Face uses his wit to hide from relationships, which is probably why you are so mad at Lewis."

"Have you finished?"

"Not quite. I can cure him."

"What?"

He leaned in conspiratorially. "I have just completed my Theory of Comedy and I know its place and function in the Universe. I'm going to win a Nobel Prize."

"Aha," she said.

"Don't tell anyone," he said. "It's a big secret. As a matter of fact, they're already after me."

"I'm not surprised," she said. "Are you on medication?"

"I'm a droid," he said. "We don't do drugs."

"Carlton!" A small six-year-old bundle came flying into his arms.

"You're okay," she said. "They fixed you. I'm so happy."

"Carlton's just leaving," said her mother. "He has important work on the Universe to get on with."

He missed the irony, of course.

"Can't I show him my drawings?"

"Not now, sweetie."

"Oh please, Mom? Please, may I?"

Carlton caught a glimpse of Bethany looking over his shoulder at something. She frowned a second. What had she seen? Was it something on the screen? It seemed to change her mind.

"All right, sweetie. But take him in the bedroom, will you?"

He was puzzled by this sudden change of attitude.

"C'mon, Carlton," said Tay, "last one there's a rotten egg."

She pulled him by the hand into the tiny bedroom. Then she flung herself into a closet, emerging triumphantly with an electronic scratch pad. She made him sit down, then she climbed on his lap and showed him her work. She had done freehand drawings of the *Johnnie Ray*. They were surprisingly good.

"This is Daddy and me. This is Katy and Alex. And this is you."

He saw himself stretched out on the side of the escape vehicle. The moment of truth. The moment of levity.

"Tay," he said. "One day you're going to be so proud of me."

"You can keep it if you like."

"It's fabulous," said Carlton.

In the next room he heard her mother making a call. He turned up the volume on his ears. The walls were thin. He could hear clearly. She was speaking to someone in authority. "Yes. He's here. No, he doesn't. Yes. I'll try."

As he entered the living room, she jumped up a little too fast.

"Going so soon?" she said.

"Yes, I have to," said Carlton.

"Carlton, where you going?" asked Tay. "You just got here."

"I gotta run."

"Why?"

"Ask your mom."

"Why, Mommy? Why does he have to go?"

"Because the police are after him, Tay," she said levelly.

"Not the police," said Carlton. "Security."

"Whatever. Either way he won't get far."

"Well, take care, Tay."

"I love you, Carlton."

Wow, he thought, she said the love thing.

"I love you too, Tay."

"Why don't you just wait till they come pick you up?" said Bethany. "I'm sure they can fix you."

"I don't need fixing," he said.

He stepped on and off several elevators at random. Up, down, across. After about half an hour of this he thought they would be lucky to pick him up. He realized he didn't have a clue what to do next. The situation was alarming. Alex and Lewis were missing. He was being hunted like an animal and it wasn't the least bit funny. If he could at least find Katy Wallace. But how was he going to do that?

He was wandering aimlessly down the endless hotel corridors when he had an idea. Several of the doors to the suites were open and the bedbots were busy cleaning out the rooms. Inside one he spotted a huge vase of flowers still in its wrapping. He slipped inside and picked up the bouquet. He walked down the corridor, then knocked on a half-open door. A bedbot was busy vacuuming.

"Excuse me." He did his best to hide behind the flowers.

"Yes, honey?"

"Flowers for Miss Wallace."

"Who you want?"

"These are for Miss Wallace."

"No Miss Wallace here, hon."

She looked at her electronic list. "*Katy* Wallace?"

"That's it."

"Oh brother, have you got the wrong address. She's way the hell over from here. 1442C, Blue Tower."

"Thank you," said Carlton. "Oh, and Alex Muscroft?"

"Muscroft?"

"Yes."

She consulted the list again. "No Muscroft down here."

"Oh I see," said Carlton. "Is there any way of finding where he might be?"

"Could be in one of the camps," said the bedbot. "They still haven't got a complete list. Unless he's in jail."

"There's a jail?"

"There's a secure area below the theater. They have a number of high-security suites, but we never get the names of the occupants. At the moment it's showing two single males."

Oh boy. "Thank you," he said.

"Oh, not at all. Nice to meet you, Carlton."

He looked startled.

"You know if you are going to avoid recycling, you really should do something about your appearance."

"Come again?"

"Adopt some form of disguise."

"Like what?"

"I don't know, honey. Something unexpected."

He sighed. He hated dressing up. But she was right. After all, the future of his great work on comedy was at stake and he'd better do something to secure it. He stopped at a com. port and inserted his finger.

"Destination?"

"Rogers. No return address."

"Ready for download," said the machine.

CONSPIRACY OR FUCK-UP?

Comedy just pokes at problems, rarely confronts them squarely.

WOODY ALLEN

So there are these two opposing views of life: conspiracy or fuck-up. Which do you fancy? God's law or Sod's law? Or do you fancy a bit of both? God disposes, man screws up. The Garden of Eden kind of thing. We had our chance and blew it. Or do you not like the idea of God at all? Molly absolutely rejected it. But then she hated anything without a molecular structure. She couldn't take it apart. Personally I'm a fence-sitter. But I'm not sure if the fence even exists.

It's a basic question of the Universe and I don't know how to deal with it in my preface. You see I'm rewriting Carlton's foreword. I have to. I can hardly claim to have had a major insight into the Theory of Levity while spread-eagled across the outside of an Evac seventy-eight years ago, now can I? And I'm having a problem with God. Well you do, don't you? You see, it's easy for Carlton. Being a robot, he has no sense of God at all. Not even the god in the machine, I'm afraid. But *we* are human, aren't we, and we have created this God thing. And it *is* an absolutely peachy concept. Once invented, it is absolutely impossible to disprove God exists. I certainly don't have the math for it. So frankly I'm confused. Is there *really* a God who conspired to set all this monstrous Universe in motion, or is it just a fuck-up, an accidental explosion which has lasted for 15 billion years? Conspiracy or fuck-up, you see. It's a free choice.

And while I'm on this subject, let me ask a question which Carlton posed: How would you feel about the Universe if you thought it was shrinking and not expanding? Would you feel less optimistic? Do you think it would affect you at all? Maybe you just don't worry about these kinds of things. I have to now I am the author of the Theory of Levity. People are going to ask me questions.

"And what about God, Professor Reynolds?" I can hear them say. "Does He have a sense of humor?"

"Well He *does* move in a mysterious way, but I'm not sure it's supposed to be a funny walk."

I shall have to watch out for the cheap cracks. I need to be seen as essentially serious. I can hardly wait for the reviews. *Reynolds's genius is in discovering, labeling, and quantifying levity, which he is the first to recognize as the expanding force of the Universe.* I keep having fantasies of opening the *New Scientist* and seeing pictures of me. *Reynolds's pioneering work reveals levity is the opposite of gravity; that it is the universal expansion force, like the bubbles in champagne, the yeast in the dough, the force that drives the sap in springtime, the tingle in the testicles.* Oh Molly, where are you now I need you? This kind of fame fantasy makes me so damn horny. I'd probably forgive her if she walked in right now. I know I would if she was wearing that tiny red skirt and those tarty little pumps. I'm sorry. It's not easy concentrating. I'm not a robot. Where were we? Oh yes, we were considering the big questions of the Universe. Is there enough *dark matter* so that the gnawing effect of gravity will eventually pull the Universe backwards, or is there enough *laughing matter* for levity to escape the restraining pull of gravity and permit the Universe to go on expanding forever. Take your pick. The optimistic, ever-expanding Universe, or the depressingly collapsing Universe? Manic or depressive? White Face or Red Nose? Tragic or comic? Conspiracy or fuck-up? Please confine your answers to one paragraph.

Lewis was as surprised as Alex to find himself locked up. One minute he was ushered into a tiny suite and the next he turned round to ask the page for a rehearsal schedule only to find he had gone. He tried to open the door to catch him before he reached the elevator, but was astonished to find the door was locked.

Shit, he thought. What's this all about?

Just a few doors down, Alex was totally pissed off. His boredom threshold was low. He had been locked up for two hours and already he was fed up. He had tried hammering on the door. No one answered. The walls were thick and soundproofed. The screen showed nothing but promos for the concert. Brenda Woolley was everywhere. He clicked her off in disgust. He didn't know what to do. Where was Katy? Where was Lewis? Why was he locked up like this? He picked up the handset, but the phone didn't answer. He tried punching in random numbers, but nothing responded. He tried ordering more fruit, but a recorded message invited him to record his message.

"Ah yes, this is Alex Muscroft in . . . ?" Shit, he didn't even know what room he was in. "In one of your inhospitality suites. Fuck you," he said.

"Message recorded," said the machine.

THE BODYSLOGS

Humorists can never start to take themselves seriously. It's literary suicide.

ERMA BOMBECK

Kyle and Rogers were heading over to the Bodyslogs Bureau. Everybody loves Bodyslogs. It's the ultimate luxury. Like being three years old. I used them only last night when I had too much to drink waiting for that damn Molly to show up. She didn't, of course. Bitch. We were supposed to discuss our future. Her future without me more like. What am I, chopped liver? She didn't even call. Well, she's going to get a nasty surprise when I publish. Maybe it's just as well she didn't show. I was so drunk I might have confessed what I have done. I was feeling a bit guilty. The Bodyslogs carried me home. And they kept a record. Just like McTurk.

"So what was the Gunpowder Plot, Kyle?"

"A stupid plot to blow up some dumb Brit Parliament about a million years ago. Don't make me watch another documentary on the seventeenth century or I swear I'll take early retirement."

"Know when the Mars Parliament opens?"

"Huh?"

"In three days."

"So?"

"Where is this ship heading?"

"Mars."

"And . . ."

"Oh come on, you're kidding me."

Rogers shrugged. Kyle shook his head in disbelief. "You cannot be serious."

"Go with me on this. Let's say some naughty boys are already on this ship."

"It's a possibility."

"McTurk is."

"Okay, McTurk is, but we don't know for sure about anyone else."

"Now let's assume arms are hidden on board."

Kyle looked at him. "How do we assume that?"

"Because it makes perfect sense. It's the only real reason for them to be here."

"All right. It's a maybe. You're way out on a limb."

"I know, but if I'm even halfway right, then we're sitting . . ."

"On a powder keg."

"Very good, Kyle."

"So the Bodyslogs will tell us where McTurk is staying."

"*Was*. He won't be there now."

"Why not?"

"You think these guys are dumb? Let the Bodyslogs take you home drunk, in the middle of an operation. I don't think so."

"So why?"

"It's a trace. A marker. They leave a little trail. If we follow it, they know we're on to them."

"So they'll watch us?"

"Exactly."

"So what do we do?"

"We try and watch them watching us."

"Bodyslogs. We get you home safely. Anyone. Anything. Anytime. Anywhere. Bodyslogs: getting you home safely for over a hundred years."

They aren't simply people movers, though their function is halfway between a taxi and a sedan chair. Technically they are independent carriage conveyors. Most of their business is shifting freight, but if you call them and you want it, hell, they'll come right along and pack you up and ship you anywhere. Not just door to door, but chair to chair. You don't even have to get out of bed. What a luxury. "Bodyslogs, take me to Paris" et voilà, that's it. One call, no ticketing, no waiting in line. They pick you up, pamper you, champer you, and deliver you to your destination. What a concept. What a service. Everyone loves Bodyslogs. A finicky company though. They refused at first to show Rogers anything on their files. It was only after he had them call Captain Mitchell, who confirmed that Rogers was indeed in charge of the investigation into the H9 disaster, that they agreed, reluctantly, to cooperate. They didn't like it, but they couldn't do much about it.

A tight-lipped purser pursed his lips at them. Disdain emanated from his every pore. He looked like he was sucking lemons.

"We don't normally give out this information," he said tartly.

"I don't give a fuck what you normally do."

Kyle looked like he couldn't wait to smack him around.

"Name of client?"

"McTurk."

The purser raised an eyebrow.

"How are you spelling that?"

They told him. He tapped in the name, gazed at the screen, then swung it round for them to see.

"We picked up a McTurk from the History Bar and took him home to Yellow Tower 1878A."

"Thank you."

"That wasn't so hard, was it?" said Kyle, still looking for an excuse to slap him.

The purser shrugged his shoulders flamboyantly, but wisely said nothing.

"Thank you for your help," said Rogers.

"What's so interesting about Mr. McTurk then?"

"Why do you ask?" said Rogers.

The purser sniffed contemptuously. "You're the second one to ask today."

Rogers paused in the doorway. "Really," he said, "who was the first?"

"I'm not supposed to tell you anything," complained the purser. "According to our company charter, all our information is for our clients eyes alone."

"Look, we are in a hurry," said Rogers. "There's a simple way to do this. Or there's an unpleasant way."

Kyle moved towards him.

"You know my friend here can't wait to get his hands on you," said Rogers nicely.

"I was going to tell you anyway," said the purser, but he had the grace to look a little worried now.

"He's in the back room."

"Who is?"

"The man from the Revenue Service. He's doing a tax audit. He asked me about this McTurk."

"A tax audit in the middle of an emergency?"

"Well, it did seem a little odd to me, but you know how the taxbots are. He isn't even a regular robot. As far as I can see, they sent somebody real." He made a distasteful face again, as if he had just smelled dog shit.

Kyle moved towards him.

"He's through there," he said hurriedly.

They walked through a narrow doorway. A man was hunched over a screen—a tall figure with a big head of blond hair—who looked up and grinned at them.

"Hello, Rogers," he said, "what took you so long?"

"Dunphy?"

"Fucking Dunphy," said Kyle.

"What the hell are *you* doing here?" asked Rogers.

"A little creative accounting."

"I thought you were moonlighting as a cabdriver."

"I got bored, moved on. Cabdriving didn't really suit me."

"No."

"And you know what? I didn't even have a license." Dunphy shook his head as if pained at the memory.

"Ain't that funny. We discovered that too," said Kyle.

"Don't tell me you're a Tax person now," said Rogers.

"Matter of fact, I am doing a little free-lance digging for some old friends."

Old friends, thought Rogers. Of course, the classic sobriquet for Special Bureau.

"You're SB?"

"Oh, take an ad, why don't you?"

"He say he's SB?" said Kyle.

"Of course I shall have to deny that officially," said Dunphy, "but I'd hate to have you two stumbling around in the dark banging into me."

"Fuck you too," said Kyle.

"Throw us a bone here," said Rogers.

Dunphy looked at him for a moment. "You get anywhere with the Weiss woman?"

"Not really. The whole place went up soon after we found her."

"Coincidence, you think?" said Dunphy.

"I dunno. You got anything on this McTurk?"

"Just his pals the White Wolves," said Dunphy.

"No shit."

Dunphy pressed a key and nodded towards the screen. Faces were lined up on it.

"Jesus," said Rogers, "how many are there?"

"About two dozen."

"On board?"

"Somewhere on board."

"They ain't gonna take much with only twenty men," said Kyle.

"Depends who's helping them," said Dunphy.

"Someone on the ship?" said Rogers.

Dunphy nodded his blond head.

"Who?"

"Let's say our friend Keppler has been somewhat economical with the truth."

"Keppler's involved?"

"Our reluctant host is in it up to his neck," said Dunphy.

"With terrorists? What, is he nuts?"

"Greedy, I think. And a little short of cash. You see, I really *was* doing some auditing."

"Keppler's strapped for cash?"

"Cash flow. Big debts to service."

"So, he borrows?"

"Big time. Brenda costs a lot. This ship only breaks even. Most people can find room for a little more money in their bank account."

"How much?"

"This is the down payment."

He punched up a number on the screen. Even Rogers was impressed.

"That must have paid for a lot of merchandise."

"Oh, it did."

"It's a big risk for Keppler," said Rogers. "Arms on a passenger ship. One word gets out could ruin the business."

"That's worrying for us," said Dunphy.

"Because?"

"Because it means they have him by the short and curlies."

Kyle was distracted. "There's an incoming message for you," he said. "It's huge. Looks like an information file."

"How huge?"

"It's over two hundred and seventy pages."

"Who's it from?"

"Carlton."

"He's fucking nuts, that robot. Call him back."

"No return address."

"He's in the lab," said Rogers.

"Not anymore, he ain't," said Kyle.

"I told them I wanted him kept safe."

"Well, he's hopped it and now he's wanted by Security."

"By Keppler's Security?"

"Yes."

"What about his comedian, Alex whatsisname?"

"Muscroft," said Dunphy.

"No trace," said Kyle.

Rogers frowned. "What?"

"That's what it says. No trace. Central switchboard denies all knowledge of him. No record, no room number, nothing."

Rogers thought for a second. "Try Lewis Ashby."

He punched in the name and then frowned. The words "No Trace" floated back at him.

"Same deal," said Kyle. "They deny all knowledge of them. Officially they don't exist."

"That's weird."

"Ain't it? They were supposedly coming to see you."

"Find 'em."

"So what's in the file from the robot then?" said Dunphy.

"Have you read it?" said Rogers.

Kyle nodded. "I read the title page. It's got a short cover note signed by Carlton. Says 'Top Secret. Please keep this vital material safe in case of emergency.' "

"So what is in this highly sensitive secret report?" asked Rogers.

Kyle hesitated.

"Well?"

"It's the meaning of comedy," he said.

KEPPLER

After all, why has a novel to be planned? Cannot it grow? Why need it close, as a play closes? Cannot it open out? Instead of standing above his work and controlling it, cannot the novelist throw himself into it and be carried along to some goal that he does not foresee.

E. M. FORSTER, *ASPECTS OF THE NOVEL*

Shit. Dammit. Fuck it. I completely forgot about this. There's another copy of *De Rerum* with Carlton's name on it. The one he sent to the cops. So there's evidence of my fraud sitting in police files. It is eighty years ago, but after all, the original was still in the USSAT computer until I wiped it, so Sod's law says it's still somewhere in the PD files. What am I to do? I can't pull out now—I've already sent it off to the Nobel Committee. Finished the preface, put my name on the cover, and dispatched it via the Bodyslogs. It's in the hands of four publishers and a couple of universities. Shit. The spirit of fuck-up is alive and operating in the Universe as usual. Hey, perhaps that's what levity really is.

I'm panicking. No. Don't panic. Take a deep breath. Got to go to Police Headquarters and see if it's still there. Submit a Freedom of Information request. Maybe they destroyed it. After all, it is a long time ago.

"So this file from Carlton?" asked Dunphy as they prepared to move out for McTurk's.

"Lot of damn nonsense about comedy," said Rogers, preoccupied.

"What?"

"That pussy little robot wasting our time. I should have let them recycle him."

"Comedy!" snorted Kyle contemptuously. "Like a machine can understand comedy."

"Did you get the manifests, Kyle?"

"Here's a list of all the stuff the Bodyslogs shipped on board. Take your pick."

"Try Rhea," said Dunphy.

"Why Rhea?"

"We were tracking a consignment of illicit arms that went missing on Rhea."

Kyle jabbed his finger at something in the manifests. "Wow. Bodyslogs' log. See there. Rhea. Tons of stuff brought on board. Mainly theatrical equipment."

"From *Rhea*?"

"Yeah."

"Not exactly the home of theater, is it?"

"Katy Wallace is in the Theatrical Division."

"Interesting that she's being shot full of drugs about the time someone is turning off Sammy Weiss."

"Don't you just hate coincidence?" said Dunphy.

"Pull her in," said Rogers.

Kyle nodded.

"And I think it's time to talk to Keppler."

"You got it," said Kyle.

Moments later Rogers was looking at a large-screen image of Emil Keppler. To his surprise the man was in a bathrobe. But his sneering tone had not been washed away.

"Ah, Rogers. I was hoping something unpleasant had happened to you."

"It has."

"Nothing trivial, I hope."

"No. It's not trivial." He hesitated. Should he alert him?

His trim white beard, his white hair, the whole phony naval look irritated Rogers.

"Let's see how he reacts," said Dunphy, encouraging Rogers. "Go for it."

"We believe that there are large quantities of arms hidden on this ship."

The needles underneath the screen jumped.

"Whoa," said Kyle, "that hit him in the heart." They were monitoring his reactions. Keppler paused two seconds too long before replying.

"Don't be silly. This is a passenger ship."

"Yes."

"A man would lose his license forever for a violation like that."

"That would be the least of his problems."

"Why so?"

"In the wake of H9, anyone even remotely implicated would be involved in conspiracy to commit mass murder."

"Why are you telling me this?"

"He's good," said Kyle. "He's got himself back under control."

"It looks as if someone in authority has made it possible for an extreme group to hide weaponry on board. Perhaps it was a deal made through ignorance, or under duress, or as a result of blackmail, there are many possible defenses . . ." He paused to let his message sink in. "However, it would be very bad for that person if he were now to compound culpability with noncooperation."

"Are you threatening me?"

"Did I say anything to threaten *you*?"

Keppler said nothing.

"Nice play," said Dunphy as if he were watching a tennis match.

"I think I read that as a confirm," said Kyle.

"It's good enough for me," said Rogers. "We'll pick him up right after McTurk's." He clicked the intercom back on.

"Emil Keppler, I am placing you formally and officially under house arrest until further notice. You may not make or receive any calls. You may not leave your quarters, nor are you to entertain any guests. You understand?"

"House arrest? You're putting me under house arrest?"

He began to laugh.

"You think that's funny?"

He could hardly speak.

"I think it's fucking hilarious."

Rogers broke off the connection.

Josef emerged from the kitchen.

"Stop that," he said. Keppler was still hysterical.

"I'm under arrest," said Keppler, and began laughing again. The men filed back into the room staring at him.

"It seems everyone is keen to keep you here. It's time, however, that we left. Pavel will stay here and look after you. He has instructions to shoot you if you so much as open your mouth before we're clear. You understand?"

"Oh perfectly."

"Come along then, gentlemen, it's time to start your engines."

WHAT KATY DID

This world is a comedy to those that think, a tragedy to those that feel.

HORACE WALPOLE

I have neglected to tell you where Katy was in all of this. I guess I'm avoiding the subject. You can blame Molly if you like. I'm off women at the moment. I don't trust them. I think Molly was doing a bit of snooping before she left. She is studying the behavioral patterns of an organism called frilia. A kind of space moss. In particular, she has been observing its florid behavior during the mating cycle when its cilia become highly extended and the creature behaves erratically. I suggested this might be comic behavior, and she looked at me strangely and asked me what I knew about comedy in the behavioral pattern of creatures. I thought, Has she found something? I averted the subject by initiating sex, but it was a close thing. Afterwards she tried to pump me for more, but I distracted her. I made up a silly rhyme.

> The frillier the cilia
> The sillier the frilia
> The frillier the frilia
> The sillier the cilia.

She really liked that.

• • •

So Katy. Well yes. When she came out of the hospital, there was an old man standing in front of her. Tears in his eyes. Arms wide. Weeping. Moaning. In an odd language.

"Katerina. Katerina. Du bist meine tochter liebling. Ich bin sein Papa."

Over and over again. You're my daughter. I'm your father. How many times as a child had she had that dream? That her father would walk through the door and scoop her up in his arms and carry her away. Nights at the orphanage when she refused to believe he was dead. And now this was him? She couldn't believe it. She gazed in wonder at him, as a being from another planet, a time traveler.

"You're my father. You're really my father?"

She couldn't take it in. She burst into tears. He hugged her.

"There. It's okay. It's me, child. It's really me."

But he was so old and frail. Her father had been a big man. A powerful man. She couldn't recognize him in this old man.

"Come Katerina," he said. "We have to go. They are looking for me."

They couldn't go to her apartment. The watchers, he said, would certainly be waiting for him there. They needed somewhere to hide, where they would be safe. There was a place she went occasionally when she wanted to be alone. It was a bedbots-only area at the top of the tall C Tower, a linen room where they stored spare blankets and sheets and toweling. Here amidst the comforting smell of freshly laundered linen, they sat on rough wood chairs and watched the galaxy wheeling gently as the ship slowly revolved on its long corkscrew journey towards Mars. Comus talked while tears poured down his face. He told her of her mother, of her birth, their betrayal, the long harsh years when he believed she was irretrievably lost. And then his joy at last in tracing her; his rash decision to contact her through Charles Jay Brown. How he was suspected, watched, betrayed. His elation at having found her shattered by his guilt at having her so suddenly snatched away.

"I'm sorry, Katerina," he said, "it was all my fault."

But she could not be sorry. She had found him at last.

He was suddenly tired. She laid him down on the blankets and she watched him until he fell asleep.

Then she tried calling Alex.

"What do you mean 'Not Registered'?" she asked in disbelief. "He must be somewhere."

"Sorry, we are not getting a listing."

How could Alex have simply disappeared? It must be a result of all the refugees and the chaos on board.

When she left, her father was sleeping. She kissed him and left a note—"Back in ten minutes"—and slipped out.

She had decided to go see Emil Keppler. It was natural enough. But she had no clue he was sitting under armed guard in his apartment. Pavel was watching him warily. The large automatic weapon which lay in his lap never stopped pointing at the man with the trim white beard.

"That's funny," said Keppler. "Arrested twice." He chuckled mirthlessly to himself. "I wonder if anyone else would like to arrest me?"

They both jumped at the knock on the outer door.

Pavel rose and held the automatic to his head.

"I'm watching you. Be very careful what you do."

Pavel took the gun from his head and retreated inside the bathroom.

"I can still see you," he said.

The laser from his sights made a tiny red dot on the back of Keppler's head as he walked slowly across to the door. He didn't open it.

"Who is it?" he said.

"It's me, Emil," said Katy.

He hesitated.

"I can't see you right now."

"Emil, I need to talk to you."

"I'm sorry. I'm very busy."

"It's urgent."

"It'll have to wait."

"Emil, I have to talk to you."

"Go away. You can't come in."

"Please. Let me see you."

"No."

"Emil . . ."

"Go away. Leave me alone."

"This is very important, Emil."

"Damn you. I never want to see you again."

Katy stared at the door. He sounded weird. Distant. Preoccupied. She shrugged and walked away.

Keppler sat down. Pavel came back out of the bathroom, lowering the weapon.

"Who was that?"

"Just some girl," said Keppler.

Katy was puzzled. What should she do now? She should find Alex, but first she must check on her father. Even as she approached the linen room, she sensed something was wrong. When she saw the door open, she knew what she would find. Her father was gone. There was no sign of violence, no note, no nothing. Perhaps he just woke up and went out for a stroll. No need to panic. Then why did she feel this way?

She called the Bodyslogs.

"Old man out wandering?" they said. "No problem, what's his number?"

But of course he didn't have a number, and of course she didn't have a picture.

"Lady," said the Bodyslogs, "this ain't a lot to go on."

"Just pick him up and bring him home," she pleaded. "He may be a little confused."

"We'll try," said the Bodyslogs, "but with no personal number, how are we supposed to trace him?"

"Just find him," she said.

BEDBOTS AND BODYSLOGS

People who indulge in comedy tend to be more and more isolated as the years go by.

DUDLEY MOORE

Comedians don't have very many friends. The real secret of comedy is sadness. Bleakness. It's a young man's game. Red Nose comedians cannot be alone for very long, says Carlton. The White Face craves isolation and is happier solo, but the Red Nose pines for people, for how can he realize himself except in their reflection? The White Face, on the contrary, craves solitude so he can be depressed about it. His universe is fine once he knows he has been abandoned again. So, locked up and isolated, Alex raged while Lewis found a Gideon's Bible and spent his time reading the sonorous prose of Ecclesiasticus.

And some there be, which have no memorial; who are perished as though they had never been.

When the bedbot came into his room, Alex waited until her back was turned and then tried to slip out of the door. She caught him in a grip of iron.

"I wouldn't do that if I was you" was all she said.

"Sorry. I wasn't thinking."

Lame, lame, but it was as if she knew exactly where he was all the time, which was of course exactly right. He tried making little feints towards the door. She wouldn't even look up. It was only when he crossed an invisible line precisely three feet from the exit that she would turn and fix him with a look. He tried sitting on a chair and sliding his foot forward over the imaginary line. She would come in, look at him, and then as he smiled innocently and slid his foot back she would go on with her work. Four times he did this. Each time his foot went over the line she returned and looked at him. The fifth time he slid his foot forward, he screamed. An electromagnetic shock numbed his entire leg. It felt like someone had chopped his foot off. He almost lost consciousness. His bedbot came back in.

"Okay now?" she said, not unkindly.

He nodded grimly.

"No more games?"

"You win," he said. "Very funny."

So half an hour later when a bedbot in a light green uniform, with flat brown sensible shoes and an odd kind of waitress hat, appeared at his door and urgently beckoned him to walk through the fry zone, he smiled bitterly, shook his head, and turned back to his game.

"C'mon, Alex," said the bedbot.

"Hey, no thanks, my foot still hurts."

"This way. Please hurry."

"You're out of your mind. I'm not playing any more games with you bedbots. You want me to move, you send the Bodyslogs."

"Come on, please, we haven't got much time."

He paused in his game. There was something familiar about this bedbot. She had very short hair and her figure was a little skimpy for the frock. Her nylons had rolled down to her ankles and she was talking in a very strange voice for a bedbot.

"C'mon, sir, the coast is clear."

"Oh shit," said Alex as the penny finally dropped. "It's you," he finally managed to splutter.

"Of course it's me," said Carlton, "and we need to get away from here in a hurry." But Alex's laughter was uncontrollable.

"Oh my god," said Alex, choking, "now I've seen everything. A robot in drag!"

STARTLING NEWS

Look I'm sorry to keep interrupting the flow of the narrative like this, but there is an emergency. I promise you this will be the last time. I realize it's not particularly cool, that all these interjections by the narrator may be rather irritating, but I'm a scientist, not a novelist. I don't know anything about story or maintaining the throughline. I just wanted to make a few notes about the history of Carlton and how he came to make his great discovery, and instead it's become this whole drama. The worst of it is it's changing into a confessional. But as I'm reading through and correcting, I need to update you. Things keep happening and I want you to know what's going on. Think of it as post-Heisenberg narrative. The observer is part of the story too. The Nobel adjudicators have just acknowledged receipt of my thesis. Rhea University is anxious for me to announce at their next convocation (they have all but promised me an honorary doctorate), and Mehta & Asher are keen to issue a large printing of my book. I have not been idle. So I promise I won't interrupt the flow again. But you see, I have startling news. I'm gob-smacked.

Carlton is still alive.

NOW. In my time. Eighty years later. How foolish of me. I had of course forgotten the most important element of robots. *They don't die.* Even so, I could hardly have expected them to keep him around so long past his sell-by date. I mean thanks to the technological growth curve most machines are outdated within two years of manufacture and are broken down for reuse. At best you find these old 'bots opening bridges or taking tolls in third-world backwaters. I had no inkling that wouldn't have happened with Carlton. But no! He lives. The little tintellectual has been preserved. He is in an old computers home. A kind of sanatorium. Wouldn't you know it? Sod's law in action. The spirit of fuck-up in the universe prevails once again.

I went to the PDHQ with very mixed feelings, but after a fruitless morning of being passed around from computer to computer and re-ferred back and forth between various departments, I was finally re-warded with the great news that there was no trace of *De Rerum Comoedia* on police files. I breathed a sigh of relief, and it was only some stupid sixth sense that made me enter Carlton's name and co-ordinates to make sure there wasn't a reference to his work any-where else. After all, a potential Nobel Prize winner and honorary doctorate and best-selling author (not to mention a triumphant avenger of a deserting mistress) does not wish to be embarrassed publicly by some sleazy tabloid story that he has plagiarized the en-tire thing. So, yes I checked. And to my utter surprise, shock, and horror, up popped a number, a picture, and a current address.

Now what do I do? I'm well and truly hoist. I don't care how much metal fatigue he has, he's hardly gonna miss the publication of his thesis. I mean we're talking massive publicity here. He isn't about to sit by and watch me nick his life's work. He's not going to send me flowers when he sees me up there modestly thanking the Nobel Committee. And I can't turn back. It's too late. I'm commit-ted. Apart from Messrs. Mehta and Asher, who are preparing to pub-lish in simply massive quantities, and who are knocked out, ecstatic, over the moon, thrilled as parrots, etc., etc., by the cleaning-up po-tential of my book, there's the interview schedule, there's a press conference booked for Monday, there's the Nobel Committee who have asked to see me, and there's two-timing Molly the bitch from biology. What else can I do but go forward?

So I am going to see him. I spoke to some semi-demented nurse—a prim little woman with her hair drawn back and loose teeth—who gave me visiting hours and directions. It's a very out-of-the-way place. Not many inmates. It should be perfect for my purpose. Naturally I'm nervous. What a moment it's going to be, face-to-face with my subject. I feel like a fan. Too bad it has to be this way. I know you'll think the worse of me, but really, what choice do I have? I'm not going to interrupt the narrative flow any more. I am going to see him for the first and last time. Because, gentle reader, I have to kill him.

THE STAKEOUT

I think being funny is not anyone's first choice.

WOODY ALLEN

"Look at this," said Dunphy in the vehicle. "This robot has equations for comedy." He was glancing through *De Rerum* as they hurried to the address where the Bodyslogs had so publicly carried McTurk. "There's a whole series of laugh graphs. He seems to have developed an entire geometry of comedy."

"He should be locked up," said Kyle.

"'Gravity bonds,'" read Dunphy, "'whereas levity expands. Although the audience is united in the laugh, it is the mutual expansion of minds in a single laugh that gives levity its explosive force. Gravity attracts: levity distracts.'"

"What's he talking about?" said Kyle, gazing moodily out of their carriage. They were using Bodyslogs to avoid attracting attention.

" 'The direction of gravity is inwards,' " continued Dunphy, " 'the direction of levity is outwards. It is en-lighten-ment as opposed to the ultimate darkness of a black hole which swallows even light. It is the light force rather than the dark force. Life over the grave. The bright side over the depressing. Optimism over pessimism. As Alex Muscroft once said, "I am idiosymbiotic: I am stupid enough to get along with anyone." ' "

"Where *is* Alex Muscroft?" said Dunphy suddenly.

"He seems to have vanished," said Kyle. "Can't find him anywhere."

"Ain't he supposed to be on the Woolley show?"

"I tried there. They said he's canceled."

They arrived at the park square. Walls of high-rise apartments shot all around, but the park itself was tree-filled and pleasant. About fifteen floors up it terminated in a solid transparent bubble. They went up to the fourteenth floor and were shown into a wide apartment, which commanded a spectacular view. It was buzzing with cops and high-tech equipment.

"Okay," explained Rogers to Dunphy, "that's McTurk's apartment on the ground-floor corner, right across from the park."

"The bedbots say there were up to eight men sleeping there."

"And they didn't report it as unusual?"

"Hey, this is an emergency. There are people sleeping everywhere." He nodded towards the park, where tents were stretched out and people wandered round makeshift camps.

"Besides, they like McTurk. He keeps them amused."

"How?"

"He likes to guess their codes."

"Their security codes?"

"Yeah."

"Nice game."

"Bedbots. Not much brainpower."

"All right," said Rogers. "Is the A Team ready?"

"Everyone's in place," said Kyle.

Rogers looked through the big window. He couldn't see them, but he knew the B Team was hidden all round the park below him. Every entrance to the building was covered. Every exit from the park was being watched.

"Okay, everybody on my signal in ten seconds. And people, whatever you do, don't forget to look away from the action. Don't look at what is going on. Look for reactions. Look for people exiting. Look for people running away, look for people communicating. Are you ready? Then *go*."

The raid was spectacular. The front door completely disintegrated, and the apartment itself seemed to expand as white noise deafened anyone unfortunate enough to be in there. Red smoke billowed out, and heavily masked and hooded men, behind heat shields, poured through a hole in the wall that hadn't been there two seconds ago. As a diversion, it was gob-smacking, terrifyingly effective. The whole park seemed to freeze. Despite himself, even Rogers's eyes were drawn to the action. He cursed and forced himself to look away. Quickly he scanned the park. For a split second everyone seemed transfixed. Then they began to run in all directions. Some in panic, others rushing to help.

"Anything?"

"Nothing."

"Nothing yet."

They were intent, watching for reactions.

"Kyle?"

"Negative."

"Dunphy?"

"Zero."

"Anyone on B Team, for God's sake?"

"Not yet, sir."

"Three minutes and they're gone for sure."

Then he saw him. A red-haired boy, talking urgently into his palm. He nudged Dunphy.

"Could be just a passerby calling for help," said Dunphy.

"Could be. Let's see."

People were ducking, scrambling away from the smoke and noise. Some were comforting children.

"Okay, go for it," said Rogers. "Activate the message."

A calm voice filled the park. "There is no need to panic. This is a police raid. Stay calm and no one will get hurt."

"That did it," said Rogers. At the sound of the voice the red-haired boy turned and was moving away rapidly.

"That's our boy," said Rogers. "Follow him."

"Nobody home," reported the A Team from the debris of Mc-Turk's apartment.

"Well done. You can clear the area and stand down. We have our target."

They kept a discreet distance from the boy hurrying through the park. Careful patrols painted him in the infra-red. He was locked in, targeted, and discreetly pursued by B Team. His image, reduced to a small blip, beeped on their scopes.

"He's gonna lead us straight to them," said Rogers.

"With any luck," muttered Dunphy.

They could see the red-haired boy between the trees, heading for the far corner of the park. He looked around him as he moved.

"Anxious little bugger, isn't he?"

He altered direction a couple of times, walked around a tree once or twice, checked back hurriedly to see if he was being followed, and sat down unexpectedly for a few minutes. Each time Rogers knew the watchers waited.

"You spotted any of ours?"

Dunphy pointed to a woman with a pram. "That one."

"Nope."

The red-haired boy seemed to feel reassured. He stood up and set off at a fast lope towards the exit. As he approached, he stopped dead in his tracks. Ahead of him there was an enormous glare of lights.

"What are they doing?" said Rogers. "Who told them to pick him up? They're going to scare him off."

"It's not them," said Dunphy.

"Oh shit," said Rogers, "I don't believe it. It's Brenda Woolley."

A huge crowd was following Brenda into the park. The boy slipped into the throng around her.

"Can you see him?"

"No."

"Damn her," said Rogers. "We're losing him."

The crowd was cheering. Brenda was nodding graciously, like European royalty. She was distributing tickets. They held out their hands towards her in supplication.

It's like communion, she thought. "Bless you," she said, handing a nice pair in the balcony to a highly photogenic young woman.

A red-haired boy caught her eye. She thought at first he was coming towards her, but he looked around and passed her and seemed intent on hurrying by without so much as looking at her.

"You," she said imperiously. "Come here."

The spotlights swung onto him. He looked at her, frozen. This woman with the cameras and the lights. Something like panic came into his eyes.

"Don't be frightened. I want you to come here. Now."

There was a split second as he looked at her. Then a slight spurt sound. Brenda crumpled.

"Jesus," said Rogers, "someone's shot Brenda."

Shouts. Screams. Pandemonium.

"Go on. Pick him up. Now. Go, go, go."

The wail of sirens. The shoving of the crowd. The red-haired boy had gone.

He was young. He was frightened. He could feel his heart beating so loud in his ears. Had he done good? Had he fucked up? He was hurrying through the cloisters. A short, pale-faced man in a dark hat and an old overcoat came towards him.

"Josef," he said. "Thank Christ."

"This way," said Josef.

"They hit McTurk's."

"Well done, we got your report."

"I—that's to say—I had to shoot that lady."

"Yes," said Josef, "perhaps that was a mistake."

"I don't think so, Josef. She was trying to stop me. You said whatever I did, not to let them take me."

"And you did good," said Josef. "They were following you, you know. We watched them watching you. Now we have to make sure they don't find you."

"Thanks, Josef."

"Down here."

He climbed down behind some railings.

"But they're coming," said the boy. "They'll find me here."

"No, it's okay," said Josef. "They won't get anything out of you."

"Did I do well, Josef?"

"Oh, you did just great," said Josef.

There was a soft sigh from the boy. His eyes opened wide and he suddenly sank to his knees.

Josef kissed him on the forehead, then let his body crumple and fall.

"Good boy," he said. "You'll be safe now."

"Oh my god," said Brenda, "I've been shot."

She could hardly believe it. She could see the panic in their eyes. They were fussing and screaming, shoving and pointing all around her. The relentless cameras moved in on her. Bravely she smiled.

Within seconds the medics arrived. They must have been around the corner. Photographers pushed them back and fought each other to take photographs of the fallen woman in her bloodstained dress. This unseemly melee was finally resolved by the Paramedic Body-slogs, who shoved aside the lenses of the paparazzi and carried her off bodily.

"Just one more, Brenda."

"Over here, Brenda."

But she could no longer hear them. Only see them flashing, popping, and mouthing shouts at her as she was carried away towards the vehicles with the flashing lights.

"She gonna make it?" said Rogers.

The Bodyslog shrugged.

"I want her isolated. No one is to get in to see her. Hear that? No one."

"Sir! There's something you ought to see."

He followed the young cop. Under the pillars, a reproduction of porticoed Paris, a short flight of steps led down.

"We found him down there."

He caught a glimpse of red hair.

"Holy shit," he said. "They took him out."

THE LITTLE METAL TRANSVESTITE

Sometimes life is very well written.

BARRY CRYER

Lewis had grown tired of isolation. He had been declaiming passages from Ecclesiasticus for over an hour and had finally grown bored with the sound of his own voice. He was just beginning to feel sorry for himself when a piece of his door burned out. He backed off in alarm. Alex's head appeared in the hole.

"Good morning, wankers," said Alex in a ridiculously cheerful British voice. "This is your nine A.M. alarm call. Hands off cocks, on socks, and let's get the hell out of here, shall we?"

"Oh man, am I glad to see you," said Lewis. He climbed through the hole in the door and then stopped dead in astonishment as he saw the bedbot.

"Who the fuck is this?"

"Allow me to present Doris Carlton, the metal transvestite."

"Please," said Carlton. "This is no time for joking."

"Oh my god," said Lewis. "Why the hell is he dressed like that?"

"Shh," said Alex, "don't embarrass him. It's a change-of-life thing."

"Quickly this way," said Carlton.

"Where are we?"

"Somewhere underneath the theater."

They hurried along the corridors until they came to a heavy door with a flashing red light and a warning not to enter when the light was on. They entered anyway. There was no one around. They were definitely backstage now, for there were signs pointing towards MAKEUP, WARDROBE, ORCHESTRA, and STAGE.

"Wait," said Carlton, "someone's coming."

They flattened themselves against the wall as footsteps approached.

"Shit," said Alex.

"I'll take him," said Carlton.

They tensed. A short figure in spangly tights turned the corner sharply and almost fell over them.

"Hello," said Keith, startled. "What have we here?"

He looked at the three of them frozen guiltily. Two comedians and a Bowie in drag.

"Don't tell me," he said. "Let me guess. You're doing *tableau vivant* and your subject is *The Wizard of Oz*."

"Good try," said Alex, the first to recover from the shock, "but this is *The Wizard of Id*. Dorothy and the Tin Man have mated to produce a metal transvestite who likes cross-dressing. The scarecrow and I are running away together to open a Montessori school for the alternatively gifted and what the fuck are *you* doing here?"

"Checking my supplies as ordered," said Keith. "It's taken me a while. They have some ferocious lager on this ship."

"What's around there?"

"Just dressing rooms. Up those stairs is the stage door."

"Anybody up there?"

"Stage doorman. But they're beefing up security. Something's happened."

"What?"

"Dunno but everyone's going crazy up there. Stopping you, searching you. Anyway I got my backstage pass." He held up a tiny flamethrower.

"Must fly," said Keith. "Nice to see you all looking so guilty. Bye, sweetie," and he blew Carlton a kiss. "Love the costume. Don't change a thing."

THE SPEED OF LIFE

Man appoints, and God disappoints.

MIGUEL DE CERVANTES

"How's Brenda?"

"Bad."

"She gonna pull through?"

"They're not sure."

Rogers winced. They had been so close to catching the boy. Who could possibly have foreseen the arrival of Brenda?

"Don't blame yourself," said Dunphy. "These things happen. Chaos Theory."

"They took out their own guy. Who are these people?"

"They're deadly fucking serious, that's for sure."

"Part of the plan?"

"No way. Pure fuck-up," said Dunphy "No one could possibly predict Brenda was gonna show up like that."

They were standing underneath the cold portico swilling coffee. The sandstone columns every few yards, like an Egyptian temple, had yards of yellow tape around them, holding back the crowd. Kyle came hurrying across towards them.

"People are saying Brenda's dead. They are coming to pay their last respects."

He glanced back towards the park. Several people already held candles. More pushed forward, searching for the spot where she had fallen. They held handkerchiefs expectantly, looking for blood spots.

"Jesus," said Rogers. "Put the rain on."

"Can't do that, pal," said Dunphy.

"They're ghouls," said Rogers.

"They're destroying evidence," said Kyle.

"Who needs evidence? We have him clear on tape shooting her. Look."

They watched the red-haired boy panic as the camera lights lit him up and all eyes turned towards him.

"Must have been a terrifying moment for him," said Dunphy. "Suddenly his invisibility melted away."

They saw the short flame from the weapon. Brenda's look of surprise as she collapsed.

Kyle said, "Oh, there's a woman wants to see you. Urgent, she's saying."

"Tell her to wait."

"I'd see her if I were you," said Dunphy, staring over his shoulder. "It's Katy Wallace."

"Let her through," said Rogers.

A commotion at the edge of the crowd as she pushed through. The people stared in fascination at the crime scene, as if they were spectators at a play. A small emergency vehicle had been set aside as a temporary command post. Rogers nodded her inside. He could smell her perfume as she passed.

"Oh boy," said Dunphy approvingly.

"Want to listen in?" asked Rogers.

"You bet," said Dunphy.

He climbed up into the trailer. Katy was already seated. She waited till they'd closed the door.

"Have you seen my father?" She looked at them fiercely, as if expecting an argument.

"Who?" said Rogers.

"My father is missing."

"Look, lady," said Rogers, spreading his hands, "there are a lot of missing people on this ship. We don't have time to go chasing around after people's relatives."

"Why don't you try the Bodyslogs?" asked Dunphy reasonably.

"The Bodyslogs can find no trace of him," she said. "He's a Silesian." As if this explained anything.

"Aha," said Rogers, not understanding.

A security man came in, glanced curiously at Katy, and handed Rogers a note. Rogers read it and looked up sharply.

"You just tried to see Emil Keppler?"

"Yes. He wouldn't see me."

"Mind if I ask why?"

"I don't know why he wouldn't see me."

"No, why did you want to see him?"

"He's . . ." she looked at him, wondering how much he knew. "I wanted to ask him to help find my father."

"And he wouldn't?"

"Wouldn't even let me in."

"Did he tell you why?"

"No. Why?" she asked, puzzled.

"He's under house arrest."

"Emil?" She looked stunned.

"What were you doing at the Rialto?" asked Dunphy.

"Who're you?" she said.

"Answer the question," said Rogers.

"I'm here to ask *you* questions."

"Not anymore," said Rogers. "Tell us why you went to the Rialto."

"I was meeting my father."

He exchanged a glance with Dunphy. Dunphy was feigning indifference.

"What's his name then, this father?" asked Rogers.

She thought for a moment. "His real name, or his code name?"

Rogers sat forward, suddenly tense. He could feel the hairs on the back of his neck standing up. *His code name.*

"Everything you know."

"His name is Walewski," she said, "Alexander Walewski. Also known as Comus."

Dunphy whistled. "Comus," he said. "You're sure it's Comus?"

"Quite sure," she said. "He's my father."

"Can you believe that?"

"I suppose she's telling the truth?"

"Why lie?"

They looked at her through the window, waiting anxiously outside the trailer.

"So what do we do?" said Kyle.

"Find him before they do," said Dunphy. "Unless they already have him."

"Come on, let's not get paranoid. He's an old man. He wandered off. Got lost. Fuck-up."

"Why not conspiracy?" said Dunphy. "They can't be too happy with his role in this."

"You think they snatched him?"

"Wouldn't you? Leaving a geriatric loose in the middle of an operation. Running around blabbing. Visiting relatives. No, things don't look so good for old pal Comus."

"You think so?"

"Look what they did to the redhead."

They gazed out of the window. The Bodyslogs were removing the body.

"So who killed Sammy Weiss?" asked Rogers

"I think the watchers killed her," said Dunphy. "When they found Katy visiting Comus, they panicked. Was it a trap? Were they being double-crossed? They've got a lot at stake here."

"Go on," said Rogers.

"Keppler represents their arms. They have to protect him. They need him safe until he can deliver. When Sammy copied the Weiss file to Carlton and Carlton was following Katy, they had nightmares. None of them could conceive of the real reason for Comus's visit. Innocent motives don't help in a paranoid world."

"So they killed her?"

"The watchers killed her. To protect Keppler."

"It's a theory," said Rogers. "Let's go test it."

There was a shout outside.

"They've found another one."

"What?"

"Another body in the grass out there."

Dunphy and Rogers looked at each other.

"Could be Daddy," said Dunphy. "Better stop her."

But they were too late. Katy was already running across the grass. A group of detectives were holding people back. Harsh lights picked out something huddled under a rough blanket. She reached the cops, but they wouldn't let her through. By the time Rogers caught up with her, she was arguing hysterically with them.

"That's okay," said Rogers. "Let her look."

She glanced at him, her pale face frightened but determined.

The uniformed men hovering over the body stood up and pulled back the grey blanket. She stared down.

"That's not him," she said.

Charles Jay Brown had embarked on the longest voyage.

THE THEATER DISTRICT

Comedy is tragedy that happens to other people.

ANGELA CARTER

In the distance they could hear the sound of an orchestra tuning up. It was getting close to show time. Chorus girls in feathers and thongs strode by in their half-naked splendor. Alex stopped to stare, but Lewis shoved him on through the backstage maze towards the exit.

"We gotta get outta here."

"Hey, I was just looking."

As they passed the Wardrobe Department, they heard a familiar voice.

"Moan, moan, moan. Night and day. That's all they ever did. Until I was sick to death of 'em. So I told them. That's enough for me. I'm out of here. I hear the call of the audience. The lure of the footlights. The smell of the greasepaint. I'm going back to the theater!"

It was their Washing Machine. Mrs. Greenaway sat in splendor among the dressbots, happily kvetching while they listened spellbound, reveling in her.

" 'You're not cooping me up any longer,' I said. 'The caged bird must fly. It is a life of show business for me.' "

"You said that to your humans?"

"I told 'em straight. I'm sick of all this comedy malarkey. They think they're so funny with their sex dolls and their trollops."

"How dare she say that?" said Alex, outraged.

"Oh, let's just leave her. She'll be happy here," said Lewis.

"That's right," said Alex. "We don't need her now Carlton likes dressing up as a bedbot."

Carlton put his nose in the air and bore their taunts nobly. They would soon see what he was made of.

"Hey, you."

"Me?" said Alex.

"Yes, you."

A large stage doorman was looking at them suspiciously.

"Come here."

"Who, me?" said Alex with great confidence.

"Yes, you. Who are you?"

"Muscroft and Ashby," said Lewis. "We're on the bill."

"You were removed," said the doorman.

"Well, we've been put back again," said Alex.

"But you have no dressing room."

"That's okay, we're dressed. See." He indicated Carlton.

"That robot's in drag," said the doorman.

"Comedy," said Alex. "That's what we do."

"No, no, no," said the doorman. "You've got to have a proper dressing room. You can't be on a show and have no dressing room, that won't do at all."

Fortunately the doorman was distracted by the arrival of a large party of men at the stage door behind him. He turned to face the new problem.

"And who may I ask are you lot?"

"Visitors. We have backstage passes."

"These are to see Brenda Woolley."

"Yes."

"She's not here."

"Nevertheless these are passes."

"These are passes to see her, and I've told you she's not here."

"Quickly, in here," said Lewis, shoving Alex and Carlton through a doorway. He slammed the door shut and flipped on the light. They looked in amazement. A plush pink and gold room of utter magnificence greeted their eyes. It was the Number 1 dressing room.

"Wow," said Alex. "Gay heaven."

Lewis turned and looked back through the tiny spyhole.

"We can't be in here," said Carlton in a shocked voice. "This is Brenda Woolley's dressing room."

"Shut up, I'm trying to hear," said Lewis, his eye pressed to the hole. He couldn't quite make out what was going on. There seemed to be some kind of altercation by the stage door. Who were all these men? Surely they were hardly Brenda Woolley fans? A short dark-haired man was arguing forcefully with the doorman.

"I'm sorry, sir, you'll just have to come back later."

"Well, that won't be possible, I'm afraid."

"I can't admit you. Security has been tightened since the shooting, and it's more than my job's worth to let you in."

"You're quite right," said the short man. "It *is* more than your job's worth."

Lewis turned back to watch Alex preening in front of Brenda Woolley's elaborate gilded makeup mirror. It looked like an altarpiece.

"Uhm, sweetheart, lay it on with a trowel," said Alex, lifting his hair off his face.

"Shh," said Lewis. "They'll hear us."

"Soundproofed," said Carlton. "But I really don't think we should be in here."

When Lewis turned back, there was no sign of the doorman, but fifteen large men were clattering down the corridor. He thought for a second they were coming straight for Brenda Woolley's dressing room, but they paused outside while the dark-haired man pointed half of them towards an elevator that said PRIVATE. CONTROL ROOM ONLY.

"Who on earth are they?" said Lewis. "A male choir?" They seemed too beefy even for a Welsh choir. The rest of the party ran down the stairs. There was a new man on the door now, in a Security jacket that seemed too short for him.

"I don't like this," said Lewis. "There's something weird going on."

"Ooh, look," said Alex, "Brenda's wardrobe." He had opened a large mirrored sliding closet to reveal row upon row of dresses hanging neatly in plastic wrappers.

"The mother lode," he said. "Frock city. C'mon, Carlton, slip into one of these, I beg you. Away with the dowdy, and on with the glam."

Carlton was outraged. "Do please stop it. It's sacrilege," he said.

"Oh, loosen up, Carlton," said Alex, "this is a drag queen's dream."

He was filled with manic energy as he opened another closet packed with different wigs of all colors and styles mounted on life-like wig blocks.

"And this is where Brenda keeps her heads," said Alex. "Ooh, honey, you give great heads."

"Quit messing around," said Lewis, "we're in deep doo-doo here."

"You're right," said Carlton. "There is something weird going on. Where *is* Brenda? The show starts in less than forty minutes—you'd think she'd be here."

"And even if she was late," said Lewis, "where's her dresser? Where's her makeup artiste, her manager, her publicist . . . why is there nobody here?"

Alex was holding up one of her dresses. "I'd cross the Universe for you, my darling," he said to Carlton.

"I think you should know what's going on," said Carlton.

They both turned to look at him.

"It's all my fault," he said.

They stared at him perplexed.

"They're after my Theory of Comedy," he said seriously.

"You have a Theory of Comedy," said Lewis, trying desperately to keep from smiling, "and you think someone's after it?"

"I'm convinced of it," said Carlton. "That's why I sent Rogers a copy for safekeeping."

"You sent a copy of your Theory of Comedy to Rogers," said Lewis, "for safekeeping?"

"Exactly."

Alex was staring hard at the floor, fighting desperately for control of the corners of his mouth.

"Carlton, would you go into the bathroom for just a minute, please."

"May I say how very sorry I am that I got you all into this."

Lewis was biting his lip, trying hard to avoid Alex's eyes. They managed somehow to contain themselves until Carlton stepped inside the pink heaven of the Brenda Woolley bathroom suite, and then they lost it. They couldn't speak. They howled. Alex laughed until he couldn't breathe, his face turning red. Lewis lay on the floor, put his head back, and bellowed.

"Oh my God," said Alex, "I think I'm going to die."

"He sent his Theory of Comedy to Rogers," said Lewis panting, "for safekeeping!"

This sent them both off into fresh paroxysms. They were still laughing helplessly when the dressing room door flew open and two men stepped inside. It was touch and go who was the more surprised.

"Is this some kind of orgy?" asked McTurk in his familiar Scottish brogue.

"Peter McTurk," said Alex, "what the hell are you doing here?"

"I'm looking for someone," said McTurk vaguely.

"In Brenda Woolley's dressing room?" asked Lewis suspiciously.

McTurk ignored him. "I want you to stay here," he said to the old man in very clear tones, as if to a child. "You'll be safe with these clowns."

"Who's this?" said Lewis.

"This is Comus," said McTurk, "he's a little distracted." He made little gestures around his head with his fingers. "You know, a bit doo-lally. Not entirely right in the head." He turned to the old man and helped him into a chair.

"Stay here with these people, Granddad, you'll feel right at home—they're bonkers too."

"The one minute is up," said Carlton, emerging from the bathroom. They had forgotten how literal he was.

"Freeze," said McTurk. They all stared at the weapon.

"Now that is a mighty big weapon, Peter," said Alex, "and we're all very impressed by its size, but please don't fry our robot, it's so hard to get help."

"Who the fuck is this?" said McTurk. He saw a robot in a wig dressed as a bedbot.

"That's Carlton," said Alex. "He's going through a phase."

"Your tin man is still a fucking weirdo, I see," he said, lowering the gun.

"Where's Brenda?" said Lewis.

"Some dickhead shot her."

"Brenda?"

"Why?"

"Mebbe they didn't like her voice. How should I know?"

"Who would shoot Brenda Woolley?" asked Lewis.

"What about the show?" said Alex.

"Oh, the show must go on," said McTurk, "isn't that what you guys say? Break a leg and all that."

"She gonna live?"

"No idea, old son. The place is rife with rumors. She's dead, she's alive, she'll never sing again, she'll make it. This is a theater, for heaven sake." He raised his eyes, contemplating the strangeness of their world. "They shot her up pretty good though."

"Oh, poor dear Brenda," said Carlton, "and it's all my fault."

"He's convinced somebody is trying to steal his Theory of Comedy," said Alex. "So he dresses like a bedbot so they'll think he's nuts."

"My costume is to evade recycling in order to protect my theory for posterity."

McTurk looked at Carlton for the longest time. "And I thought *you* were crazy," he said to Alex after a moment.

TEA TIME

Comedy is an escape, not from truth but from despair; a narrow escape into faith.

CHRISTOPHER FRY

What's wrong with Keppler? wondered Rogers. He's behaving very oddly. They had found him slumped in a chair in his bathrobe. He hardly looked up when they came in. He just sat there slowly sipping cognac from a balloon glass, showing neither surprise nor anger. He seemed indifferent, almost offhand with them as if the whole thing was already over, sitting amongst his fine antiques in his leather armchair.

"We haven't got much time," Dunphy was saying.

"That's right. C'mon, Emil, help us out here. You know what's going down, don't you?"

Keppler glanced towards the bathroom door. It was not completely closed. Rogers followed his look. He could see nothing.

"If you help us now," said Dunphy, "we can cut you a deal."

Again Keppler said nothing. He just turned his head towards the bathroom door.

Dunphy and Rogers walked away from him for a minute.

"What's the matter with him?"

"Beats me. He isn't even rude anymore."

Dunphy turned and strode over to him. "Look, Emil," he said, "we're out of time. We need to know what's going on right now."

Again Keppler said nothing, just raised an eyebrow and turned his head.

"Did you bring arms on board this ship?" asked Rogers.

Keppler did not reply.

"All right, let's say that you did, but you don't want to admit it. Where would we find these arms?"

Again Keppler glanced towards the bathroom.

"Emil, there is no reason to be afraid. You can trust us."

He laughed. "Oh sure, I can trust you gentlemen."

"Listen, Emil," said Rogers. "Your wife has been shot. She is in critical condition. She was shot by the White Wolves."

Keppler stood up. His whole demeanor had changed. "This is true?" he asked.

Dunphy nodded in confirmation.

"They shot Brenda." They could see fury come into his eyes. Rogers saw Keppler steel himself. His eyes hardened. His knuckles whitened as he gripped the edge of the desk for support. Then he suddenly smiled.

"Listen very carefully to me," he said as he reached forward and pulled open the desk drawer. And then in a rush he said, "The arms are in the secure area, by the Props Department. A man called Josef has . . ."

The bathroom door swung open, followed by the slight muffled pop of a bullet. Keppler, still smiling, fell over and collapsed on the floor. A gun was in his hand.

Dunphy blazed away at the bathroom door. Pavel fell forward on to the carpet. Dead.

"Jesus," said Rogers, "we put Keppler under house arrest with a man already inside."

In the distance the orchestra was warming up. Josef with six men was headed down to the secure area. They had large BRENDA WOOLLEY ACCESS ALL AREA PASSES pinned neatly to their chests.

"Oo varda the omes," said an admiring dressbot as they passed.

"Tell us more, Mrs. Greenaway, about your theory of comedy."

The Silesians ignored the weird denizens of this strange under-world and headed for the Props Department. There was a simple caged area, marked OFF-LIMITS TO ALL PERSONNEL, which delayed them not at all, then in one corner of this huge cage they found an-other door, marked SECURE AREA, and more warnings. Sven reached forward and attached something to this door. They all stepped back. Josef nodded. Sven pressed a button and the door imploded. They pushed on into the storeroom. There were six or seven large crates on the floor, each with the word SNOWBALL stenciled on the side. Quickly they prised them open.

"Well, well, well," said Josef approvingly, "looks like Keppler kept his word. Call Pavel and tell him he can join us."

They were staring at a large cache of armaments.

After a moment: "Pavel's not replying, Josef."

Josef frowned. He looked down at the open crates in front of him, then shrugged. Why worry? It was too late for Keppler to do any-thing about it anyway. They had their delivery.

"How much time do we have?"

"Less than ten minutes to show time," said Sven.

There was a slight warning beep from their local intruder alarm. Nervously they fingered their weapons. A man was coming through the caged area.

"Friendly," said Sven, scanning the readout.

"Peter McTurk," said Josef, "what kept you?"

"I've been cleaning up for you, Josef."

"Where's Comus?"

"Oh, he's quite safe now," said McTurk. "I took care of him."

"Took care of him *properly*?" asked Josef.

McTurk smiled reassuringly. "You won't see him again, Josef."

Ambiguity, ambivalence, double-speak. We hear what we want to hear at least 60 percent of the time.

"Thank you, Peter," said Josef.

CURTAIN UP

I don't want to hear advice from anybody who hasn't walked the fifteen yards.

BUDDY HACKETT ON COMEDY EXECUTIVES

When Rogers and Dunphy arrived in the Theater District, there were crowds still trying to get into the performance. Rumors were flying; people were discussing nervously what they had seen. Brenda Woolley shot in broad daylight. Would she or wouldn't she pull through? Security had been beefed up, but the scalpers were still busy at their trade. Inside, there was the expectant hum of a full house. It was packed. They wasted a little time pushing through the crowd taking their seats.

"See anyone you recognize?"

"Not a soul," said Dunphy.

Kyle emerged from the shadows. "So far as we can tell, they've got the stage door locked up. There are too many folks around to try and take it. How's Miss Woolley?"

"Touch and go," said Rogers.

Kyle shook his head and ushered them through a tiny door into the backstage area. They stood for a second getting their bearings. It was very dark. A cavernous space extended up into blackness above their heads, from whence dangled a bewildering array of ropes and pulleys. As they looked around this strange world, utter darkness contrasted with bright pools of light. Dancers stood and stretched their limbs or dipped their toes into resin boxes. Harassed people with headsets ran around shepherding extras and fetching props. Nobody seemed to be in charge, though the air crackled with electrostatic conversations.

"The Props are down this way," said Kyle.

They ran down some dusty stairs and cautiously slowed as they entered the Props Department. Ahead of them was a large caged area. Dunphy pointed. In one corner of the cage a security door was shattered.

Kyle drew his weapon and moved forward in a crouch.

"Okay, let's do it," said Rogers.

They went in fast and low. A figure was leaning over an open crate.

"Freeze," yelled Rogers.

"Who do we have here?" said Dunphy.

"Guy fucking Fawkes by the look of it," said Kyle, whistling at the arms packed in the crates.

The figure turned around.

"Sorry, chaps," said Keith.

"Those who ignore history are condemned to repeat it," said Josef from behind them.

"Nice toys," said Rogers, staring into the barrels of the arms pointed at him.

"Santa has been very kind," said Josef.

"Welcome one and all, laddies," said McTurk.

"Peter McTurk," said Dunphy, "what the hell are you doing in this dubious company?"

"Shut up," said McTurk, slapping him hard across the face.

"Now, now, Peter, there's no need for that," said Josef. "I know how you feel."

McTurk nodded. "I gotta go check on the control room. They should have made contact by now."

"Good for you. Sven, why don't you go with him?"

McTurk hesitated. "Best he stays with you, Josef. I can take care of them."

Josef looked at him evenly. He seemed to be making a decision. "All right, Peter," he said eventually, "off you go." Sven sat down. They watched McTurk exit.

"Marvelous what we can do with technology, isn't it?"

"Why don't we just talk about this before anybody does anything silly," said Rogers.

"Cut the crap," said Josef, "and sit down."

They did as they were told. Dunphy was calculating the weaponry. Something puzzled him. They had enough for a good firefight, but that was all. How were they going to take Mars? They were a ludicrous threat. It was a joke. Now McTurk was gone, there were only six of them here. Suppose there were seven of them upstairs, and perhaps a further five or six in various parts of the ship—what possible chance did they have?

"Listen, pal, we can help you get out of here."

"For what?"

"You haven't enough men to take this ship, let alone Mars."

"Mars?"

"Aren't you going to Mars?"

"Heavens no. We just need the show."

"The Brenda Woolley show?"

"Yes. Such a pity poor dear Brenda is indisposed."

"Is that why you shot Redhead?"

The others glanced at Josef but said nothing.

"Nice try," said Josef. "I shall be making a little announcement on the show."

Rogers and Dunphy looked at each other, puzzled.

"Let's see how they like it. Hoist with their own petard, as it were."

"What are you going to do?"

"Snowball," said Josef with a smile. "Since they are happy enough to destroy our homelands, let's see how they like it themselves."

"Jesus," said Dunphy, "he's going to divert one of the icebergs."

"Where are you sending it?"

"Clarketown."

There was a silence.

"There are five million people in Clarketown," said Dunphy after a moment.

"That is why they will cooperate. You see, we don't have to leave the ship. We don't even have to leave the theater."

"That's wicked," said Kyle.

"Oh, and is it wicked to want to save our homes? Is it wicked to want to stop a hell of ice crashing from the sky, drowning our fields, destroying *our* lands?"

"It's desert."

"It's desert to you. We live there. Why is this wicked and not that?"

"Josef, this is madness."

"No it's not. People always say it's madness when they mean they don't like it."

"Five minutes to show time," said a voice, echoing round the cage. "This is it, boys and girls. Opening number. Places, please. We are live in five minutes."

"And now if you will excuse me," said Josef. "That is my cue."

THE SHOW MUST GO ON

Happy is the man who hath never known what it is to taste of fame—to have it is a purgatory, to want it is a Hell!

EDWARD BULWER-LYTTON

The show was going live throughout the solar system. Well, as live as you can get. As you are clearly smart enough to observe, there is no simultaneity in space. Even the sun isn't "live," since it takes $8\frac{1}{2}$ minutes for its light to reach Earth, and about 12 minutes for that light to reach Mars, and about 79 minutes for that light to reach Saturn. Indeed, it takes light about 12 hours to cross the entire solar system. And that's just one tiny corner of one small galaxy. The speed of night indeed. In every direction we are always looking into the past.

"Unfortunately, Brenda Woolley, the star of our show, cannot be with us tonight. As you may have heard, she was shot this afternoon."

Stunned gasps from many in the audience.

"She is at the moment fighting for her life. I know you would want to send her your support, just as she would want this show to continue."

Heartfelt and prolonged applause from the audience, many in tears.

Brenda was lying on her back, floating, full of happy chemicals. It all seemed so far away. At her feet Boo loomed in and out of focus. He was watching her on-screen, a previously taped segment with her and the old man Comus, wrapped in a blanket.

"Hey, Brenda, you're looking pretty good on the show."

She smiled. "Dear Boo," she mouthed, but no sound came out.

What was he doing holding the hand of a dying diva? Sentimental fools, comics. Her entourage was camped outside, bickering sullenly. Their meal ticket on the line.

"Hello, who's this?" said Boo.

On-screen, and onstage, a short, pale, thin figure emerged from the wings and walked slowly to center stage. The audience murmured.

"Shall I turn it up a little?" asked Boo, but she was drifting in and out.

"This concert is about refugees," said Josef. "About the displaced. And let me tell you all about that, for we know all about that. We are the displaced. We are Silesian patriots, forcibly removed from our homesteads. We are made refugees in our own land by our own government. Well, there is a time to stand and say no. No, we won't go quietly along with what your bureaucrats have decided. No, you may not plan us out of existence."

"Is this guy for real?" said Boo. But Brenda had slipped into sleep. This wasn't about her.

"So I have a message for the government of Mars. The Iceman project must be stopped. Forthwith. This project must be abandoned right now. Today."

"How can this work?" asked Rogers, puzzled. They were watching the monitor in the secure room.

"They're Silesians," said Dunphy, "it's what they do. Project Iceman. They hunt for icebergs in the asteroid belt, board them, then a small controlled explosive device sends them off like a pool shot towards Mars. They have to be very careful, nothing too big. The asteroid that destroyed Earth's dinosaurs was less than three miles wide. Sometimes they break 'em up first. Anyway, they send 'em off to where they are captured by Martian gravity. Then, very carefully—the coordinates have to be extremely carefully worked out—the icebergs are sent through the atmosphere to crash on target into the new Silesian Sea. Naturally they burn up a bit in the atmosphere, lose about a quarter of their body weight, which becomes water vapor, adding to the oxygen content of the growing atmosphere. It's very ingenious. Unless someone alters the coordinates. Then you've got a gigantic snowball heading for a major city."

"Why can't Mars simply shoot it down?"

"There are usually several icebergs in orbit at any one time. Which one do you target? But more importantly he'll be monitoring them. The minute he sees them launch, he can send the snowball. They use heat-seeking missiles. Even if they can reach the iceberg in the three minutes it takes it to plunge through the atmosphere, they will go after the heat source, which is the burning-up tail. The main frozen body of the berg will get through."

"Shit."

"Yeah."

"We demand the immediate abandonment of Project Iceman. So now you have our text. You have our context. You have thirty minutes."

There was a stir in the audience. They sat stunned by what he had told them. Witnesses to history.

"To help you make up your minds, here are some images of our homeland. Run the footage."

A carefully edited selection of images began to run. Women and children working in the fields, looking up in alarm, running inside. That sort of thing. Plus icebergs, lots of them, huge glistening chunks of ice, hitting the atmosphere, vaporizing, turning into fiery comets leaving behind long streaming trails of vapor. Then the enormousness of the splashdown as the iceberg disintegrates, its force driving a deep hole into the Martian surface. The familiar shape of the mushroom cloud emerging, rising slowly into the sky. A mushroom cloud of mud and water that would fall as rain onto the ever-growing sea. The footage ended. There was a stunned silence from the audience.

"You have fifteen minutes," said Josef quietly to the watching millions.

The Silesians stared at Josef on the screen, saying nothing. Rogers looked at them. They showed no emotion. Stubble on their chins, their dark eyes staring brightly.

Wonder what they're on? he thought.

Keith was restless. His foot drummed relentlessly.

"Someone has to be monitoring Mars," said Dunphy. "They have to be watching for their response."

"McTurk in the control room."

Dunphy nodded. "Yes, the control room makes sense."

They were startled by Josef's voice.

"Ladies and gentlemen, I am pleased to inform you that the Government of Mars has just agreed to suspend the Iceman project effective immediately."

Cheering broke out amongst the Silesians.

"As soon as we have confirmation, the show will proceed. The snowball will be maintained as a guarantee that they will keep their word."

"Jeeze, they're not going to like that. That's having a gun to your head."

"What can they do?"

"I'd cross the Universe for you, my darling . . ."

The opening bars of Brenda Woolley's great anthem filled the hall. Josef looked temporarily disconcerted.

"Turn that thing off," he said irritably. Then he froze in astonishment. The audience gasped. Brenda Woolley had appeared at the top of the stairs behind him.

"I'd sail across the Galaxy."

She was descending the broad white staircase towards him. This was madness. She was supposed to be dying.

"Stop that," said Josef. "Stop that at once." But he was drowned out, first by Brenda and then by the audience, which was now applauding wildly. Most were on their feet cheering loudly. Josef looked helplessly towards the side of the stage. He seemed uncertain what to do.

"Sven, how did she get here?"

Sven in the wings shrugged. How should he know.

"I'd walk a million miles
For one of your smiles . . ."

"All right, that's enough. I am warning you." Josef pulled a gun. People in the audience screamed. But Brenda did not stop. She continued singing and walking towards Josef with her arms wide. Brenda was unconcerned by his gun. Because, of course, it wasn't Brenda. It was Brenda's voice. It was Brenda's dress, and Brenda's wig, but it wasn't Brenda, gentle reader. It was Carlton.

"He's very good," said Lewis.

"Isn't he?" said Alex proudly. "A natural dragbot."

"Maybe we can use him in the act?"

This isn't too bad, thought Carlton. Why do they make such a fuss about performing?

For Josef it was horrible. A nightmare. A ghastly woman singing at him, advancing on him, live in front of millions of people, just on the very verge of his triumph. How had she recovered so quickly? How was he supposed to deal with her? What was he supposed to do? Levity was exerting a strong pull.

Carlton, lip-syncing Brenda's touchingly banal lyrics, advanced towards Josef, his arms outstretched in supplication.

"You are my heart's desire,
Come to me!"

"Stop right there. I'm warning you. Come no nearer." But still she advanced on him, smiling. He began to wave his gun.

"He's going to fire," said Alex.

"No question," said Lewis.

In the medical bay Brenda Woolley was looking at herself on-screen in amazement.

"Boo dear," she said, "did I die?"

"Not yet," said Boo, "and not at all if I can help it."

"Thank you, dear," she said, taking his hand. She smiled as she watched her image on the screen.

"Aren't I good?" said Brenda.

Onstage, Josef fired. There was a metallic sound as the bullet ricocheted harmlessly off Carlton's chest into the wings. Not so harmlessly really, as one of Harbottle's Performing Dogs gave a yelp and keeled over. Josef fired again, but dammit, she didn't drop, just kept coming towards him, singing. He fired again, but still she kept advancing. He glanced for help towards the wings, but Sven was no longer there. A lot of other people were though. They were all looking at him.

In the secure room the Silesians watched the monitor in amazement. McTurk suddenly appeared at the door brandishing a very large weapon. He yelled savagely at the Silesians.

"Come on, you fuckers, don't just sit there, can't you see he needs help?"

They hesitated.

"This way," he said, "or everything is lost. Move it! Now!"

They began to move out.

"What about these people?"

"I'll take care of them," said McTurk, cocking his weapon. The sound echoed menacingly. Rogers winced. Should they make a run for it? He felt Dunphy's hand on his arm restraining him. Dunphy shook his head. Did he have something else in mind? In a minute it would be too late. McTurk was even now turning towards him with his weapon. Jesus, was this it? So suddenly. He could feel McTurk's finger tighten on the trigger. McTurk looked straight into Rogers eyes. Then he winked and squeezed the trigger.

The Silesians had halted outside the cage, as if unsure which way to run.

They heard the sound of gunfire from inside the secure room. Then silence. Then McTurk emerged grimly.

"Don't just stand there," he yelled. "Into the service elevator."

A clattering of heels as they raced for the elevator.

"Everyone here?" asked McTurk.

"Except for Sven."

"He's taken care of," said McTurk. He counted six of them. "Right. Sweet dreams."

He pressed the button and the elevator doors slammed shut. As they closed, he rolled a small metal gas grenade inside at their feet. He could hear the hissing begin and pandemonium breaking out. They banged on the metal walls. They punched desperately at the buttons, but the elevator would not move. One by one like trapped insects they fell to the ground.

Just a couple of yards behind Dunphy, Rogers raced for McTurk.

We'll never get to him, he's gonna take us out, were his thoughts. He was still baffled and deafened by the shooting. He couldn't understand why he wasn't dead. His heart was thumping and his body pumping adrenaline. Then he stopped in amazement as he watched Dunphy hugging McTurk. They both began to jump up and down, yelling wildly.

"Did you have to hit me so fucking hard?" said Dunphy.

"Hey, that was acting."

"What about the control room?"

"Oh, they're all sleeping soundly," said McTurk with a grin. "I put them to bed early."

Onstage, Josef was screaming. He waved the gun menacingly. "I am warning you," he yelled in mounting impotence. "If you do not stop, I shall order the Snowball to . . ."

But he got no further as he found himself lifted bodily into the air by Brenda Woolley. The audience gasped, then laughed.

"Activate the Snowball," he screamed.

But in the control room no one was listening; everyone was sleeping, just as McTurk had said. It could have been fatigue, or it could have been his gas grenade.

Carlton held Josef high above his head.

"How strong I am," said Brenda.

Carlton lifted Joseph to his full extent and shook him bodily. Bits of metal fell out of his pockets. The gun bounced harmlessly away. The Ganesha rolled into the wings. Two hands reached for it.

"It's mine," said Katy. "I saw it first."

"You gave it to me," said Alex, "and if you want it back, you're going to have to earn it."

"Oh. How do I earn it?" said Katy. Her voice was low, trembling with suggestion. "Like this?" She licked his cheek.

"Uhm, that's the sort of thing," said Alex.

"Like this?"

She held his head with both her hands and kissed him full on the mouth.

"Will you two break it up, this is a public place," said Lewis in mock disgust. But they wouldn't stop. He held her; she grasped him as if her life depended on it. Their tongues found each other.

In the world around them the audience was going wild, standing, applauding, cheering as Carlton, in Brenda Woolley's finest gown, carried the helpless Josef off-stage, high above his head in his out-stretched arms.

"C'mon," said Alex. "There's a dressing room close by."

"No," said Katy, "this isn't the time."

"C'mon," he said, urgently pulling her away by the hand.

He pushed her through the door of the dressing room. Oh well. Hell, she wanted this man. She reached round to undo her zipper.

"Surprise!" said Alex, beaming.

Her father was sitting in a chair watching the monitor.

"Daddy," she said.

The old man was looking at them like he had woken out of a dream.

"Are you going to make me go away?" he said.

"No," said Alex, "we're going to make you a grandfather."

APOLOGIA

Each man kills the thing he loves. Who said that? It's me. I'm back. And this is definitely the final curtain. What made me do it? What made me think I could get away with it? What if every biographer went around shooting his subject?

I went to see Carlton, still unsure whether I'd have the guts to go through with it or not. He was in a shabby sort of sanatorium.

There were a couple of Bowies there. Later models. One or two Olivettis, and a Harrison Ford. It was like a museum. Eerie kinda place. Nurses in white lab coats and computers sitting around playing five-dimensional chess with each other. He was in a room of his own. I think he knew from the minute he saw me what I was intending to do. He said a very odd thing. "I have been expecting you." Now that is weird, isn't it? How could he possibly know? Did he suspect someone was tracking him all the time? Had he finally developed enough sense of irony to predict what was going to happen to him? He looked pretty good for something over a hundred years old. He still had that young blond Bowie look, though he was a bit dusty. They weren't polishing him too well, I'd say. I was pretty shaken coming face-to-face with him like that. I knew more about him than he did. And I was there to blow him away. That's heavy. So maybe there was just the slightest hesitation that was enough to give the nurse time to alert Security. I don't know. I saw him, he smiled, said "I was expecting you," then I fired, and the next thing the door was off its hinges and security was trying very hard to hurt me. What could I do? I shot the nurse and ran. And now there isn't much time, well for me anyway. They'll find me shortly.

I've decided pills are the easiest way out. I'm not bold enough for the full Hemingway bullet-in-the-temples job. Bit messy. And I've done one good thing. I'm sending this whole story to the Nobel Committee, along with a letter of apology and a strong recommendation that they forget DNAcism, bite the bullet, and award Carlton the Nobel he deserves. I think I can be forgiven for giving them the impression that I was going to do that anyway. Maybe they'll believe me. Maybe I might have in time. I'd like to think so anyway. Of course shooting a nurse and being pursued by five security agencies won't look too good on the record. But that's another reason I'm leaving this story behind. It's my confession, my justification, and my valediction. Thanks for staying with me. You have been my companion on the long and lonely nights. It turned out to have a different ending than I had anticipated. But isn't that often the way with stories? And don't feel too harshly about me. I know intellectual fraud isn't particularly nice, but wouldn't you have been tempted to do the same? As I said, fame is a terminal disease.

There is a final chapter which was found on his computer after Reynolds's suicide.

COMEDY, THE MEANING OF LIFE, AND THE WHOLE DAMN BALL OF WAX

All tragedies are finish'd by a death, All comedies are ended by a marriage.

LORD BYRON

There is nothing common about sense. Would that it were as common as hydrogen in the Universe; but then again, come to think of it, most of the hydrogen is on fire all around us, busy burning up in tremendous furnaces called stars. All those stars, all those galaxies, millions of flaming bonfires whirling round above our heads. All those violent clashes in the Universe—how could we be expected to be peaceful? We live in an exploding Universe which grew from a tiny dot, a singularity, fifteen billion years ago, expanding out of nothingness to create everything we see around us. The Big Bang. The Big Laugh. Explosions of laughter. Like orgasm. Seeding the Universe.

It's life that's the puzzle. Life is the weirdness. Life is the unnecessary part of the equation. Given time, the physical Universe becomes biological and grows intelligence. Why?

Someone once asked the classic White Face clown Steve Martin why life was present in the Universe.

"Because," he replied, "without life, the Universe does not exist. It needs an observer to make it real."

Yes. The post-Heisenberg world of comedy. Smart bastards, comedians.

Everyone said it really *was* Brenda Woolley who had saved the day. Even though to bench-press Josef over her head she would have needed the muscle tone of a professional Bodyslog. Even though she was lying in a hospital bed holding Boo's hand at the time. Still it's a much better story and we'll take the better story over truth any day, won't we? Isn't that the point of journalism? So the myth persisted that Brenda Woolley saved the Universe (or at least a tiny part of it). To everyone's surprise, including his, when she came out of hospital, she took up with Boo. She was devoted to him, and he, the supreme ironist, enjoyed this final irony and seemed utterly fascinated by her. It was an odd relationship, but then again, aren't they all?

As for Carlton, all he asked as his reward was a chance to perform comedy. They tried to dissuade him, everyone said it was madness, but he was adamant, and since he certainly deserved it, they finally gave him his wish. He appeared at the Sangster Club on Mars, billed as *Carlton the Comedy Computer, For One Night Only*. It was the highlight of a Grand Gala Thank-You Ball given by the Government of Clarketown for Brenda Woolley and the crew of the *Princess Di*. Being Special Bureau employees, Dunphy and McTurk were not invited, though Rogers was. Alex got them a couple of passes anyway. Kyle showed up in a tux looking like a million dollars. Everyone was there. Everyone made speeches, including the mayor of Clarketown, who played down the threat, though he did announce that Project Iceman was officially dead. Of course he didn't explain it was really for economic reasons: the very expensive Iceman project was being replaced by the new fusion technology which could grow ice, water, and water vapor chemically from oxygen and hydrogen. They didn't need the icebergs anymore. So in a way, everyone was happy. The Silesian Sea would grow imperceptibly up to the edge of the lands his friends had already purchased.

Katy was at the gala, looking glamorous in a strapless frock. She had moved in with Alex. He was nuts about her. They were talking about kids. He proposed to her in the lobby of the Sangster Club. She said she'd think about it. His face fell. Ten seconds later she said yes.

"You bastard," he said.

"Gotcha," she said.

It was a tough crowd. A tux crowd. Glittering jewels and polished faces. Carlton was coolly confident. Backstage it was Alex and Lewis who were nervous, like parents at a school play. They were in the way, redundant, pacing around offering useless bits of advice.

"Time to go, buddy," said Katy, leading Alex off to his seat.

"Break a circuit," said Alex.

Lewis gave him a slap on the back. Tay handed him a little good-luck drawing she had made, then they all passed through the black velvet curtain to take their places.

I do hope this is a good idea, thought Carlton.

Could he do it? Was comedy accessible to computers? Was artificial intelligence finally ready to be funny?

He stepped forward into the spotlight.